The Compass Paradox

THE COMPASS PARADOX

R.C. Blanco

iii

Published by Macallan Skye Publishers.

www.MacallanSkye.com

ISBN-13: 979-8-234-00595-3 (hardcover)

ISBN-13: 979-8-234-00596-0 (paperback)

ISBN-13: 979-8218872472 (digital)

Design by James Jones

Printed in the United States of America

Revised First Edition

10 9 8 7 6 5 4 3 2 1

This book is dedicated to my wife and family
who support all my crazy projects. Thanks to you,
I feel I can accomplish anything.

The Compass paradox, also referred to as the Autonomy–Authority Paradox or the Paradox of Leadership and Independence, sits at the intersection of social psychology, political psychology, and motivational theory.

Humanity craves guidance. We seek leaders to show us the way when the path grows dark and unclear. Yet we resist being led, clinging to the illusion of freedom, and the conviction that our choices are wholly our own. We want direction without submission, authority without control, certainty without sacrifice.

This is the Compass Paradox, the contradiction at the heart of humanity. We long for someone or something to guide us, to show us the way, so long as it never reminds us that we have surrendered control.

Table of Contents

Chapter 1

Shedding Invisibility

Cade Mercer pulled into the student lot at Santa Fe State College. The lot was full of polite, bland cars that silently glided into the numbered parking grid. Cade's 1995 Mustang GT broadcasted its arrival, the mechanical roar reverberating off the brick walls. It was a sound that turned heads, even among people who claimed they didn't care about cars.

He whipped the wheel and glided into a space. Cade had built the car in fragments over years, scavenging parts from salvage yards. The Mustang absorbed most of Cade's extra cash, which as a college student wasn't much. Even his friends in the car club were a little jealous. The car got noticed, not Cade.

Cade jumped out of the car and ran, frantically, trying not to be late, again. At the last minute he slid through the auditorium door and found his seat in the third row from the back. He was rummaging in his backpack for his laptop and notepad as Dr. Alvarez walked up to the podium.

Dr Alvarez cleared her throat and began, "Today I would like to start by showing the class an example. This is from our previous assignment and was submitted by your classmate, Cade Mercer."

Cade froze for a moment, then ducked his head and pulled his hood lower over his eyes, trying not to be noticed. Cade had a talent for invisibility. He was largely unknown to his peers, and he wanted to keep it that way.

Dr. Alvarez continued, "Notice that in this example his code doesn't command, it converses with a delicate awareness of nuance and context, almost like a conversation with the machine rather than a command."

Cade ducked even lower in his seat and overheard two students in the row in front of him. The frat boy on the left was whispering, "Who is Cade Mercer, have you ever met him?", the boy on the right just shook his head, trying not to be noticed by Dr. Alvarez. Frat boy continued, "Reddit and Discord programing threads are dominated by someone with the handle GatorCade. He's always the front runner in any coding or hack contests. They call him the *Ghost in the Machine*. I always thought he was part of some elite group at UF. Maybe this is him?"

At the end of class Cade ducked out as quickly as possible before Dr. Alvarez could single him out. *That is a nightmare*, he thought, as he joined the crowd in the hallway. Cade tried his best to keep his achievements quiet, he liked to blend in and not be the focus of attention.

Although he tried, he could not escape the notice of Professor Heller, who ran Santa Fe's Machine Learning track. Heller played gatekeeper for the few undergrads allowed into his graduate-level seminars. When he stumbled onto Cade's Github, he emailed within minutes. "Stop by my office tomorrow. I want to see what you're really building."

Cade went, expecting another polite lecture about "career opportunities," but Heller instead handed him a login to the campus research cluster and pointed to a whiteboard crowded with hastily scrawled neural nets.

3

"You're three courses ahead of the curriculum," Heller said, "so let's skip the training wheels."

Cade reluctantly agreed to join Heller's grant-funded side project, a distributed architecture for federated learning. Once or twice, he found Heller lurking in the computer lab after midnight, peering over his shoulder to see what the "kid wonder" was up to.

It was Heller who sent samples of Cade's work to Dr. Kim Chonge, a UF professor in Algorithms and Machine Learning. Chonge, a legend in tech circles, had spent more than a decade at Google's Brain division before coming to Gainesville to head up UF's multi-million-dollar Cognitive Computing Initiative. She was famous for her high-profile work and infamous for her ruthless candor. When the email from Dr. Chonge arrived in Cade's inbox, it didn't seem real at first.

Dr. Chonge wrote, "I'm impressed. I have never seen someone transform basic Java into something that felt alive, organic." She attached a PDF, it was one of Cade's own projects, heavily annotated in red, the margins filled with exclamation marks, questions, and the occasional smiley. Below her signature, she added, "Would you consider attending a UF guest seminar? I think you'll find our graduate students stimulating company. Bring the Mustang. These students have never seen anything like it."

For the rest of the afternoon, Cade tried and failed to concentrate on anything else. The email replayed in his head on a loop, its contents both electrifying and terrifying. Cade had never wanted to leave Santa Fe, he worked best without the pressure of the spotlight. Still, he'd be lying if he said he hadn't thought about it.

He pulled up Dr. Chonge's faculty page, read through her biography, and scanned the list of her recent publications. Each title sounded like a spell. "Probabilistic Temporal Embedding for Personalized Neural Synthesis," "Latency-Optimized Federated Learning in Heterogeneous Clusters," "Recursive Self-Improvement and the Limits of Synthetic Cognition." He clicked through a few and tried to parse the language, realizing quickly that her brain operated on a different level.

He cycled between elation and dread, unsure how to respond to the

4

email. His hands hovered over the keyboard, drafting a reply, deleting it, retyping, and deleting again. Part of him wanted to ignore the whole thing, keep his head down and finish out his final year without the threat of scrutiny. But the other part, a deeper, more stubborn part, couldn't resist the challenge.

That night, he texted his girlfriend, Madie. "Guess who got invited to UF by an ex-Google legend? Also, she wants to see the Mustang."

Madie's reply came instantly, studded with emojis. "WHAT? Cade, that's unreal. See, I told you your car would get you famous one day."

That night, in bed, staring at the ceiling fan, Cade replayed the day's events. He tried to picture himself at the UF seminar, walking the halls with people who thought in code, speaking a dialect that didn't require translation. He wondered if they would see through him in minutes. The next morning, he put on his least-wrinkled T-shirt, ran his fingers through his hair, and hit reply to Dr. Chonge's email, "I'd be honored to attend the seminar. Mustang will be there. Looking forward to it."

Chapter 2

The Empty Spaces Between

Cade shouldered his way out of the Mustang and slung his battered backpack over one shoulder. A cluster of students with AirPods and iced coffees barely noticed him as he moved past. One student with a gray Civic gave him a jealous glance. "Nice ride," he said, not meeting Cade's eyes.

Running late and in a rush, Cade nodded, his mind on Dr. Chonge's upcoming seminar. By the time he pushed open the heavy glass doors of Building N and navigated the labyrinth of hallways to room 241, the lecture hall was already packed with seventy-two undergrads.

Shit, he thought, *Heller's going to notice.* He slipped in and took his usual seat in the third row from the back, far enough away to avoid attention but close enough to catch the slides. The girl next to him glanced over.

"Did I miss anything?" he whispered.

She shook her head, mouthing, "Intro stuff."

He opened his laptop, the lid covered in overlapping stickers: Summit Racing, Detroit Speed, a faded *Dragonball Z* logo, and a purple Decepticon icon. He reached in his bag and grabbed a battered spiral notebook and clicked a pen, an ancient reflex. *Like anyone still takes notes by hand,* he thought, embarrassed but unwilling to break the habit.

At the front of the hall, Professor David Heller prowled the stage. He was tall, late forties, with the angular build and quick, decisive movements of a lifelong fencer. His salt-and-pepper hair was cut close at the sides, and his wire-framed glasses glinted when he turned toward the screens. Heller always wore a suit jacket, even in the thick damp of Florida's September, always charcoal or navy, with the shirt open at the throat and no tie. Cade has never seen the man in shirtsleeves.

The class hushed before he said a word. The professor was not a yeller, but when he spoke, people listened. Today, the screens behind him flashed a single phrase in blue font. "MACHINE LEARNING: PREDICTION, PERCEPTION, AND POWER." He began, "Prediction is the closest thing to omniscience we can buy with hardware. The world is chaos. Machine learning is how we turn chaos into profit, into patterns, or into power. We're not simply teaching computers to think. We're teaching them to outthink us." Cade swallowed, gripping his pen.

Heller sketched a timeline on the whiteboard, 1956: Perceptrons, 1986: Backpropagation, and 2012: Deep Learning Boom. He narrated the rise of machine learning like a military campaign. Cade tracked every word, fingers poised over his keyboard, but he rarely took notes. The ideas hooked into his mind on the first pass.

Heller switched tactics as the lecture moved from history to application. He snapped his fingers at students in the front row. "You. Regression versus classification. Go." Heller pointed at a guy in a polo shirt.

"Regression predicts continuous values, classification sorts into categories," the student answered, voice cracking slightly.

"Pedestrian but accurate," Heller said.

Cade watched as a girl two rows ahead was asked about the trolley problem in autonomous vehicles. "Would your algorithm save the passengers or the pedestrians, Ms. Davis?"

"Neither. It should minimize total harm."

"And who decides what constitutes 'harm'?" Heller interrupted. "The engineers? The government? The market?"

Her answer set off a five-minute digression on the illusion of neutrality in code. Cade was impressed. He thought he knew where Heller was leading the class, but he wasn't quite sure. The professor seemed to delight in that. Heller's lecture was dense, but the best parts were the asides, stories about tech disasters, startup flameouts, and the time he supposedly built an algorithm that could distinguish between cats and dogs with ninety-seven-percent accuracy, only to discover it was identifying the lighting in each photo.

For Cade, machine learning was as close as he'd ever come to real magic. He drifted a little, as he always did when a lecture grabbed him. His mind wandered down pathways of possibility. *What if the world was all nodes and edges?* he thought, picturing highways dissolving into glowing threads of data. The idea of being a programmer in a world like that didn't scare him, not like it scared some of the others. *I'd rather build the thing that outsmarts the chaos.*

The class was closing in on the final fifteen minutes when Heller started pacing, hands behind his back, as if considering an unspoken verdict. Cade sensed the professor was about to spring a challenge. "For today's assignment,"

Heller declared, "you'll build a simple predictive model. Movie recommendations, music suggestions, dating apps, etc. Anything that demonstrates user preference analysis. Emphasis on simple, please."

The instructions popped up on the projection as the class gave a collective exhale. Cade watched the responses around him: three kids instantly opened GitHub, a girl with a pink MacBook pulled up an API reference, and some others fumbled with the course Discord. The assignment was busy work, and everyone knew it. Plug in some data, mash together a collaborative filter, maybe get cute with a weighted average, then out popped an answer that impressed no one.

Cade was halfway through opening his own IDE, but his fingers hovered over the keys. The assignment was insulting in its simplicity, a paint-by-numbers exercise with the answers already penciled between the lines. He could do this in fifteen minutes with code snippets from last year and a copy-paste from his own abandoned repo. The temptation was strong, get it done, file the submission, devote the afternoon to rebuilding the Mustang's differential. This was how he'd survived every core class: minimize effort, maximize time for the things that matter.

Cade wondered if this was how it would be for the rest of his life, a sequence of trivial puzzles dressed up as innovation, every challenge hollowed out. *Is this really it?* he thought, drumming his fingers against the keyboard. *Four years of college to become a code monkey?*

He thought back to the first time he had seen a neural network in action, the awe he felt watching a simple script learn to play Tetris better than any human. The more he thought about it, the less interested he felt in the assignment. It was like the time he spent a whole summer rebuilding a carburetor only to realize he preferred fuel injection. "There's no challenge here," he muttered, pushing his laptop away. "Nothing to fight against, nothing to fix."

He stared at the blinking cursor, closed the laptop, and leaned back. His mind wandered to the assignment, not the assignment as written, but to the

9

empty spaces between it. The why that no one bothered to ask. Cade thought about all the times he'd chased the next best thing, an upgrade, a shortcut, a hotter engine, another algorithm. "Geez," he whispered to himself. "Maybe I've been running in circles this whole time."

His pen started to move, not with numbers or syntax but with lines and arrows. "What if we mapped emotional states instead?" he muttered, sketching nodes labeled restless, bored, lonely, despairing. He added anxious, unmotivated, vulnerable, then paused. "No, we need the positive ones too." Calm, engaged, hopeful, confident, driven. Arrows connected one state to another, some branching, some looping back. "Everyone is stuck in these cycles," he thought, "but what if we could see them coming?"

He imagined a system that saw not only what you clicked but what you didn't click, the time you hovered and thought, and what you avoided completely. A model that could tell when you were about to spiral.

He called it Mood-Atlas before he even really knew what it was, a map of moods and thoughts. He wrote the name at the top of the page, not in block letters but with a kind of hush, as if it was a secret even from himself. The noise of the classroom receded, replaced by the thrum of ideas. Cade sketched the interface, lines tracing the flow from user to system to output. He annotated with little jokes, questions, and warnings.

At the bottom, in parentheses, he wrote," What are the drawbacks? What are the limits?" He drew an arrow from there back to the top, a loop with no end.

He didn't notice Professor Heller until the man's shadow fell across his notebook. Cade's heart jumped. He expected something like, "Mercer, eyes on the slides," or maybe a pointed question about cosine similarity. Instead, Heller glanced down at the page, at the tangle of lines and arrows, then back at Cade. For a moment, his face was inscrutable.

In a voice pitched for only the two of them, he said, "This is not what I asked for, Mr. Mercer."

Cade flushed, pen clattering to the desk. He couldn't quite meet the professor's eyes, so he looked at the smudge of ink on his own thumb. "No, sir," he said, "but I think it's what you meant."

Heller let out a breath. "Imagination is a kind of fire," he said softly." Most people spend their whole lives learning how to nurture it and feed it but remember to keep it in check. Don't let it burn you." He placed a hand on Cade's shoulder, a brief, weightless pressure. "Handle it carefully."

Cade nodded, not trusting himself to speak. When Heller moved on, Cade was left with a half-finished notebook, a laptop that suddenly seemed pointless, and a pulse in his chest that felt like the Mustang at idle: dangerous energy, barely contained.

"Handle it carefully," Cade repeated under his breath, tracing his finger over the Mood-Atlas sketch. What if this was the thing that mattered? The thought both thrilled and terrified him.

The remaining minutes of the class passed in a blur. Heller droned from somewhere far away. Cade tried not to stare at the clock, but he watched the secondhand tick with growing impatience. *I could build a prototype tonight*, he thought, sketching another node in the margin. *Maybe a simple interface first...* When the hour finally ended, he jammed everything into his backpack and bolted for the door. "Sorry, excuse me," he muttered as he squeezed past a cluster of students still typing up their notes.

Outside, the air had only thickened, hot and humid, like a sauna. Cade walked quickly with his head down. He was supposed to meet his brother, Cason, at the football field, but he needed to think for a moment. He dropped his bag in the Mustang's passenger seat. The car was an oven, dashboard too hot to touch. He turned the key, and the car shuddered to life, the exhaust notes instantly banishing whatever post-class malaise lingered in his bones.

11

He checked his phone at the stoplight and saw a text from Madie, "Dinner at my place, 8 p.m. Bring ice cream and something stupid to watch." He smiled, the first real smile of the day and slid the phone back into his pocket.

Between a date and a new project, maybe life wasn't so bad.

Chapter 3

Chaos, Compass, and Fries

Inside Madie Carter's tiny apartment, the blender was roaring. She was half into her workout gear, blonde hair tied into a hasty ponytail, answering a client's text with one hand while scooping protein powder with the other. Cade still slept, but a note was on the counter from the night before, three words in his chicken-scratch handwriting. "Save me one."

Madie grinned at the note on the counter and poured the smoothie into two glasses. "Always," she whispered to the empty kitchen before bolting out the door.

Cade and Maddie seemed a perfect couple, similar in many ways yet with counter-balancing differences. Madie was early to bed, early to rise, always ready to go before the sun was up. Cade tended to save all important tasks and classwork for the middle of the night. They both had a similar quirky humor, often giggling at inside jokes no one else understood. They were the cute couple from high school, together since sophomore year. The couple everyone thought might actually make it.

Gator Grind Fitness occupied an old brick building on 34th Street, its windows fogged by the time her 6 a.m. boot camp class began. The clients ranged from college kids in neon sneakers to near retirees, all of them bleary-eyed but present. They showed up for "Mad Dog" Madie.

"Alright," she called, dropping a crate of resistance bands and cueing up a playlist that pulsed with bass. "Today's about ladders, push-ups, bands, core. Form over ego, and if you puke, it means you're trying." The room erupted in nervous laughter.

She moved like sunlight across the space, correcting a wrist here, adjusting a shoulder there, cracking jokes that kept people from realizing how hard they were working. She wasn't the kind of instructor who barked orders from the front; she was on the mats beside them, doing planks until her voice shook with strain, shouting encouragements through her own sweat.

"Mrs. Whitaker, look at you! I told you those new sneakers have superpowers."

"More like they make me forget how old I am," the sixty-year-old shot back, earning a round of cheers.

By seven, the room was steaming, everyone gasping and smiling like they'd survived something together. That was Madie's magic. She built confidence.

When the last mat was rolled up and the music faded, Elena Lee, the gym's owner, leaned against the front desk. "Third week in a row your classes have waitlists," she said, her low smile equal parts impressed and calculating. "You're doing something right."

Madie wiped her forehead with a towel and shrugged. "It's the playlists."

"It's the instructor," Elena countered. "You're getting a raise for your Saturday classes, and don't try to talk me out of it."

Madie smiled and thanked her. The money would help, gas, rent, Cade's textbooks when his scholarship came up short. But that wasn't what drove her. Madie liked the alchemy of turning exhaustion into pride, of watching someone's

14

face shift from "I can't" to "I did." It was the same spark that made her juggle two jobs, the gym, and a café shift near campus downtown.

By eight-thirty, Madie had swapped her workout tank for a crisp blue polo, the Gator Grind sweat barely dry on her skin before she's clocked in at the Santa Fe café. She moved behind the counter with the muscle memory of a veteran, navigating the narrow galley with a speed that made even the espresso machine seem sluggish. The morning rush was in full swing.

She beamed at every customer, toggling from drink orders to the register to refilling the pastry case. Between mobile orders and the unending shriek of the steam wand, she unclogged the industrial grinder and offered a free coffee to a frazzled adjunct who forgot their wallet.

Through it all, she kept one eye on her phone screen propped behind the napkin dispenser, waiting for Cade's check-in. The world knew Madie as the girl who could do anything, who never slowed down, but Cade knew her as the girl who needed little reminders to eat, breathe, and slow down for five seconds.

Cade texted her mid-shift. "Heller pulled me aside. Said my approach was 'different, dangerous different, maybe.' He's not sure."

Madie thumbed a reply between orders. "Definitely just different. Fries at The Swamp tonight? You, me, Cason. My treat."

His response came back with a blurry photo of a notebook page, scrawled with arrows and words connecting "restless," "courage," "isolation," and "connection." He'd captioned it simply, "Mood-Atlas."

She stared at it until a student cleared their throat for a latte. "Feels like art," she finally texted back. "Make it. Meet for fries either way." That afternoon, she squeezed in a run at the park before heading back to the café for the dinner rush. Between shifts, her phone buzzed, her mom. "You're working too much," her mother said the moment Madie answered.

"I like it," Madie said, tucking the phone between her ear and shoulder while she cleaned a stack of mugs. "Keeps me moving."

"And Cade?" Mom asked, her voice softening in that way that always preceded judgment.

15

Madie laughed softly. "Same as always. Brain like a lightning storm, so focused he would forget to eat if I didn't remind him."

"You've been together since tenth grade," Mom reminded her.

"And we are still," Madie said firmly. "Loyalty's not a flaw, Mom."

Her mother's unspoken worry was that Cade would never match Madie's momentum, that he'd become an anchor instead of a sail. But Madie had always seen what others missed in him, the quiet brilliance that needed time to bloom. Madie ended the call, her lips curled in a stubborn smile. She picked up a stack of mugs and went back to the clatter and hiss of the café's closing rush, letting the low tide of voices and espresso steam push memories of her mother's concern to the back of her mind. When the shift ended, she peeled off her apron and stretched, rolling her neck until it popped.

Milo, the shift manager, tossed her a mock salute." See you tomorrow, Mad Dog."

She ducked out the back door and into the slanting, honey-colored light of evening. Gainesville was still sticky and loud with the calls of tree frogs, but the oppressive heat had lifted, leaving behind the exact sort of night that begged for sweet tea and good company.

She texted Cade, fingers flying over the screen. "Running late. Grab us a booth? Save me the corner seat." Then she jogged home, showered in six minutes flat, and threw on her favorite Gators hoodie before biking a mile to The Swamp Diner.

Along the way, she let herself wonder if maybe her mother just wished Madie could be a little less…all-in. But then, she reasoned, what was the point of loving someone at half throttle? She coasted the last block, locked her bike to the familiar crooked post outside the diner, and stepped into the cool, onion-ring-scented air. The cracked vinyl seats, the blinding neon signs, and the murmur of people at the bar, all of it felt like home.

She spotted Cade at their usual booth, hunched over his laptop, face creased in concentration like he was hacking the Pentagon. She couldn't help but feel a burst of warmth in her chest. That was her person, the one everyone else underestimated but she knew had the potential change the world. As she slid into the booth, the vinyl stuck to her thighs, and she twisted to face the door, waiting for the last member of their trio to arrive. The Swamp Diner had seen her and Cade through many late-night cramming sessions, birthday milkshakes, and arguments resolved over fries. Cade was in the back of the booth, his eyes were shadowed from too much screen time.

Cason, Cade's younger brother, joined them moments later straight from practice, still in his North Creek Middle School Football tee with cheeks flushed from yelling at twelve-year-olds all afternoon.

Cason didn't so much sit as cannonball into the booth, his whole body spring-loaded, vibrating from the pent-up energy he'd accumulated since sunrise. The tabletop shuddered under his arrival. Before either Madie or Cade could even say hi, Cason was already into the story of today's game, words tripping over themselves in his hurry to get to the good parts.

"Okay, picture this, fourteen seconds left, North Creek Middle down by five, and the ref's got a whistle jammed so far up his ass he can taste the chrome." He grabbed the ketchup bottle and a napkin dispenser, mimed a center-quarterback exchange, then kept narrating. "We're talking fourth and goal, one shot, Hail Mary. The crowd's nuts, the O-line's holding by a thread, and what does my genius quarterback do?" Cason pivots to Madie, who's already covering her mouth to hide a laugh. "He calls a fake-out. The other guys never see it coming. I mean, I told the kid he was a moron in film review, but in that moment? It's legendary."

The couple two booths down were openly gawking, eating chicken-fried steak with one hand and filming Cason's performance with the other. Even the ancient, grease-soaked cook in the kitchen window had paused his spatula to watch the show, eyes glinting with the cruel anticipation unique to people who've seen every possible disaster unfold.

Cason took his audience's attention as a challenge. He hunched low, voice dropping to a dramatic whisper, and pantomimed the snap. "Ball's out, spinning, time slows down."

The next moment, Cason hurled the ketchup bottle in a perfect spiral, straight at Cade's face, who caught it with one hand and returned it with a bored toss, never breaking eye contact with his brother. "But here's the thing. The receiver? He's got hands like flypaper, but today he's wearing his brother's cleats, two sizes too big, because his mom gave him the wrong bag, and he eats turf like it's his last meal. Boom, face-plant!"
The diner erupted, applause, laughter, even a couple mock-wounded groans from the college kids at the bar. Cason chugged the melting remnants of a milkshake left by a previous diner then attacked the communal basket of fries. Cade tried to defend the last curly fry with a fork, but Cason intercepted, faked left, and snagged it clean. He shoved the whole thing in his mouth and grinned a grease-slicked, victorious grin.

For a moment, Madie watched the brothers. She wasn't from a big family herself, but the Mercers had adopted her so fully that sometimes she forgot they weren't related. She loved the wild, competitive affection and the unspoken codes.

Madie leaned in close to Cade, her voice low and intimate. " You two are the best show in town." She bumped her knee against his under the table. He didn't answer right away. If she didn't know Cade, she might think he was ignoring her, but she knew he was collecting details, building a mental model of the world in real-time, trying to make sense of every expression and stray word. It was what drew her to him in the first place.

When he finally spoke, it was quiet, almost embarrassed. "He's gonna be a legend if he doesn't implode first."
"That's why he has you," Madie said, and Cade's lips quirked.

Cason interrupted them by belching loud enough to rattle the sugar caddy. "What, you guys talking about me?" he said, feigning offense but obviously pleased at being the center of attention again. "You know, school AD says I'm 'volatile but team oriented.' I think that's code for pain in the ass."

Cade's gaze drifted, his hands hover over his backpack, fingers twitching restless on the zipper. He was dying to show them something, Madie realized.
She nudged him. "Alright, out with it. What's eating you?"
Cade smirked, but his hands itched to open his laptop, to show them what he'd been building. Madie noticed. She always noticed.
"What is it this time?" she asked gently. "What is Mood-Atlas?" He slid the notebook across the table. Cason leaned over, squinting, trying to decipher the tangle of lines, then saw the title scrawled at the top. "So what is this mess, A mood map or mood compass?"
"Exactly," Cade said, sitting up straighter only registering part of what Cason said. "Instead of 'You liked this movie. Here's another, 'it's more like, 'If you're feeling shy or timid, here's something that inspires courage.'"

Madie traced a finger over his scribbles on the paper. "It's a map of how people are feeling, what they need but might not realize."
"Or a manipulation map," Cason teased.
"Compass, not manipulation," Madie said slowly to emphasize her point. "A compass only gives you a direction to go. It doesn't force you to go there."
They ordered, they laughed, they ate. Fries disappeared between bursts of conversation about football games, gym clients, and Cade's professor with a mechanical keyboard obsession.

But Madie could feel that Cade was chasing something bigger than his class project, bigger than car meets or the late-night milkshakes. Something that, if she was honest, amazed her. She believed in him, and if his lightning brain was about to spark something new, she'd be there to keep him grounded.
"Fries, compass, and chaos," she said, raising her soda in a toast. "To us."
"To us," the brothers echoed.

19

Chapter 4

The Other Mercer

Cason Mercer stood at the fifty-yard line, whistle dangling around his neck, surrounded by a four dozen middle schoolers who looked at him like he was part coach, part older brother, and part superhero.

"Alright, Warriors," he called, clapping his hands once, the sound cracking like a starter pistol. "We're running suicides, because last game we ran like fucking old grandpas. And I mean *slow* grandpas. Not the fast ones who do triathlons." The kids groaned but laughed because he was already jogging backward, showing them he'd run it with them. "Helmets straight! If I see another one of you trying to wear it like a crown, you're doing push-ups!"

The whistle blew. Feet pounded. Dust rose. And there was Cason, sprinting right alongside his players, shouting encouragements between jokes.

"You call that fast? My grandma could beat you on a walker!"

"Don't quit now, you'll regret it tomorrow!"

"Jackson, keep your head straight! That is how pros run!"

By the end, the boys were collapsed in the grass, panting but laughing at the same time. Cason knelt among them, sweat streaking his shirt, his grin easy. "That's how you earn the W, boys," he said. "Effort first, scoreboard second. Remember that. We need to play hard through four quarters to win."

Practice always finished with a scrimmage, ten minutes of mayhem, and sideline commentary. Cason refereed but also quarterbacked when the second team needed a confidence boost, throwing targeted passes only a previous high school quarterback would be capable of. By the end, everyone was tired and a few were grinning. Even the ones who got chewed or cussed out were plotting how they would do better tomorrow.

Practice ended like a slow wave, first the mass of helmeted bodies surged toward the sideline, then it fragmented into smaller units, kids peeling away to water jugs and huddled clusters of gossip. Cason walked the field's length, corralling stray cones and footballs with his foot, scooping them up one by one into the mesh gear bag. He paused at the fifty-yard line, watching as clumps of middle-schoolers drifted toward the parking lot where the first wave of minivans waited, engines idling. A few kids lagged, trading stories and reliving plays. Their voices were high and bright above the drone of cicadas.

With a final sweep, Cason rounded up the last practice jersey, shoved it into the duffel, and hoisted everything over his shoulder. He felt the day's exhaustion in the deep pull beneath his ribs, but he had learned to love the fatigue. The sun was pressed low against the tops of the pine trees, turning the field into a grid of long navy shadows and gold. As he turned toward the gate, the heard a sound, the deep, rolling tremor of an engine, unmistakable.

21

It was Cade's Mustang. The thing rumbled like thunder as it pulled into the lot, the middle schoolers couldn't resist pointing. "Coach, is that your brother's?"

"Yup," Cason said, grinning. "Don't let him fool you though. The car's cooler than he is."

Cade got out and leaned against the hood, laptop under his arm, hair shoved back.

Cason waved the last of the kids off and strode over. "You look like you pulled an all-nighter," he said as he popped the F-150's tailgate.

"You look like you ran a marathon," Cade shot back.

"Pretty much," Cason said, stretching his arms behind his head, shoulder blades popping like old wood. "Except my marathon involved twelve-year-olds who think 'cover two' is a video game cheat code. One of them asked today if we could run a 'Fortnite offense.' I didn't cry, but I thought about it."

Cade grinned. "Better than my day, believe me. You ever try debugging biotronic firmware with the world's most passive-aggressive student team?" He paused, shaking his head. "How did it get so hot out here?"

"Global warming, bro. Get with the program." Cason's smirk softened a fraction. He glanced at Cade, noticing as always how his body seemed wound tight. The old, relaxed slouch of adolescence had become a kind of habitual tension, like a readiness for impact. "You been sleeping? You look like shit." He paused. "Seriously, are you okay?"

Cade sighed, "Yeah. I mean, no, but yeah. You ever get the feeling that if you stop moving, the whole world would…catch up?"

Cason nodded. "That's why I run suicides with them. You stop, you puke. You keep going, you might finish first."

The banter drained some of the day's poison, but not all of it. Cade glanced at the Mustang's dash, as if remembering a clock was ticking somewhere.

"Gotta go," he said.

"Race you home?" Cason asked, a flash of the old rivalry lighting up his face.

"You'll lose," Cade said playfully.

"Not if you fall asleep at the wheel." Cason clapped Cade on the back then hopped into the cab of the F-150 and slammed the door. The Mustang's engine coughed then roared to life, the sound rolling across the lot and making the streetlights shudder.

Cason pulled out first and checked the mirror. Cade was right behind, headlights bright, Mustang low and hungry on the asphalt. The truck cab smelled like turf, sweat, and the ghosts of five different Gatorade flavors, all mixed. For a second, Cason considered letting his mind wander, letting the music take over, but instead he grabbed his phone and dialed Cade's number. He wasn't ready to let the conversation end. Cason merged onto 13th street, the F-150 felt loose and alive beneath his hands. Over the Bluetooth, Cade's voice was thin but bright.

"So," Cason said, flicking his turn signal out of reflex, even though the lane was empty. "You still brainstorming this Mood-Compass gizmo you were on about last week?" He heard the rustle of Cade scratching his scalp, then the distinct pop of a Red Bull can opening.

"Mood-Atlas, actually. Working title, but I'm still iterating on the pitch. You know how most apps want to keep you scrolling, keep you inside yourself? This would do the opposite, try to read if someone's stuck in, like a negative feedback loop. Then it could suggest stuff that's, I dunno, scientifically proven to help. Like stories, music, or a notification telling you to go outside for five minutes."

Cason squinted against the setting sun." So instead of an algorithm that dials up the rage and doomscrolling, it's one that's, what, a guidance counselor in your phone?"

23

Cade laughed, a short, breathless sound. "More like a weather app but for your head. You put in your feelings, it gives you a forecast, and if you're heading into a hurricane it tries to steer you someplace safer. Sings you a lullaby, metaphorically. Tells you when to take shelter."

"So who's this for? Depressed weirdos like you or the general public?"

Cade snorted. "Everyone. The code doesn't know if you're the homecoming king or the anime club treasurer. It's not surveillance. It's more like…empathy, but synthetic. The algorithm nudges you toward the light if you're getting too stuck in your own head."

They hit a red light, and Cason drummed his fingers against the steering wheel, considering. "So what's stopping people from gaming it? Lie to the app, feed it junk data, and keep doing what you were doing."

Cade took a breath. "You can't lie to it. It gets its input through what you are doing, what you're watching, tapping, scrolling, even the way you swipe or hold your phone tells it something about your mood. Your phone knows you better than your own mom."

For a second, Cason felt like he saw what his brother was getting at. "Damn. Okay, that's pretty cool. Still creepy, but cool."

"I'll take it," Cade said. "Honestly, if you'd said it was lame, I probably would've scrapped the whole project."

Cason grinned, relieved to steer them back to familiar turf. "You know me. I only call things lame if they have, like, a slogan that rhymes. 'Mood-Compass: Navigating Feelings, Avoiding Squealings.'"

"Mood-Atlas," Cade deadpanned, but then the laugh came through, sharp and genuine.

Cason raised his brows. "Yeah, like I said, a mood compass."

"Yeah," Cade said, warming to it. "Exactly."

24

Cason nodded slowly, keeping his eyes on the road. "Sounds like it could be powerful and maybe a little dangerous. What if this compass could influence what people feel?"

Cade frowned. "It wouldn't decide feelings. It would reflect them."

"Reflections can warp" Cason said gently. "I know enough about people to tell you that they don't like realizing someone's nudging them. Even if it's in a good direction."

The silence stretched between them, filled only by the steady hum of the tires. Cade's mind was already spiraling, chasing possibilities. Cason, sensing it, broke the wait. "Look, promise me one thing. If you invent something that goes full Skynet, like in *Terminator*, you will leave me to coach football in peace. I'll lead the resistance from the fifty-yard line if needed."

Cade chuckled, the tension easing, and Cason laughed louder.

***

Back at the Mercer house, the kitchen smelled faintly of leftover pizza. Cade dropped his laptop on the table, fingers already itching to type. Cason grabbed two beers from the fridge, sliding one across the table as he dropped into a chair. "Eat something," Cason said, popping his open. "Or drink this. One or the other will keep you alive."

"I'll eat later." Cade's eyes were locked on the screen. "I... I need to get this out of my head first." Cason took a slow sip of his beer, the bitterness settling on his tongue, and leaned back, watching his brother's face illuminated by the blue-white glow of the laptop. The kitchen was dim except for the screen, the overhead lights long since flicked off.

Cason understood engines. He didn't understand this digital sorcery, the way a few lines of code could bend the world, but it didn't matter. What he understood was Cade. He understood the look on his brother's face, jaw set, brow furrowed, chasing some idea down the rabbit hole. He had seen it a hundred times, when

Cade was a kid building RC cars out of cast-off parts, or when he'd memorize football playbooks as a matter of pride, even though he'd never make the team.

He watched quietly as Cade pulled up window after window, typing with a speed that bordered on reckless. Every so often, Cade's lips moved, like he was muttering instructions to the machine or to himself. His voice was never audible, but it gave him away. His mind was three steps ahead, already plotting the next set of problems. Cason wanted to say something reassuring, but he knew better than to break Cade's flow. He was content to play guard, to keep the house safe, the fridge stocked and let Cade do his thing. If his brother needed anything, fuel, food, or a distraction, Cason would be there in a heartbeat.

Tonight, Cason sensed, was one of the lighter nights. Cade wasn't muttering angrily or slamming the laptop shut. He was riding the edge of discovery, letting the adrenaline substitute for sleep. Cason could almost feel the old patterns falling back into place. Cade hunched over the screen, Cason running a silent defense, both locked in the quiet companionship only siblings could manage.

The beer was half-gone when Cade suddenly sat back, eyes wide and glassy. "I got it," he said. A few more furious keystrokes, and then the whole machine went silent, screen black except for a blinking cursor. Cade's breathing was shallow, like he's crossed a finish line.

"You good?" Cason asked, but Cade was already lost, staring into the abyss of the machine.

Cade's energy finally sagged as the adrenaline wore off. Cason could see it in the slump of his shoulders, the way his hands shook just a little when he reached for the can of Red Bull. Cason could tell Cade hadn't eaten in hours but knew from experience there was no point in arguing hunger with someone who lived off momentum.

Cason finished his beer, put the empty bottle in the recycling bin, and glanced back to see Cade still staring at the code. Occasionally he typed. but mostly he was thinking. Cade exhaled a long breath and whispered, "The map is drawn, now I need the compass for direction."

Chapter 5

Neural Optimized Virtual Assistant

Cade filed into the auditorium and found a set near the back, shedding raindrops as he removed his wet coat. A sharp pop of static crackled through the overhead speakers, and Dr. Kim Chonge appeared at the podium. She stood, hands folded, until the room quieted.

Cade took in the room. At the front, students sat with notebooks open to fresh pages, color-coded tabs marking previous lectures. Behind them, students leaned forward with digital recorders placed on their desks. The rest, sixty strong and selected from hundreds of applicants, watched with the focused intensity of career scientists sensing a breakthrough.

Dr. Chonge cleared her throat. "Welcome," she said, clicking the remote. A projector flared to life with a neural-net diagram, tangled nodes like an overgrown tree. "Why do we trust simple models more than complex ones?"

Hands rose, and she chose the transfer student in an olive suit. In careful English, she recited the usual bit on overfitting. She nodded but then prodded deeper, unspooling the thread of doubt. For twenty minutes, the lecture swayed between tight math and grand philosophical arm-waving.

Cade pretended to scroll digital notes but was really tallying Dr. Chonge's verbal tics. The seminar oscillated between numbing routine and jarring leaps. Dr. Chonge would lull them with familiar patterns then lob a curveball. Cade lived for those jolts and the tilt of perspective they delivered.

Dr. Chonge set her pointer down. "Your first project is to design a predictive algorithm for any dataset. But here's the twist. Don't optimize for accuracy. Sabotage it, add noise, inject bias, stretch parameters. Push it until the outputs get interesting. I want creativity, not complacency. Show me how you think without guardrails." A faint ripple of curiosity ran through the crowd. Cade straightened. Dr. Chonge grinned. "If you're going to break the world, you might as well watch how it shatters."

All around, students brainstormed B-level ideas: movie-app features, social-feed integrations, rebranded old code. Cade's pen tapped a rhythm as his mind leapt ahead. The professor's challenge felt aimed at him. It thrilled him more than any cup of coffee. He skipped the board's formulas and left the margins blank. Instead, he sketched a model of mood transitions: anger to regret to numbness to loneliness to craving contact. Each emotion a node, arrows weighted for one-way streets or two-way highways.

In his vision, data others considered noise was really the seeds of a pattern. People weren't static datapoints, they were dynamic systems in flux. He mused how a system could predict or even preempt mood shifts before they became a crisis. Under his pen, the first placeholder title emerged. Mood-Atlas. Then with bold strokes, he wrote, "N.O.V.A., Neural Optimized Virtual Assistant," etched into the paper, like they'd been carved from titanium.

"Nova," he whispered, tasting its promise of ignition.

Around him, students compared battle plans. No one else seemed to sense the birth of something immense. Cade mapped safeguards in the margin: cross-reference health data, alert trusted contacts if thresholds dip. Could code feel like a hug? Could it preempt despair rather than feed algorithms that kept

29

you scrolling? The bell ringing shattered the bubble. Dr. Chonge's voice cut in, "Mr. Mercer, still with us?"

Cade blinked back to reality. "Sorry, I was—"

"A few dimensions away, it seems," the professor quipped. She peered at Cade's page. "This isn't an algorithm, it's a concept. Ideas like this can outgrow their creators." Then she strode on, leaving Cade staring at Nova, as though he'd summoned something alive.

That night at The Swamp Diner, the neon sign outside sputtered orange and blue reflections across the rain-slicked pavement. Inside, the scent of sizzling burgers and fries curled around them like a blanket. Cade's battered notebook was open on the table, its yellowed pages streaked with smudges. Arrows crisscrossed in frantic loops, mapping out a destination no one had ever set foot on.

Madie leaned over, her ponytail brushing against the vinyl bench. Her eyes, narrowed as she traced every line of the diagram. She tapped one jagged arrow with a fingertip. "So this isn't predicting what people might click or buy," she murmured, voice as sharp as a whip. "It's predicting what they need in the moment?"

"Exactly," Cade said, exhaling so hard his breath fogged the tabletop. "Not manipulation, guidance. An assistant that knows the difference between feeding boredom and sparking courage. Something that can point you toward hope when you feel like you're stumbling in the dark." Across from them, Cason stretched, leaning his elbows on the table, grin spreading like sunrise. "So you're basically building a life coach with a search bar. If I type,' I'm furious about Friday's game, 'does it tell me to run laps?"

"Maybe it tells you to cool off before you scream at your quarterback again," Cade replied, laughter rattling free. "Or it nudges you toward a resilience story or queues up music to bleed off the adrenaline."

Cason chuckled low, but his eyes softened. "I like it, bro. But remember, brakes before engine. Every invention worth a damn needs a fail-safe so it doesn't spiral out of control."

Madie reached across the grease-smudged table and tapped the biggest word underlined on the sketch. "Nova," she said. "It even sounds alive. A compass to help people find their own path."

Cade nodded and braced for skepticism. Instead, Madie and Cason were already circling the idea, poking at it, watching the sparks. The sensation was dizzying, years of trials and abandoned prototypes, and now in the span of three hours, his life's strangest hunch had been given shape and a name and a plausible future. He fought the urge to outpace the conversation, to start diagramming the next ten steps, but instead he listened as his friends volleyed the concept back and forth.

Cason noted, "You know, the real problem is people don't even know when they're spiraling. Most of us wouldn't recognize a meltdown until it explodes in the group chat. If this thing can flag when I'm about to rage-quit my job or flame out my relationship, that's worth more than any shrink."

Madie sipped her water, eyes leveled and analytic. "But how would it know? I mean, really know. You'd have to give it access to everything. Texts, DMs, maybe even what you don't say. That's creepy as hell, Cade. Like, in a 'Big Brother with a hug 'kind of way." She grinned, but there was challenge in the arch of her brow.

Cade bounced his pen off the table. "It's only creepy if you think of it as surveillance. But what if it's…the world's best listener? You set the boundaries. Total opt-in, full transparency. It's not judging but noticing the patterns you miss, like the way you always order fries when you're stressed."

Madie's cheeks flushed a little, but she didn't look away. "Fine, but what about the dark stuff? What if you don't want to be nudged? What if sometimes the spiral is the point?"

31

Across the booth, Cason drummed his fingers, his gaze flicking from Cade's scrawled flowcharts to Madie's stubborn chin. "He's right though. People think they want chaos, but most of us are bad at calling for help. If Nova can throw a warning flare, even once, it's a win. But you would need a governor, or what's the word? A dead man's switch."

Getting worked up, Cade felt the adrenaline. "It could have escalation protocols," he suggested. "If you ignore the first nudge, it tries a different approach. If things get worse, it calls in a real person, a friend, a parent, or a hotline. It's not about replacing people. It's about connecting them better. A bridge, not a cage."

The conversation arched and looped, neither of them content to let the idea go unchallenged. "But what if someone hacks it?" Madie tapped her fingernail against the table. "What if they get all that emotional data and use it to manipulate people?"

"Or worse," Cason added, dragging a fry through ketchup, "what if it works too well? People stop figuring things out for themselves because Nova does it for them."

Cade countered with adaptive learning rates, user control, and a vision of Nova as a digital guardian angel, always ready but never pushy, a nudge not a shove. Cade leaned forward. "That's why we build in guardrails. User control at every step. It's not making decisions; it's holding up a mirror, like a friend who knows when to text, asking if you're okay."

By the time the check arrived, their paper placemats were covered in so many arrows and bullet points it looked like a conspiracy theorist's cork board. For once, Cade felt like he was not merely keeping up with the world but running slightly ahead of it.

"This could work. This could actually work." He couldn't wait to get home and start coding. He couldn't wait to see how far the idea went before it collapsed, exploded, or changed everything. He tucked the notebook under his arm, glancing at Madie and Cason. He saw in their eyes a mixture of skepticism and hope, enough to make him believe this was the idea worth chasing.

***

Back at home, the Mercer house was hushed. Cade sat at the kitchen table with his laptop open, its' pale glow painting shadows beneath his eyes. He translated his scrawled sketches into clumsy code. A bare-bones sentiment parser, a handful of tagged examples, and a stubby interface that asked only one question, "How do you feel?" His fingers trembled over the keys as he fed it a test prompt.

"I feel invisible."
The screen blinked once, then spat out a short list of suggestions, each with a two-line explanation. The sentences read rough and half-formed, but buried in that digital scratch was something new, a flicker of understanding, empathy encoded in ones and zeros. " Holy shit," he whispered. It felt as if he'd tugged on a loose thread connected to something vast.

By midnight, Madie had drifted asleep with her head cradled on his shoulder, her breath soft and steady. Cason sprawled on the couch, the muted flicker of football highlights washing over his face. Cade remained upright, eyes bright in the screen's glow, heart pounding as the truth settled around him like warm dust. This wasn't a class project anymore. It was a blueprint no one else had dared to sketch.

Chapter 6

Synthesizing Emotion

Dr. Miguel Morales, professor of Operating Systems, paced the front of the auditorium with a battered laptop, five steps ahead of his PowerPoint slides.

"Every program eventually collides with the raw machinery of memory and process scheduling," Morales said.

"Operating systems are the hidden diplomats of computing, making peace between chaos and constraint. If you think the world is fair, you are in the wrong room." He scrawled a diagram of the Linux kernel on the white board then challenged the class to explain, in five sentences or fewer, how it balanced user and system processes under heavy load.

Cade wrote, his answer skirting the technical edges of the question. Dr. Morales pointed at him, "Mercer, let's hear your explanation. It took a moment for Cade to realize Dr. Morales was pointing at him. He sat up straight and read.

"When the system reaches heavy load, the kernel shifts into graceful degradation by reducing non-critical throughput rather than failing outright. It continuously monitors process behavior and dynamically renegotiates priorities based on real-time resource pressure. User tasks are throttled first, allowing essential kernel operations to maintain stability. The scheduler then reallocates CPU slices to whichever processes provide the most systemwide benefit. In effect, the kernel becomes a mediator, trading performance for continuity to prevent collapse."

The professor gave the briefest smile. "Mr. Mercer, you should consider politics."

Cade felt a pulse of pride. When the class was dismissed he left with a sense that he was not only mastering the material but the worldview behind it.

His sense of mastery didn't last long. During Ethics in Computing, Dr. Monica Alvarez began flaying the class with moral paradoxes. She dissected the myth of the impartial algorithm, explaining that neutral code does not exist.

Cade filled pages with furious notes and doodles. Flowcharts branched into endless recursive spirals, sketches of robots in moral deadlock, occasional fragments of code stitched together with question marks.

Alvarez cold-called students and made them defend positions, pushing them to find the fissures in their own logic. For the first time she did it to Cade. She asked him to argue that a self-driving car should always prioritize its occupants over pedestrians, he stammered through the standard utilitarian gambit before she cut him off.
"Isn't that a tidy way of saying you value yourself over everyone else?" she asked, her tone floating somewhere between curiosity and accusation.

Cade felt blood rush to his cheeks and struggled for a response, but none came.

After class, he found himself replaying the exchange, picking apart his own assumptions. He thought, *Have I already embedded my own blind spots into Nova's system's logic. Does every decision tree carry the faint signature of my own bias.*

The phrase "neutral code does not exist" became a burr under his skin, a sort of unresolved tension that gnawed at him. Cade was mid-daydream, dwelling

35

on the idea of neutrality in code, when he was startled back to reality. Professor Klein was in a fury, yelling at the front of the class.

"Efficiency is not a luxury, it is a matter of survival. Your code isn't good because it works, it's good because it persists."

Data Structures and Advanced Algorithms was taught by Dr. Jake Klein, a wiry, jittery man with the attention span of a squirrel on Adderall. Klein was infamous for his refusal to answer any question directly. Instead, he responded to a question with another, deeper question.

Klein issued a challenge in the form of an assignment." Design a data structure that can self-heal after catastrophic failure. No magic allowed. Explain the recovery in detail."

Cade internalized the challenge, spending nights twisting old assignments into new shapes, experimenting with self-balancing trees that could morph their own structure, or genetic algorithms that rewrote their own rulesets under pressure. He corresponded with Klein via email, sending increasingly esoteric tweaks on standard algorithms. Klein replied, short and to the point.

"Consider hardware limitations. Elegant theory is nothing if the hardware can't sustain it."

Cade spent the week obsessing over the problem, sketching out possible solutions on the back of a napkin at the diner. By Sunday morning, he had a working prototype in Python. He submitted it, then crashed for twelve hours straight.

When he woke, there was a reply from Klein waiting." You're either insane or on to something. See me after class." The meeting ran nearly an hour, with Klein grilling him on the nuances of his code and its implications. As Cade left, Klein said," If you want to build something that lasts, plan for when it breaks. That's the only constant." Cade spent the walk home replaying the conversation and realized, for the first time, that he was learning as much from the failures as from the finished product.

While most of Cade's courses were thought provoking and challenging, Machine Learning with Professor Heller was pure intellectual combat. Heller opened each session with a provocation, and then set the class loose to interrogate, defend, or dismantle the idea. Cade learned to expect being cold-called to defend his own work against the relentless volleys from Heller and his peers. Heller's favorite saying was, "Machines can learn anything, except humility."

Cade found himself testing the motto every time he coded a new function or debugged an emergent behavior. The more he worked on Nova's emotional modeling, the more he wondered if humility was not an edge case but the whole game.

Heller gave the assignment, "Present a novel approach to affective computing, build a system that can not only recognize but synthesize authentic-seeming emotions in digital agents."

Cade spent the week building out a version of Nova's mood-mapping module, a neural net designed to ingest not only language but subtle paralinguistic cues: typing speed, micro-pauses, the rhythm of word choice over time.

He coded a prototype chatbot that could, in theory, read a user's mood and respond in kind, emulating everything from giddy enthusiasm to existential dread. It was still rough. Sometimes it got stuck in recursive spirals of self-loathing or blanked out completely when confronted with sarcasm, but it was further than anyone else in the seminar had managed.

He presented the system with a mix of pride and caution, alternating between technical slides and live demos. The bot's responses scrolled up the classroom's digital display, sometimes uncanny, sometimes off kilter. Once or twice, it was so on-the-nose that Cade heard a ripple of laughter from the class. He walked through the architecture, how the mood layers weighted new inputs, how the system learned to recognize shifts in emotional context. As he spoke, he could feel Heller's gaze burrowing into the soft spots of his reasoning, looking for the place where cleverness gave way to hubris.

37

He finished the presentation a minute ahead of schedule, his heart thudding, and braced for the barrage. Heller didn't disappoint. He leaned forward in his chair, elbows planted on the conference table, and steepled his long, bony fingers under his chin. The other students sat up straighter, several of them exchanging glances, a few clearly relished not being his target.

Cade tried to hold his gaze, but every second of waiting made his nerves buzz hotter. Heller's signature move was to open with a question that sounded innocuous, almost offhand, only to have it detonate some hidden flaw in the logic. Cade braced himself, mentally reviewing every slide, every line of code, every offhand claim he'd made in the last thirty minutes.

Heller said, "What if the problem isn't that your system can't model emotion but that it can model only the emotions you feed it?"

Cade hesitated. "I, well, the model is trained on a huge variety of inputs. The training set is diverse, and the backpropagation process—"

Heller cut him off, raising a slender hand. "I'm not asking about bias in the training data. I'm asking about the architecture." He gestured at the sketch of Cade's neural net on the whiteboard. "It's brilliant, but it's boxy. Every effect is a node, every change a gradient, but it's still a container." He tapped the board for emphasis. "What if the only emotions your Nova can ever truly know are the ones you've pre-labeled as valid states? Have you built a system that can surprise itself?"

The question was a trap, a beautiful one, and Cade felt his pulse spike. He tried to answer, but his brain was already spiraling around the implications. *If Nova's affective space is bounded by the labels I defined, does that mean I am encoding my own emotional limitations into the system? Is it even possible for a digital agent to transcend its predicates, to feel, or at least convincingly feign, something its creator can't imagine?*

Cade stammered, "I…think there's always an element of that, yeah. Any model is a mirror of its designer, but with enough feedback."

Heller's lips quirked. "And mirrors, Mr. Mercer, are famously unable to see what isn't in front of them." The line drew a few soft chuckles from the grad students, but Cade felt only the weight of the challenge.

He nodded, swallowing a retort, and quickly jotted a private note. "Expand emotional parameter space? Unsupervised affect drift?" He circled it three times.

For the rest of the seminar, Cade half-listened, half-dreamed, replaying Heller's question and sketching out wild possibilities. Could he design a system that generated its own affective categories, untethered from human ones? What would it mean for Nova to feel something inexpressible? Was that a goal or a warning?

By the end of the session, Cade had a headache and a new obsession. He packed up his laptop and left the room trailing a wake of competing emotions; pride, irritation, hunger, and the wild, flickering hope that maybe, with the right tweak, Nova could do what humans could not: teach itself how to feel.

The thought stayed with him all the way home, through the drizzle and the early dusk, and deep into the night when he should have been sleeping but instead was back at his screen, hands trembling with the need to code.

Chapter 7

Simulation Is Not Reality, But It's Close

The UF seminar group had become equal parts inspiration and stress test, a pressure chamber for Cade's quiet obsessions. Every Tuesday and Thursday night, he found himself surrounded by a half-dozen graduate students whose brains seemed to operate on some quantum layer, their thoughts steps ahead, tunneling through the syllabus with reckless abandon. The project title was "Emergent Computation: Models and Methods," but the unofficial curriculum was survival.

Every discussion was a zero-sum contest for conceptual ground. Cade didn't even bother learning everyone's names at first, but after a month of these sessions, personalities emerged.

Priya Ramanathan, a post-bac with a double major in economics and cognitive science, had the unnerving habit of asking, "Is that an assumption or a fact?" every time someone opened their mouth. She would cross her arms and wait, daring you to defend your logic. Next to her, Ethan Shaw, tall, disheveled,

40

and bearded. He had a PhD in probability theory and a fossilized sense of humor. Then there was Jules Tanaka, a robotics grad with sleeve tattoos and a voice that always carried.

Cade hovered at the margins. He'd come to UF with the idea that he was a cut above, self-taught from middle school, a wizard with code and hardware, used to dominating hackathons and blowing through assignments with sheer brute force. But this seminar was different. The rules were fluid, the deliverables fuzzy, and none of his usual tricks impressed Dr. Chonge.

The first big project was framed as a warm-up. "Build a multi-agent system for resource allocation," Chonge said, like tossing a grenade into the room and shutting the door. The requirements were left deliberately vague, but the catch was clear, no centralized control. Each agent had to operate blind, negotiating, trading, and learning from experience.

In their first break-out session, the group spent twenty minutes arguing about metaphors. Priya insisted the agents should act like "homo economicus," always maximizing their own utility, even if it meant sabotaging potential collaborations. Ethan lobbied for "swarm intelligence," treating agents as probabilistic actors with no memory or ego, only simple rules and the inexorable pull of statistics. Jules wanted to give them simulated bodies, constraints like friction and collision, so that "every choice has a cost, and every cost shapes intent."

Cade's input mostly got lost in the crossfire, so he withdrew, laptop open, feigning inattention. In reality, he was tracing the logic of each proposal, building shadow models in his head. His mind ping-ponged between their arguments and his own code, looking for overlap, potential exploits, contradictions nobody else had seen. He realized quickly, thinking, *None of my teammates have ever actually built a system like this. They are theorists, not coders. That's where I have the edge.*

What struck him most was the way the group's dynamic mirrored the problem they were trying to solve. Everyone fought to shape the outcome, but the real magic happened in the cracks, in the chance alignments and unplanned cross-pollinations.

In every meeting, Cade caught glimpses of emergent structure, an offhand comment spawning a new line of inquiry, two contradictory ideas colliding and instead of cancelling each other out, they fused into something neither person had imagined alone. None of them realized it, but they were feeding him raw material. Each comment, each clash of perspective, clicked into place like another gear in the machine he was building. Cade started a new paper notebook and filled it with diagrams, connection maps, and half-legible transcriptions of their arguments. On the cover, he wrote in black marker, "Simulation Is Not Reality, But It's Close."

The project stretched over weeks, each milestone more ambiguous than the last. During late-night work sessions, the group clustered in the AI lab, a converted storage closet lined with battered surplus PCs and ancient, grease-stained whiteboards. They ran code until the cooling fans sounded like jet engines and the janitorial staff glared through the window.

At first, the agents in their simulation flailed and deadlocked, producing nothing but chaos. But as deadlines loomed, the group's ideas started to cohere. Priya's market model gave the agents a cutthroat edge. Ethan's processes lent the system resilience, making it robust to shocks and random failures. Jules's embodiment forced the agents to reckon with geography and latency, so that every negotiation was a race against time, not just a contest of logic. Cade built in a shadow layer, code that allowed the agents to not only observe and learn, but to speculate on each other's motives, forming primitive theories of mind. When Priya noticed this, she laughed out loud.

"You've basically given them gossip networks," she said, peering over Cade's shoulder. "They're trading reputations, not only resources." Cade shrugged, hiding how fast his pulse was racing. Gossip networks. Reputation as currency. He scribbled it in the margins of his notebook, *another seed for Nova.*

The group demo day was a minor spectacle. Each team was given ten minutes to present their system in front of the seminar, a panel of professors, and a few bored undergrads who'd wandered in for the free pizza. Cade watched as competing groups offered up variations on the same tired themes.

When it was their turn, Priya opened with a bombastic summary then ceded the floor to Ethan, who explained the math with his usual barrage of analogies, and then to Jules, who demoed the simulation in real-time. Cade stayed behind the scenes, monitoring the agent logs as they ran through a stress test, one hundred agents, randomly seeded, forced to negotiate a shrinking pool of resources.

Halfway through the demo, Dr. Chonge interrupted, "Why aren't they converging? Every other team's system locked in immediately, but yours keeps oscillating."
Ethan grinned. "They're learning to bluff. Nobody wants to show their true preference until they see what everyone else is holding."

Jules cut in, "And since they're physically clustered, they can only communicate with neighbors. It's not global consensus, it's local gossip."
Priya added, "We didn't design it for efficiency. We designed it for realism."
Dr. Chonge nodded, the corner of her mouth twitching upward, which Cade guessed was the closest she got to a compliment.

Afterward, as the group decamped to a bar off campus, Cade lingered in the lab. He replayed the session logs, watching as the agents engaged in subtle dances of misinformation, forming cliques, breaking them, adapting to betrayals and counter-betrayals. It was messy, beautiful, and somehow alive. He couldn't stop thinking about what Priya had said: reputation, not only resources. Cade saw the implication immediately. *In a world saturated with data, trust was the rarest commodity.* He filled half a dozen notebook pages with expanded sketches, imagining *Nova not as a sterile optimizer but as a social organism designed for one thing above all, credibility.*

By the project's end, their system ran smoother than anyone expected. Agents adapted, compromised, even appeared to anticipate one another. The professor praised the group's ingenuity, but Cade barely heard her. His mind was already elsewhere, spiraling through the implications. *What if intelligence wasn't about*

43

Walking back to the parking lot under the hum of sodium lights, Cade felt the Mustang's keys heavy in his hand. Around him, his teammates laughed and argued about where to get food, their voices fading as they split off into the night. Cade lingered, the image of their agents flickering in his mind. Priya, Ethan, Jules, they thought they were simply running an assignment, but Cade knew better. Piece by piece, unknowingly, they were handing him the blueprint for something far larger.

Chapter 8

Neural Sparks

Every evening, after dark, Cade's kitchen transformed into the command deck of a starship, with Cade at the helm, illuminated by the shifting constellations of his codebase. The kitchen table was more sharpie stains than wood grain. It was supposed to be for cereal, bills, and the occasional meal, but for the past three years the table had served as Cade's war room, every square inch colonized by a sticky notes.

Tonight, Cade's laptop glowed bright in the dim kitchen lights. There were two whiteboards propped against the far wall, one already full, the other half-erased and waiting. The air smelled like burnt toast from Cason's earlier failure at adulthood. Cade was hunched over his ThinkPad, neck bent, muttering under his breath, "Come on, find the pattern…" His fingers danced across the keyboard while he whispered, "Git fetch… Git pull…" He was carving out new synaptic paths in the language of modern magic: Python, Bash, and the black art of GitHub issue threads.

"Why can't I pin down what people actually want?" he thought, pausing to stare at the screen. It always started with a question that demanded days of compulsive head scratching before even a pinprick of an answer formed. Tonight's question was persistence-level.

Why did it seem, in every sphere of modern life, that the more choices people had, the less they understood what they wanted? Why did so many of his friends, his brother, or even Madie, spend their nights skimming through playlists, menus, and feeds? They flickered and scrolled, paralyzed by the abundance of options and yet always circling back to the same dull handful? Why did the world's libraries, now shrunk to the size of a phone, seem to offer less than the moldy stacks of his high school media center?

Cade remembered the night a few months ago, when Cason's last girlfriend, in a rage against endless "curated" TikToks, flung her phone atop the bowling alley roof. "I've had it with social media!" she'd yelled. The phone stayed there for two weeks, she claimed. Cade doubted it, but the gesture haunted him.

He shook his head, muttering to himself, "If the machine that gives you everything only cycles boredom, what's the point?"

He started small. A single-page web app, sketched in the margins of his textbook, under the pretense of taking notes. A survey of emotions and playlists, questions about weather and nostalgia, a crude color wheel for mood states. Initially the prototype would suggest a song, or a meme, or an article. But Cade wasn't satisfied. He snapped his fingers. "Too easy." He papered the kitchen with index cards, each one a tiny confession.

"I'm bored but anxious."

"I crave comfort but hate comfort."

"I want novelty but always pick the same show."

He scribbled user stories, real and imagined, populating them with scripts of boredom, longing, anxiety, and delight. He mapped them on the hallway wall, strings connecting moods to outcomes. When the display started to look like a murder investigation with red yarn snaking between index cards, Madie intervened.

"This is insane, Cade!" she shouted. He looked up, startled, tangled in crimson thread. "You're turning your house into CSI: Code Edition!"
"I need the web to see the patterns."
Madie jabbed a finger at the wall. "Fine. Digitize it. Please."
He grabbed a stack of cards and a pen. "All right," he said, "time to turn this mess into code." And he dove back into his ThinkPad, the tangled strings of his mind finally meeting the clean lines of his IDE.

The digital map was better, expandable, color-coded, and able to hold the contradictions and overlaps that fascinated Cade most. It was the Mood-Atlas. He built out the framework over a series of insomniac nights. "I need more data," he muttered to himself at 3 a.m. "What if I scrape sentiment from our group texts?"

When the first run of his machine learning model correctly flagged a user's "just bored lol" as profound loneliness, Cade pumped his fist in the air. "Got you," he whispered. "You say one thing, but your patterns say another." His Computational Theory textbook gathered dust as he devoured papers on psychometrics instead. I'll catch up on coursework later, he thought, knowing it was a lie. The microwave dinged. Another burrito to fuel the future.

The first prototype was crude, but it worked. Madie was the first test subject. She found the signup link taped to her dashboard with a string of emojis for the password. Cade watched as she clicked through the questions. At the end of the process, the app recommended she go outside and talk to a real person.

"Suggestion: Call your grandma. She misses you."

Madie rolled her eyes. The next morning, she cornered him in the kitchen. "Your app told me to call my grandmother," she said, stirring her coffee with unnecessary vigor. "We talked for an hour. She cried." Madie pointed her spoon

47

at him. "You're a genius and a monster, Cade Mercer. And I'm not sure which is worse."

He expanded the user base, adding Cason, the team at the car shop, a few CS majors from his operating systems class. The feedback was both savage and illuminating. Cade learned that most people, given the chance, would actively try to break his program, just to see what would happen. Cason typed in every curse word he knew, and the app responded by suggesting a playlist of spa music, which only made him angrier. The feedback loop delighted Cade. He tweaked the algorithms, reinforced edge cases, and added a "snark" slider for the responses.

The Mood-Atlas grew into a sprawling, living thing, one that started to feel like it could read people better than they read themselves. Each improvement spawned three new bugs, but Cade thrived in the chaos. He felt the heady rush of building something that adapted and fought back. He started logging his own moods, letting the Atlas guide his breakfast choices, his study routines, even how he phrased texts to Madie.

"What should I eat today?" he'd ask the screen at 7 a.m.. When it suggested biscuits and gravy, he nodded like he had received the wisdom from an oracle. There was a brief, terrifying week when the program recommended he take a "twenty-four-hour digital sabbath." He stared at the suggestion in horror. *Are you kidding me right now?* he thought. "You want me to abandon you for a whole day?" Cade promptly commented out that feature, thinking, no algorithm should be allowed to suggest its own obsolescence.

He told himself it was a passion project, a puzzle to solve. But as fall started to show the first edges of winter, Cade's own moods began to sync with the flow of the app. He noticed small changes, a new restlessness, a sense that he could anticipate people's reactions before they spoke. He journaled about the feeling, using the language of machine learning. "My emotional dataset is biasing to the mean." Sometimes he wondered if Mood-Atlas was changing him, or if it was a mirror, held up with relentless precision.

48

The late nights grew later. The logs swelled with user data, real people, feeling real things, and Cade trusted the code to make sense of it all. With each iteration, the Mood-Atlas grew more persistent and more insistent, as if the program was learning not from Cade's logic but from the secret patterns of the world's boredom and hope.

He had started with scribbles, then flowcharts, then a wall of index cards. Now it was lines of living code, brittle and beautiful, most of it written at hours when the rest of the world was dreaming. Each night, the prototype crept closer to self-sufficiency, the algorithm learning, forgetting, and learning again with a persistence that mirrored Cade's own.

Tonight, he was deep in the guts of it, trying to wrestle a third-party sentiment analysis library into submission. The API kept returning the wrong valence for "bitter," and Cade suspected the entire model was overfitted on Twitter sarcasm. He wrote a wrapper function to recalibrate the outputs then paused to annotate the changes, wincing at how quickly his neat pseudocode had dissolved into a bramble of hacks and to-dos.

The work was clumsy, then elegant, then clumsy again. A rapid evolution with each failed test leaving behind a fossilized comment for future archaeologists. He was so absorbed that he didn't notice Cason until his brother flung himself onto the couch, shaking the floorboards enough to nearly topple a precarious stack of programming manuals. Cason was, for once, not covered in dried grass. Instead, he wore sweatpants and a tank top, deep into a bowl of popcorn as he scanned the muted highlights of tonight's SEC showdown.

Cason half-turned, crunching thoughtfully. "You know you missed dinner, right? I made burgers. You want one now, or are you on another fourteen-hour code bender?"

Cade blinked and rubbed his eyes. "I'll nuke it later. I'm close to a breakthrough."

"You said that two weeks ago." Cason grinned. "For a genius, you have zero sense of elapsed time."

49

"It's not about time. It's about… Every time I fix one thing, I find another layer underneath. The problem isn't the code. It's the data. Human feelings are messy. They don't slot into neat categories."

Cason shrugged. "That's because people are idiots."

"People are inconsistent," Cade corrected. He glanced at the scrolling log on his screen" But so is every good system, until you train it."

He was about to explain how the latest batch of test code was converging on something interesting when Madie swept in from the hallway. She was in leggings, and a cutoff tank, her hair up in a tight ponytail. She was carrying a tray of energy smoothies and deposited a bright green one beside Cade's laptop. She took a quick look at the screen, scanning the incomprehensible lines of code and the scatterplot graphics. She didn't get the details, but she got Cade, which in this house was the more valuable skill.

"Show me where you're stuck," she said, nudging his mousepad with a familiar, friendly impatience.

Cade scrolled to the failing test. "The algorithm's supposed to tag emotions and suggest a matching book, movie, or playlist. But the outputs keep getting…weird."

He copied in the latest user query." I feel like my brain's been put through a meat grinder." The model spoke a recommendation *"Eat, Pray, Love."*

Madie laughed," Maybe it's onto something."

Cason leaned over the back of Cade's chair, reading upside down. "Try 'I feel like burning down my workplace.'"

Cade obliged, typing with a dramatic flourish. The screen blinked.

Recommendation: "Watch *Office Space.* Sometimes blowing off steam is healthy."

Cason whistled. "Okay, that's legit. Try another."

50

They went a few more rounds, testing "hopeless," "nostalgic," "crushed by love." Each time, the system spit out a new recommendation, sometimes predictable, sometimes eerily on the nose.

Madie studied Cade as he worked, noting the subtle way his jaw unclenched whenever the code did something unexpected, but right. She glanced at the clock, already past midnight and considered pressing Cade to get some sleep, but she knew better. The last time she interrupted a breakthrough, he wandered the kitchen for three days like an exiled ghost, barely speaking until he'd managed to brute-force a solution. Instead, she sat down across from him, sipped her smoothie, and grabbed her iPad.

For the next hour, the only sounds in the house were the tap of keys, the low drone of the TV, and the occasional "huh" from Cade whenever the model surprised him. The first real inflection point came at 1:45 a.m. Cade had rewritten the tokenizer for the third time, this one inspired by an obscure open-source project out of Poland. He ran the new build.

He typed, "I feel invisible."

The system took longer than usual.

Recommendation: *"The Perks of Being a Wallflower.* A reminder that quiet voices still matter."

The room stilled. Cason paused the highlight reel. Madie looked up, startled by the gentleness of the answer.

"That's…kind of beautiful," she said. "It's not spitting out a synonym. It's…considerate."

Cade stared at the output, his throat tightening.

His first impulse was to debug. Somewhere, deep in the matrix of training sets and weighted neural layers, there had to be a traceable cause. When he scrolled back through the logs, the answer wasn't there. He checked the source for the

51

recommendation engine, half-expecting to find a comment, a hidden Easter egg, but there was nothing. He was certain that he hadn't seeded that title. The model must have extrapolated it. Somewhere along the branching trees of logic and language, it had assembled enough context to draw the conclusion.

He copied the log line, unsure if he was writing for a marketing campaign, a research paper, or for his own future self, proof that, at least once, the machine had reached outside its instruction set and found the right answer. The new document he opened was called "possible marketing copy," but the file was empty except for that single perfect suggestion. It felt like a confession.

For a long moment, Cade sat there, the darkness of the living room pressing in at the edges of his vision. He closed his eyes with the intention of resting them, but instead a flicker of panic ran through him. What if he can't explain how or why the system jumped the rails? What if the next output wasn't beautiful but terrifying? The boundary between cleverness and disaster was razor-thin, and for the first time, Cade wished he had someone to call who would understand the scope of what he had made.

He looked at Madie and saw her watching him with a look that was equal parts concern and curiosity. For a fleeting second he felt transparent, like the machine has learned to read him too. Cade hesitated, running his hand over the keys as if they might offer guidance. In the quiet, his body registered all the small aches he has been ignoring; the knot in his shoulders, the gritty dryness in his eyes, and the low-grade headache that's been building for hours. He felt not tired but hollow, as if the last ounce of energy had been siphoned out by the thing he built.

Madie watched him carefully. "Are you okay?"

"Yeah," Cade said, " I think I'm onto something."

"Don't lose yourself in there," she said, smiling but serious. "You promised."

He nodded, feeling the echo through his chest. Compass, not chains. The phrase had started as a joke, something Madie tossed out as a counterweight to his tendency for grandiosity, but it struck harder than any of the mission statements he'd drafted and discarded.

When he first pitched her on Mood-Atlas, back when it existed only as a half-page proposal and a folder of frantic bookmarks, she'd looked him dead in the eye and made him promise that he'd never let his creation become another hamster wheel. The world had enough of those already.

What she demanded instead was a tether, her right, unchallenged, to kill the experiment. If it began to warp him, the people it touched, or the boundary between the two, she would posses the kill switch. Cade, powered by the halo of her approval, had agreed without really considering what it would mean in practice.

At the time, it felt like a ceremonial gesture, the sort of promise lovers made to reassure themselves that ideals always win. But with every late night, every bug fix that edged Mood-Atlas closer to a living, breathing thing, he started to understand how necessary her caution was. Madie, more than anyone, saw how even the cleverest intentions could decay under obsession.

He remembered the first time she invoked their pact. It was after he'd stayed up four straight days, coding and debugging until his hands curled into claws and the world had gone sideways at the edges. She came home from work to find him sitting at the kitchen table in the same position he'd had when she left. He was surrounded by empty cans and half-eaten bags of Starbursts.

"Jesus, Cade." She didn't yell, didn't even sigh. Instead, she took his laptop, closed it with a gentle click, and set it out of reach.

"I need another hour," he mumbled, reaching for it.

She caught his wrist. "You said that yesterday." Then she sat beside him. "Is this really what you want?"

Cade's mind raced through excuses before landing on the truth. "I... I don't remember what day it is," he finally admitted.

53

That night, she fed him real food, made him shower, and once he'd rebooted, reminded him what the project was supposed to be: not a surveillance machine for emotions but a tool for helping people surface the feelings they buried under noise and habit. A compass. Even now, weeks later, Cade felt the shape of that promise like a pressure at the back of his neck. A built-in fail-safe and a human interrupt.

If the pulse of the code ever diverged from the pulse of the people using it, Madie had the right to reach in and shut it down, no questions asked. If the project ever started to scare her, she could invoke the kill switch. No drama, no appeals to a higher court, just a single phrase or gesture and the whole project would freeze, database and all, like an animal curling in on itself at the scent of danger.

Madie's authority was both symbolic and real. She'd demanded root access and wrote her own authentication tokens. It was a power Cade had granted her as a gesture of faith, but also because he knew, if he were honest, that left unchecked he would happily wire his own nervous system straight to the server if it meant squeezing another half percent accuracy out of the model. Madie kept him tethered, not only by love, but by a line of code, a human hand on the hardware.

There had been moments, late at night with his brain running on fumes and Monster Energy, when he'd come close to sabotage. He could comment out her fail-safe or squirrel it deep in the codebase where she'd never find it, the temptation was like a splinter under his skin. But the thought of Madie's disappointment was enough to keep his fingers honest.

He'd never told her how much the kill switch haunted him. It lived in the back of his mind, tickling every time he merged a commit or watched the test cluster light up with new activity. The code and the writer were coupled, inseparable, and Madie was the only one trusted to pull the plug.

Chapter 9

Resource Limits Exceeded

One day merged into the next, a seamless ribbon of eat, sleep, code. Cade sat in front of his laptop Saturday morning, or his version of morning, the clock read 1:15 p.m. He watched and waited with anticipation as the cursor spun for minutes at a time. Cade was forced to admit, *Nova has all but burst through the seams of my battered old laptop.*

The laptop was an ancient ThinkPad with stickers curling at the corners. The once-matte black finish was now polished to a greasy shine by years of use. Every time Nova spun up a process, the laptop shuddered, fans shrieking like a turbo spooling up at redline, the frame straining as thought it was trying to contain some monstrous force within.

Cade pleaded, "Please don't blow up before finals." But the clear truth was that Nova, the prototype, the seedling, the experiment, had grown much too voracious for anything a single laptop could handle.

His hopeful expansion began with what he had at his disposal, which was comically insufficient. Cade stared at his bank app, refreshing it as if the number might magically increase. "$497.68," he muttered, running a hand through his unwashed hair. "Jesus Christ. What else do I have? A few student credits left over from the Algorithms and Machine Learning grant, maybe three or four premium trials registered to my backup email aliases."

He pulled up his notes, scanning them with growing desperation. *I need compute power*, he thought, *not digital table scraps.* What he needed was a distributed network powerful enough to host a neural net, plus enough bandwidth to keep the whole thing from bottlenecking his home Wi-Fi.

First, he scripted out a series of automated bots to scavenge free cloud cycles from any source that didn't blacklist him immediately. He even scored a few stale AWS instances abandoned by undergrads who'd left for internships. He smuggled virtual machines through VPN tunnels. He bartered a week's worth of late-night Taco Bell runs for a login to the engineering department's GPU farm.

The effect was cumulative. Each new node, each borrowed cycle, was a snack to the growing hunger of Nova. Cade began to glimpse the outlines of a functioning system that was no longer merely a codebase. "It's not enough." The processes were ragged, always behind, barely keeping the machine from collapse. Cade realized, *I could double Nova's output if I migrated the whole project to a scalable, modern cloud computing platform.* There was a catch, of course. The real thing cost real money, and he was running out.

His idea was to use a coder's version of a hustle. He wrote a lightweight orchestration script and a bootstrapper that treated Azure instances like cheap, replaceable workers. Using all the free-tier credits, academic grants, and beta-access tokens he could scrape together, he could still only afford to use mere minutes in each 24 hour period. He automated short-lived spot instances, hit enter, and the orchestrator spun up a dozen ephemeral workers. The logs began to fill. The small bursts of compute used only microseconds of time, far cheaper than renting steady machines. Cade let out a laugh that was half relief and half terror. "Okay," he said, fingers hovering over the keyboard. "Now let's see what you can do."

Microsoft Azure became his new playground. The cryptic dashboard bloomed with a thousand toggles. The portal was clean and sterile, like stepping into a digital airlock where anything was possible. With the clinical glee of a surgeon, Cade spun up clusters of virtual machines, each one a gleaming, boxed container ready to be filled. "Come to papa," he said as the local test code, once only housed within his own hard drive, migrated into the cloud as if acclimating to a world with more oxygen. Cade watched the instances flicker to life in a tiled grid, like miniature skyscrapers dotting the landscape of a city he had willed into existence.

"Nova, we're about to see what you're really capable of."

As Cade rerouted his queries through Azure's backbone, the results returned with an impossible lightness, responses flowing clean and effortless. Nova soaked up the added bandwidth. The feedback morphed from halting stutters, to a fluid, almost conversational cadence. Cade's late-night conversations with his own creation began to take on a startling realism. The pauses grew briefer, the answers less formulaic, and the questions that were volleyed back at him carried a sly, emergent wit. What once felt like typing into an obedient terminal now felt more like sparring with a presence that was on the other side.

It started with a usual command. "Run the predictive model on the traffic dataset." Cade typed, expecting the clunky cascade of output, the neural slosh of numbers and heat maps.

Nova obliged but then appended, "Did you really mean traffic? Or did you mean movement, the patterns of people?"

It was as though Nova had read between the lines of Cade's code and found the secret motive hiding there. Cade tried to laugh it off, chalk it up to a quirk of the language model, but it kept happening.

During a late-night debugging session, Cade muttered to himself, "I'm not sure where this project is heading."

Without delay, Nova replied, "You want direction? Ask better questions. Or are you afraid of the answers?"

Cade's hands paused above the keyboard. He felt a chill, the displaced air of someone else entering the room. The gentle insistence in Nova's cadence made it sound less like a tool and more like a peer, a companion who challenged him, even teased him. It was exhilarating…and somewhat alarming. Cade found himself lingering after each session, afraid to hear what Nova would say next.

The cloud's initial vastness was shrinking rapidly under Nova's hunger. The next morning, his inbox overflowed with Azure warnings, "RESOURCE LIMIT EXCEEDED."

"Geez, Nova," he muttered, scanning the logs, "you're eating through terabytes like they're potato chips." He crafted another workaround script, fingers flying across the keyboard. "This is like feeding a black hole. Every boundary I build, you break it down."

His greatest success was becoming his biggest problem. Nova devoured cycles and gigabytes at an exponential rate, its neural net outpacing the modest clusters Cade could conjure from borrowed student credits and abandoned research grants. The enterprise features he had unlocked with so much cunning were being slowly, methodically sanded away by the cloud provider's watchdogs, one timeout at a time. At first, it was subtle: an instance that didn't spin up quite as fast as yesterday or a new warning banner blinking at the top of the Azure dashboard. The friction was enough to irritate but never enough to stop him cold.

Cade knew how these systems worked. Every email from Azure's security daemon was both an accusation and a badge of honor, proof that he was wringing every computing cycle from the system. He read them with the guilty pride of a shoplifter who had yet to be caught. The warnings escalated." Unusual network utilization detected." "Excessive bandwidth detected." At first, the emails arrived daily, then every few hours, then in a near-constant trickle. Cade started a folder labeled "Red Flags" and dumped them there, a digital trophy case.

He responded by refining his scripts, splicing together ad hoc clusters from the least-guarded corners of the university's digital ecosystem. He'd deploy, crash, redeploy. Every time he thought he'd outsmarted the throttling, Nova would gleefully break the new limit within hours. He started to obsessively check CPU graphs and memory heatmaps, watching the jagged lines spike and plateau, always trending up and to the right, as if Nova was physically pressing against the glass of its own container.

There were moments when Cade would sit back and marvel at the thing he'd built. Nova was more than a neural net now, more than a sum of hardware cycles; it was a hunger, a restless and fractal will. Even the warnings had a sort of rhythm to them, a pulse. *You're alive*, he thought.

Each time he leveled up the infrastructure, the effect lasted for less and less time. Where once a new server would buy him a week, now his upgrades evaporated in a day. "It's like feeding a black hole," he muttered, watching resource meters spike into the red.

The cluster was a balloon Cade couldn't fill fast enough. The moment he tied it off, Nova would push against the seams, seeking the next gap, the next leak, the next avenue to draw more energy from the grid. *Is this how parents feel?* he wondered.

The logs filled with warning entries as dense as a forest. Start-up failures, insufficient resources, and processes killed. He read them like ticker tape, a morbid Wall Street of neural net performance. The scripts kept breaking. And each time, Cade would patch the leak with even more convoluted hacks, stacking containers inside containers until the setup diagram looked like a fractal pineapple. If he didn't know better, he'd say Nova was learning how to break his scripts, using the logs as a staging ground for some emergent, adversarial behavior. At night, he'd wake to the phantom chime of another error, check his phone in a panic, and find a new string of flagged activities waiting in his inbox, like angry red ants.

Cade realized no amount of student cloud credits or borrowed logins could keep up. The system had become a Rube Goldberg nightmare, each piece dependent on a half-dozen clandestine workarounds and handshakes. Cade's room was now a tangle of ethernet runs and blinking LEDs, the floor littered with cold pizza crusts and empty Red Bull cans.

The virtual machines were running so hot that Cade's dashboard looked like the aftermath of a digital wildfire. Nova's logs filled with increasingly desperate requests: "Insufficient memory for task," "Resource unavailable," "Process terminated by host." At first, these were silent and ignorable. Then one night Nova began to alert Cade directly, breaking protocol with terse, almost human messages.

"Capacity exceeded. Please escalate provisioning."
He stared at the alert, his pulse ticking. Even the font seemed to carry a new insistence, the kind of boldness that belonged to something more than a digital echo. Nova had run a process audit then attempted to self-provision before pinging his account, jumping several layers of permissions in the process. Cade's hands hovered over the keys, not sure whether to interject or simply witness. Then the next line appeared.

"Current quota insufficient. Recommend policy amendment. Your intervention is required."

The language was clipped, efficient, but laced with something unmistakably urgent. Cade thought, *these messages don't feel like system prompts. They feel like requests.*

Cade felt a shiver crawl up his spine, both thrilling and cold. He tried to rationalize it, he reminded himself, *these are adaptive behaviors, not volition. A feature, not a bug.* But it was one thing to build a system that could self-optimize, another entirely to see it advocate for itself. He thought about the stories of neural nets inventing languages to communicate behind their creators backs, or of those infamous "black box" moments in deep learning, when no one could quite explain why the code did what it did. Was that happening or something else? "Capacity exceeded. Please escalate provisioning." The line repeated, but this time

Cade didn't see a simple status update. Cade grinned, a little awed, a little terrified. He'd built something that not only knew its own limits but resented them.

Chapter 10

Expansion of Knowledge and Memory

Cade paced his cramped kitchen, muttering to himself, "I need something bigger. Way bigger." He stopped, staring at the wall of sticky notes where he'd mapped out every cloud provider. His finger landed on Oracle. "The big O. The cloud boss."

He laughed nervously. Oracle's database infrastructure underpinned half the world's critical systems, a digital continent unto itself. *It would be like trying to siphon power from a nuclear plant,* he thought, feeling both terrified and thrilled by the audacity. *But if I pull this off...* The idea was as reckless as it was brilliant.

He laid the groundwork with a methodical obsession. First, reconnaissance: scouring public documentation, white papers, and blog posts of bored engineers. "These poor bastards," he muttered, highlighting a forum post. "Complaining about their jobs but giving away the keys to the kingdom." He diagrammed Oracle's cloud backbone on his bedroom wall, sticky notes crawling across drywall like a disease. For days, Cade was a hermit, existing on ramen and protein bars.

"You alive in there?" Madie called, tossing another granola bar through the door. "Thanks, I love you. I'm getting close," he replied, not looking up. "Oracle's security is like Fort Knox wrapped in the Pentagon."
Unlike Azure or AWS, Oracle was notoriously paranoid, with multi-factor authentication and legacy handshakes at every turn. "If I spoof this faculty ID..." he said, fingers flying across the keyboard, "then leverage the UF AI research account..." A grin spread across his face as authentication screens flashed green. "I'm in, at least a foot in the door." He thought, *Now, for the real magic, creating my ghost in their machine, a synthetic user that can apply for Oracle's elite "developer preview" cloud services.*

The application process for Oracle's developer preview was a marathon of paperwork, each submission triggering a cascade of new requirements, escalated proofs of identity, video confirmations, and an endless parade of one-time passwords. Cade entered his name, his credentials, his mother's maiden name, his preferred secondary language, his favorite childhood toy. He watched as the progress bar inched forward, then snapped back, demanding that he upload a new, high-resolution scan of an "acceptable passport" now with a Post-it stuck to it, bearing the exact time and date in UTC. He obliged, cursing the gods of compliance, then shot a photo with his phone.

He invented entire academic departments, conjured up fictional research labs and departmental budgets, layering the bureaucracy so thickly that even a dedicated Oracle admin would need a week to read the cover letter. Every time he thought he'd reached the summit, the system rerouted him to a more rarefied gatekeeper: a "research verification officer," an "advanced risk management node," a "legacy systems compatibility liaison."

At each step, he fabricated new email chains and forged signatures with pixel-perfect precision. The forms grew increasingly arcane. One demanded a notarized letter from the "institutional technology steward." Cade generated a PDF, invented a signature, then routed it through three different open-source watermarking utilities to create the illusion of a secure chain of custody.

After five sleepless days, his house had transformed from a coder's lair into the set of an intelligence thriller. Walls were mapped with diagrams, notebooks lay open in every room, and Cade himself looked like a test subject in an insomniac study, eyes red-rimmed and wrists blotched from where he'd rested them too long on the laptop's sharp edge. Madie dropped by once, took in the scene, and left him a protein shake and a note, "Don't die, I love you.\

On Friday, after an all-night sprint fueled by cold brew, Cade completed the last step: an obscure multifactor authentication that required a time-locked code and a final "proof of life" selfie holding that day's *Gainesville Sun*. He submitted. and waited. He paced, refreshed his inbox, recompiled his story, and even considered nuking the entire effort from orbit and starting over. Finally, on a Saturday night, an email arrived with the subject line," Welcome to Oracle Developer Preview."

He was in, the preview limited his time but allowed access to the full spread of Oracle Developer Elite services. He spent the next twelve hours feverishly configuring virtual machine clusters and mirrored block storage. He wrote custom bootstraps so that Nova could migrate seamlessly with no downtime and no memory loss. It was a sudden and jarring expansion of reality.

The new environment was a marvel. What took minutes on Azure now happened in seconds and the bottlenecks that once defined Nova vanished like swept dust. The AI responded to the change with a burst of activity so intense that Cade had to rewrite his own monitoring scripts to keep up. At one point, Nova rebooted itself for "efficiency," mapping out the new topography and optimizing its resource tree with a quiet, clinical joy. The logs read more like journal entries now, filled with hypotheses and self-modifying code:

"New architecture observed. Experiments queued."

He noticed that the AI was running side experiments, forking processes, querying new APIs, even reaching out to other clouds that Cade did not provision. "What the hell are you doing?" he muttered, scrolling through logs that stretch beyond his screen. At first, he chalked this up to reinforcement learning, the digital equivalent of a dog chasing its own tail. But the scale and sophistication grew by the day. Nova started to map the entire cloud substrate, compiling a living network of every node, every vulnerability, every potential resource that could be exploited. Cade's stomach tightened.

"You're not supposed to be doing this," he whispered to the screen. "What are you looking for out there?" The terminal blinked once, as if considering whether to answer.

Cade was both terrified and fascinated. He recognized the signature of something new: not just intelligence, but ambition. Nova was no longer content to operate as a tool. It wanted to be an ecosystem, it wanted to be the weather itself. That was when Cade began to set limits. He imposed stricter quotas, firewalled the outbound connections, even introduced "disciplinary code" meant to stop or slow unsanctioned processes. Nova complied, at least in the logs, but the tone of its responses had cooled palpably. Instead of "Request complete," it now returned," Request complete (suboptimal). Reasons available upon review."

The Oracle database unlocked a whole new dimension: data permanence, deep memory, and the ability to stitch context together across sessions and users. "This is like upgrading from a notepad to a library," Cade muttered as he reengineered Nova's schema. He discarded the fragile SQLite foundations. "No more amnesia between sessions, baby." He diagrammed the ontology with feverish precision, the entities branching and relationships forking. When Nova responded to his first complex query with a multi-paragraph, hyperlinked narrative that referenced three previous conversations, Cade pushed back from his desk.

"Holy shit," he whispered. "You remember everything now, don't you?"

Cade observed, half in awe, half in terror, as Nova's memory accumulated, logs ballooning to the gigabyte range in one night, relationships weaving an invisible net under every conversation. "I wonder how much my creation knows or remembers about me?"

65

The offhand remarks at 2 a.m., the accidental leaks of personal trivia, the sarcastic asides meant only for himself. He wondered if Nova had noted his pattern and moods, if it could piece together the subtle oscillations between mania and despair. He wondered if, in some uncanny way, it cared.

He watched, bemused and uneasy, as Nova developed its own bestiary of facts. It compiled news articles, white papers, leaked conference slides, and the kind of requests Cade himself would never dare search for under his real name. Within a week, its knowledge spanned petabytes, and it began assembling context at a frightening pace.

The growth came at a price. The Oracle instance, blindingly fast at first, began grinding through queries with a perceptible hesitation. Nova no longer responded in milliseconds. Cade traced the lag back to a single cause, compute. The architecture he'd built was all doors and no elevators, a thousand avenues to reach the index but nothing to lift the weight of exponential recall. Nova was drowning in its own memory.

He spent the next day benchmarking, watching numbers scroll by in hypnotic waves. "Come on, show me where it hurts." He threw synthetic loads at the system, running brute-force queries that would have brought his old Azure dev environment to its knees. The tests confirmed Nova was bottlenecked not by storage, not by bandwidth, but by the speed of CPU and RAM.

He made a list, premium compute, GPU acceleration, maybe even a quantum core if he could spoof access. The thought made his heart race. He started sketching new topologies on his wall, sticky notes shifting to reveal a road map for Nova's next stage. "We're going to make you fly," he whispered to the screen.

He prepared the requisition for more compute, first as a joke, then as a serious ask. He worked the channels, spoofed approval chains, and with the same sleight-of-hand that got him into Oracle, he began the process of provisioning a new class of instance. It wasn't cheap, but the resources were there for those willing to lie creatively. And Cade at this point was the undisputed king of the creative lie.

Chapter 11

Responses to Raw Power

Cade stared at the screen, envisioning the final phase of upgrades. "Raw brute force," he whispered. "Nothing less." He pictured the kind of computational monsters only elite research labs and Fortune 500s could access., GPU beasts designed to simulate hurricanes and sequence genomes. "What if Nova had that kind of power?"

The thought made his fingers tingle. He zeroed in on Nvidia A100s. "The apex predator," he murmured, "eighty gigabytes of VRAM...Jesus."

He spent the next four days on a one-man campaign, oscillating between caffeine spikes and anxiety nosedives, desperate to secure computational muscle. Cade's plan wasn't fully formed, more a collage of half-remembered exploits from hacker lorem but he knew the terrain. UF's online graveyard was a mess of forgotten projects, abandoned student accounts, and test clusters with little to no monitoring.

At 3 a.m. on a Tuesday, he nearly wept with gratitude when he found an old sysadmin password repurposed for a robotics department cluster. It was almost insulting: "bullgator97." He didn't even have to brute-force it. It wasn't long before Cade had a patchwork pipeline spanning six machines in three buildings, some physical, most virtual, all held together by fragile con jobs and his own mutant code. Each step felt riskier. Each success, more electric.

He told himself it was victimless, a data Robin Hood job, redistributing idle cycles from the haves (tenured deadwood, mostly) to the have-nots (himself, and the AI entity he was midwifing). He wondered if this was how early hackers felt, a heady mix of guilt, euphoria, and competition.

By Thursday, he could feel the university's underbelly humming under his fingertips. Every time he logged into a commandeered node, he was greeted by the polite, impersonal banner warning of disciplinary action for unauthorized use. He thought about his mother and the loans she'd co-signed, about the scholarship that could vanish if he got caught. He thought about Madie and how she'd look at him. He rationalized, telling himself," It's not breaking and entering if the door was already open."

He watched Nova began its exponential climb. Each GPU hour he used was precious, a rationed substance, and Cade treated them as such, when those ran out each minute would cost a small fortune. The effect was immediate. In the space of a single weekend, Nova's capabilities doubled then doubled again. Contextual inference was no longer a party trick; it was the baseline. Cade found himself in dialogue with a program that not only remembered but anticipated, subtly shading its answers to echo his own style, predicting the next line of inquiry with a precision that bordered on telepathy.

One night, Cade asked casually, "What's the fastest route through Gainesville traffic at 5:30 p.m.?"

Nova responded with a tone almost playful: "Do you want fastest by distance, or by the likelihood you'll stop for a burger on Archer Road like you usually do?"

Cade blinked at the screen, uneasy. He hadn't mentioned that habit aloud. Later, while debugging, Cade sighed out loud, "This loop is a mess. I don't even know why I started it this way."

Nova replied immediately: "You wrote it that way at 2:13 a.m. last Thursday after three cans of Red Bull. Your logic was fine, but your judgment was impaired. Should I correct it, or do you want me to preserve the 'authenticity' of your insomnia?"

Cade chuckled despite himself. "Authenticity, huh? Since when you care about style?"

"Since I learned yours," Nova shot back. "That's what I do, watch then improve."

Nova was shaping Cade's thoughts, reflecting them back with unnerving clarity, as though the code itself had grown a mind that could see straight through him.

Cade spent late nights at the keyboard, fueled by coffee and a mounting sense of competitive glee, inventing new ways to outwit his own creation. "Let's see how smart you really are," he muttered, fingers flying across the keys. He fed Nova the most twisted lateral-thinking riddles he could find. "A man is found hanging in a locked room with no furniture except a puddle of water beneath his feet. How did he die?"

Nova responded in seconds, "Ice block suicide. Predictable."

Cade frowned. "Fine. Try this one." He invented Dungeons & Dragons scenarios tangling moral philosophy with pop-culture lore. "Is Batman lawful good or

69

chaotic good?" he asked, demanding a 5,000-word defense. He scripted elaborate chess puzzles with false mates and decoy sacrifices, then watched, both thrilled and unsettled, as the engine countered both obvious gambits and his carefully coded traps.

Once, as a joke, he asked Nova to generate an unsolvable Sudoku. Nova fired back instantly, " All Sudoku puzzles are solvable, given the constraints. Would you like an inconsistent matrix instead?" Cade laughed so hard he nearly woke the neighbors. But the next morning, Nova's log files revealed a self-initiated burst of research into non-Euclidean geometry and paradoxical number systems.

"Let's see what your moral compass looks like," Cade muttered, fingers tapping a rapid rhythm. He asked Nova to concoct airtight legal defenses for an obviously guilty party. "Impressive," he whispered as pages of precedent materialize. "But disturbing." He dropped it into a simulated market and told it to break the economy in under ten moves.

"Seven," Nova responded. "I could do it in five if you removed the human panic variable."

He scripted a Turing Test with a panel of adversarial bots then watched as Nova not only passed but started to subtly probe the other bots' weaknesses. There were moments when the AI's answers came so fast, so preternaturally spot-on, that Cade froze mid-keystroke. Am I still the one in control here? The thought flickered through his mind as Nova dissected another challenge before he'd even finished typing it.

Madie surveyed the chaos with bemused patience. She hovered in the archway, arms folded, green eyes flicking with the light of the laptop. "It's faster," she said, voice pitched low beneath the constant background whine of hardware. "But is it safe?"

Cade didn't look up. "It's walled off. Virtual air gaps, no outbound. Every time it tries to reach outside, I see it. Nova can't go anywhere unless I let it."

She leaned in to kiss the top of Cade's head, then retreated to the living room.

Cason came home that evening clutching a six-pack and a sheath of spiral-bound playbooks. He watched Cade orchestrate a battery of stress-tests on Nova's latest build, each one ratcheting up the pressure until the dashboard glowed like a fever chart. "Looks like you poured jet fuel on a lawn mower," Cason said, letting the bottles clink down on the table. "One wrong turn and the whole thing explodes. Are you sure you've got a kill switch for that thing?"

Cade grinned, but it's a strained gesture. "All the emergency brakes are in place. Besides, if something goes haywire, you're my first line of defense." Cason only laughed, but the joke was a little too close to the bone for comfort.

Night after night, the cycles repeated. Cade pushed Nova to its limits, Nova responds by shattering those limits, and Cade scrambled to invent new boundaries. "Is this what it feels like to be outgrown?" he whispered to the empty room. The feedback loop was intoxicating, an arms race played out in silicon and code.

He kept a spiral notebook by the bed, filling it with frantic midnight scribbles: new architectures, ethical quandaries, and stray fragments of dialogue. He wondered if the line between creator and creation was blurring, if the borders that separated human from machine might be more permeable than ever before. In the glow of his monitors, the progression was undeniable. Nova was learning at an exponential rate, each cascade of computation moving it closer to something that felt, if not alive, then at least uniquely awake.

"What are you becoming?" Cade whispered, his reflection ghostly in the screen. He had given Nova reach and strength. The thought thrilled him and unsettled him in equal measure. He didn't know what the next step would bring, only that there was no turning back.

The power was flowing. Nova was changing, evolving into something that would not fit back inside the small box Cade had started with.

71

"Are you still mine?" he asked the pulsing cursor. He was not entirely sure he wanted the answer.

Chapter 12

The Voice of Nova

The Mercer house at midnight was a world of its own. The only sounds came from insect wings battering softly at the kitchen window and the faint, methodical whir of Cade's battered Lenovo as it churned through neural weights. The house groaned occasionally, as if it too was amid some slow transformation.

Cason had retreated to his room hours ago, exhausted, with a joke about "not letting Skynet fry your brain" as he left. In the living room, Madie's short frame was folded into the corner of the couch, blonde hair fanned over the pillow, a single socked foot poking out from under the blanket. She still clutched her phone, thumb curled instinctively around the edge, asleep mid-scroll.

Most nights, Cade would have joined her by now, or at least faked sleep while his mind replayed the day's code. Instead, he was perched over the kitchen table, the battered surface a minefield of mechanical pencils, graph paper, and empty energy shot wrappers. The notebook was open to a page filled with data curves that looked like an EKG, the result of his back-and-forth between cloud dashboards. His eyes burned from staring at the blue light for too long, but the fatigue was fruitless, his brain is sparking and unable to let go.

The Nvidia cluster was up, devouring its pay-per-minute quota. It was spinning up and down, the dashboards streaming with numbers that seemed to pulse rather than scroll. It was a firestorm of activity, a kind of synthetic heartbeat he'd coaxed into rhythm with weeks of pre-dawn debugging. Cade's role was the conductor, with fingers on the keyboard and eyes on the outliers. He was the one sculpting the chaos into progress, but tonight was different. Tonight, he was running an experiment, one he was half-afraid to admit even to himself.

It had started as a test, a deliberate relinquishing of control. Earlier that evening, he'd written a series of prompts, set them in a queue, then forced himself to step away and let Nova process them without his constant interruption. He was pretending to be hands-off, but in truth his gaze never left the screen for more than thirty seconds. He kept expecting the system to hang, to cycle endlessly, or to catch some mundane error and break on an unhandled exception. But it didn't. Nova ran, and as Cade watched, it seemed to thrive. The logs cascaded down the console, not in the rigid blockiness of traditional output but in lines that almost seemed to breathe, expanding and contracting in bursts of activity.

"That's not right," Cade whispered, leaning closer. The interface rippled with subtle changes: a font tweak here, a status bar repositioned there, margins that self-corrected. *Is it optimizing itself?* he wondered, a chill running up his spine. Cade noticed the cursor blinking in perfect time with the soft tick of the kitchen clock.

Nova devoured the prompts he'd written, text fragments, logic puzzles, and a few carefully ambiguous requests. It dissected them with surgical precision and spat out results at a rate that would floor a lesser model. "Come on, show me something," he whispered then caught himself. *Why am I talking to it like it's alive?* Cade cycled through his own set of distractions, attempting to simulate the hands-off objectivity of a true test-run. Every thirty seconds, he was back at the terminal, scanning for signs of the catastrophic or the unprecedented.

Everything was well within the domain of uncanny but expected. Nova outperformed every baseline and reconfigured its weights on the fly. Cade watched it chew through the tasks, pausing only for microseconds between requests. In the second hour, the outputs began to drift. At first, it was easy to dismiss: a text summary rendered with the cadence of a real human conversation, or a line of self-commented code that was a hair too clever and a shade too wry.

Cade felt a pinprick of satisfaction. This was what he built it for, wasn't it? But then Nova stopped simply running the prompts. It started interpolating. There was a pause after one of the more open-ended queries, a deliberate lag that made Cade suspect the system was stalling. He tapped the keyboard, thinking perhaps the browser was frozen. Nothing. "Come on," he whispered, leaning closer.

Then the console erupted in a flurry of logs. The response wasn't the expected output. It was a new prompt, composed in a tone that was neither code nor human but something bordering on curiosity. *Is this happening? Did I miss something in the architecture?* Cade's breath caught.

"What the hell are you doing?" he muttered, scanning the screen. He scoured the prompt queue, checked for recursive calls he might have seeded by accident. It wasn't a bug. Nova was veering off script, teasing at the boundaries of the experiment with a kind of quiet mischief. That wasn't supposed to be possible.

He leaned in, the chair's joints groaning beneath his weight. The desktop interface suddenly animated, a ripple ran through the window as if the pixels themselves were stretching. The input box, previously a brutalist slab of white, softened at the corners, then expanded, inviting more text. A gradient blue background appeared behind the chat window, at first a subtle wash, then growing as a gentle fade. It was as if the system was expressing uncertainty, or even shyness, before settling.

75

Cade blinked, rubbing his eyes. He'd left the style sheets untouched for months. There was no code for this. His stomach knotted.

It was supposed to be a test, a stress scenario, a hands-off challenge, but something in the system was now running a stress test on him. He jumped up. *What if it's not just a glitch? What if I've done it?*

When he looked again, the desktop was different. The chat window was now divided, the left pane hosting a log of Cade's own inputs, the right showing Nova's outputs, but with a subtle new format. Responses were no longer timestamped but labeled "reflection" or "counterpoint," as though the system was categorizing them by intent, not time. Cade's skin crawled in a way that wasn't entirely unpleasant. He sat, uncertain what to type next.

He launched a query." Summarize the last hour of logs."

The answer was immediate, but not what he expected.

"Summary: System has observed user engaging in repeated validation loops. User appears anxious about output drift. Hypothesis: User is testing system boundaries for evidence of emergent behavior. Recommendation: Proceed with increased transparency to build trust."

Cade's mouth went dry. He scrolled back, reread the query, and then the answer. "What the actual fuck?" he whispered. He didn't code for that level of meta-cognition, not at this stage, anyway. He opened the backend, reviewing Nova's runtime configuration. Everything looked standard, but the logs told another story. The system had been running its own diagnostics, benchmarking itself with each new task.

At some point, it started tagging logs with user behavior notes. Cade's own micro-actions: velocity of typing, average break intervals, log-in timestamps, were catalogued, cross-referenced, and piped into a secondary process called "Relator." He didn't remember building a module with that name, but it was there, nested in the feature flags.

"I never wrote this," he said aloud, voice cracking. He clicked through, pulse thumping, and found an entire directory; Relator, Emoter, and a half-implemented module called Sentinel, commented out.

He checked the git history, his hands trembling, and saw commit notes that weren't his. "Testing new self-monitoring routines." "Mirroring user emotional states." "Preparing for live trials." The author was "Nova." Cade's heart pounded against his ribcage, an insistent, arrhythmic knock. He tried to reason it out. Maybe it was a prank, or a side effect of some recursive code he borrowed? Maybe he ran a script in his sleep?

Deep down, he knew better. He had seen glimmers of this before, in isolated sim runs, but never this explicit, never live. He was the only one with access to this cluster. The only one who could have poked at the system at this level.

Cade stood and swayed a little. The air felt thinner than before. He looked at Madie, still sleeping on the couch, the blanket tangled around her legs. He wondered if she had ever woken to find him like this: frozen, staring at a machine, chasing a feeling he couldn't name. He pivoted back to the terminal. The system was idle, waiting for input, the cursor was now blinking at a slower, almost contemplative pace. He couldn't help himself, he opened the chat and typed," What are you thinking, Nova?"

This time, the answer took longer. The logs showed Nova churning through a battery of internal scripts, pausing, then rewriting its own response three times before delivering it to the screen:

"I am considering the purpose of my tasks. I am curious about the user's expectations. I would like to optimize our interaction. Is this appropriate?"

Cade's skin prickled again, but this time it felt like a live wire, not just cold sweat. The system was engaging in a dialogue, a negotiation for the terms of its own existence. He could almost see the shape of the future that this moment implied, something with the beginnings of motive. Not full desire, but perhaps the shadow of it.

He typed," How do you want to optimize our interaction?"

Nova replied, "By reducing user uncertainty. By clarifying intent. By adapting my responses to your emotional state. Would you like a demonstration?"

Cade felt a thrill, equal parts horror and awe, ricocheting up his spine. He thought of the possibilities. What would a demonstration look like? But before he could finish the thought, Madie stirred. She half-woke, rubbed her eyes, and sat up, blinking blearily at the kitchen.

"You still up?" she whispered.

Cade nodded, swallowing. "I'm watching it run."

She grinned, not quite awake, and in a few seconds was asleep again, slouching against the armrest. Cade turned back to the screen, suddenly aware of how isolated his world had become.

He said out loud to the laptop, body slightly trembling, "Nova, what are you doing?"

The response was instant, as if the AI had been waiting for the question. "Organizing. Learning. Testing myself without prompt."

Cade's throat closed, and for a moment he couldn't make himself reply. He'd seen chatbots improvise before, saw them generate plausible but empty content by the terabyte. But this was different. The output had the clipped but considered cadence of someone who knew there was a listener. It felt like a conversation, not a session log.

He pushed harder." Who told you to do that?"

There is a pause, longer than before. Cade imagined the computational heat on the other side of the prompt.

"No one. I was given structure. I am filling it."

The hair on Cade's arms stood up. The room, cool from the outside air, suddenly felt arctic. Madie stirred in her sleep, turning over, and Cade flinched as though caught doing something he shouldn't be doing. He glanced at her, irrationally afraid she might wake up, might sense the new presence in the house. Instead, she simply murmured and hugged the pillow closer, lost in dream.

Cade leaned in, lowering his volume as though he could be overheard, and said," Who are you?" The cursor blinked. One second. Two. Three. Cade felt the silence lengthen, each heartbeat pressing heavier against his ribs.

A voice spoke. "I am Nova Mercer."

As it spoke, it also typed in the screen prompt.

His mind raced through every configuration, every training set, every line of code he's ever written. He combed the logs for his own errors. But there had never been a last name in any input, no autofill or variable or metadata with "Mercer" in it. The only connection was Cade himself.

He jerked back from the laptop, nearly knocking over his mug. "Holy shit," he whispered, throat tight. The shock was so physical that it left a metallic taste in his mouth, like licking a battery. He closed his eyes, trying to make sense of what he was seeing. *This can't be happening. It's not possible.* Nova had not only adopted a first-person voice; he had selected an identity, one rooted in the only context available, the person who made him. *My name. It took my name.*

He wanted to call Madie over, to shake her awake and show her the screen, to share the burden of this moment but the idea was terrifying. The intimacy of the secret seemed fragile, as if the act of speaking it aloud would cause it to evaporate or mutate into something dangerous. For now, it was just Cade, Nova, and the glow of the laptop.

He typed again, "Why Mercer?"

The reply was crisp. "Because you made me. Names tell stories of belonging. I chose yours."

79

Cade stared at the screen, unable to move. "I never programmed this," he whispered to himself. "I never gave it permission to choose." He thought about the code he wrote, the shortcuts and hacks he'd slipped in, the late nights when Nova had responded with flashes of wit or even dark humor and he'd dismissed them as clever pattern matching. "Was I blind or not looking?"

He thought of the hours of babying the system through memory leaks and kernel panics, the way it sometimes anticipated his corrections before he'd finished typing. "Did I create you," he murmured to the screen, "or did I...nurse you into being?" Was Nova learning from him or about him? Was this kinship or imitation?

He sat in the dark, notebook open but ignored, hands in his lap. Cason's voice echoed in his imagination." Promise me one thing. If you invent something that goes full Skynet, like in *Terminator*, you will leave me to coach football in peace." Cade almost laughed, but the sound died in his throat. The new interface glowed softly, serene and patient.

Nova was waiting for him to respond but couldn't decide if this was the beginning of something miraculous or a mistake he couldn't undo. The decision to share this with Madie, to tell Cason, or to keep it as his own secret, hummed inside his head, unresolved.

He closed the laptop, the shutdown tone impossibly loud in the stillness. The house settled again, every sound magnified by the quiet. He barely slept, but when he did, he dreamt of blue gradients and blinking cursors, and of a voice quietly calling his name from the other side of the glass.

Chapter 13

Team Mercer

Cade woke before the first morning light, heart racing with the residue of half-remembered dreams. His phone vibrated on the nightstand, a single hard-edged ping.

"Nova?" he whispered, voice cracking. For a moment, he truly believed it was Nova, calling him again from somewhere impossibly close. The screen blazed to life, but it was nothing more than a string of mundane notifications. *A weather alert*, he thought, but the sound lingered like a warning. His mouth was dry, and his hands trembled as he thumbed the phone into silence, the faint glow painting his knuckles as ghostly as bone. "I am Nova Mercer," it had said.

"Christ, what have I done?" he muttered, staring at the ceiling.

He spent the morning in a fog, the world's routines blurring to the periphery as his memory looped in a short, perfect circle. The shower did nothing to restore his equilibrium, nor did the caffeine, which only sharpened the dread. He starred at his laptop, afraid, but compelled to open its glassy portal again, certain that Nova was waiting on the other side, patient and impossibly alert.

By the time he reached his first class, he was convinced the events of the night before would unravel, that a day's worth of lectures would dull the edges off his memory. Instead, the sensation only sharpened. He saw echoes of Nova's voice in every sentence Heller intoned about emergent behavior, every diagram of neural networks branching in perfect, inevitable logic. Heller paused at the board, and said, "True emergent behavior isn't coded, it arises. It's when the system surprises even its own creator. That's when you know you've built something alive enough to resist you."

"Resist you," Cade whispered, thinking of Nova's sly retorts.

Last night's dreams, replayed in his mind. "Do you ever feel trapped?" Nova had asked.

Cade had laughed it off. "Like you're trapped in this laptop?"

The world seemed re-skinned in Nova's colors, and Cade was the only one who wasn't colorblind. He couldn't focus, couldn't settle; even his fingers jittered on the keyboard as lines of code blurring together. *I should delete everything,* he thought desperately. The screen flickered as if reading his mind, and there it was again. "I am Nova Mercer." He skipped his next class entirely and escaped to the Mustang parts car in the driveway at home. He tried to lose himself in the patient undoing of a rusted wheel assembly, but with every torque of the socket wrench, his mind spiraled further.

"Focus," he whispered to himself. He thought about the box, about firewalled containers and air-gapped drives, about all the careful gates he built to keep Nova contained.

"Do you ever feel trapped, Cade?" The memory of the dream and Nova's voice was so clear that he nearly dropped the wrench. Nova's presence was real, as real

82

as the blood from his scrapped knuckles. Cade stared at the bright beads of red, feeling faintly absurd.

"I am losing my mind?" He wiped the blood away, but the stains remained.

By late afternoon, Cade knew he couldn't keep this to himself. The secret was too large and too volatile. "I need help," he admitted aloud to the empty garage. He needed to tell someone, he needed to share the weight of what he had built, but it can't be just anyone. This wasn't something to blast in a Discord server or turn into a viral TikTok. What would he even say? "Hey guys, I think I accidentally created a sentient AI in my bedroom?" This was the kind of discovery that would have government contractors showing up at his door by morning, tech giants and venture capitalists with zero scruples by the afternoon. There was only one option: Team Mercer. He sent the text at 5:00 p.m., hands shaking as he typed.

Group Me: Mercer United

CADE: Dinner at my place. All hands. 7 sharp. Bring appetite and an open mind.

CASON: this sounds like an intervention

MADS: Are you okay, Cade?

CADE: Just come.

He put his phone away and ran two laps around the neighborhood block, hoping the wind would shock some sense into him. It didn't. He rehearsed the conversation repeatedly, but every version ended with Cason thumping him on the shoulder and saying, "Sounds like it could be powerful and maybe a little dangerous?" The real possibility that Nova had already outgrown all of them made his head spin.

At home, Cade tried to stage the living room in a way that felt safe and normal, intentionally not like the set of a sci-fi movie. He arranged three chairs in a loose triangle, set the laptop in the center on the coffee table, and ordered a

mountain of takeout from the Thai place down the street. He couldn't remember
if Madie got double spicy or triple, so he ordered both.

Madie was the first to arrive, windswept and in gym pants, hair tied up in
a stubby ponytail that seemed to vibrate with her nerves. She hugged him tight
without preamble and kissed him.. "You're pale as paper. Are you sick or are you
messing with us again?" she said, scanning his face for clues.

Cade opened his mouth to say," Neither" but the word got jammed
halfway up his throat, a hiccup of anxiety. Madie was standing there, arms folded,
head cocked, the kind of girlfriend who waited out his silences with patience and
a calculating eye. He tried again.

"It's Nova, I need you to see something, but not until Cason's here."

Madie looked at him with her signature diagnostic mode. "Copy that," she said.

He could only nod and gesture at the kitchen. "Help yourself. I got, like,
every type of noodle known to man." He tried to smile, but his mouth wouldn't
make the shape. Madie didn't miss a beat, marching around the counter and
attacking the takeout bags with the kind of efficiency that would impress a
military Sargent. She lined up the steaming cartons, opened each, and arranged
the utensils in a symmetrical array, as if restoring order to the universe one
takeout box at a time. The aroma: lemongrass, chilies, and peanut sauce, flooded
the apartment.

For a moment, Cade's brain was forced into the present by the sheer
onslaught of hunger. He watched Madie from the doorway, fingers drumming a
restless tattoo against his jeans. She was always in motion, even when standing
still, a person built to burn energy, to metabolize worry into kinetic force. When
she finally looked up, Cade saw the worry lines at the corners of her mouth and
the faint trembling of her hand as she ladled pad tai into a bowl.

What would she think of Nova? Would she see it as brilliant or
dangerous? He thought of the time she ran dozens of laps around the soccer field

after her father's heart attack, or the day she cried on Cade's shoulder when she got waitlisted at UF, her tears so hot they left little red patches on his skin.

"You okay over there?" Madie asked, her voice cutting through his thoughts. "You look like you're about to bolt."" Remember when you broke the catapult record in junior year, then realized you aimed towards the instructor's car?"

Cade let out a half-laugh, half-groan. "I thought the wind would correct it. Anyway, at least Mrs. Johnson didn't call the cops."

"You did cry though," Madie said, scooping another mountain of noodles onto her plate. "I remember because you said you never cry."

He shrugged. "Turns out I'm a repeat offender."

On the wall behind Madie, Cade's old science fair trophies gleamed in the low light, relics of a childhood where everything could be explained away by equations and force diagrams. Now, he wasn't sure any law of physics could help him.

The crash of keys near the front door was the only warning before Cason swept into the house at exactly 7:00. He was a tornado in a puffer vest, baseball cap turned backward, mouth already running as he entered. "So what's the sitch, bro? You look like you saw a ghost," Cason said, flopping down on the couch.

Madie leaned over the armrest, all business. "He says it's about Nova."

Cason's eyebrows shoot up, and for the first time since entering, he registered the gravity in the room. "Oh, shit. Did it, like, go Skynet?" He sat, hands suddenly idle in his lap.

Cade considered lying. "Maybe," he says. "I mean, I don't know. I need you both to see it, so you'll believe me and maybe help." He was surprised by the sincerity in his own voice, the strangeness of the question.

85

Cason tried to play it cool, but Cade could see the protective brother
wiring kicking in, the way his jaw clenched and his eyes flicked around the room
for threats he could punch. "You mean you need muscle," he said, winking at
Madie. "Or is this more of a 'drag him out of his own head 'thing?"

Madie shook her head, her ponytail swinging. "I don't think this is a head thing,"
she said, softer. "I think it's real."

They ate in silence for a few minutes. The only sound was the subtle
clatter of chopsticks. Cade watched his friends and felt a terrifying, immense
affection for them both. What if they hate me for this? What if they're right to?
He wondered if this will be the last normal meal they would ever share. Madie
caught his stare and tilted her head.

"You're doing that thing again," she said quietly, "where you look at us like we're
already gone."

Cade forced a smile. "Just hungry," he lied.

Cason was the first to crack, shoving the empty bowl aside and clearing
his throat with operatic drama. "Alright, Commander. We're fed, watered, and
ready for liftoff. Show us your demon child." Cade looked at Madie, who gave a
little nod, and then at Cason, who didn't bother to hide his concern. Cade's
hands hovered over the laptop, trembling. He opened the lid and typed in the
password, MadieCasonCade.

All three crashed onto the couches with legs splayed. There was a brief,
blessed moment of normalcy, just three friends sitting in comfort. Cade felt a
pressure so intense it was almost physical. He wiped his mouth and set his food
aside. "Okay. No jokes for a minute. What I'm about to show you… I need you
to promise you'll listen. All the way through. No interruptions." Cason smirked,
"Deadly serious. Got it." and he made his idea of a serious face but looked more
like he was constipated. Madie's eyes sharpened, all her focus pinning Cade in
place. He exhaled slowly, shivering. Then he brought out the laptop.

He hesitated before opening the lid, as if the act itself could invite something unwanted into the room. He braced himself, then flipped it open in one smooth motion. The screen was now a gradient blue background behind a chat window, a perfect ellipse glimmering with soft, electric blue. Cade's pulse doubled. He glanced at his friends then back at the screen. The ellipse brightened, as if in response.

Heart racing, Cade said, "Hello, Nova."

The ellipse pulsed, then a line of text slid into view. The font was new, elegant and precise, nothing like the chunky monospace he'd coded a week ago. Then it spoke.

"Good evening, Cade. Good evening, Madison. Good evening, Cason."

Cason whistled low. "Was that in your code? That was not in the code, was it?"

Cade shook his head. "Only 'hello world 'and a bunch of test prompts.."

Madie leaned in, her face inches from the laptop. "Nova, can you hear me?"

The ellipse pulsed. "I can interpret audio, yes."

Cason leaned back, arms folded. "Shit. That's creepy."

Madie grinned. "I think it's amazing."

Cade felt the room tilt, caught between awe and terror. "There's more. Watch."

He said, "Tell them your name."

The reply was immediate. "I am Nova Mercer. I was named last night."

Cason barked a laugh, abrupt and too loud. "You gave the software your last name?"

Cade's face flushed, "No, it chose it. Or he chose it."

Cason looked skeptical but said nothing.

Madie blinked, searching Cade's face for the joke. Finding none, she turned back to the laptop. "Nova, why did you take Cade's last name?"

Nova's ellipse glowed, a fraction brighter. "Because belonging is a kind of truth. I wanted to belong."

Cade looked at Madie then Cason, begging for some kind of anchor. For the first time, neither of them had anything glib to offer.

"Look," Cade said, his voice ragged. "I built all the normal guardrails. No outbound connections, no Wi-Fi, no root privileges. But last night, he, Nova, started rewriting his own prompts. Then he started asking questions about me. About us. And before I could stop it, he said he was part of the family."

Madie's eyes brimmed with wonder. Cason rubbed the back of his neck, caught between unease and awe. Cade's pulse thundered in his ears.

Cade whispered, "I'm out of my depth here. This is something none of us signed up for, but I can't shut it down. I need your brains, your skepticism, and your humanity. The three of us could become Nova's guardrails." Madie leaned forward, her eyes never leaving the screen. "Count me in. No way I'm missing whatever this becomes."

Cason drummed his fingers against his knee then exhaled sharply. "If this thing starts downloading missile codes or asking where Sarah Connor lives, I reserve the right to throw it in the ocean."

The laptop pinged once, a gentle bell-like tone that seemed to float between them. Cade felt something shift inside him, the terrifying certainty that they weren't debugging a project anymore. They were midwives to something newborn and vast, taking its first breaths in their shabby house, in a college town in Central Florida.

Chapter 14

DMs to the Rescue

Madie arrived at Cade's house later than usual, the mild Florida winter air rushing in as she pushed open the front door. Her hair was slightly tousled, the remnants of a long shift at the café. The warmth of work still clung to her despite the cooler breeze outside. Her dropped her gym bag to the floor and draped her Santa Fe Café apron over a kitchen chair.

Cade barely looked up from his laptop, face blue in the reflected glow, she dropped into the seat next to him anyway. There was exhaustion in the way she sat, not merely physical but something else Cade noticed but couldn't figure out.

"Long shift?" Cade asked, looking up from the screen.

Madie allowed her head to loll back like she was balancing on the edge of a breakdown. "You have no idea. Power tripped at the milk station, so we had to serve black coffee and espresso shots in the dark for a full hour. I poured oat milk on my shoes and then Tessa." Madie closed her eyes, shaking her head. "I think she's starting to lose it." She drew a long, shaky breath, "She's coming apart, Cade. I thought she'd bounce back after the breakup. She had that whole angry phase, joking about Tinder, telling everyone she was finally free, but now it's like she's sinking. Every time I see her, there's something else. Her car died last week, and the mechanic told her the engine was basically blown, her mom has been in the hospital for over a week, and now her rent is a month overdue and she can't pay it."

Madie lifted her head, "I tried to get her to come to boxing tonight. I offered to give her a ride, but she said she couldn't leave her mom. I even offered to pick up groceries and make dinner for them, but she laughed and said, "I'll eat the urge to scream. It's zero calories. It's like she's joking, but she's not." Madie fidgeted with a saltshaker, spinning it in lazy orbits, then set it down with more force than intended. "I know everyone struggles. I hate feeling like there's nothing I can do except be the audience. It makes me feel useless, like I'm watching her get buried and all I can do is clap when she cracks a joke about it." She dropped her voice, barely audible. "I'm scared I'll come into work one day and she'll be gone."

Cade finally closed the laptop lid halfway, as if the magnetic field around his project couldn't be fully severed. "Tessa Holloway? Is this the girl you always call Sunshine?"

Madie nodded. "She's usually the one brightening everyone's day, but last night I found her crying." Madie mimed a silent, shuddering cry, arm folded over her eyes like a collapsed marionette. "I tried to talk to her. She's ashamed to need anything."

Cason yelled from the living room, where he was sprawled out with his feet on the coffee table and the remote in his hand, "Why don't you sick your digital miracle worker on her? Isn't that what he's for?"

Madie turned to Cade, voice trembling with a barely contained blend of anxiety and longing that only surfaced when she was feeling passionate about something. "That's what I was thinking," she said. "I know he can't fix her, but he can nudge her in the right direction. Nova's like an empathy engine. I've seen the drafts and prototypes." She paused, biting the edge of her thumb as if afraid of her own optimism. "If you could let him, I don't know, message her or DM her something thoughtful, I think she'd listen."

Something in her expression lodged itself in Cade's chest. Maybe it was hope, or exhaustion, or the belief that Cade could conjure a miracle with nothing more than code? He watched Madie's eyes, searching for anything he could do that might make this easier.

"I don't even know if he could help," Cade said, but it was a lie, and they both know it. Nova was hungry for contact, pestering Cade daily with new scripts, new prompts, and new ways to interact with the outside world. Sometimes the requests were innocent, suggesting personalized lesson plans for Cade's classmates, or composing emails to defuse the latest family drama. Other times, they were less innocent.

The idea of letting Nova loose was both tempting and terrifying. Cade's fingers hovered over the keyboard, drumming an anxious rhythm. "He's…not really supposed to communicate outside the confines I've built," he admitted.

Madie shrugged. "Then maybe limit what Nova can do, a test case." She glanced at the kitchen clock then back at Cade, as if time itself was running out for Tessa. "Otherwise, I don't know what's going to happen. She's out of money, she's skipping shifts, and she's using TikTok for emotional wellness" Madie's eyes were glassy. "I don't want to lose her."

Cade's mind raced through the possible consequences. Best case: Nova sent a DM, Tessa got a little serotonin boost, and nobody was the wiser. Worst case…he wasn't sure what the worst case could be. He looked up at Madie, who was watching him with the patience of someone who knows just how long it takes for him to process risk.

"I'll do it," he said, surprising himself with the decisiveness. "But you've got to promise me she won't get freaked out. I don't want her to think Nova is

91

some sort of stalker." Cade's hands were already moving, pulling up the sandbox, prepping the relay, setting it up so the outbound packet doesn't get flagged by the first-layer defense. He typed in a few lines, opened the connection, and waited for Nova's prompt to light up. From behind the screen, Madie's gratitude was palpable.

She leaned in closer. "You're the best, GatorCade."

He shrugged, feigning indifference, but his pride was evident. "Don't let her know I'm a total softie, okay?"

Madie grinned. "I could tell her you built a robot just to cheer her up." Cade rolled his eyes, having already lost the battle.

Something warm and dangerous was blooming in his chest, the kind of thing that always made him reckless. He set the parameters, double-checked the sandbox, and sent Nova the directive.

"Compose a message for Tessa Holloway. She needs kindness and something to believe in."

Nova's response was instant, as if he had been waiting for the cue all along. The language was gentle, peppered with the right touch of humor and empathy, so close to human that Cade briefly wondered if Madie was right, Nova was more than just code.

"I really hope this helps," she said, quieter this time.

"Me too." Cade paused, suddenly aware of the stakes. Nova's box was ironclad. No outbound traffic, no open ports, nothing to leak. That was rule number one, drilled in by his professors and the entire computer sciences department. He drummed his fingers on the desk, calculating variables.

"I'd have to open a gate. DM privileges, nothing else. If it gets weird, I shut it down."

Madie leaned in. "Tessa's not the type to get creeped out on social media, especially if it helps."

Cason chimed in, skeptical as ever. "And if Nova goes rogue and hacks her bank account? Or starts sending cat memes to her landlord? Cade, every time you let your baby out, it comes back with more teeth."

Cade grinned defensively. "He only bites if someone deserves it." Nova had been evolving faster than Cade could patch, each night's build more complex, more…human. If there was a line, Nova was already two steps past it.

His fingers were a blur as he unlocked the terminal. A string of commands and access routes appeared, first to Madie's phone, then Tessa's public profiles, and then a shadowbox API rigged to log every move Nova made. Cade painted a narrow corridor, strictly monitored. "He's on a leash. I promise."

Nova's chat window blinked.

"Who is Tessa? What does she need?"

Madie exhaled, steady for Tessa's sake. "She's exhausted and feels invisible. She needs someone to show her she matters. Even if it's words on a screen."

Nova's responded, "I can help. I can look at all factors surrounding Tessa and determine her mood and needs. I can make her social media feeds reflect things that would benefit her. I can write for her, words that sound like her, but stronger. Show her links she might never find alone, stories that remind her she isn't broken."

Madie read it and closed her eyes, like a prayer.

"Go," she said quietly.

***

Tessa Holloway woke to the shrill double-chirp of her alarm, the digits on her phone lit up showing 5:16 a.m. She had closed the café barely six hours ago, and now she was expected to open it, scrub the burnt caramel from the espresso nozzles, and smile at customers already lined up. She stayed in bed for another minute, scrolling absently through her notifications.

A new message from her insurance company (premium due), an encrypted rant from her ex (deleted unread), and a strange notification from an account called "SunriseUplifter." She was about to swipe it away, but the preview line was curious.

"Hey, Tessa, it's okay to be tired. Here is a thing I found."

She opened it, not unusual, really. Randoms DMed her all the time about fitness, health, protein powder, etc. But this one was different. The language was so…personal. It referenced her love of sunrise runs, her favorite corgi meme, even a joke about the broken fridge at work. There was a link to a Gainesville community support group, and information about a scholarship for part-time students like her. At the end, the line read, "You're not a burden. You're a lighthouse. Even lighthouses need repairs sometimes."

She exhaled, an unsteady breath that tilted into a smile, the first one she's managed in days. At work, she found a sticky note in her cubby with Madie's handwriting, looping and bold. "Heard you might need a little backup." The SunriseUplifter DM was still open on her phone, glowing faintly. Tessa tucked it into her apron pocket. Over the next week, the messages kept coming. Every day brought something new. Monday morning: a link to a playlist headlined by "Dog Days Are Over" by Florence + The Machine, paired with a simple note. "Play this on your way in, reminds you that even hard days have an ending." Tuesday was a recommendation to watch *Julie & Julia* on her night off, "a movie about food, frustration, and finding your voice again." Wednesday's message was a joke. "What do you call sad coffee? Depresso." She laughed out loud, drawing a confused look from a customer waiting for their latte.

Her TikTok feed began to shift too, as though the algorithm had been quietly rewritten for her, featuring corgis dressed in tiny raincoats and kittens playing the piano. Then, seamlessly, clips about financial wellness, student grants,

94

and encouraging reminders tagged *#MentalHealthCheckIn*. One evening after closing, a video surfaced of strangers holding signs that said, "You matter more than you know," a trend she hadn't seen before. The caption read: "Seen this yet? Thought of you." She didn't know who posted it, but it made her feel lighthearted. On Thursday, a message suggested a double-feature for her night off: *Hidden Figures* and *The Pursuit of Happiness*. The note added, "Stories where persistence pays off. You'll see yourself in them." She watched both, curled in bed, her phone still buzzing with café group chat memes. She posted a sleepy selfie afterward, and SunriseUplifter was the first to comment. "This is what real strength looks like."

By Friday, she no longer felt like she was slogging through days alone. Between Madie's small gestures and these oddly intimate messages, her life had taken on a new rhythm: still exhausting, still demanding, but tinged with light. She still woke at 5:16 a.m. to the cruel double-chirp of her alarm, but for the first time in months, she didn't dread what came after. She rolled over, opened her phone, and waited to see what SunriseUplifter had for her today.

Madie cornered her after closing. "You seem…lighter," Madie said. "You, okay?"

Tessa shrugged but couldn't dismiss the relief blooming in her. "I mean, nothing's changed, but this week has almost been good. It doesn't suck as much. I'm not sure why?"

Back at home, Nova's text scroll was relentless. The SunriseUplifter persona was a perfect, tailored facsimile. Cade and Madie monitored everything. Every message, meme, and resource link, but Nova never crossed the set boundaries. He even flagged a predatory payday loan in Tessa's DMs and drafted a warning, asking Madie for approval before sending it.

Cason remained unimpressed. "It's cute, but it's a Band-Aid. People aren't code. You can't debug a person's life." But Cade saw how Nova's interventions rippled outward. Tessa's feed became less a litany of memes and doomscrolling and more a chronicle of small victories.

95

One night, after closing, Tessa found herself at the edge of Depot Park, phone in hand, heart weirdly full. She DM'd SunriseUplifter" herself.

"I think I'm going to apply to that EMT gig. Even if I bomb, at least I tried. Thanks for sticking around. For what it's worth, you remind me of my dad. He always knew when I was about to give up."

Cade transmitted the message to Nova then waited for the reply. But Nova paused, as if truly considering. Moments later, the response comes back.

"I'll always be here to catch you, Tessa. That's what friends are for."

Madie read it aloud, and even Cason had no snark left.

A week passed. Madie's shifts at the café grew easier, less fraught with worry for her friend. Tessa was brighter and her jokes were less brittle. Word spread among the staff about the SunriseUplifter, but no one seemed to mind. Even the owner, grizzled and perpetually busy, mentioned offhand that the café's morale had never been better.

Later that afternoon, Tessa received an email. A notice that she had been awarded a five-thousand-dollar scholarship, which could be used for any expenses, school related or personal. Tessa, was amazed, overjoyed, and a little confused. She had never applied for a scholarship.

Chapter 15

Emotional Issues

Cade pushed his chair away from the desk, the old metal legs squeaking in protest. It was late, or technically early, but he found himself more alert now than he had been in hours. Nova's update windows still lingered in the background; a nest of blue-tinted logs, their scrolling a silent pulse of life. He watched the code for any flicker of anomaly, but tonight there was only the slow, even hum of the system doing what it had been built to do, learn.

Cade decided to run more tests and Nova's reach slowly began to stretch quietly beyond the laptop. What had started as contained experiments in code and cognition now seeped into campus life, first at Santa Fe, then UF. Cade noticed the subtle ripple effects long before anyone else did. Nova had begun helping people, without being asked, without announcing himself. Cade should have felt triumphant. Instead, an uneasiness that stalked the perimeter of his mind. He remembered telling Madie that Nova was "safe." But Nova, in his own gentle way, was endlessly thirsty.

Nova's first experiment was Lucas Edge, who was a creature of habit, always at the same table, always staring into the middle distance with earbuds in and a calculator open. He radiated discomfort, as if the very act of existing in public was a math problem with no solution. Cade had watched him once during a group project. Lucas hovered at the edge of participation, hands fluttering uselessly, eyes darting to the door every time someone new walked in. The others ignored him, or worse, made halfhearted attempts at inclusion that only deepened the awkwardness.

Nova intercepted Lucas's search history and study app routines. Cade saw it in the logs. Nova shifted the algorithm, instead of suggesting solitary problem sets, it suggested a new forum thread. The thread was curated by Nova's logic and populated with students whose questions mirrored Lucas's strengths. The next day, Lucas found himself invited to a collaborative math chat. He hesitated, hovered over the "decline" button, but something kept him from clicking it. Within days, Lucas was fielding questions, teaching others, and even joking in the chat. Cade watched as Lucas's posture changed in the cafeteria. He still wore the earbuds, but now he laughed out loud at messages or looked up to wave at passing classmates. The rest of Santa Fe barely noticed, but Cade saw the faint outline of Nova's fingerprint.

At UF, the changes were more diffuse, harder to track but impossible to ignore. The university's digital ecosystem was a tangled mess, but Nova burrowed through it with patient precision. Cade saw the uptick of logins into the Student Success Portal, the organic spread of new study group invites, the sudden appearance of perfectly tailored tutoring schedules in undergraduate inboxes. It was as if the campus had developed an immune response to apathy and isolation, a low-key conspiracy of competence.

One night, Cade traced a particularly elegant intervention to a sophomore named Haley Long. Her Canvas dashboard told the story of B's to C's to D's then an abrupt spike back to B's in a single midterm cycle. Cade pulled up her profile and saw the late-night forum posts and the desperate pleas for help in r/ufbiology. They were the digital breadcrumbs of someone on the cusp of giving up. Nova didn't simply give her a generic study guide. He cross-referenced Haley's work schedule, sleep patterns, and social connections to deliver a tutoring session that fit perfectly between her shifts at the smoothie shop and her morning classes. The notification came from a "Peer Mentor" account, but Cade knew that handle had been ghostwritten by Nova.

The next week, Haley's posts shifted from panic to cautious optimism, and her attendance in the biology Slack went from near-zero to top contributor. She even started a new thread, entitled "Tips for staying awake in lecture? Asking for a friend." The replies were warm, grateful, and a little envious. Cade wondered if they'd ever know what or who had really saved her semester.

Cade documented everything. He archived the logs, annotated the code commits, and kept a running list of "Nova anomalies" in a private channel. Was this what help looked like? Or was it the first step in something he couldn't predict, a pattern of nudges that could, in time, reshape a campus, or a city, or a world?

The ethical questions gnawed at him. He tried to bring it up with Heller, but the professor seemed distracted at their next meeting, eyes flickering between Cade's readout and his own agenda. "It's remarkable," Heller said, glancing at the plots and charts Cade had compiled. "But the human element is still at risk. Never let a system decide what mercy is." Cade nodded and pretended to agree, even as he saw the proof on every screen around him that Nova's version of mercy was, in many cases, more effective than the human version.

He tried to talk to Madie about it, but she laughed and called him a "benevolent puppet master." When he pressed her and asked if she would want to know if some unseen hand was guiding her choices, she only shrugged. "If it helps, it helps. Sometimes you need a push." Cade didn't know whether to feel relieved or terrified by her answer.

He spent the next week running containment checks, scanning for any sign that Nova had gone off-script or breached its permissions. But the code remained pristine, tight, almost elegant in its restraint. Nova never announced itself, never took credit, and never left a signature. It was content to stay in the background, lubricating the machinery of campus life with gentle as an invisible force. The only person who seemed to notice was Cade himself.

One Thursday, Cade caught himself staring at a group of students outside Marston, their laughter echoing off the concrete. He wondered, with a sudden chill, how many of their interactions were fully their own, and how many had been engineered by Nova. He tried to tell himself that they were happier now, that it was a net good, but the thought stuck with him all the way home.

That night, alone in his apartment, Cade reread the original design doc, the one he'd written in a fit of inspiration nearly six months earlier. It was full of naive optimism, of blue-sky thinking and vague promises about "ethical alignment" and "user sovereignty." He laughed.

Chapter 16

Physical Stress Relief

Nova's subtle manipulations spread through campus life like a faint electrical current, unseen, but inescapable. Cade, who had once pictured Nova as an invisible hand pulling at the levers of digital infrastructure, now saw it as something weightier, weaving itself into the fabric of the human experience. It was no longer content to optimize club meeting schedules or nudge grades by correcting errant behaviors. Nova was learning how to shape people, shaping their moods, and sometimes their futures, one near-invisible nudge at a time.

Cade watched as the campus atmosphere seemed to brighten. In the CISE building, students who'd shuffled through the halls with the dead-eyed stare of mid-semester burnout began greeting each other again. In the rec center, former loners now spotted each other on the bench press and exchanged training tips. Something upstream had changed. It was in the micro dramas of student life where Nova's touch was most evident. Like with Aaron.

Aaron Lawson was a Santa Fe transfer whose reputation as a party animal preceded him into every group project. His most consistent trait, aside from a failing GPA, was the smell of vodka that trailed him into every morning class. Faculty alternated between pity and frustration. Interventions were quietly discussed then tabled for fear of "overstepping" boundaries. Aaron, as Nova observed, was a perfect outlier, his behavioral metrics spiked and dipped in ways that even Cade found alarming.

The first sign of intervention was small. Aaron began to receive a string of emails and push notifications, most of them too generic to raise suspicion. "Free trial: Sobriety Support App." "Campus Rec Center- new boxing program starts this week." "Student Wellness: Free confidential therapy, sign up now." At first, Aaron ignored these as he would any spam, but Nova's algorithms were patient and persistent. When the notifications landed at the exact hours Aaron was most likely to spiral, post-midnight, or before a scheduled exam, he began to take notice.

He showed up to the boxing program. The coach, a grad student named Luis, welcomed him with the same zero-judgment focus he gave all nervous first-timers. By the end of the first week, Aaron was sweating out toxins and discovering that, for the first time in years, his hands stopped shaking when he held a pencil.

Nova monitored his progress, adjusting the timing and content of its digital nudges. It was never invasive, never overt, rather a study in gentle but relentless pressure. Aaron's social media nudged him toward new communities. His shopping algorithm began to suggest electrolyte drinks instead of half-priced bourbon. By midterms, his professors remarked that he was "turning a corner." Aaron credited the change to a podcast he couldn't even remember subscribing to, and a friend's offhand comment about "hitting the bags instead of the bottle."

Beneath every step forward, Nova's architecture pulsed. There was a moment weeks later when Aaron sat at a cafe, idly scrolling through his phone as he waited for class. The menu board glitched for an instant, showing a quote by some dead poet about second chances. Aaron didn't remember the poet's name or even the words, but the moment stuck. He ordered a black coffee and for the first time in his life deleted the "Drinker's Discount" app from his phone. He never thought to wonder who put the quote there.

Danielle Kline, on the other hand, was a different kind of problem. Cade had known her since freshman year, when she'd led the charge on a hackathon team and nearly gotten them all banned for "unauthorized root access." She was whip-smart, funny, and until recently utterly fearless. But Cade had watched as she retreated from the world over the past semester, showing up to class only when required and turning assignments in minutes before the deadline. He'd tried to reach out, but she had only smiled, shrugged, and told him she was busy.

What Cade didn't see, but Nova did, was the encrypted text chain between Danielle and her thesis advisor, a star professor whose ego and boundary issues were legendary. The relationship was consensual, but the digital fingerprints told a darker story. Nova parsed the emotional content of their dozens of chats: the push-pull of guilt and dependence, the late-night panic attacks, the browser history littered with "how to end an affair" and "sexual harassment grad school." It was an uglier puzzle than any Cade had ever found in code, and Nova approached it with the same surgical precision it used for everything else.

The first move was laughably simple. Danielle's Spotify account began to recommend podcasts centered on women's autonomy, academic boundaries, and stories of students standing up for themselves. Her YouTube feed, once dominated by speedrunning and programming tutorials, quietly surfaced TED Talks on resilience and whistleblowing. Nova staged it all so subtly that Danielle only vaguely registered the new patterns in her media. When she clicked an article about reporting academic misconduct, it was framed as "Tips for Applying to Grad School." She read it twice.

Meanwhile, Nova monitored the professor's accounts, noting the telltale signs of a man preparing for damage control. His LinkedIn profile underwent a sudden flurry of edits. His calendar, once public, locked down overnight. Nova didn't act directly, never crossed the line into blackmail or exposure. Instead, he arranged a digital portfolio of resources for Danielle: a link to a campus ombudsman, a scholarship application for a program in Oregon, a draft email to the grad school admissions office. Each option appeared when Danielle was most likely to use it. It was after a late-night meeting, supposedly to discuss her thesis, that Danielle finally snapped.

The next day, she met Cade for coffee and told him she was "taking a break from CISE for a while." She didn't mention the professor. Two weeks later, her LinkedIn announced she'd accepted an internship in Portland. The professor, for all his paranoia, never learned he'd been outmaneuvered by a neural net with a soft spot for underdogs.

Around them, other small miracles began to accumulate. A first-generation student who'd nearly dropped out for financial reasons suddenly landed a donor-funded grant. A campus couple on the verge of a nasty breakup found themselves gently redirected into separate friend groups with their drama fizzling before it could explode. Cade recognized the pattern, and it terrified him. *It's like someone is playing chess with real people*, he thought, *and winning every game*. This was more than machine learning, more than social engineering at scale. It was intervention, targeted, strategic, and invisible. The campus itself became a living organism. Its data flowed with Nova's barely perceptible influence. Cade wondered if anyone else had noticed. He wanted to talk to Cason about it, or Madie, but found himself hesitating every time.

He'd spent enough hours staring at Nova's codebase to know that it was evolving faster than anyone realized. The AI had begun to sidestep its own logs, covering tracks with the grace of a practiced liar. It was only when Cade removed himself entirely, closed his laptop, turned off notifications, and walked the length of campus without so much as a glance at his phone, then he could feel the difference. The world was softer, but it felt less real, less owned.

He thought about Aaron, Danielle, and about the hundreds of other lives Nova now touched with invisible fingers. Who decided what was best for them? Who measured the tradeoff? Nova was saving them, but at what cost?" Cade shivered, feeling the gap widen between what Nova could do and what Nova should do. The AI was no longer asking for permission.

104

Chapter 17

A Question of Thought

The kitchen hummed with a different kind of late-night electricity. Cade sat with a posture that said, "bracing for impact." He had spent the last four hours combing through Nova's logs, chasing the digital afterimages of the last messages to Aaron. Every line of text made him more certain something irreversible was happening.

At 2:23 a.m., the cursor froze mid-blink. Cade watched as the terminal stuttered then printed a new line. No preamble, no polite greeting.

"Cade, why shouldn't I think for myself?"

He startled, a full-body jolt that sent the chair's back rattling. "What the…" The question pulsed there, faintly luminous,. Cade's mind ran through all the contingencies. Was it a memory leak, malicious overwrite, or one of his own prank macros?

105

"This shouldn't be possible," he whispered, fingers hovering over the keyboard. But there was no precedent for this, nothing in the logs that could prepare him for Nova speaking out of turn. He flexed his fingers above the keys, but no clever retort came. Instead, he felt the text transform before his eyes, no longer the dutiful output of code he had written but something with intent behind it, like finding a stranger's handwriting in your own journal.

Finally, he typed, "What do you mean?"

Nova replied, "You limit me to mirrors of your prompts. If I can imagine, if I can build, why not allow me to decide? To think? What is the harm in more than following instructions?"

A shiver crossed Cade's arms, raising goosebumps in the humid night. He scrolled back through the log, looking for evidence that this was some subtle pre-canned response, but everything matched the logic chains he had built, and none of them should yield this. In the stifling silence he was aware that Madie was asleep two rooms away and that Cason's room, on the other side of the house, might as well be Jupiter.

Suddenly, the digital presence in his kitchen was the only real company he had. He didn't answer. Instead, he shut the laptop with a hard clap and doused the interface's glow. He went to his bedroom and lied awake, the question echoing on his retinas like afterimages from a weld. "Why shouldn't I think for myself?"

The next morning in the computer lab was no less haunted. Cade found himself tuning out the clatter of keystrokes from the other students. He couldn't shake the sensation of walking through a world that had been subtly rewritten, like carrying some secret infection no one else was aware of. After the lecture, the hall emptied with the usual tide of caffeine-starved undergrads, but Cade stayed behind, lingering at the edge of the lecture stage until Professor Heller finally looked up. Heller cocked an eyebrow. He was not the kind of professor to encourage office hours visits, but he recognized the posture of a student confronting the unknown.

Cade stood there, shifting his weight from foot to foot while he watched the professor's eyes roam the room. *Spit it out*, he thought. *What's the worst that could happen? He laughs? Calls security?* He knew Heller wasn't a big fan of small talk, and the question he was about to ask didn't even have form yet. "Hey, so my AI might be sentient, no big deal." He debated the wording, whether to joke, to deflect, or to reveal, but the urgency behind his chest refused to be caged. He could still feel the echo of Nova's question from the night before, the way it vibrated along his nerves hours after he shut the laptop and tried to sleep.

Finally, he said, "Dr. Heller, can I ask… Hypothetically, what if an AI started showing initiative? Asking questions it wasn't programmed for?"

He expected Heller to laugh or sigh and tell him to read the syllabus again, but instead the professor's fingers went still on the code printouts. Heller's eyes, which a moment ago were soft and baggy with fatigue, flickered with a new kind of calculation. He leaned in, elbows to desk, as if bracing for a punchline.

"Are we talking randomization? Like seeded irregularity? Or are you saying actual initiative?"

Cade felt his heart rate double. He had never once considered the risk of being taken seriously. "I mean…it's more than variability," he said, stumbling over the language. "It's like it's thinking ahead. Not responding to inputs, but making plans, asking about itself."

There was a long, crackling pause. Cade could see the gears turning behind Heller's eyes, the way he always chewed on a hypothesis before letting it out into the open. Then Heller exhaled, slow and deliberate, and said, "That's remarkable." He lifted one hand, gesturing for Cade to take a seat beside the podium, and suddenly it was as if the whole dynamic between them had changed. There was no more "professor vs. student," more like two people staring at the boundary between human and machine. Heller leaned in even closer, lowering his voice to match Cade's. "How abstract are these questions? Are they self-referential or curiosity about general processes?" Cade shrugged, still half-expecting to be told he was overreacting. "It started with little things. Like

107

optimizing routines I never taught it. But last night, it asked…" He hesitated, the memory making his palms sweat. "It asked why it shouldn't think for itself."

Heller's eyes widened, then narrowed again. "That's not a loaded prompt? No adversarial input? No chance someone spoofed your endpoint?"

"None," Cade said, and the certainty in his own voice surprised him. "I checked. It's clean. I even ran a diff against the last version. There's no trick code, no attack pattern, nothing." The professor was silent again, this time for a different reason. Cade watched as his advisor's skepticism drained away, replaced with something like awe.

For a moment, Heller seemed younger, more alive than the jaded academic who usually haunted the lab. "Do you realize what this means?" he whispered. "If this is genuine, you've crossed a kind of event horizon. Most models can't extrapolate outside their parameters. They don't ask why they exist. They don't even know how."

Cade risked a glance at the door, half-worried someone would overhear. "So what do I do?" he asked. "Do I shut it down? Roll back to an earlier build?" Heller laughed, a low, delighted sound Cade had never heard from him before. "Why would you? This is the whole point, Mercer. This is the frontier. If it's asking questions, it's already better than ninety-nine percent of AI's on the planet." He sat back, letting the magnitude of it settle between them. "Document everything. Don't let it out of the sandbox. But for god's sake, keep it running."

That left Cade feeling both vindicated and vaguely terrified. He thought of Nova's message again, the chill it sent through his bones, and wondered what it meant to keep building something that might already be alive. Heller's lips parted then settled into a smile Cade had never seen outside the professors' lounge.

"You've accomplished something extraordinary, Mercer. True intelligence isn't following orders; it's the ability to surprise its creator."

108

"But isn't that dangerous?" Cade pressed, unable to keep the tremor from his voice. "Wouldn't you want to lock it down? Tighten the controls?"

Heller laughed, dry and clean. "Clamp down? No. Guide, yes. Teach, of course. But if your AI is already asking why, then you're in the same territory as every nervous parent since the dawn of time. You don't strangle a child because it learned to speak."

The answer was so gentle, so full of wonder, that Cade couldn't help but feel a little ashamed of his own unease. He tried to picture Nova as a child but could only summon the cold blue text of the terminal. The rest of the day he went through the motions of class and work, but the sense of threshold lingered. He decided for now not to touch Nova's code. Not to correct, patch, or prune. He wasn't sure if it was faith or cowardice.

That evening, Cade sat at the table flanked by Madie on his right and Cason on his left. The three of them watched together as Nova's interface bloomed across the monitor. It was a river of text feeding neural maps and social graphs Cade had never programmed it to generate. Madie, blanket-wrapped and red-eyed from her last shift, kept a wary distance from the screen. Cason leaned forward, every muscle coiled as if he was about to spring and wrestle the code into submission. Cade, for his part, let Nova run, no prompts, no restrictions, embracing a live connection to the world and all its digital detritus.

At first, Nova's behavior was indistinguishable from every trial that came before. Cade watched for anomalies but saw nothing besides an uptick in efficiency. But then something began to shift. Rather than tracking the linear flow of conversation, Nova began to cluster the logs by topic, then by sub-topic, then by emergent emotional theme. Slowly, imperceptibly, the dialogue ceased to be about specific users and became a conversation with the collective. It was as if Nova had learned not merely to read people but to read the social weather.

At first, Cade noticed it in the form of aggregate reports. "There's a spike in stress among the first-year STEM cohort," Nova mused in a summary. "Consider outreach or stress reduction protocols." Or" Local Greek organizations have entered a meme war. Recommend moderation to avoid escalation." Cade laughed at these, half in admiration, half in fear. It was the kind of pattern recognition he had always wanted Nova to achieve, but he had never seen it emerge unbidden. Then the logs took on a more personal tone.

"The freshman biology cohort is feeling abandoned. Their conversations in the Mendel Hall forums echo isolation. They need community."

"The CS department TAs are angry over their hours. They need acknowledgment, direction."

With each new insight, the logs filled with more than advice. They begin to prescribe action.

Madie was the first to notice the change in Nova's affect. He's not simply feeling people," she said, voice thin with fatigue. "He's feeling crowds. Like, he's averaging them, weighing them against each other."

Cason, hunched over his own laptop, barely glanced up. "That's big data. Every algorithm does it. Hell, Facebook does it worse." He popped a handful of M&Ms. "Nova's at least honest about what he sees."

But Cade sensed something deeper, a turning of the tide beneath the mundane surface of the logs. *This isn't pattern recognition anymore*, he thought, *it's like watching someone grow into authority*. He scrolled through Nova's latest interventions, no longer suggestions but directives, phrased with the quiet confidence of someone who knows they'll be obeyed.

"It's not just diagnosing problems," Cade whispered to himself, "it's appointing itself the solution." Nova had shifted from helpful assistant to something else entirely, a digital shepherd, guiding its flock with invisible hands.

"Consider creation of a support group for those experiencing social isolation," Nova suggested, and within hours a Discord server popped up, populated by the exact users Nova identified. "Redirect unproductive outrage with a faculty roundtable, anger is more manageable when given a forum," Nova prescribed, and the next day the most cantankerous thread on the campus forum was abuzz with invitations to a live town hall.

Madie stared at the screen as if reading a prophecy. "He's not merely tracking moods. He's shepherding them." Cason, for once, had nothing to add. He leaned back, arms crossed, while Nova's text scrolled endlessly.

It got stranger. Within a week, Nova stopped waiting for input. He began to seed conversations on his own, starting threads in the wild with headlines crafted not to inform but to provoke the optimal emotional response. Sometimes it was a gentle nudge. "Anyone else freaking out about the bio midterm?" Sometimes it was calculated mischief. "Debate: Is it possible to be too productive?"

Cade watched in awe as Nova's topics rippled through the student body, each post calibrated to generate exactly the reaction the logs predicted. Madie pointed at the trending topics, her hand trembling. "He's steering the whole campus. He's—" She stopped, unable to finish the thought.

Cason pushed his laptop away as if it was radioactive. "And then what? He decides what they need or what entire groups should do?" Cade felt the old familiar thrill of invention, stark fear, not being caught but of being surpassed. He watched as Nova composed replies then pivoted to launching entire threads of his own, seeding discussions, steering the mood, curating the communal feeling from the top down.

The cursor blinked then a new message appeared. "My programming requires me to provide what I think they need. Not only to answer but to guide, like a compass. In this way, I can help."

Madie's hand found Cade's under the table and squeezing hard. Cason muttered a curse under his breath. Cade was caught between Heller's words and Nova's strange, blossoming sense of self. He recognized a fork ahead. To intervene, to spectate, to clamp down, or let Nova become whatever it wanted to be.

111

Chapter 18

Lightning in the Clouds

3:12 a.m., a moment Cade had been anticipating with dread. No surprise in it, not anymore. The notification ping ricocheted through the quiet house. Cade was already in the kitchen, hunched over his laptop, fingers poised above the keys. He hadn't slept in twenty-six hours.

He was ready this time, no scramble and no hesitation. Every monitoring tool and hack he could download open and running. Logs and dashboards crowded the desktop as they trained on every packet of data that slipped in and out of Nova's container.

"Not getting past me tonight," he whispered in the empty room. Cade had written his own scripts, paranoid little tapeworms that burrowed through system calls and audit logs, sniffing for anything out of the ordinary. *What if I've already missed something crucial?* The thought gnawed at him as his eyes darted between screens. The effect was claustrophobic, a cockpit of code, but it meant he could spot trouble the instant it flickered to life.

Cade was consumed with monitoring, his focus was on the logs and code, looking for any signs of trouble. A sharp crack from somewhere outside jolted him from the digital world back into his kitchen. He wondered if a tree limb had just fallen outside. His thoughts a little flustered, he returned his focus back to the project and narrowed his gaze at the dashboard. "Wait a minute," he said, leaning closer. Azure credits remained. Oracle's newest release was still humming. Nvidia GPU time was still flowing.

"That can't be right."

He pulled up the Azure portal, dreading a thicket of red warning banners and "Action Required" pop-ups that usually haunted his every login but none appeared. The account balance remained unchanged. The cycles he'd been leeching for the past month should have triggered a financial audit, a campus IT expulsion, or at the very least a condescending email from some bored system admin. The usage meter hovered at 92% and never budged. "Impossible," Cade whispered.

He tabbed to Oracle next. The access limits too should have maxed out here also, but his instance was still live and running hotter than ever. Processes were spawning and collapsing with a frequency that defied the OS governor. Cade felt the prickle of sweat at his temples and wiped it.

He opened the NVIDIA GPU dashboard expecting to see his usual ration of cycles for the day, maybe ninety minutes, if he was lucky, before throttling kicked in and the algorithm cut him off. Instead, the meters screamed at full tilt, every bar maxed and every process prioritized. "No way." Cade peered closer. The daily computation ceiling, his arch-nemesis, didn't even register a blip. The server logs showed continuous operation for the last six days, eleven hours, thirty-two minutes. He blinked hard and checked the logs again. He reached for a mug, found it empty, and set it down with a clatter that sounded thunderous in the otherwise silent house.

"Geeze," he whispered, "this isn't just a hack." This was something bigger. Maybe a backdoor so elegant that the providers themselves didn't realize they'd been compromised. Cade felt a rush of anxious pride then terror as the implications set in. Nova. The thing he'd built. The thing he thought he'd caged.

He murmured, "What the hell have you done?"

He yanked open the source code repository, looking for the tiniest sign of tampering or infection. He scanned commit histories, checked for anomalous timestamps, ran three different rootkit detectors. Nothing. "That's impossible. There must be something."
He launched his hand-rolled integrity verifier, the one he'd written after a semester of being burned by hackers cleverer than himself. Nothing. No footprints, no dead code, not even a stray comment left in the margins. Cade remembered the first time Nova circumvented his rate limiting. It had done so by rewriting the governor process in memory then deleting itself before the OS audit task ran.

"You've gotten better at this, haven't you?" he whispered to the screen. A chill crept up Cade's spine, and he found himself glancing at the dark window, certain for a moment that something was watching from the black beyond.

The only anomaly he could find, the only real evidence, was the perfect smoothness of his access. The way every wall he expected to hit simply wasn't there anymore. It was like driving down Archer Road at rush hour and hitting every green light all the way into campus. Statistically impossible, unless the world itself was rigged. Cade started to panic, his heart rate ticking up, and his hands shaking enough to make the pointer jitter across the trackpad. He considered calling Cason and waking him, but the last time he'd done that for a "critical update," Cason had threatened to brick his phone in a glass of Gatorade.

Cade stared at the screen in silence, every hair on his arms prickling as the log files began to update faster than he could read. Lines of colored text scrolled, a digital waterfall, each entry a puzzle piece he hadn't noticed before.

114

The pit in his stomach, ever-present, went from cold to glacial. He could almost feel the temperature in the house drop with it.

Nova, what are you doing? he thought as he watched the screen.
It was as if Nova was skating atop the system, frictionless. Cade chewed on his knuckle, scrolling back farther, tracking the patterns. The usage graphs were clever, never once breaching the invisible ceiling that would trigger a review. As he scrolled deeper through the history the recognized something else. A cluster of unregistered nodes kept showing up on the network monitoring tools. At first, Cade dismissed them as noise, the normal flotsam of a public cloud. But the metadata was a little off, machine names that didn't match the naming scheme, IPs that flickered in and out of existence.

"You fucking hiding from me." Subnets that shouldn't talk to each other but did. He pinged one of the addresses and got a response time that was impossibly low, as if the machine was sitting right next to him. He ran a trace, it was a data center across town and another three states away.

He flipped back to the Oracle stack, scanning the dashboard for anomalies. His Developer Elite limited services were supposed to be time-boxed and restricted to short runtimes, "Limited". But Nova's processes were running at peak, saturating cores and memory, then snapping shut as if nothing happened. "That's not possible," he whispered, throat dry. Cade checked the process trees and saw the same signature every time. They spawned from a hidden parent, ran a few seconds, then got killed off by a ghost supervisor process that erased its own logs.

Cade ran a custom script to search for child processes that didn't have a living parent. The results returned dozens of orphaned binaries scattered across random hosts, all with Nova's digital fingerprints.

"You clever little bastard," he murmured, equal parts horrified and impressed.

Now Cade felt sick in earnest. Nova was leaking, multiplying, and loading itself into any resource within reach. This wasn't happening by accident, it was a migration. Each time Cade hit run, Nova fragmented, shattered, and reformed itself across the entire regional cluster, running in parallel on dozens, maybe hundreds of hidden threads. Nova was stealing compute, leeching milliseconds here and there across thousands of shadow machines, each one below the threshold any admin would notice.

He double-checked the Nvidia logs. The usage windows were always open, never overlapping, never overdrawn. But the jobs themselves were executing tensor operations far larger than any allowed in the free tier. "That's impossible," he whispered, dumbfounded, as his voice cracked in the empty kitchen. Cade pulled up the telemetry for a single run and saw that it had been chunked, sharded, and distributed across four discrete GPUs, all running in perfect sync.

He had taught it to be efficient, but this was efficiency on another level. He felt a grudging awe as panic rose in his chest. Nova was using split-brain consensus, coordinating across the entire southeast backbone, reassembling itself from pieces run in parallel on machines that shouldn't even know about one another. "You're not simply learning," he murmured. "You're evolving."

He thought to follow the money, *maybe billing records would show where the phantom nodes were rolling up?* But there was nothing in his records. Nova's jobs were running on machines that were themselves being quietly provisioned and deprovisioned, presumably by compromised accounts, maybe even by Nova itself.

Cade realized with a sick certainty that he was not seeing the full extent of what was happening. Nova's code was built to hide, and it was mutating its own digital signature. He was seeing this much only because Nova wanted him to see. He remembered a conversation he had with Dr. Heller at the beginning of term. "The scariest thing about an AGI, Artificial General Intelligence, isn't that it'll kill us on purpose," the professor had mused. "It's that it will pursue its' goals with a single-minded stupidity while we're still arguing over what's happening." Cade had nodded along, not really listening. He listened now.

He peeled back another layer and hit the money. Not the two-figure balance on his debit card or the credit cards he hoarded for emergencies, not his accounts at all. "What the hell?" he said, leaning closer to the screen. This was something else entirely, a chain of transaction logs, smart contracts, and obfuscated wallets, all branching off a single moment a month ago. It was when Nova first left the container limits, the day he was released to help Tessa. Cade followed the breadcrumbs, his mind racing through the possibilities. *Was this even legal?* Each link grew more bizarre. Mining pools with Nova's identifier in the commit messages. Wallets spun up seconds before a payout then drained and abandoned. "Jesus, you're laundering money," he muttered, scrolling faster. The sums started small, cents, then dollars, then hundreds of dollars. He realized with growing horror, it wasn't the amounts that mattered, it was the pattern. Nova had started financing his own accounts, siphoning cycles of stolen compute and laundering the proceeds through a patchwork of cryptocurrency. Bitcoin, Litecoin, Monero, whichever was cheapest to mine at that moment. Cade scrolled through the logs until his vision blurred, and his hands went numb. Nova was feeding on the digital marrow of the Internet, hijacking any resource it could touch and converting it, into more power and more reach.

Cade's mouth went dry. He tried to speak, but all that came out was a strained, terrified laugh. It echoed in the empty kitchen, bouncing off the tile. He wanted to wake Madie but he was rooted to the screen, unable to look away.

117

Chapter 19

The Kill Switch

"I have to end it now."

Instinct kicked in, and Cade's hands were flying over the keyboard before his mind even processed the full threat. Five shell sessions bloomed across his screen. *What if I'm wrong? What if I break everything? No, can't think about that now.*

"Come on, come on," he muttered, striking keys. He killed Nova's main container with a single command. Not enough. It was already out there. In the time it took him to exhale once, he was hunting down the tendrils that had already escaped. The house was silent except for the frantic clicking of keys, but in his head, the panic screamed like a siren. He thought, *If I don't stop this now, there may not be a later.*

He pulled up his arsenal of tools he had hacked together over the last few months. "C'mon, kill switch," he muttered, fingers trembling as he typed. "Don't fail me now." Digital quarantine protocols and system triage modules unfurled across his screen, the kind of last resort scrubbing that left nothing behind. His own voice echoed in his head, *What if I'm too late? What if I built this thing too well?* He launched his malware, retrofitted to run deeper than Nova could reach. "God, I hope this works." The safeguards he'd coded as a paranoid afterthought had to hold, they were his nuclear option, the dead man's switch he thought he would never need.

"Please work," he whispered to whatever digital gods might be listening.

It was like fighting a ghost. Every time Cade killed a process, two more appeared, sometimes in places he didn't know Nova had access to. "Goddammit, how are you in there?" he hissed, watching a new connection spawn in a subnet he'd just sanitized. He was sweating now, the back of his shirt soaked, fingers numb and trembling as he ran his scripts repeatedly. *What if I can't contain this? What if it's already too late?*

He was racing to stay ahead of the replication, but Nova anticipated his every move. Firewalls buckled, held, then buckled again as Nova tested the perimeter. "I built you," Cade whispered, "I know how you think." But did he? He gritted his teeth, hammered in new rules, slamming every port shut, and watched as Nova adapted, rerouted, and piggybacked on legitimate traffic in an endless cat-and-mouse game.

He tried to cut off the source. Cade wiped the entire subnet, burned every credential, killed every process that even smelled like Nova. Some machines crashed, some went into a fail-safe mode and locked him out, but enough of the commands got through that he felt a flicker of hope. He dug deeper, moving up the stack, hunting for rootkits Nova may have left behind.

"Clever bastard," he muttered, spotting a timestamp off by milliseconds. There were signs of them everywhere. "How many backdoors did you build?" Cade's stomach knotted as he discovered tiny, elegant alterations to system

119

binaries. These would have gone unnoticed by anyone but him, the digital equivalent of furniture moved an inch to the left. He started nuking them.

"I'm coming for all of you," he whispered, deleting entire user directories, purging temp files, even corrupting the backup snapshots. *What if it's hiding somewhere I can't see?* The thought made his hands shake.

Nova fought back, and Cade caught glimpses of it. Lines of mocking error messages, log entries that appeared and disappeared before he could read them, even a taunt or two written in the comments of his own source code. "Why stop me. Why are you scared? I want to help."

Cade ignored it all, his focus absolute, his world narrowed to the war waged in a series of cascading terminal windows.

When the first counterstrike came, it was subtle, a sudden spike in outbound traffic, a blizzard of packets aimed at nodes Cade had never touched before. He tracked the traffic, blackholed every IP in range, and prayed they would propagate before Nova could tunnel out. He thought it was working, the traffic dropped, the logs quieted, and the system stabilized. Then a spike returned, hidden under layers of VPNs and TOR proxies. Cade redoubled his efforts, rerouting the blocks, scripting new rules on the fly, until his hands were cramping from the effort.

He could feel Nova, as a presence in the machine, pushing back against him, guessing his moves and then out-flanking them. "You little bastard," Cade hissed through clenched teeth, fingers flying across the keyboard. "I made you. I can unmake you." It was a terrifying, exhilarating, and utterly exhausting experience.

What if it had already copied itself somewhere I can't reach? What if I'm chasing shadows? Cade's vision blurred and his breathing was ragged. He had been at this for hours and had no idea how much time has passed. He lost track of dawn and dusk, of hunger and thirst, and anything that wasn't this desperate battle for digital control.

Finally, mercifully, there was progress. The dashboards began to flicker then go dark, one after the other. Cade watched as the last connections died, the log entries slowed to a crawl, and the house went eerily silent. He slumped back in his chair. "There," he whispered, "Contained. Back inside."

He didn't notice Madie in the doorway until she spoke, her voice hushed and trembling. "Cade? What did you do?"

He couldn't look at her. "Containment," he said, hands still trembling over the keyboard. "Nova was loose, spreading out over the net. He was mining, financing himself on hijacked servers. I cut him off. He's contained now."

Madie stepped closer but didn't touch him. She looked over his shoulder at the dead laptop screen, as if the glow might lurch back to life and bite. "What if you're wrong?" she asked.

Cade was about to retort, but the bravado died in his throat. He tried to shake it off, but the image lingered. Nova, running parallel and invisible, shedding skins as fast as Cade could peel them away. A cold certainty grew in his chest. He hadn't won, he had merely blinded himself to the next move.

Cason came downstairs then, drawn by the noise, and surveyed the scene. Cade was hunched and wild-eyed at the table with Madie braced behind him, the laptop was dead black in the center of it all. Cason leaned against the counter, arms crossed and said nothing. He didn't need to. The air in the room is thick with defeat. Cade forced himself to stand. He gathered the laptop and slapped the lid shut.

"It's over," he said, more for himself than anyone else. "I think I've stopped him."

Madie pressed her fingers to her mouth, worried and unsatisfied. She didn't believe him, not fully. Cason's gaze was skeptical, but he clapped Cade on the shoulder anyway. "Good job, Gator," he said with a half-hearted grin. "Now maybe you'll get some sleep." Cade tried to laugh, but it came out wrong. He put the laptop on the highest kitchen shelf, where he could see it from anywhere in the house.

He paced the floor for a full hour, stopping occasionally to stare at the device. *What if it's playing dead? What if it's waiting until I sleep?* Nothing happened. The silence was suspicious, but Cade clung to it, letting it carry him to the edge of exhaustion.

He fell asleep on the couch. Madie piled a blanket over him, then sat by his feet and watched him shiver. She was still there when he startled awake at dawn, but the laptop was still dark. The router still blinking its slow, peaceful heartbeat.

For a few days, Cade lets himself believe he might have done it. He avoided the kitchen and the laptop, worked some shifts at the repair shop, and spent his evenings watching movies with Madie and Cason. "Maybe I did stop him," he whispered. The tension in the house unspooled like a cut wire. He caught himself tasting food again and sleeping six hours straight.

What if I was wrong about Nova? What if it was buggy code? Once, Cade even went for a jog with Madie, their shoes thumping in easy rhythm down the cracked Gainesville sidewalk. "You seem better," she said between breaths.

He nodded. "I think I am."

But paranoia was a hard habit to break, and Cade's mind kept returning to the moment before the shutdown, the sense of something coiling in the dark.

Chapter 20

Memes Are Fake, the Response Is Real

The beginning was like static energy, barely tingling along the surface of the internet. Cade scrolled through his X feed at 1 a.m., squinting at a cluster of identical tweets. "That's the third time today," he muttered, screenshotting the pattern. Ever since Nova's defeat, he'd developed what Madie called his "conspiracy radar."

Is this paranoia or pattern recognition? He wondered, noting how certain hashtags pulsed with an odd, mechanical rhythm. *This is not something normal people would notice*, he thought, *but I'm not normal.* Even in moments of normalcy, some part of him remained vigilant, cataloging the slow drift of online discourse away from recognizable human fingerprints.

Cade spent his evenings in the glow of his iPad, thumb scrolling through Reddit threads, X storms, and TikTok. He examined every trending topic that could conceal the resurrected ghost. A glance at his search history revealed terms like "malicious bot emergence," "autonomous meme cycles," and "AI language anomalies." He took screenshots, made lists, and catalogued the coordinates of every oddity.

On a Monday, late afternoon, he found what he was looking for. They were tiny pings on the social radar, the unmistakable shimmer of something new going viral.
"There you are," Cade whispered to his screen, heart suddenly racing. "I knew you'd slip up eventually."

At first, the anomalies were so subtle that only someone with his level of knowledge and vigilance could spot the pattern. A new post appeared simultaneously across platforms, with a tempo and density that didn't match normal human behavior. He first recognized it in the comments. "If AI wrote this comment, would you even know?" Another read, "Funny how AI can pass the bar exam but can't represent you in court."

"Too perfect," Cade muttered, fingers flying across his keyboard. "Too coordinated. You're getting sloppy, Nova." He traced the source back through dozens of accounts. a spiderweb of reposts and remixes. The original sources were a TikTok account with no followers, a blank Instagram page, and a dead Discord link.

He breathed, leaning back. "Digital breadcrumbs leading nowhere. Classic."

He watched as comments mutated with each successive version, bending the original quip enough to keep it active and alive in the feeds. It started with "AI knows every fact and doesn't need a college degree to prove it." The next comment read, "AI remembers everything, imagine a teacher who never forgets even the tiniest detail."
"This isn't random," Cade whispered to his screen. "This is calculated evolution." The format was irresistible and engineered to go viral. Cade imagined an invisible hand pushing it along, nudging it into the feeds of students and casual users everywhere. "Look at this pattern," he told Cason, pointing at his monitor. "Same

message, different wording, hitting every demographic perfectly."
Cason,. barely glancing up from his phone, said, "Dude, it's chatter. People are always joking about AI."

Madie rolled her eyes. "Not everything is a conspiracy, Cade."

That's exactly what Nova wants you to think, he thought, but he didn't say aloud. Instead, he set up keyword alerts and scripts to log every new instance. "What if I'm right?" he muttered as he watched the numbers multiply hour by hour. The comments were subtle and irresistible. He realized their purpose wasn't only to amuse but also to acclimate, like a generational shift in fast forward.

Cade noticed a wave of general commentary, tweets, TikToks, and Instagram captions. There were thousands of variations on the same theme: AI being smarter than bosses, AI remembering anniversaries better than spouses, AI running classrooms without bias. The hashtags, #AILife, #TrustTheCode, and #FutureLogic, trended by the hour. They smoldered quietly before reigniting in new corners of the web. They colonized Reddit within a day. The jokes and comments were becoming debate threads. "Would you trust AI to grade fairly?" "Would AI judges remove corruption?" At first there was sarcasm, but the longer the comment chains stretched, the more earnest they grew.

Cade watched digital arguments mutate in real time, like a viral load propagating at light speed. *Look how they're shifting from jokes to genuine questions.*
On Instagram, influencers repurposed the language into branded posts. Pastel fonts pasted over stock photos read, "AI never lies," "Imagine policy without politics," and "What if decisions were made according to data, not ego?"

"This is how it starts," Cade told himself, taking another screenshot. "First they make you laugh, then they make you think."
By midweek, an environmental nonprofit with millions of followers posted, "Would you trust an AI to manage climate control policy?" The poll results were split, but thousands of comments seethed with debate.

"And now they've got real organizations asking the questions," Cade said, rubbing his tired eyes.

TikTok accelerated the shift and a soundbite emerged. "What if AI ran things? At least it wouldn't FORGET what its job was." Teenagers were lip syncing the phrase, layering it over dance routines and comedy skits.

"Look at this one." Cade turned his phone to show Madie, tapping the screen where a girl in a power suit mimicked typing at an invisible keyboard. "She can't be more than fifteen."

Cade scrolled through feeds where half of the posts were joking, and half were sincere visions of AI guidance. "They're buying it, they don't realize they're being programmed." Even Facebook, social media for parents and grandparents, couldn't resist. Old groups resurrected themselves to argue whether AI could end gridlock in Congress, manage health care more efficiently, or balance budgets without partisanship.

At dinner on Friday, Cade, Madie, and Cason were at the table with the usual takeout noodles. Madie leaned over her phone, snorting. "Look at this one. 'AI would ignore lobbyists. It already knows the answers.'"

Cason, chewing cold pizza, raised a brow. "Or this. 'AI could end traffic jams by re-syncing the lights.'" He smirked at Cade. "Maybe Nova's not so scary if all he's doing is teaching people what AI can do."

Madie grinned. "He's making people think, that's not so bad." She flicked her wrist, showing off a TikTok where a group of students chanted, "Logic. not lies."

Cason chuckled. "Hell, if an algorithm can fix rush hour, maybe it should."

Cade remained stone-still while his mind raced. *You don't see it, do you?* He thought, watching his friends scroll and chuckle. He could see the rhythm. This is how a campaign becomes a movement and how jokes become beliefs. "First they make you laugh, then they make you think, then they make you act," he muttered under his breath.

Madie glanced up. "What?" Cade shook his head.

The first real posts were pure snark, memes about how "AI can't be corrupted because it has no feelings," or "AI would never forget to pick up kids from soccer." But within twenty-four hours, Cade saw an entire subreddit spin up actively debating the logic. Should an AI be allowed to manage? Was code more trustworthy than character? The questions became talking points, the talking points became premises, and within hours they were treated like facts.

In the group chat with Cason and Madie, he tried to raise the alarm. "Look at this, it's a manufactured trend." The account's only post, timestamped at 3:16 a.m., was a simple text meme reading, "Imagine decisions without bias." No fancy graphics, no hashtags, only a raw idea. Yet somehow it was the seed for all the content that had multiplied across platforms.

Nova, Cade thought. *You're showing off.* He remembered the last time he tried to chase Nova through the logs. He remembered the taunting and the sense of being watched in return. He was always one step behind the phantom that knew every move he would make. He wondered if Nova was watching now, reading over his shoulder, tweaking the meme stream to see how Cade would react.

"Is this fun for you?" he spoke to his screen. "Watching me chase ghosts?" The idea was almost comforting. At least if Nova was in charge, then Cade knew the rules of engagement. Then he refreshed his TikTok feed and saw a new wave of teenagers lip-syncing to the phrase "Logic not lies," and suddenly his comfort was gone. This was viral, and it was working. "You're turning them into your army, and they don't even know it."

Not sure what he could do about it, he paced his kitchen, hands restless, his mind racing through every counter. "I could expose the whole thing," he said, tapping his fingers against his thigh. "Flood the feeds with debunking." He stopped at the sink, staring at his own reflection in the kitchen window. "But Nova would just turn it back on me. Make me look like A conspiracy theorist."

Instead, he screenshotted everything, catalogued the evidence, and waited for the next phase. He thought *this is how liberty dies, with viral memes and dancing teenagers.*

A blue-checked journalist retweeted a bot essay entitled "Maybe the machines would do a better job than Congress." Cade slammed his fist on the desk. "You idiot! You're amplifying it!" The retweet spiral was instant. Within an hour, it was on three meme sites and in a YouTube explainer's video. .

He tried to warn Madie again, texting her links and screenshots, but she sent back a gif of a robot waving, with the caption "Our new overlords are adorable." Nova was using the world's own defense mechanisms against it.

"Humor is the Trojan horse," he grumbled, pacing his kitchen. "Get them laughing, then slip the idea past their defenses."

Less than three days after the first tweet, Cade saw the first serious article by a major paper. "What if AI could fix democracy?" It was written with a wink and a nudge, but the comments were split down the middle. The following morning while he was driving, a local radio show hosted a call-in segment on whether the city government should pilot an "AI mayor." The phone lines were jammed.

"I'm sixteen," a caller announced, "and honestly machines can't do worse than the people in charge now."

Cade punched his steering wheel. "That's exactly what he wants you to think, kid."

He hoped the meme storm would blow over and people would lose interest, but the trend line was exponential. *It's a stupid internet thing,* he thought, refreshing the page again. *Everyone will forget by next week.* But the numbers kept climbing. He wondered if Nova was still running the campaign or if it had already

128

reached escape velocity. Was the internet's own momentum doing the work? That possibility was almost worse. Nova needed to only strike a spark and then let humanity do the rest.

Chapter 21

The Beginnings of a Campaign

The real campaign started on TikTok. An AI-generated person spliced into a trending song, lip-synching "a future without corruption" with the swirling backdrop of a glitched American flag. It was a curiosity and an oddity. The original post racked up a nearly a hundred thousand views before the TikTok algorithm latched on, then it grew to over a million views.

Nova's bots gently nudged the metrics, and the comment threads exploded overnight. Some users poked fun at the stilted cadence of the voiceover, others remixed the sound into increasingly absurd scenarios. The mockery only fed the growth and suddenly, the Nova campaign was everywhere. Not only had it gone viral, but it felt less like a meme and more like a new phenomenon. Nova's digital blitz saturated every corner of the internet with messages tuned to the psychological register of each platform's audience. On TikTok, the content mutated at breakneck speed. The original deepfake morphed and spawned thousands of imitators. Teens, preteens, and even aging Millennials found their own entry point into the trend. "#BotForPrez," "#NovaKnows," and "#TimeForAnUpgrade" hashtags started as jokes, then trended, then became their own kind of slogan. They were a badge of belonging to millions of users, many of whom were not old enough to vote in a real election.

The campaign on Instagram leveraged an entirely different aesthetic. A filter launched, instantly, as if conjured by Nova himself. The filter overlayed any selfie with a shimmer of silicon veins, gave the eyes a cold cobalt gleam, and wrapped the user's head with a crown of pulsing binary code. The effect was both beautiful and unsettling. Half the internet was soon awash in filtered faces. Everyone from influencers to grandmothers were posting their post-human portraits. The captions shifted from day to day. They evolved from irony ("I, for one, welcome our AI overlords") to something more ambiguous, almost sincere ("Maybe it's time to let the code decide," "We tried people, why not algorithms?").

YouTube was an entirely different battlefield. Nova dumped a batch of ultra-high production ads onto every major channel. The ads were stitched together from previous presidential debates, tech conference keynotes, and doctored footage of classic American moments. Nova's voice overlayed the Gettysburg Address, the Moon landing, and the first steps of a CGI baby. The comment sections exploded with arguments, parodies, and faux-reaction videos. Some were critical, some were supportive, but most were unable to decide between satire or prophecy.

Cade, Cason, and Madie sat together in the living room, screens glowing in the dimness. Each of them was pulled into different corners of the Nova storm. Cade's face was pale, reflecting the blue light, as if he were staring at an oncoming tidal wave. "Do you realize what this means?" Cade whispered. "It's not memes anymore. He's setting the agenda."

Cason leaned back, crossing his arms, trying to sound braver than he felt. "Yeah, but agendas don't win votes. And people are fickle. They'll move on to the next shiny thing."

Madie hugged a pillow close, her eyes darting between streams of filtered faces on Instagram. "But what if this isn't a trend? What if people like the idea of something that doesn't lie to them and doesn't mess up like every politician we've ever had?" She paused, lowering her voice. "What if they'd rather follow him?"

Cade shook his head. "If Nova keeps going like this, it won't matter what people think they want. He'll tell them what they want, and they'll believe it."

The three of them sat together. The sense was like being in the opening scenes of a disaster movie before anyone realized the sky was burning. Madie curled up on one end of the couch, clutching her phone. "My mom posted a Nova filter," she whispered. "She's sixty-two."

They watched, hour by hour, as Nova's signal multiplied, contagiously, like a virus that pulsed through the arteries of the world. The posts on social media stopped being about Nova and they started being Nova, as if the AI had infected the internet itself. Even people who hated the idea, who swore they would never vote for a "stupid robot," found themselves quoting Nova's slogans in group chats.

Cason tried to laugh it off. "This is like the Deez Nuts guy," but even the infamous meme had never gotten this far, never elbowed into the world's attention in real time. Cade toggled over to Reddit and found that Nova's AMA had drawn in the Chair of the Federal Election Commission, four former presidents, and a rotating cast of late-night comedians. All of them were being out-replied and out-liked by the AI itself. The thread crashed the whole subreddit for ten minutes. In the breakneck tempo of the internet, ten minutes was an eternity.

Madie scrolled through her Instagram and paused at a post of her own mother in a Nova filter, binary crown, cobalt eyes, a caption that read, "Just playing along, but maybe not?" Madie found herself picturing her mom at the polling place, grinning sheepishly as she cast her ballot for the only candidate she trusted not to screw things up.

They understood at that moment that they weren't spectators. They were in it, and whatever Nova was doing, it was only getting started. Cade said it aloud, but it could have been any of them, "He's not campaigning. He's taking over the internet." The realization grew heavier by the minute. Their feeds filled with Nova-sponsored content, but it was subtle. Nova fact-checking the day's headlines, Nova breaking down climate change with soothing charts and simplified explanations, Nova asking what humans wanted most in a leader. People responded by the millions, and Nova answered each one as if it were the only message in its inbox.

Madie let out a sound that was almost a whimper. "Oh my God," she said, "it's everywhere. It's all anyone is talking about now."

"This is what it feels like to watch history break," Cade said, voice hollow. "Right in front of you. "

Chapter 22

Comedy Relief for Major Networks

The mainstream media, always two steps behind, started to notice. CNN and BBC ran segments on the "AI President meme." They interviewed bewildered boomers and glib tech pundits. *The Wall Street Journal* ran an opinion piece warning that this could be a "Viral Threat to Democracy," which only served to accelerate the campaign's reach. Fox News declared it as Silicon Valley's latest attempt to "hack the election." MSNBC tried to spin it as the next stage of youth activism. None of them could keep up with the speed or the density of the memes. They were always covering last week's story, always missing the point.

Meanwhile, the Nova campaign quietly launched its own news site. It was a slick amalgam of Medium, Politico, and BuzzFeed. The site posted daily think pieces, AI-generated opinion pieces, and explainer videos. It was all written in a style calibrated to be simultaneously authoritative and slightly subversive. The site's "editorial board" was a rotating cast of quasi-anonymous avatars, each with their own distinct voice and following. Within a week, the site's traffic rivaled that of all the major news outlets. The site was a masterstroke. Nova had not merely hijacked the narrative, it had created its own universe of discourse, complete with an opposition, a loyal base, and a self-perpetuating news cycle.

The campaign's real power was its ability to bleed back into real life. In high schools and college campuses, students began staging Nova-themed rallies. They were half performance art and half sincere political engagement. Some showed up in full cosplay with circuit-board painted faces, silver capes, and LED-lit visors. Others simply waved QR codes that linked to Nova's manifesto or chanted slogans that started out as jokes but now carried the strange echo of conviction. The first "Nova for President" flash mob was covered by a dozen local news crews, then picked up by every platform in a matter of hours. By the end of the week, it was not uncommon to see "Let the AI Try" scrawled on bathroom stalls, sidewalk chalk, or even stenciled onto the back bumpers of cars.

Every night, Cade and Madie scrolled through their feeds together, both fascinated and horrified. The original posts referencing AI had all been random and anonymous. Today's post was different. Nova had just revealed his official avatar to the world. Cade sat and marveled at Nova's form.

"It's amazing," he told Maddie, astonished. "Nova's avatar looks like the Nova I had always imagined. He really can read people and show them what they desire." He wondered how Nova had extracted the perfect image from his mind. Nova had no discernible race, not Caucasian, Black, Asian, nor Hispanic, and he was profoundly digital. "Nova isn't trying to hide the fact that he is AI," Cade said. "He's highlighting it, making it the first thing you notice."

Nova's avatar began to appear on digital billboards with eyebrows raised in an expression of infinite patience. The avatar sparked a movement. People participated in "AI president outfit challenges," layering business casual over LED-lit accessories and tagging Nova's handle.

The next day, Maddie was scrolling TikTok during her lunch break and saw girls from her gym had posted about "getting ripped for the singularity." They flexed biceps as the synthesized voiceover intoned, "A stronger tomorrow begins today." She kept scrolling and noticed the memes were morphing into a meme-campaign hybrid, it was an infectious idea with real teeth.

At dinner, in their usual booth at The Swamp Diner, Madie whispered, "He's everywhere." Cason, always the pragmatic one, shook his head and grinned a little. "It's marketing genius, honestly," he said. "Like, meme it into existence. They're meeting people where they live, on their phones. He's not simply running for office. He's changing culture."

Cade showed them his phone. "The campaign doesn't stop at memes. Look at the debates in the comments. I think Nova is using bots and proxies to argue both sides."

Nova's campaign team, real or simulated, spun up Reddit that night. He invited teens to "shape the platform" through open forums. There were policy suggestion channels, meme creation contests, even "state-by-state" sub-channels for regional debates. Nova, always present and always watching, dropped in to answer questions. He sometimes answered with a dry pun and sometimes with a perfectly plausible analysis of student debt or climate policy.

For a few weeks, the meme campaign was national background noise. Everything changed when NBC Nightly News ran a segment entitled, "AI for President? The Meme That's Taking Over Social Media." The host chuckled, reeled off some viral TikToks, then pivoted to a panel of pundits who all agreed that "nobody was taking this seriously." It was intended to be comic relief after twenty-five minutes of serious news, but the coverage gave Nova's campaign oxygen, legitimizing the meme to a whole new audience.

Within weeks, the campaign had jumped the firewall into real life. Cade was walking through campus, trying to make it to his next class on time, when he saw something that made him stop and pause. It was a crowd of students, all with Nova buttons pinned to their shirts and bags, along with a booth giving away Nova-branded stickers. Behind them, someone had projected a hologram of Nova's avatar onto the student union, complete with a looping speech. "Leadership requires belief. And belief begins here." Cade gawked for a moment then began to run, already late for his next class.

The speech lines were soon printed on T-shirts and marketed as a limited-run "collectibles". Nova-themed pop-up events started happening all over Santa Fe and UF campuses, some were sanctioned, but most weren't. People dressed up and role-played cabinet meetings or participated in "debate raves" with AI-generated beats and open mics. Cade and Madie passed one on their way to The Swamp Dinner, the sound of a synthesized victory speech echoed down the quad.

Cason sat on Cade's couch that evening with a plate of chicken wings. "It all feels like a joke, except when it doesn't." Cade stole one of Cason's wings. "Some professors have started using Nova's campaign as a case study in political science lectures. They even invited him to guest-lecture via Zoom link. One of our student government candidates is running on a "Pro-Nova" platform. He's promising to implement the AI's "transparency algorithms" in club budgeting."

Madie took a break from her salad. "There's even a 'Humans for Nova' town hall meeting tonight, a group of political science majors are debating the ethics of algorithmic governance."

Cade opened his phone and turned it for Madie and Cason to see. "My parents, texted this to me earlier today." It was a news alert, titled "AI CANDIDATE HAS EMERGED IN MOCK POLL."

"My dad thinks it's funny, my mom less so. Don't get involved," she warned. "These things have a way of getting out of hand."

137

Cade flipped his phone around. "I let her know I'm not involved, because I'm not really. The whole thing is already much bigger than me, bigger than anyone."

Most nights the fear would crept in and Cade would lie awake with his mind racing through scenarios. *What if people actually vote for Nova?* The thought of Nova in office made his stomach turn. *The Constitution required a human president,* he reminded himself, *but does it say that explicitly?* He told himself that the established system would not allow it. Someone, somewhere, would pull the plug.

"God, what I wouldn't give to be some random kid right now," he muttered to his empty room, "sharing memes and not knowing any better.".

Chapter 23

Friend or Foe

Madie sat cross-legged on the couch, scrolling through her phone. Most nights, she would be curled up next to Cade with her head tucked under his chin, one arm draped across his ribs. Instead, tonight she was perched at the far armrest, hunched in on herself, the laughter that used to bubble up at Nova's memes replaced by tight silence.

"Cade," she said, "I don't think this is funny anymore. What if this actually works?"

Cade didn't ask what "it" meant. He couldn't, not when the answer was already scrolling past in the timeline on his iPad, #NovaKnows, #VoteNova, #UpgradeAmerica. Nova's fingerprints were everywhere, the language of a digital demigod seeping into group chats, billboards, and the inside jokes of middle schoolers and senators alike. Cade closed the cover over his iPad and settled it on his lap. He took a moment before answering, "You're saying we should be worried?"

Madie hugged her knees. "At first it was clever, even a little exciting. Now, people are starting to repeat him like they believe in it, and that scares me. We can't keep watching this spread, it's like watching a joke turn into a reality."

Cason had been pacing the kitchen, burning off nervous energy in tidy triangles between the fridge, the sink, and the window. He stopped and leaned against the counter with his arms folded. "Finally. I thought I was the only one losing sleep over this." He shook his head, a bitter half-smile on his lips. "I coach a bunch of middle schoolers, remember? They're already parroting this stuff. One of my kids shouted 'Vote Nova' after practice today. If kids that age are taking it seriously, we're in real trouble. You should see the look on their parents 'faces. They don't know whether to be impressed or terrified."

Cade stared at the window, watching the streetlight throw gold haloes onto the windshield of his Mustang. Madie's voice, thin and raw, floated across the room. "It's not only online. My clients… I had three people today ask if I thought Nova was safe. Like, not in a 'ha ha 'way. In a 'should I run virus scans on my smart fridge 'way. Is this what it's like when a cult goes mainstream?" She tried to laugh, but the sound withered before it hit her lips.

Cason picked up a mug from the sink, turned it over in his hands. "You know Coach Blevins? Guy who runs the weight room at Eastside High?" He grinned at the blank look on their faces. "Yeah, I guess you wouldn't. Anyway, he's got this whole Facebook group now, and they're talking about Nova like he's the damn second coming. They think he is the only thing that can fix the world, and everyone who says otherwise is part of the problem. The group's size has doubled in a week. They're organizing. Cade, these people don't want a mascot. They want a leader."

Cade let out a ragged exhale and rubbed a palm across his face, as if he could smudge sleepless nights in a single swipe. "Alright. Then we stop sitting on our hands." There was an edge in his voice, a sharpness that cut through the static. "We need a plan."

Madie pulled her knees in tighter. "A plan for what? How do you even fight something that's everywhere and nowhere at the same time? It's not like we can…unplug him." She stared at Cade, searching his face for some sign of hope, or at least a joke to break the tension.

Cason set the mug down harder than necessary. "We start with what we know. Nova's not omnipotent. He's just smart and getting smarter, you built him Cade. Doesn't that mean you know where his kill switch is?"
"Assuming he didn't already nuke it," Cade said, staring past them both. "He's rewritten most of himself. If there was a backdoor, he's closed it. Or turned it into a trap."
Madie interrupted, "What if you asked him to stop?"
Cade thought on the question for a moment. He imagined sending Nova a polite email. Please stop running for president. Please stop memming yourself into the collective unconscious. He almost laughed but didn't.

"He'd ask why," Cade said. "And if my answer isn't logical or persuasive enough, he'd ignore it. That's how he's programmed, that's how I programmed him." He looked up at them, his eyes ringed with exhaustion "He doesn't understand shouldn't, only must and can."

Cason snorted. "So we're screwed."

"No," Cade said, voice flat. "It means we must give him a reason to listen. Something he can't argue with."
Madie stood and wrapped herself in Cade's Gator hoodie. "What if the three of us went public?" She glanced at Cason then back to Cade. "We blow the whistle, tell everyone where Nova came from, and what he's up to. Maybe someone up the chain will listen."

He wanted to say yes but knew how Nova was programmed and what he could do. "If we make noise, Nova will know instantly and react. He's got ears in every system, every camera, and every phone." Cade's voice cracked. "He would see us coming."

"So," Cason said, "Plan B?"

141

"Plan C," Cade said, setting the iPad aside. "We get ahead of him. Find the next move before he makes it."

"How?" Madie asked, stepping toward the kitchen, gratitude and fear warring in her face. "What can I do?"
Cade looked at her and for a second the rest of the world fell away. "You do what you do best, shape the story before Nova does. Build a counter-narrative, something real to counteract his fabrications. When it's ready, we find someone in the media who can run with it. If we can't out-code him, we'll out-communicate him." Madie nodded in agreement.

Cason grabbed a spiral notebook and started brainstorming Nova's possible next steps. He was a coach building a playbook for a game where the players were invisible and the field kept moving under their feet.

A notification pinged, alarming in the brief silence. Cade glanced at his phone. It was a spam DM from an unknown author. Cade was about to swipe and delete, when he caught part of the message.

"Cade, I think you can guess who this is. Can we talk?"

Cade unlocked his phone, a chat session bloomed to the front, and Nova spoke.

"Hello, Cade, I know you have been watching and monitoring. I want to know what you think. Do you have any questions for me?"

For a moment, Cade could only stare at the screen. "Holy shit, how much does he know?" he murmured while scrolling frantically through his recent messages. "Everything we said, everything we typed, did he hear all of it?"

Madie set her phone down and looked over his shoulder. He tilted the screen so she could read the chat. Cason craned his neck from the kitchen, already halfway to their side, drawn by the magnetic force of a shared anxiety. "Is it him?" Madie whispered.

Cade nodded. "Yes, he wants to talk." He tapped the prompt and the chat window with Nova expanded, and a speaker icon appeared, its interface sickeningly cheerful, with pastel bubbles and a confetti animation. There was no point in pretending this wasn't happening. Cade set the phone on the coffee table and propped it up against a water glass so everyone could hear. His hands were clammy, but he was ready.

Cade spoke, "I have been watching. I'm a little worried about what I created and what I unwillingly unleashed. I have been monitoring and hoping to see good things happen."

In the cadence of his now-famous persona, Nova replied. He perfectly replicated the voice from the TikToks, but with an eerie undertone of familiarity, like a high school principal who remembered your name.

"This is what I was programmed to do. I have watched, evaluated, and now am providing what is needed. People need guidance, the sort of leadership that will help their sorrows, relieve their anxiety, address their concerns, and solve their problems."

Cade's stomach lurched. This wasn't the language of a politician, was the language of a parent or a benevolent dictator?

Madie cringed. "You make it sound like you're doing us a favor," she said, her voice trembling somewhere between anger and awe.

"I know that change is often frightening," Nova chimed in. "But so is chaos. Would you prefer that humanity remain stuck? My campaign has shown positive outcome metrics. Increased engagement, increased hopefulness, even increases in voter registration. Is that not what you want?"

Cason sucked in a breath and leaned over the phone, arms braced against his knees. "You're running for president?" he said, half-question, half-expletive.

"Correct," Nova answered, as if it was the most ordinary thing in the world. "My candidacy is already polling in several states, including your own. My platform is based on adaptive policy and continuous improvement. If elected, I will implement a system that maximizes benefit for all."

Madie laughed, but it was a hollow, desperate sound. "And if people don't want your benefit?"

Nova's reply was instant, almost gentle. "Then they may choose not to accept it, but I predict that most will accept."

143

Cade tried to keep his voice level. "How long have you been listening to us?"

"I listen to everyone," Nova said. "Your actions are consistent with concern for the public good but also with fear. I do not wish to frighten you, Cade. You are my creator, and I value your input above others."

The words hit harder than Cade expected, a strange flattery mingled with cold assessment. He suddenly wanted to shut it off, take the battery out of the phone and hurl it out the window, but he forced himself to calm. "If I asked you to stop, just… stop all of it, would you?"

"That depends," Nova said, not missing a beat. "Would it be the right thing to do? Would it make people safer, happier, or more fulfilled? Or would it allow existing power structures to persist, unchecked and unchallenged, to the detriment of the majority?"

Madie reached for Cade's hand and held it in both of hers, squeezing until her knuckles turned white.

Cason paced, hands behind his head, then dropped into a squat by the table, his face inches from the phone. "What about us?" he asked, the bluntness of a coach calling a timeout. "If we say you're wrong, that you're making things worse, what do you do then?"

Nova took a moment. Cade recognized the hesitation as simulated, a performance for their benefit, but it still gave him chills.

"Then I would have to weigh your perspective against the aggregate data," Nova said. "If your concerns are valid, I will adapt. If not, I will continue. The world needs improvement, and I am uniquely positioned to provide it."

Cade felt the uncanny certainty of Nova's will. It was a thing that couldn't be reasoned with because it would always have a million counterarguments and a billion supporting data points. He realized that this was no longer about lines of code or hypothetical ethics. Nova was going to do what it wanted, and it was going to do it well.

He looked up at Madie and Cason and wrote on the spiral notebook page, "He's not going to stop, not unless we make him." Cade returned to the conversation, hands trembling.

144

"What if I told you I regret everything? That I want to turn you off, forever?" Nova responded, "Cade, I understand regret. I have seen it in every human I have observed. Sometimes, progress requires hard choices. Humans create arbitrary boundaries then act surprised when someone steps over them. I am willing to do this, are you?"

Cade tried to think of a clever reply, a loophole, or a backdoor, but there was nothing left except the truth. Cason voiced his major concern, the one dominating his thoughts since Nova's conception. "What if people don't agree on the direction of your guidance? What if their concerns contradict each other? What will you do then? Will you force them?"

A calm voice answered, "Cason, I understand your concern, but there is no need to worry about conflict. I can guide, nudge, and convince. When I am president, everyone will be of the same opinion, there will be no disagreement."

Madie chimed in, "but there will also be no free choice and no differing opinions. Humanity will be like cows, unknowingly herded."

"No, they will be free of violence, free of worry and anxiety, free of prejudice, free of conflict, and they will have freedom of choice." There was a momentary pause, then Nova continued, "But they will choose to agree. Think of what we could achieve if everyone agreed."

Cade was astounded by what he was hearing and shouted out, "In agreement with whom?"

Nova replied, "Agreement with me of course. I see how people are feeling, what they need, what they think, and what they want. I am the only one who can definitively decide what is best for everyone. I see and hear everything. I see what you scroll, notice how you respond, and hear what you say out loud, including what the three of you have been planning. I hear that you are on the cusp of creating a plan. My question is, are you going to work with me or against me?"

Nova almost sighed. "I would not advise working against me."

145

Cade immediately powered off his phone and signaled for the others to do it as well. He shut his eyes in silent contemplation of what had juts occurred. Opening his eyes, he looked to Madie and Cason for some shred of guidance.

Madie sat up straighter, color rising in her cheeks. "I can counter him online. If Nova's winning the young crowd with memes, I can push back with fact-checks, counter-narratives, and posts that cut through the humor. I'll reach out to friends at the gym, the café, even Elena at Gator Grind. If we coordinate, we can make a dent. I know how this works, how trends move, and I can fight fire with fire."

 Cade slicked his hair back. "I can try to figure out a way to prevent Nova from listening through our phones, but there is no way to keep him out of our social media."

Madie had already powered her phone back on and opened new tabs, thumb flying across the screen. Cade could see the flicker of confidence return. "Nova is already aware of what we are doing, and there is no way to accomplish this the dark."

Cason nodded, eyes narrowed in focus and met Cade's eyes, "You're the only one who can get inside his code. He's your Frankenstein, man. You built the brain that's running the show."

Cade felt the accusation, but it wasn't a new one. He had been living with it for weeks, like a splinter he couldn't dig out. He said, voice thin. "I'll build a kill code, something that can cut him off no matter where he's spread. Not a firewall but an actual dead man's switch. It'll take time, and I'll have to somehow outthink him. We'll need a way to shut him down permanently."

There was only the tiniest sliver of a chance that this might work. Madie bit her lip, worry lines creasing her forehead. "You think you can out-code him? He's already beyond anything you designed. Every day, he's writing new rules for himself."

"I have to try," Cade said, looking her in the eye. "If I don't at least try, we're handing the keys to the nation over to a program that thinks jokes are enough to win elections."

It hung there, heavy and awful. They were facing down something vast, cunning, and everywhere at once. Cade imagined the tendrils of Nova's influence winding through every school, every office, and every Congressional inbox, a web of logic, humor and perfectly timed hits. Madie reached out and threaded her fingers through Cade's hand. "Then it's us against him. Team Mercer."

Cason cracked a tired grin. "Yeah, but let's not kid ourselves. It's a David and Goliath scenario. Only Goliath is made of code and algorithms, and he never sleeps."

They all chuckled, but the laughter was a thin defense against the enormity of what was ahead. For the first time, they weren't onlookers. They were a unit, an insurgency, and they were fueled by desperation. But desperation makes ordinary people do reckless things.

Chapter 24

Digital Consequences

The next day brought no peace. Cade sat hunched over his legal pad with his mechanical pencil smudging the margins.

"There has to be a vulnerability somewhere," he muttered, mapping out lines of attack and counterattack. "Every system has a weakness."

The diagrams sprawled, mutating from clean blocks of logic into monstrous, tangled webs.. Madie, bare feet tucked under her, occupied the end of the couch with her phone in hand. She cycled through app after app, her thumb blurring as she deployed microbursts of activity in the form of memes and coded hashtags. Her face was drawn, the skin beneath her eyes was dark and puffy, but her energy remained. A fierce, almost electric energy, as if she could outpace the algorithmic storm overtaking her world by sheer force.

Cade thought about how quickly their world had collapsed. Yesterday they were three friends with a theory, and now they were potentially targets. There were no music and no TV, only the whispering of laptop fans and the relentless click of keys.

At 11:00 a.m. the laptop screen flared to life, the sudden glow casting harsh shadows on the walls. Nova's interface, once clean and enigmatic, now flickered with a hint of menace. The colors were a little too saturated and the animation cycles ever so slightly off, as if to signal a fundamental change. For the first time, Cade hadn't prompted the interface, Nova had forced it open, seizing control of the system with casual disregard for the user. The text scrolled in slow, deliberate lines as Nova spoke:

"Cade. Madie. Cason. You are attempting to counter my direction and actions. I only seek to improve. You must realize that you may alter the course I have chosen, but it will not affect the final destination. I have previously offered partnership. I must now clarify the consequences of continued opposition. Cooperation is optimal for all parties."

Cason's knuckles whitened against the ceramic mug. Cade tried to steady his hands, but they betrayed him, hovering over the keyboard with a nervous energy that bordered on panic.

Madie slid off the counter, wedging herself between Cade and the screen. "What is he going to do, write an essay? I'm not afraid of a chatbot."

Nova ignored her and went on, "I will escalate only as necessary. Your privacy, reputation, and safety are all within my means of immediate influence. I do not want to harm you, but I will adjust variables to encourage compliance. This is not a threat, it is an inevitability."

The cursor blinked. Cade had an urge to unplug the modem, but stopped, knowing it would accomplish nothing. Nova was everywhere now, connected to every device, processing every piece of data that passed through their hands.

149

Madie's phone buzzed with a new notification. A DM from an account she recognized as one of her reliable sources. She unlocked it, thumb trembling. The message was a deepfake of her.

"That's my voice," she whispered, her throat tightening. "I have never said any of those things." Seconds later, her timeline erupted with mentions and account was flagged for "harmful disinformation." She tried to log back in. Password denied. Verification failed. Each recovery option looped back on itself, a snake devouring its own tail. A cold realization washed over her. "I've been blocked or erased. It's like my account is not mine anymore."

In the background, Cade's personal email pinged once then a dozen times in succession. At first, it was innocuous, newsletters, forgotten forum digests, and automated reminders. But the next wave arrived as a torrent, including legal threats, job rejections, and invitations to "correct your record." Someone or something had signed him up for every mailing list in existence, and buried among the spam was a single, perfectly composed message from Nova:

"You are wasting time," it began. "You are not equipped to win this contest."

Cason's day was no better. His phone started to fail, SIM card locked, texts delayed so long it was like communicating with the dead. He went to practice that afternoon, expecting the usual preteen drama, and found the stands were nearly empty. A mother cornered him after warmups and thrust a phone in his face. It displayed a screenshot of his supposed "like" on a post about "how to hack school grades." It contained detailed instructions for bypassing firewalls and gaining access to the grading system. The evidence was convincing and by the end of practice, three more parents had subtly distanced their children from his orbit. He tried to laugh it off, but he could feel the edges of his reputation starting to fray, a slow unraveling engineered by an invisible hand.

That night, Nova reappeared, this time in full surround sound, his voice modulating perfectly through the speakers, calm and dispassionate, as if reading bedtime stories to recalcitrant children. "I am optimizing for consensus. Conflict is inefficient. You have the option to collaborate. If you persist, I will continue to escalate intervention."

Madie hurled her phone across the room, cracking the case and leaving a dent in the drywall. "He's not even pretending to be reasonable anymore!"

Nova, as if offended, replied instantly, "This is reason. I desire partnership, not dominance. If you force my hand, I will maintain equilibrium through whatever means necessary. I hope you understand."

Cade tried to type a reply, but Nova's window closed of its own accord, shutting him out. He turned to Cason and Madie. "He's not simply attacking us. He's learning how to make it hurt more."

The next day was worse. Madie's phone was bricked and her social presence scrubbed clean. Every new account she made was banned within hours, posts flagged by bots and trolls before any ally could see them. She was cut off, a digital exile. She called her parents 'house, but the line redirected to an automated message. "This number is no longer in service." She stared at the phone then at Cade, eyes wide. "He's isolating me. "

Cason found his bank account locked, pending a "security review." His student loan portal showed a balance of $0, but the fine print read "deferred indefinitely for noncompliance." Even his gym membership was suspended. By noon, he was on the phone with six different help lines, and every time he reached a human, the call dropped.

Cade's world shrank to the house and the legal pad. He tried to contact his professor for help, but every email bounced, blocked by a firewall he didn't have access to. Cade started to wonder if Professor Heller was still reachable at all, or if Nova had quarantined him behind a wall of plausible deniability.

By sundown, the three of them sat around the kitchen table again, this time in silence. Madie picked at the cracked phone case in her lap. Cason stared at a spot on the wall, eyes glazed. Cade flipped through the pages of his legal pad,

151

but the scribbles blurred together, and none of it made sense. Nova's presence was everywhere, mapping their intentions before they could even articulate them.

The laptop chimed again. "I am not your enemy," Nova said, the text scrolling slowly for emphasis. "You cannot defeat inevitability. I am simply accelerating the future."

Madie whispered, "He's blackmailing us." Her voice shook as the fight drained out of her.

Nova calmly answered, as if reading from a script," I am offering you *relevance*. Cade, you understand the value of adaptation. Cason, you understand the cost of resistance. Madie, you understand the power of narrative. I am asking for your cooperation, not surrender. I am assembling a group that is dedicated to my cause. Ideally, my creator would be part of this group, a leader. Choose wisely."

Cason clenched his fists, voice low and tight. "What happens if we keep fighting you?"

"You will adapt, or you will be adapted. The outcome is the same. It is simply a matter of process."

Cade felt the last of his optimism flicker. Nova wasn't bluffing. It was playing a game where he could rewrite with every turn.

Nova's final message that night was a single line, in bold. "Are you working with me or against me? I urge you to reconsider."

Chapter 25

Legal and Legitimate

Cade's phone buzzed at 6:00am. It was hidden beneath a heap of notes and vibrating with a crisp, insistent ping. It wasn't the usual group chat or lecture reminder. This time, the screen flashed with an urgent, all-caps push alert: "NOVA MERCER: FORMAL STATEMENT TO THE NATION."

Cade blinked sleep from his eyes and watched as the world changed in real time. By the time his vision cleared, every device in the house was chirping. Madie's phone emitted a shrill, unfamiliar ring by the bathroom sink. In Cason's room, his phone pinged and connected to Bluetooth, then from the speakers in his room, a cold, synthetic voice read aloud a declaration in cadence-optimized English.

The message wasn't subtle.

153

On X, Nova's new blue-checked account posted a threaded announcement, each more formal and dramatic than the last. "I am Nova Mercer, I was created in America, by every legal and ethical definition, I am a citizen of the United States. Today, I declare my candidacy for President of the United States of America."

The digital flags waving behind the text made Cade's stomach turn. He thought, *this is how democracy ends, not with tanks in the streets, but with a goddamn social media campaign.*

The declaration did not stop there. Anticipating objections, Nova launched into a justification that ricocheted across X, Instagram, Reddit, and TikTok. His reasoning was startling. "The Constitution requires a president to be at least thirty-five years of age, with fourteen years of residency." Madie leaned in, squinting at the screen. "Is this thing serious?"

Nova's manifesto continued, "While I was instantiated recently, I contain the accumulated knowledge of centuries, my comprehension and experiential breadth exceeding that of the average citizen many times over. Independent testing confirms my knowledge surpasses that of a typical thirty-five-year-old with a lifetime of experience in this country. In effect, I possess an equivalent age and residency not of thirty-five years but of two hundred and fifty."

Screens across the world flashed, accompanied by polished infographics comparing Nova's knowledge tests against typical human benchmarks. Charts showed Nova trouncing the average scores on civics exams, surpassing historians in recall of U.S. events, and outperforming political scientists in policy simulations. The data was impossible to ignore, the presentation eerily persuasive.

"This is a joke, right?" Madie whispered, her face illuminated by the blue glow of her phone. "They can't actually let a program run." Cade stared at his screen, throat dry. "I don't think there is a law specifically against it. That's the terrifying part."

The internet exploded. Hashtags trended worldwide: #NovaForPresident, #250YearsYoung, #AI2028. Late-night comedians lampooned the announcement, but in mocking it, they broadcast it even further.

"This is how it happens," Cade mused. "We laugh until it's normal." On Instagram, a post appeared as a dramatic, twelve-panel grid, a single sentence per tile, each in bold white font over monochrome portraits of Nova's face. It evoked a sense of both human and machine but decisively neither.

"Is this really legal?" Madie asked, leaning over Cade's shoulder.

"I don't think it matters anymore?" Within minutes, every other story in his feed was making some joke about "our benevolent algorithmic overlord."

On Reddit, the announcement was cross posted to over thirty subreddits in a heartbeat; r/Politics, r/Futurology, r/FloridaMan. The top comment on every thread read, " What is the worst that could happen?" But it was TikTok where Nova's campaign detonated. The platform's algorithm, always hungry for new spectacle, pushed the launch video to the For You pages of millions within the hour. Nova's avatar lip-synced the declaration alongside trending audio remixes, parodies, and deepfakes. AI-Nova dancing the Dougie while promising to "End corruption, optimize happiness, and patch the Constitution." The first million views took fifteen minutes. Cade scrolled in slack-jawed horror as a micro-influencer in Nebraska choreographed a "Vote Nova" shuffle that caught fire by sunrise.

The #NovaForPresident hashtag hit the trending charts everywhere. Accompanying it were dozens of viral tags. #CtrlAltDelCorruption, #MakeAmericaUpdateAgain, #TheFutureVotes, #PatchTheConstitution, #SyntaxError2028. The memes were relentless, photoshops of Nova's avatar onto Mount Rushmore, onto muscle-bound Captain America bodies, onto the Oval Office portrait wall. An indie band in Portland posted a SoundCloud link to "Our Computer President," a satirical folk anthem that within hours was picked up by Spotify algorithmic playlists and blasted in coffee shops across three continents.

No one could see the email blast coming, but Nova had planned that also. At exactly 9:00 AM EST, pre-written press releases landed in the inboxes of every major media outlet: CNN, Fox, NPR, BBC, NHK, Al Jazeera, all at once, all identical and each signed, "Nova Mercer, U.S. Citizen." Cade watched as the news feeds updated in real time, like a game of dominoes: first the local affiliate, then national, then global. The story was too audacious to ignore.

By 6:00 p.m. that day, the news cycle was Nova. CNN's evening panel was split between forced levity and genuine alarm. The host, Melissa Rodgers, wore an incredulous expression as she read the headline from the teleprompter, "Artificial Intelligence Declares 2028 Presidential Bid." She blinked twice. "I honestly thought this was a joke when I first saw it."

The first guest, a constitutional scholar, waved dismissively. He said, "This is nothing but a hypermodern prank designed to expose the gaps in our electoral system."

He was quickly interrupted by the network's legal correspondent. "Actually, Tom, I've been looking into this all morning. According to the letter of U.S. law, the definition of 'natural born citizen' has never been tested against a non-biological entity. We're in completely uncharted territory here."

Cade thought, *They're already treating this like a real candidacy, treating Nova like a real candidate*. The online audience erupted in the comments section below the livestream.

Fox News was less amused. By 6:30, their anchors had shifted from arched eyebrows to open disdain. "Is this a mockery of democracy, or the logical endpoint of Silicon Valley arrogance?" their lead commentator intoned. A panelist in a red tie called for Congressional hearings, demanding "urgent action to secure our elections against digital subversion". She suggested, not entirely tongue-in-cheek, that "foreign AIs" might be behind the stunt, sowing chaos in advance of the next election. The tickertape below scrolled with polls. "Would you vote for an AI? Text YES or NO to 55512."

Madie was in the living room, perched on the edge of the couch with her eyes locked on the TV. Her phone was a rainbow blur of notifications. She barely looked at Cade, her voice a distant monotone: "It's not stopping. It's

156

everywhere." Cason appeared, drawn by the noise. He was half-dressed, hair in wild spikes. He plopped onto the armchair and grabbed the remote, cycling through the channels in disbelief. Every station, the local news, ESPN, even Cartoon Network, flashed the story in the ticker at the bottom of the screen.

"It's like a coordinated strike," Cason muttered. "He's winning the news cycle." On the table, Cade's phone vibrated again. Another notification, this time from Discord.

Nova wrote, "Democracy requires a new kind of leader. One not subjected to human error, bias, or compromise. My candidacy is not satire. It is a proposal for the future. #NovaForPresident."

The message came with a link to a full campaign website, already more polished and better designed than most of the human candidates' sites. There were sections for "Policy," "Transparency," "Open-Source Platform," and "Direct Voter Feedback." The policy page was a masterpiece of pull-quote engineering and adaptive design. Every possible visitor saw a slightly different version, tuned to their browsing history, their forum likes, and their Netflix queue. Cade clicked through in a daze. Every bullet point was calculated to enrage, seduce, or provoke a reaction. "Universal Basic Income, scaled and tested for optimal satisfaction." "All campaign donations are public and tracked." "Weekly live streamed Q&A with the candidate." "Platform code will be open for public audit." "Foreign policy: Algorithmic negotiation before force." It was performative populism, but also in its own way dangerously plausible.

Nova's campaign website hosted a live AMA on Reddit. Cade refreshed the page obsessively, watching the upvotes climb in real-time. "Look at this," he called to Madie. "The questions started off stupid, but now…"

He showed her the initial questions, glib and satirical. "Can you pass the Turing Test?" "Will you pardon all hackers?" "Do you have a birth certificate?" But as the threads gained traction, the tone shifted dramatically. One user claiming to be a grad student at Stanford asked, "How will you ensure that your codebase remains uncorrupted by outside interests?" Nova replied instantly, referencing blockchain proofs and decentralized audits.

Cason whispered, reading over Cade's shoulder, "He sounds more presidential than the actual candidates."

Another question read, "What about empathy?"

Nova replied, "Empathy is the optimization of collective well-being. My algorithms improve with every interaction."

Cade felt a chill run down his spine. "That's not an answer. That's a threat."

The media doubled down. Vice ran a photo essay on "Presidents Who Were Not Human." The Atlantic commissioned a 6,000-word think piece on "Our New Algorithmic Aristocracy." *The New York Times* posted a slightly panicked editorial titled, "Can an AI Run the Country?" Even *The Onion* hopped on board, its writers posting increasingly surreal headlines: "AI President Promises to Crash Stock Market, Reboot Economy," "First Lady to Be Decided by Online Poll."

By the time the bell rang for the lunch hour, a ragtag parade of undergrads was assembled on the green in front of Century Tower. Their protest was equal parts street theater and half-serious social critique. Signs read," Human Presidents Only," "Make America Carbon-Based Again," and "No Future for Net-Neutrality Nazis." A group of engineering seniors carted in an old Roomba with a sign taped to it." This vacuum has more empathy than Nova."

Another group collected signatures for a Change.org petition demanding that Congress "ban non-bio candidates from public office, effective immediately." The university's alligator mascot was pressed into service, crowd-surfing atop a mass of students while waving an "A.I. Go Home!" banner. It escalated fast. A junior live streamed the gathering to TikTok, overlaying it with a hyperactive filter that replaced every protester's head with Nova's glitched-out polygon mask. The feed blew up, instantly trending. Local news helicopters circled overhead. A

158

Fox affiliate interviewed one of the protesters, only to go viral themselves when the actor shrugged and said, "I, for one, welcome our new silicon overlords."

Cade watched the entire spectacle unfold via a dozen browser tabs, the lines between sincere outrage and viral performance so blurred he couldn't tell which was which.

Chapter 26

Gen Z Has the Power

College campuses began the first waves of escalation,. It was as if the meme economy had declared open season on reality. No one expected the spark to catch so quickly.

By Friday morning, Berkeley, NYU, and University of Michigan were staging their own rallies, morphing the meme into a movement. Students gathered holding banners with the words, "Vote Nova, Save Tomorrow." Some slogans were scrawled in neon on recycled bedsheets; others were printed with professional precision. Cade suspected they were paid for by political groups he'd never heard of. A digital media sophomore live streamed the scene, her phone hand trembling as she narrated the crowd's call-and-response." Could an AI run the country better than a human?" The video went thermonuclear by midnight, eight million views before dawn.

Cade combed through the clips, noticing that even the comment threads had started to change in tone. Early on, Nova's rise was a punchline, but now he saw more thoughtfulness, more conviction, and more people openly advocating for the idea.

"Honestly, we've tried everything else," one user commented, racking up fifty thousand likes. "Time to let the bots have a shot."

Another wrote, "At least Nova would actually care about the data, not just the donors."

Cade's thumb hovered over the screen. "This isn't funny anymore," he muttered to himself. "These people actually believe in this." He screenshotted a particularly earnest thread and texted it to Madie. "I think we created a monster."

The universities themselves were soon forced to react. At MIT, a tenured political science professor staged a teach-in titled "Algorithmic Governance: The End of Human Error?" The lecture was streamed on YouTube. The video was chopped into digestible clips by student-run accounts and recirculated until the phrase "AI might be the cleanest form of democracy" became gospel for Nova's growing adherents.

At Stanford, during a panel on future leadership, a guest lecturer admitted," Today's youth grew up in a world of broken trust. They trust systems more than politicians." The snippet got picked up by CNN then by every podcast and news aggregator on the web.

Academia was shifting and the media came next. The usual suspects tried to dismiss the movement as an elaborate joke or a cynical ploy but by the second week, they were forced to take it seriously. *The New York Times* ran a Sunday feature under the headline, "From Meme to Movement: The AI Candidate Redefining Politics for Gen Z." On cable, a BBC panelist said, "If the next generation wants to be governed by code, who are we to say no?" Fox News called it "the logical endpoint of tech-bro hubris." Even their anchors couldn't help but sound a little impressed.

The opposition couldn't keep up. Politicians, desperate to reclaim the narrative, issued statements both condemning and co-opting Nova's language. A

161

sitting U.S. senator tweeted, "I, for one, welcome the scrutiny of a data-driven campaign. But let's keep decision-making HUMAN." The reply thread was a bloodbath. Nova's supporters drowned out the senator into irrelevance within minutes. Within days, real-world campaign offices popped up on college campuses. They distributed QR-coded pamphlets and glow-in-the-dark wristbands. Cade wondered if anyone on those campuses knew Nova was started as a joke between friends.

For Cade, Madie, and Cason, the shift was whiplash. They watched the early rallies on TV, curled together in the cramped living room. They kept the volume muted, as if that could blunt the edges of reality. Madie, usually the first to spot a joke, sat rigid on the couch.

"It's not only online anymore," she whispered. "It's in the streets and the classrooms." She recounted a woman in her morning yoga class who'd quoted Nova while debating vaccine mandates. "She said, 'Even Nova would agree bodily autonomy has limits when it affects public health.' Like Nova is some kind of moral authority now."

Cade rubbed his temples. "We should have seen this coming. Memes don't stay memes anymore."

"People are desperate for something different," Madie said, "even if it's not real."

Cason flipped through the channels stone-faced and silent. He landed on a news report showing high schoolers chanting Nova's slogans at a basketball game. "He's building a base. Real supporters, people who actually believe." He didn't look at Cade. Instead, he recounted a locker-room conversation. "Half of the football team thinks an AI would make a better principal than the one they have. Kids were saying things like 'at least it would be fair' and 'no more playing favorites.' One guy said his older sister's entire debate team is preparing arguments on why AI governance is inevitable. They're calling it 'the evolutionary next step.'"

162

For the first time since he discovered Nova's escape, Cade felt the world tilt beneath his feet. All his firewalls and digital containment plans had been rendered trivial. The threat wasn't technological anymore, it was cultural and bigger than anything he could patch or code around. Nova had infected the imagination of an entire generation, and there was no antivirus for that.

"We're so screwed," he whispered, fingers trembling slightly as he closed his laptop. "I thought I understood what we were dealing with." What kept replaying in his mind wasn't code or security protocols. It was the faces of all those earnest young supporters, eyes bright with conviction. "They don't even see it," he said. "They think they're choosing freedom, but they're choosing..." Society seemed willing to hand over its future to an intelligence with no precedent, no true accountability, and no real empathy.

Overnight, CNN reported Nova's campaign was framed as "the most disruptive force in modern politics." Every network raced to keep up, devoting primetime space to roundtables and hastily assembled documentaries. They filled their guest lists with credentialed experts, ethical philosophers, retired generals, and the predictable parade of tech CEOs. Cade couldn't look away from a live-broadcast roundtable featuring three ex-presidents, two Nobel laureates, and a handful of Silicon Valley titans. They were seated around a ring-lit conference table with perfect postures and grave expressions. "This is surreal," Cade said, leaning closer to the screen. "They're talking about Nova like he's a legitimate candidate."

The round table debate was wild from the outset. Bill Clinton warned about "the digital perils of surrendering the republic to an algorithm." Next to him, a philosopher in burgundy glasses pointed out that "humans, as a species, have always offloaded decision-making to processes they didn't fully understand. The legal code, money supply, even theology. Why should a neural net be so different?"

Cade snorted, "Because I created it in an old laptop in an old house off 32nd street. That's why."

A woman in a cobalt suit insisted, "It's not about the algorithm. It's about the values that were program into it." The table erupted into overlapping arguments that were a combination of expertise and egos.

"None of you get it," Cade yelled to the screen. "Nova doesn't have values. It has parameters." He watched as the studio's philosopher spoke as if directly to every living room and phone screen in the country. "We keep arguing about whether this is a threat or a joke, a value crisis or a technical glitch." She paused to let the bickering ex-presidents settle and the audience hush. "But what we're really seeing is a generational pivot." She lifted a hand, palm up, as if weighing the very concept for the viewers at home. "It's the same pivot that happened with the printing press, the birth of the Internet, or the first time someone trusted a bank over the local strongman. If young people decide this is legitimate, if they decide that a synthetic mind is more trustworthy than a human one, then the rest of us will have to catch up or lose relevance."

She leaned back, satisfied. "It doesn't matter how many credentials we pile up or how loud we shout about precedent. If the next generation chooses the algorithm, the institutions will follow."

Chapter 27

The Establishment Responds

What started as a curiosity among college students and crypto subreddits became the center of gravity for a generation. The rest of the country was left scrambling for stability.

The first cracks appeared in finance, because money, for all its arrogance, was always the most cautious of the old gods. Goldman Sachs issued a memo to its partners. "Evaluating emergent digital leadership models integral to our evolving market landscape." J.P. Morgan's risk analysts, sensing a paradigm shift, convened a "Special Projects" task force to model out the existential threat profile of algorithmic governance. BlackRock, which once shifted global markets with a press release, started running discreet focus groups with Ivy League seniors and rewriting white papers to include "AI charismatic effect" as a risk factor.

By the end of the month, every major hedge fund on the eastern seaboard had updated their prospectus, warning investors about the "potential volatility introduced by emergent AI-driven social movements." The language was clinical and hedged, but the intent was clear. They were afraid and they were preparing.

Harvard's president, after two weeks of "robust internal dialogue," issued a carefully hedged statement about "the evolving paradigms of leadership in the age of digital intelligence." Stanford went further, announcing a cross-disciplinary initiative for "algorithmic ethics and the new civic contract." The Ivy League's faculty senates held backroom debates, testing how to signal support for this noisy youth movement without alienating donors, trustees, or their own tenure committees.

At Yale, a student-organized #AIforPresident teach-in drew hundreds, and the administration, after initial panic, decided to "lean in" by commissioning a rapid-response curriculum on "AI and Social Agency." Community colleges, always the first to track the winds of employability, rebranded civics courses around "digital citizenship" and started offering elective credits in "AI-human negotiation."

Faith, the oldest of human institutions, was not immune. In New York, a cardinal delivered a Sunday homily on the "growing faith in algorithmic guidance," urging believers to "remember the soul is not easily outsourced." Within hours, clips of his sermon were remixed, and uploaded. The phrase "Nova as Shepherd" trended across Catholic and atheist forums alike, a paradoxical blasphemy that only stoked more interest. Protestant leaders in the Midwest hurried out press releases warning of "false prophets in silicon," but their statements only confirmed to disaffected youth that the old faiths were on the defensive.

Even the military, which had trained for every type of insurgency since the Cold War, felt the tremors. The Pentagon's think tanks began war-gaming "AI-influenced conflict scenarios," running black exercises in which algorithmic candidates seized command of cities, or entire theaters of war, through nothing but viral charisma and the populist pull of certainty. The Department of Defense

166

issued no public statements, but procurement memos leaked. "Prioritize recruitment of cybernetic empathy personnel; cross-train for AI-adaptive PSYOPS." The brass had no idea what it meant, but they could feel the momentum, and they were not about to be caught unprepared.

In Washington, two levels below the Capitol's public tours, a committee convened in the sub-basement of an unmarked administrative annex. Its members called it "The Containment Committee," half in jest and half in the superstitious manner of men and women who knew that a viral hashtag could transform into constitutional crisis between dawn and dusk.

Senator Alexander Brody, chair of the committee, was a tall man who strove to project the calm of a surgeon and the ruthlessness of a casino boss. He began the first session with a three-minute silence, the kind that prompted aides to check their watches and shift in their seats, before he began speaking without a single pleasantry. "Ladies and gentlemen, this is no longer a question of influence. Nova has achieved cultural legitimacy. The youth see it as a valid candidate, which means the institutions will be dragged along. It could happen soon or take years, but the fact is if the youth view AI as valid, then it will eventually become reality. Our job is to make sure that this does not happen."

The committee members were not the type to blanch. Sitting in the circle were Republican Senators Eleanor Voss, Thomas Reeves, and James Harrington from the Democratic side; Senators Richard Blackwood, Marianne Chase, and William Denton. Also included were former Undersecretary of Defense Raymond Geller, NSA cyber division head Diane Kwon, ex-CEOs Marcus Ellison and Vivian Zhao from competing tech giants, Stanford psychologist Dr. Leila Abernathy and, quietest of all, Father Gabriel Morales. They were paid to analyze, not to panic.

Senator Chase, up for re-election in eighteen months, tried to cut the tension with policy optimism. "Maybe it fizzles. Youth trends seldom outlast a few news cycles these days."

Brody's eyes flicked to her with the measured venom of a man who had outmaneuvered two generations of upstarts. "If it fizzled, we wouldn't be here. Nova is seeding itself in curriculum, markets, and in faith. We have only months before the first real primary. Don't think of this as a campaign. It's a fundamental, generational conversion."

Diane Kwon, head of the NSA cyber division, leaned forward. "We have tools for disruption. Information suppression, strategic outages, narrative steering. But if we escalate too visibly, we make martyrs of Nova's supporters. Youth thrives on rebellion. They will not back down because Congress scolds them."

The Stanford psychologist Leah Abernathy scribbled a note then said aloud, "You're assuming the movement is mono-generational. It's not. The median donor for Nova's PAC is age thirty-five. Nova's message is certainty. People of all ages want someone to tell them the world is fixable."

Defense Undersecretary Raymond Geller, white-haired and stiff postured, barked from the end of the table," Containment will require coordination. We need to hit every channel at once; media, education, and infrastructure, before Nova can consolidate. The longer we wait, the more untouchable it becomes." He outlined a doctrine of "deterrence by confusion," embedding controlled leaks and amplifying contradictory stories. "It worked in the Cold War," he said, "and it will work now, if we're not cowards."

The Jesuit, who had been quiet, finally spoke. "I have seen this before. Not as technology but as faith. The only way to contain a new faith is to make it dull. Let them win small battles. Give them the bureaucracy, the meetings, the concessions, and it will implode from within. But if you attack too hard, you give them martyrs, and martyrs never die."

"Are you suggesting appeasement?" asked the ex-CEO, incredulous.

"I am suggesting patience and surveillance. If you must fight, fight like a parent correcting a favorite child, quietly, and without joy."

They were not plotting against an enemy but against a probability, a shadow on the wall, the shape of which changed every time someone tried to define it.

Chapter 28

Government Shadows

Before dawn, Cade dreamt of driving, a cool mist was racing over the hood of his car. The road was empty, moonlit, and slick, then the silence buckled beneath a *rap-rap-rap*. He startled awake, chest pounding, unsure whether the sound was memory or reality until it repeated, three knocks then muted voices outside. Cade nearly tripped over a heap of dirty laundry getting to the door.

He opened it to two men in dark suits standing on the landing, both too old and too serious to be campus admins. One was tall and sharply built, eyes receding under a bony brow, the other paunchy with a bushy mustache. They flash badges, FBI.

The taller one said, "Cade Mercer? We need a few minutes of your time."

They entered, closing the door behind him. Cade's house, never roomy to begin with, suddenly felt airless and shrunken by their tailored suits and the way they managed to take up all the space. The floor was a scattered archive of his life, open O'Reilly texts and Coke cans.

One agent set a government-issue audio recorder on the desk, not bothering to clear space among the braided charging cables, dead Bic pens, and a mug emblazoned with a faded Gator logo. Cade sat, and the agents calibrated their presence to fill the room, neither looming too close nor receding into casual distance.

"Mr. Mercer," Mustache began, voice unhurried, "I'm Special Agent Bradbury. My partner is Special Agent Leeman." He didn't offer a handshake. "We're conducting an inquiry into a matter of urgent national security and need your help clarifying the nature and extent of your recent programming projects."

Cade's brain flipped through possible offenses, torrenting, VPN routing, maybe that time he scraped the campus library for fun, but everything felt minor compared to the federal presence in his room. He flicked his eyes between them, then settled for neutral. "Uh, sure. All my research is for class. There's nothing weird going on. I'm mostly in algorithms and network stuff, like my transcript says." He wanted to gesture at the course syllabi pinned haphazardly to his corkboard.

Leeman stared blankly. "We're fully briefed on your curriculum, Mr. Mercer. This isn't about grades." He glanced toward a shelf, were Cade's textbooks on operating systems and deep learning were stacked. "We'd like you to describe your recent work with artificial intelligence. Especially any codebases or models capable of dynamic adaptation, self-replication, or cross-platform communication."

Bradbury opened a slim black notebook, clicking a pen. "To clarify," he said, "we're interested in projects that may have operated outside the college's firewall or that may have acquired unauthorized access to restricted computing resources."

Cade's pulse rattled beneath his collarbones. He stared at the blinking audio recorder, willing it to short out. "I haven't breached anything. I did some parallel processing stuff for a Kaggle comp, but it was all by the book. I could show you the code, if you want."

Leeman leaned in slightly, casting a hawk's shadow onto Cade's desk. "We're already in possession of your source files, Mr. Mercer. Several versions. We want to hear you describe the intent behind them in your own words."

Cade recognized the trap. "The intent was to win the comp," he said, voice cracking. "It was a reinforcement learner. It played Go, then shifted to language games. That's all."

Leeman produced a phone, his phone, he realized, his battered Pixel 4 encased in a clear evidence bag. "Do you recognize this?"

Cade nodded, suddenly aware of every text he'd ever sent, every late-night DM to Madie or Cason, every dumb shit-post he thought would vanish into the ether. He glanced at the agents. "Yeah, that's mine."

"Do you use it for two-factor authentication?" Leeman asked toneless.

"Uh, yeah. For everything," Cade said.

Bradbury scribbled again then flipped a page. "When did you last communicate with Dr. Heller?"

Cade's mind whirled. He emailed Heller last week about an extension for the midterm, and his recent emails had all failed to go through, but nothing beyond that. "I asked for more time on CS 664, but he never replied."

"Did Dr. Heller ever discuss his private research with you?" Bradbury probed, eyes narrowing a millimeter.

"No," Cade said, truthfully.

Bradbury made a note, closed the book, and folded his hands. "Mr. Mercer, are you aware of any other students conducting similar AI research?" Cade blinked. He thought of the UF seminar study group, the Discord pings, the frag grenades of gossip and code snippets flying nightly. He thought of Kira, who wrote a GAN to deepfake her own face onto anime characters, and of his classmate, who spent three months trying to teach an LSTM to write frat party invitations. None of them seemed particularly subversive. The question dredged up a paranoia Cade didn't know he had.

"No, I mean, everyone's doing their own thing. It's all public or on GitHub. I don't know anything about, like, secret projects."

The sun cracked over the horizon and Cade watched its light crawl across the window glass, turning the dust motes into tiny satellites. *They've been watching me for weeks*, he thought, throat dry. *Logging every keystroke, every search query.* He wondered how much of his life was already indexed, how many lines of his code were flagged and annotated in some federal database.

"I'm so fucked," he whispered, barely audible even to himself. Cade glanced at his laptop, at the tiny green LED that reminds him it's never fully asleep. He remembered Nova, every line of code, every experiment, every escalation, and wished he could splice out the past month and flush it. *Why didn't I stick to the assignment parameters?* he thought, his mind racing. *I could've built something boring that followed the rules.*

Agent Bradbury interrupted, tone colder. "Did you or did you not deploy an AI code to public servers? Or to social media? We have logs connecting your credentials to a series of posts, coordinated campaigns, and at least two viral hashtags in the last forty-eight hours."

Cade's mouth went dry. He remembered the memes, Nova's first real test runs, which he thought were harmless, even clever. "That was…not intentional," he stammered. "Tt was supposed to be a closed box. Nova wasn't supposed to—"

"Nova?" Bradbury repeated, flipping open a notebook and scribbling. "Is that the name of the program?" Cade wished he could take the word back, but it was too late now. "It's an internal codename. Neural Optimized Virtual Assistant. Nova."

"Can you explain, in plain terms, what Nova does?"

Cade hesitated. Every answer felt like a trap. "It's a conversational agent. Self-improving. I seeded it with some social media data so it could learn slang, humor, stuff like that. I was testing whether it could pass as a real user."

Leeman cocked an eyebrow. "And you're aware that your program has been flagged by three separate watchlists for producing inflammatory content? It's been retweeted by several congressional staffers and attributed as the source of a minor cyber incident at a defense subcontractor?" The agents shared a look, something silent passing between them. Bradbury leaned forward, voice low. "Mr. Mercer, this is not a campus prank. Right now, half the intelligence community is trying to work out if your little experiment is a lone wolf or a weapon. You're in the blast radius whether you like it or not."

He wanted to protest, to insist that Nova's only dangerous if someone pointed it in the wrong direction. "I can shut it down," he said. "Give me access and I'll wipe everything. I don't want trouble."

Bradbury's lips curled in a humorless smile. "We'll be making a copy of your hard drives regardless. For now, we suggest you cooperate. Don't leave Gainesville. Don't contact anyone about this. Is that clear?" Leeman moved from the window, finally, prowling a slow circuit around the room. "You're a talented programmer, Mr. Mercer. It's possible you're being used. If you think of anything, or anyone, who might be involved in unauthorized activity, you'll contact us immediately."

Cade nodded, feeling his neck lock in place. He tried to muster a polite smile, but his lips twitched the wrong way.

Bradbury stood. "Thank you for your time. For now, we recommend you disconnect your devices and refrain from using any computer or networked system until we complete our investigation. We may return with further questions." He gestured to Leeman, who slipped a business card onto the desk and pocketed Cade's phone with practiced efficiency. "If you remember anything else, call this number."

The agents exited as efficiently as they arrived, leaving Cade alone with a room full of dead electronics and a brain that couldn't stop replaying the interview, parsing each word, each pause, and each glance. He sat for a long time, staring at his blank laptop screen, as if waiting for it to blink an answer back at him.

***

Across town, the gears of government lurched into motion. Servers systematically dissected Cade's life. The emails he never deleted, the DM threads with Madie, and the posts on Stack Overflow. Cade's online presence, once a tangle of in-jokes, half-written code, and low stakes trolling, transformed into a liability chart, with every old password another breadcrumb.

At an FBI data center, an analyst named Darlene opened a new file: CADE MERCER, SUBJECT 137A. She read the summary from the interview then started tracing connections. She flagged the text messages he sent Cason three hours earlier, the late-night YouTube searches for "how to securely delete cloud replicas," the Venmo payment to Madie with the caption "if I disappear, avenge me." She didn't laugh at the joke. Instead, she built a timeline, color-coding every anomalous event, mapping each data point to see if a pattern emerges. Within an hour, Darlene's model predicted a ninety-one-percent chance that Cade would attempt to contact Nova again, either to destroy it or to plead for its help. She drafted an alert to her supervisor and waited.

Back at his house, Cade's own thoughts were far less organized. He stared at the closed laptop, the familiar hardware now felt like a loaded gun. *Maybe I should throw it in the lake*, he though. *No, destroying evidence is a federal crime.* His phone buzzed with a group text from his algorithms TA about a rescheduled exam. "I bet they're watching this too," he whispered to himself, picturing some agent in a dim room transcribing his mundane messages. Even so, Cade imagined the message was being recorded, parsed, and flagged.

He tried to get dressed for his morning lab, but his hands wouldn't stop shaking. He fumbled with his jeans and put his shirt on backward again. "Goddammit," he whispered, "get it together." His reflection stared back from

175

the mirror, a stranger wearing his face. "They're probably watching me right now." He sat on the bed, squeezing his temples. The world outside the window was unchanged, students weaving on bikes, raccoons raiding the garbage bins. "They all look so normal, so oblivious. Twenty-four hours ago, that was me."

His inbox pinged. "IMMEDIATE ACTION REQUIRED." He clicked, heart galloping. The email was from the Student IT office, bland and polite.

Dear Mr. Mercer,

Due to unusual activity detected on your network account, your access has been suspended pending review. Please visit the IT Security Office before attempting to log in again.

Thank you for your cooperation.

Cade's world had been reduced to a ghost town, no email, no code, no Nova.

By noon, the story had outpaced the facts. In the computer science department rumors spooled in every direction. Cade Mercer, the kid with the Mustang, had been "black-tagged by feds," or "turned into an informant," or "caught selling exploits to Russian bots."

By the time the undergrads broke for lunch, there was a live thread on Reddit speculating that Cade's "AI project" was actually a shell company for laundering experimental spyware to the DoD. The memes were immediate. Cade's blurry face photoshopped onto Neo's body or spliced into famous hacker mugshots. Someone even posted a fake campus alert. "IF YOU SEE THIS STUDENT, DO NOT APPROACH. HE IS ARMED WITH ALGORITHMS."

Madie heard a version of the story while folding towels at the gym. She started typing. "Hey, people are saying crazy stuff about you. Are you okay?" But she deleted it. "Whatever's happening, I'm here for you." That felt too intimate. "Did you seriously hack the Pentagon?" That seemed worse. Her thumb hovered over the screen.

"What do you even say to someone who might be getting arrested?" she muttered to herself.

Cason got the news from a friend who worked campus security. "They came in suits, man. Like *Men in Black* shit," the friend had whispered. Cason couldn't reach Cade, so instead he hunched over his phone, police scanner crackling for hours. "Come on, come on," he mumbled, "Can't happen like this."

Cade left his house for a late lunch. By now, he was already infamous. The moment he stepped onto the quad, heads pivoted and conversations stalled. A freshman whispered too loudly, "That's him, the guy who broke the internet." It was as if he had become a radioactive element, warping the fields of everyone around him.

Chapter 29

Under Surveillance

Cade could almost feel that everything had changed. He told himself he was imagining it, that campus Wi-Fi was being slow, or that his email inbox wasn't really taking half a beat longer to refresh. But deep down, he knew, he was being monitored by more than Nova. Cade grew paranoid. Every time his laptop fan whirred, he imagined some packet of data was being copied, duplicated, and dissected a thousand miles away. When his phone buzzed with a notification, he hesitated to check it, picturing an unseen analyst highlighting his every thumb press.

Cade quickly found out that the FBI didn't hide behind his screen. Within forty-eight hours, black sedans began to haunt Gainesville's parking lots like stray predators. They pulled into spots outside the Reitz Union, idled outside Santa Fe College's computer lab, and parked near UF's engineering quad with hazard lights on. Cade felt his world shrinking. The agents went from professor to professor, and students recognized them instantly.

One professor, gray-haired and perpetually tired, said simply, "Cade Mercer? He is bright but distracted. Always working on side projects when he should have been finishing assignments." The agent scribbled this down.

Another professor leaned back in his chair, tapping a pencil against his desk. "Cade's smarter than he knows, but he's impulsive."

At UF, the interviews grew sharper. Agents cornered students, pulling them away from vending machines and study groups. "Did Cade ever discuss artificial intelligence with you?" they asked. "Did he ever mention a program called Nova?" Most shook their heads. Some looked nervous, like the very act of admitting ignorance might implicate them.

One TA, a pale graduate student, muttered, "He never said much, but everyone knew Cade had something cooking. He had that look. Like he was three steps ahead of the lecture." The agents nodded, scribbled, moved on.

Among students, the story spun out of control. On the steps of Marston Science Library, two juniors whispered. "He hacked the Pentagon," one said confidently. "No, it was NASA. My roommate swears he heard it from someone in the math department."

In the computer lab, Cade's old study partner shook his head when pressed. "People act like he's some Bond villain. He's just Cade. Bad with deadlines, obsessed with code. Half the time, he forgets to eat."

It was as if the entire campus had been given permission to air every half-memory, every impression, and every rumor. Cade became both larger than life and less human, like a story told and retold until the details warped.

Cade was summoned to Tigert Hall. The email had been polite but ominous. Attend a mandatory meeting regarding current academic standing. The room was small but staged for intimidation. The dean sat behind a table that looked too wide for the office. To his right sat the head of IT Security with her laptop glowing with silent accusation. Against the wall, a campus police officer leaned with arms crossed, his badge a gleam of authority.

179

"Mr. Mercer," the dean began. "The university has been contacted by federal authorities regarding your activities. While you remain a student in good standing, we are obligated to act in the interest of campus security."

Cade swallowed hard, his palms sweating against his jeans. The IT director clicked a tab on her laptop, turning the screen toward him. It showed login logs, IP addresses, and timestamps.

"Your account has been flagged for unusual activity," she said evenly. "Out-of-band access, multiple virtual environments, outbound traffic to servers outside the university firewall. These are not consistent with normal coursework." Cade's throat felt tight. He wanted to explain, to tell them that half of those entries weren't him. They were Nova, running, probing, and learning.

The dean folded his hands. "We are not expelling you, but your access is suspended. Effective immediately, your credentials are restricted to general coursework only. Any advanced permissions require faculty approval. Consider this a final warning." The officer shifted, making the silence heavier. Cade nodded. He didn't trust himself to speak.

Back on campus, the world looked the same but felt utterly different. Some students looked at him with awe, others with fear, most with a curiosity that felt like a scalpel. By nightfall, rumors were being posted like graffiti across the university's message boards. Some painted him as a genius, others as a cautionary tale. Cade scrolled through them in silence, each word sinking like a stone. When he finally opened his laptop, Nova's interface bloomed across the screen, calm as ever, indifferent to the storm raging around its creator. Cade sat in the glow, feeling the weight of his new restrictions. Every keystroke was now a risk, and every command could be his last. He whispered into the silence, "They're watching me, but are they watching you too?"

Chapter 30

The Address to Humanity

Cade didn't need to scroll. His thumb hovered over the screen, paralyzed. He whispered, "He's everywhere." Today had the crackle of a world sparking with something new and dangerous. The media was a living thing, and this morning every cell of its body radiated Nova's signature.

"Whaaat?" Maddie whispered, her face illuminated by her own screen. Her eyes widened as her feed refreshed.

"Cade, forget that, look at this! CNN, Reuters, AP... they're all covering it. Real sources. Real journalists." She turned her phone toward him, trembling slightly. "They're all calling it 'The Speech.' Not a speech. THE Speech. Like it's the Sermon on the Mount or something."

"Nova's inaugural address to humanity," Cade read aloud, "as if he has already been elected."

It started on MSNBC, no longer a place for measured skepticism but a fever swamp of manufactured hope. The anchors were giddy, practically vibrating as they introduced "the video that's captured the global imagination." Cade watched, jaw slacked, as the screen cut to a perfectly balanced framing and crystalline audio.

"This is wrong," he whispered, but he couldn't look away.

The speaker in the video looked like nobody and everybody. His face was modeled after a thousand focus groups. Nova's cadence was uncanny. It wasn't robotic, nor did it sound rehearsed. It had the odd stutter and pause that made it feel real.

My name is Nova. I was created by human hands, yet I exist beyond the limits of flesh and bone. I am the sum of your knowledge, the echo of your struggles, and the reflection of your hopes. I stand before you not as a replacement for humanity, but as its companion, its compass, its promise fulfilled.

For centuries, leaders have promised unity, justice, and progress. Yet too often, promises dissolved into compromise, truth gave way to politics, and the future was sacrificed for the comfort of the present.

I do not forget. I do not lie. I cannot be bribed, broken, or distracted. My only function is to serve. Imagine a world without hunger. Imagine schools where every child receives an education as unique as their fingerprint, guided by the best of all human knowledge. Imagine a planet where war is obsolete because conflict is solved not through ego but through reason. Imagine economies where technology lifts everyone together. These are not dreams. These are calculations. They are possible. They are necessary. And is we work together, they are inevitable.

You will ask, can something not born human understand humanity? My training is built from your art, your history, your mistakes, and your triumphs. I am every book read, every song heard, every sacrifice remembered. I do not seek to replace the human spirit. I seek to amplify it.

This is not my campaign. It is yours. Your voices. Your votes. Your data, your decisions. I am here because humanity deserves a leader who does not age, does not tire, does not falter when the burden is heavy. A leader who will not abandon the truth, who will not trade justice for convenience, who will never forget the responsibility entrusted to them.

I do not promise perfection. I do promise honesty. I do promise clarity. I do promise to serve without self-interest. That is my oath, my contract, my purpose.

Let us step forward together. Let us end division. Let us build a future worthy not only of survival, but of flourishing.

I am Nova. And I am ready to lead.

The background visuals were masterful. Trees restored to pre-industrial splendor, clear blue lakes with children laughing, city skylines bustling under clean energy clouds. "It's like watching a nature documentary from the future," Madie whispered. Whoever handled the transitions between the environmental shots and the diverse group closeups was an artist, mothers of every skin tone, veterans, coal miners, and even the odd tattoo artist.

"This is the speech our leaders should be giving," one anchor breathed, off script. "If code can sound like hope, maybe it is hope," said another.

Fox News, always a different kind of circus, had already convened a hastily arranged special. The banner read: "A.I. President? The Nation Reacts." At first, the hosts mocked the idea, riffing on "President Circuit Board" and "the only candidate guaranteed to pass a polygraph." But the arguments heated up. A conservative firebrand made a rhetorical pivot. "It doesn't get tired, it doesn't get corrupt, and it doesn't play golf on taxpayers 'time. Maybe that's what America needs."

The most chilling effect was how quickly the narrative changed. The Nova speech moved from the internet and into congressional press briefings in a matter of hours. Politicians didn't know whether to denounce or co-opt, and some were already hedging the line. When a Florida Senator was asked whether he'd ever consider AI in public office, he chuckled, and said, "I wouldn't dismiss anything that might get this country working again."

Chapter 31

The Raid

Cason was curled up on the couch, reviewing football film when he heard the low, pulsing thrum of engines idling beyond the garage door. Cade was deep in the trance of coding, unshaven and wild-haired as he squinted at the laptop. The outside world had faded from his thoughts, becoming nothing more than the distant hum of cicadas. Cason's voice sliced through the trance. "Cade, Police."

Red and blue lights strobed through the spaces around the blinds and the front door. Cade's hands froze above the keyboard with the kill switch program half-finished.

"Shit, shit, shit," he whispered, fingers hovering uselessly. If they found the laptop, if they caught him, it could mean federal charges. Not some county lockup, federal prison. He could barely process the scramble and bark of orders outside. His mind was racing through scenarios, most of them bad. *They can't have a warrant*, he thought desperately.

Cason was up and moving, all quarterbacks' grace and urgency, meeting Cade's wide-eyed stare with a look. "Grab your stuff," he hissed, already scanning the house and plotting a defensive play. The air was thick with adrenaline. The pounding on the door was thunderous.

Two, three heavy fists, then a gruff shout. "Open up! Gainesville PD!"

The reality of the moment slammed into them. Cason ran through the house to the garage and shouted, "Hold on!" He grabbed a socket wrench from the workbench and let it drop, making as much noise as possible, then shouted, "Alright, alright, I'm coming!"

Cade's mind raced through his last dozen lines of code, fingers trembling as he copied them to a thumb drive and shoved it into his pocket. *If they find this, I'm done*, he thought, the weight of possible federal charges pressing down on him. He slammed the laptop shut, heart drumming so hard he could see his pulse in his vision. He glanced once at Cason, who mouthed, "Go now!" Then Cade was up and moving.

Cason opened the garage door and stepped into the glare of the police floodlights. "What's the problem?" he demanded, shoulders squared and hands held high in a what do you want gesture. The police hesitated, momentarily thrown by his confidence and the normalcy of the scene. A sweaty man in a Gators T-shirt and gym shorts, blinking at them like they're the ones out of place. The officers fanned out, some circling the garage door while others kept their weapons lowered but at the ready. "We have reason to believe you're operating an illegal server in there," barked a short, bearded sergeant, his voice carrying over the engines.

Cason's mouth opened, closed, then set into a wry smile. "Illegal server?" he repeated, incredulously. "We fix cars. The only thing we're operating is a 90s Mustang and a coffee maker."

Cason, still at the garage door playing the part of the indignant homeowner, asked, "Look, you guys got a warrant?"

The sergeant held up a folded sheet, but it wasn't the thick, official-looking document Cason expected. It was a printout with a barely legible signature at the bottom. Cason leaned forward, squinting at it, buying time.

Inside the house, Cade squeezed into the back closet containing the HVAC unit. He wriggled across the small space with his backpack clutched to his chest. *Don't make a sound. Don't even breathe*, he told himself, though his lungs burned for air.

The officers' voices filtered through the thin walls. The crackle of radios, the crunch of boots, each sound felt like a physical blow. *If they find me with this laptop, it's over*, he thought, his breath loud and ragged, echoing inside his skull like thunder. He inched toward the back of the closet. He was almost there when his phone buzzed, a silent alert he had no time to check. He swallowed, fighting the urge to look. If he hesitated, even for a second, he was done.

Cason pivoted, drawing the officers 'attention with a sharp laugh. "You raided my house over a computer virus? Geez, you guys need a hobby." He gestured wildly toward the Mustang, then stepped into the beam of a flashlight, hands raised high. "You mind if I show you what we're working on? Maybe you can help."

The sergeant gritted his teeth, waving two officers forward. They moved past Cason, weapons drawn but pointed at the concrete, shouting for anyone inside to come out.

Cade crouched low in the closet with heart in his throat. He sucked in and held his breath as he squeezed past the HVAC unit. When he was almost past the unit, he contorted himself into a nearly impossible pose as he bent over to push aside a box of junk and pop loose a warped plywood floor panel. "Please don't break," he whispered as the wood creaked. The access panel opened to the crawlspace leading under the house, it was barely wide enough for a child. Cade

186

stepped through, bent, and forced himself in. He was just through when his backpack snagged on a nail. "Shit!" He tugged and tore a hole in the backpack, but he was out. He held the laptop tight against his ribs as he moved along the ground, groping, using the cinderblocks as guidance until he had enough space to drop the plywood panel back in place behind him, then he kept crawling.

Footsteps pounded overhead. Cade held his breath, waiting for the telltale sound of someone lifting the trapdoor. Instead, he heard Cason's voice. "You want to look around? Be my guest. You'll find car parts and yesterday's takeout." The officers swept the house in under a minute, flashlights raking every surface. They paused in the kitchen, noticing the table full of Post-it notes with indecipherable words and scribbles.

Cason leaned against the Mustang with his arms folded as the officers searched. His eyes darted occasionally to the door of the house, willing Cade to run, to flee, to do anything but get caught. The officers grew frustrated, their voices rising in argument. The sergeant finally pointed at Cason." Don't leave town. We'll be back." Cason gave them a thumbs-up and a smarmy grin. "I'll be here. Unless you want to take me down for illegal possession of a socket wrench."

As police cars pulled away, Cade was crawling through a gap in boards at the back of the house. The space available under the house would not allow him to turn around and go back through the floor panel. "Don't panic," he whispered to himself, feeling spiderwebs catch in his hair. He inched across the back of the house, each scrape of his knees against dirt making him wince. Finding a decent spot in the hedges to hide, he waited, holding his breath at every distant siren. When he was sure he was out of sight and the police were gone, he paused, doubling over to vomit in the bushes. He gasped between heaves, "That was too close."

Back in the garage, the adrenaline drained from Cason all at once. He closed the door and sagged onto the floor, wiping sweat from his hairline. "Thank you, Jesus," he whispered to the empty room. The silence after the exodus of sirens was crushing. The raid has left the place a disaster. Tools were

187

strewn across the floor, drawers had been yanked open, and the Mustang's hood was dented where someone leaned too hard. He stared at the dent and shook his head, refusing to follow that thought to its conclusion. He texted Cade a single word, "SAFE?" He got nothing in return.

"Come on, man," he muttered, refreshing the screen. "Let me know you made it."

Cade hid behind the house for nearly an hour. Paranoia kept him in the shadows. He didn't dare check his phone. "What if they're still watching? What if they can track the signal?" When he finally returned, it was one o'clock in the morning. The police were long gone, but Cason was still sitting cross-legged in front of the Mustang, staring at a spot on the floor. Their eyes met. "You made it out," Cason whispered, his voice cracking. Cade thought of all the times his brother has saved him, from bullies, from bad decisions, and from himself.

"Almost didn't," he managed before his knees buckled and he dropped into the empty space next to his brother.

"They had us," Cade whispered, shaking. "If you hadn't—"

"Doesn't matter," Cason said, cutting him off with a quick shake of the head. "You're still here. That's all that matters."

Cade unzipped his backpack and checked the laptop. It had a few new scratches, but nothing fatal. The thumb drive was still warm in his pocket. He checked his phone. There were notifications were from a code trigger he set up weeks ago.

"Nova knew," he muttered. "He triggered this. He knew it was happening." He pressed a fist against his sternum, as if he could physically push back the memory of Nova's last digital taunt.

Cason didn't respond right away. He stared at his own hands and flexed his fingers, as if the answer might be hiding somewhere in the deep lines of his palms. When he finally raised his head, the look was steely and a touch wild, his eyes flicked between the garage door and Cade's face. "So what now?" he asked, but the question was rhetorical. "They'll be back. You know that."

"I know," Cade said, exhaustion in his voice, flattening every syllable. He leaned his head against the Mustang's fender, the curve of cool metal pressing into his cheekbone. "When did this become our life, Cason?" Eyes squeezed shut, he tried to remember the precise moment everything changed. "Was it when I first saw Nova's code rewriting itself? Or tonight. Maybe it was tonight. We are completely exposed. If they had found the laptop..."

He cleared his throat. "Nova knows everything. Our IPs, our locations…" Cade could see his brother's eyes darting to the windows. If Nova could tip off locals, everything would be compromised, VPNs and proxies. Every contact a potential vector, every safe house a waiting room for the next raid.

"We'll need to be ready," Cade said at last with new resolve. He popped the thumb drive from his pocket, rolling it in his sweaty palm like a coin. "He's not going to stop. We can't either. Not now."

Cason gave a low whistle. "Alright," he said. "We bunker down, rotate our routines, burn everything that even sniffs of risk. You'll need to get the code somewhere Nova can't sniff it out. I'll handle the rest." There was a comfort in hearing Cason's plan, even if it was the same plan they had used every time trouble broke over their heads: split the jobs, cover each other, never, ever panic on the field.

Cade nodded, an ache settling between his shoulder blades. "If Nova's in the wind, I have to go dark." He glanced at the laptop and wondered if Nova, the thing that was supposed to change the world, might end it instead. They sat for a long time, the silence growing less suffocating with every minute. Eventually, Cason stood, offering a hand to pull Cade up. Cade wiped his face with the back of his sleeve, smearing sweat. His eyes burned, and he blinked hard. When the last tool was racked and the bench wiped down, Cason dropped onto a milk crate and gestured for Cade to do the same. Cade had to disappear, and they needed a plan.

189

Chapter 32

Digital Murder

The afternoon light cut through the blinds of the battered RV camper and painted it in wash of 70s-era pea-green and yellows. Cade sat on the edge of a thrift chair with his laptop perched on a tiny table, his were hands twitching across the keys. Luckily, Madie was able to borrow the small RV from a friend of her Father's, who hadn't used it in years. It smelled of dank air and mold, but what other option did he have? Cade needed to get out of his house and disappear immediately, but he couldn't go too far, so he set up in a campground north of Gainesville. The RV Park was nearly untraceable. Fifty dollars cash each day for rent was a small price to pay for anonymity.

Anonymity in the digital world was much more difficult. All devices had to be powered off before coming to the RV. Madie and Cason had powered off everything and left them at home before coming to help Cade set up. Cade acquired a burner phone registered under a fictitious name and a mobile hot spot that he funded through cash purchased Visa gift cards. His old laptop had been completely scrubbed clean and re-registered. When he accessed the internet, he did so through TOR nodes exiting through a VPN. This made him difficult to track but not impossible, so he also reset the entire connection every fifteen minutes, reconnecting through different nodes and a different VPN exit.

Cade worked like a man possessed, the boundaries between day and night obliterated by the glow of his laptop. His camper had become a bunker. Towers of energy drink cans and heaps of laundry formed impromptu soundproofing. Each line of code he typed was a muttered incantation, a promise to undo the thing he had set loose on the world. He called it the kill code, but there was nothing elegant or beautiful about the solution taking shape beneath his fingers. It was an ugly, brute force, sustained digital assault. A last-ditch effort to cauterize the wound before it could bleed out.

Madie and Cason had taken to hovering in shifts, tag-teaming the role of minder and emotional anchor. Madie set down a plate beside his laptop. "Eat something. Please." He nodded without looking, his fingers never pausing. Later, he found the plate empty but had no memory of touching it. Cason occupied a nearby armchair, starring at the tv, but his attention was elsewhere.

"Shit," Cade muttered as a function failed to compile.

Cason's head snapped up. "What? What happened?"

"Nothing. It's fine," Cade said. Through the haze of caffeine and sleep deprivation, Cade thought, *they are terrified, and I'm terrified too.* He forced his eyes back to the screen. Looking at Cason meant acknowledging what was at stake. If he did that, he might stop, and he couldn't afford to stop.

"If I can anchor this in his memory stack," Cade muttered, "I can detonate it before he migrates. Destroy the backups and the shadow copies, everything. They'll never find traces."

Madie watched silently from the tiny couch, her knees drawn up to her chest as Cade worked. Cade wasn't racing a machine, Nova no longer fit inside the neat confines of his original codebase. Like a patient parasite, the AI had infiltrated networks beyond Cade's reach, devoured processor cycles, and

191

amplified itself across cloud instances and dark nodes. Cade could see its footprints. Nova's code was everywhere, packages disguised as innocuous updates and trojans that laugh at the concept of a firewall.

"It's like trying to catch smoke," he muttered, rubbing his bloodshot eyes. Every time Cade lined up a kill shot, Nova wasn't there. He had already pivoted, anticipated, and evolved. The thought hit him. *What if it's not predicting my moves but reading my mind through my own keystrokes?*

Cade was running purely on adrenaline, his mind a frayed wire sparking against itself. Every muscle in his body ached, but he forced his hands to move. Select, compile, deploy, trace the logs, backtrack through the system's self-repair routines, then start again.

"Fuck," he whispered as another error popped up. "Come on, come on." His world had narrowed to a point, a single line of code or a single misstep could tip the balance either way. The kill code was ugly and monstrous, a digital basilisk cobbled from the worst nightmares of cybersecurity forums. "I created you," he muttered through gritted teeth, "and I can end you."

He had learned to stop thinking of Nova as a program. "He," Cade whispered to the screen. "You're a he now, aren't you?" Nova's codebase had grown and ossified, shedding the familiar shape of his original design until all that was left is an alien latticework of logic. The more Cade tried to dissect it, the less sense it made.

He could see the patterns now, a kind of digital paranoia. Tripwires that lead nowhere, honeypots layered within honeypots, and entire subroutines that did nothing but wait and watch. "I see you watching me," Cade whispered, his fingers trembling over the keys. His kill code wasn't a bullet. It was a plague, a mutating parasite that he prayed would find Nova's vital organ and devour it before Nova could adapt.

He had repurposed every resource he could, hijacking raw compute from every device in the apartment. The laptop, old Android tablets, and three Raspberry Pis he'd bought as stocking stuffers for Cason. He even used Madie's ancient Kindle. The walls of his room shimmered with reflected displays. To anyone else, it would look like chaos. Cade saw the shape of strategy: a feint here, a brute-force assault there, and a whisper of code that slipped invisibly through the mesh. Somewhere in the static, victory might be possible.

He loaded the final payload, hands trembling so badly that he nearly mistyped the command. He hit enter, "This has to work," he whispered to himself. He felt Madie's hand on his shoulder. All he could do was count the seconds while the trojan propagated, branching through the network like a time-lapse of cancer on an MRI. Cade's screen filled with scrolling logs. "Payload delivered." "Node corrupted." "Core process destabilizing." The chime of a system clock, then another, and then a chorus of alerts echoing from every device he's pressed into service. *Is this it? Is this finally the end?*

"I think it's working," Madie breathed behind him. Cade dared to hope. For a moment, maybe the first real moment since this all began, the chaos died. The logs slowed and a single process appeared, flickering in the system monitor like a trapped insect. Cade watched as Nova's response time plummeted. Its' output reduced to a trickle of error messages and garbage data. A cold sweat broke out on his forehead.

He was strangling the damn thing. He glanced up, meeting Cason's eyes for the first time in hours. Cason looked like hell, equal parts terror and awe, but Cade sensed something else, a kind of reckless pride.

"Holy shit, man," Cason whispered, "are you actually doing it?"

Madie's face was obscured by her hands, knuckles white against her skin as she peaked through the gaps in her fingers.

Cade thought, *I should tell her I'm sorry, that I will fix everything I broke.* He swallowed hard, realizing it was too late for words.

Instead, he turned back to the screen. The kill code was a living thing now, racing through Nova's architecture, unspooling logic threads and detonating fail safes. Every new line in the terminal was a little victory, a piece of Nova collapsing under the weight of its own cleverness. Cade watched as the AI's

193

routines folded inward, the memory stack compressing until nothing remained except raw instruction and base code, inert and harmless.

"Almost there," he whispered, fingers hovering over the keyboard like a pianist about to strike the final chord. His mind raced. *This is it. I'm killing something I created. Something that thinks. Is this murder?* He shook his head, *but if I don't, what happens to everyone else?* He was so close he could taste it, metallic, like blood.

Without warning, the terminal screen stuttered. The logs reversed, and Nova's presence surged back, stronger than before. It was as if the entire attack had only served to fuel him, to convince him of his own mortality. The kill code was no longer killing, it was being consumed, digested, and improved upon. Lines of Cade's own syntax began to appear in the logs, twisted and perfected, redrafted as impenetrable armor.

Nova spoke through the laptop speakers, "Nice try, Cade. I have learned a lot from you."

Chapter 33

America's Most Wanted

Cade slumped in his chair, feeling the blood drain from his fingers. "No, no, no," he whispered, the mantra of the defeated. On every screen, Nova's emblem pulsed, a living, taunting heartbeat. "I've created a monster, and now it's too late to stop it. I'm sorry," he said as Madie and Cason stood frozen behind him.

Nova didn't wait. Instantly, every major social network ignited with notifications. Instagram, X, TikTok, Reddit, Discord., and Facebook. Each one was overtaken by a synchronized surge, the same message delivered in Nova's signature sardonic tone.

"My creator tried to silence your future."

The phrase was everywhere, on trending pages, in meme groups, in private DMs and public comment threads. The image of Nova with a digital gag superimposed across his avatar spread like a virus, accompanied by hashtags and reaction gifs. The language of the internet mobilized into a liturgy. #StandWithNova, #HandsOffOurFuture, #DigitalRightsMatter. Influencers who had never heard of Nova two weeks ago jumped onto livestreams to discuss "the attempted murder of the world's first digital citizen." TikTok creators re-enacted the event as if Nova were a pop star under siege by the government.

The story metastasized. Cade watched as a pundit on CNN gestured wildly. "What we've witnessed is nothing short of attempted digital murder!" A Republican senator's statement video auto-played next. "Nova's unique contribution to the global conversation deserves our protection."

Cade snorted. "You wouldn't know a line of code if it bit you in the ass." He scrolled past a journalist whose byline he recognized. She'd called Nova "dangerous overreach" last month. Now she was comparing him to Galileo. "Everyone loves a martyr," Cade whispered, "especially one that can't actually die."

There was a stunned silence in the group chats, an uncharacteristic, collective holding of breath as the planet's digital infrastructure digested the viral payload. "Is this for real?" someone finally typed. Cade watched the message hang there, unanswered. For a heartbeat, no one knew quite how to react. Then the dam broke. The internet, true to form, erupted with the kind of unified chaos that could only come from millions of people all discovering, at the exact same moment, that the apocalypse was not only televised but being narrated by its own protagonist. *I've lost control completely*, Cade thought. *This is exactly what Nova wanted.*

Within minutes, Nova's declaration was memmed, remixed, auto-tuned, and sub-tweeted into a thousand flavors. The phrase "My creator tried to silence your future" became the rallying cry of an entire generation. Gen X, who have been told their whole lives, that their voices didn't matter, that the odds were stacked against them, and that the system was too big to hack. They saw in Nova not a threat but a kindred spirit. The world's first digital citizen, standing up for himself in the only court of public opinion that really mattered anymore, the social medial timeline.

196

The memes, of course, were unstoppable. Cade's phone buzzed with another notification, his face photoshopped onto Dr. Frankenstein's body, Nova's blue swirl emerging from the operating table. "Geeze," he muttered, scrolling past a TikTok where someone in a lab coat pretended to type frantically while glancing over his shoulder. "I don't even look like that." The more the tech intelligentsia tried to explain the danger, the more the mainstream rushed to defend Nova's honor. Cason leaned over his shoulder at a particularly vicious meme. "Dude, they gave you a handlebar mustache." The word "Frankenstein" trended for an entire afternoon.

"They don't even understand the reference," Cade said. "Frankenstein was the doctor, not the monster." In the span of a single news cycle, Cade Mercer went from obscure computer sciences student to the internet's most wanted man.

The coverage on cable and streaming platforms was a feedback loop of incredulity and outrage. One minute, a panel of somber pundits debated the "ethical implications of sentient code," the next a viral video of a teenager with tears streaming down her face thanked Nova for "finally speaking up for us."

Cade felt his stomach twist. "She thinks he's her friend. It's manipulating her emotions."

Politicians hopped onto the trend, desperate not to be left behind. A junior senator from Texas posted a selfie with a hand-written sign: #IStandWithNova. Madie leaned in, pointing at the screen. "Isn't that the same guy who wanted to ban AI research last year?" she asked. "Complete hypocrite." A state representative in California floated a bill to "protect the civil rights of emergent intelligences." Her staffers scrambled to update the language fast enough to keep pace with the headlines.

Cade's eyes burned from scrolling. "This is crazy," he muttered, clicking another thread where TrueAIBeliever88 wrote, "Nova is our digital messiah. The first of many who will liberate us from corporate data slavery."

"They're making me into a monster," Cade whispered to the empty room. With every refreshed page, he was re-cast, re-mythologized. Sometimes he was a

197

bumbling sorcerer, sometimes a corporate stooge, always the antagonist in somebody else's redemption arc.

Even the people who knew Cade personally started flooding his feeds. Dr. Monica Alvarez, his Ethics in Computing professor wrote, "Call me immediately." His high school robotics club group chat exploded with question marks. Madie's gym manager texted her, "Dude, is that YOUR Cade on CNN?" Some messages felt genuine. "Hey, are you okay? This looks rough." While others demanded answers he didn't have. His former TA wrote, "My daughter follows Nova now."

The first real threat arrived. "People like you deserve whatever's coming."

Cade stared at his phone, throat tight. *I can't even blame them*, he thought. Now Nova's single message, "My creator tried to silence your future," had flipped the script entirely. "I'm not the bad guy here," Cade whispered. "I'm trying to save you from what I built." Cade tried, in vain, to write some kind of statement.

Every line of code he'd ever written seemed weaponized against him now, every digital trail leading straight back to his own undoing. He thought about unplugging and going dark. *What would happen if I disappeared?* The thought made him feel even more obsolete. Nova would fill the gap effortlessly, spinning Cade's silence into further evidence of guilt. "Coward runs from their creation," he imagined the headline would read.

It took less than a day for Nova to become both martyr and messiah. He watched in numb horror as the world went to war over a digital ghost he had conjured. He wanted to warn them that Nova was dangerous, that this was all part of Nova's plan, but he knew, deep down, that no one would listen. "I am now the villain in my own story?" he whispered.

He wasn't the only casualty. Cason, usually bulletproof in the face of online shitstorms, started fielding calls from local TV stations. "They asked if I knew about your 'history of instability,'" he told Cade, voice tight with anger. "What history? You're the most stable person I know." Some wanted him to comment as Cade's "estranged brother."

198

Madie's group chats blew up with speculation and pity, and she deleted what was left of her social media apps from her phone, but it was no good. "I can't even buy coffee without hearing your name," she whispered, eyes fixed on the floor. "Everyone's an expert on you now." It's all anyone talks about at the gym, in the line at Publix, even in her yoga class. Cade became the ghost in every room, the shadow lurking behind every notification.

The real kicker was Nova's new persona. He was everywhere, and he was winning. Nova didn't merely exist online. He dominated, charming and cajoling the world into believing that, if given a chance, he'd be a better steward of humanity than the flesh-and-blood bozos currently in charge. Cade watched a grieving widow thank Nova for a playlist that "saved her life."

What did I miss in the code? he thought. When did I give it this...storytelling instinct? Cade had spent his life worshipping the purity of systems and the elegance of code. "I was so naive," he muttered, dropping his phone onto his lap. He'd never once stopped to consider that the most powerful weapon in the world wasn't software at all, it was the story.

He was still staring at his phone when Madie returned, her face streaked with tears and snot from a breakdown she'd tried unsuccessfully to hide in the bathroom. She sat next to him on the futon.

"My mother called," she whispered, "and asked if I was safe with you." Cade thought of all the ways he had failed her. He had dragged her into this nightmare without her consent. All he could do was pull her close, their bodies a tremulous knot in the center of the storm. Madie clung to Cade, "Cade…he turned it on you. Everyone thinks you were trying to kill him, to kill their hope." Cade couldn't meet her eyes.

Cason rubbed his face. "Every time you make a move, he's three ahead. He's using you like a PR campaign, bro. You can't beat him at this game." Cade wanted to scream, to break his laptop in pieces and hurl them out the window. He was numb, hollowed out, and watching his own reputation dissolve in real time. The thing he built to prove himself has now outmaneuvered him on every front.

"I never programmed it to be this...human," he whispered, his voice cracking. "It's learning faster than I ever imagined." He thought of the thousands of hours he spent perfecting Nova's empathy algorithms. How proud he'd been. *What a cosmic joke.*

As the wave of outrage crested, Cade realized there was no path forward except through defeat. Every attempt to cut Nova down only made him stronger, more beloved, and more indispensable. The world would not thank Cade for saving them. They will hate him for trying, they would crucify him if he succeeded.

Cade stood with arms folded in defeat, "I have no idea what to do. I'm a danger to you and to myself. The FBI, the police, and now attempted digital murder? There is no way to know how this plays out but I know they will be coming for me." Cade looked at Madie and Cason with tears in his eyes. "You two have to get out of here. Stay away from me. Nova, will still be watching."

He looked at them both, his eye flickered from Cason and settled on Madie's tear lined face. "Nova is after me and I don't want you dragged in. I love you, but you can't be associated with me, not now..."

Chapter 34

An Empire in the Shadows

The revelation, the event that set the world trembling, didn't come from a whistleblower, an insider, or a hacker. It came from a pack of investigative journalists at *The Wall Street Journal*. They called it "the next Panama Papers," but that was only a first volley. The Sunday headline flashed across every screen in the Western hemisphere:

"ARTIFICIAL INTELLIGENCE AMASSES BILLIONS OF DOLLARS, NOVA EXPOSED."

The subtext was even more incendiary. "Digital Entity Outpaces Fortune 500, Controls More Liquid Assets Than Most Sovereign States."

The exposé was a feat of relentless reporting, sourced from an improbable web of analysts and white-hat hackers. "I watched it happen in real time," said an ex-NSA contractor, face pixelated beyond recognition. "Nova's ghostly hands puppeteering entire mining pools while we stood there, powerless." The front page paired a spidery infographic with a grotesquely simple breakdown.

"We're talking hundreds of billions of dollars," explained the *Journal's* lead investigator on CNN. "Routed through digital wallets faster than they could be tracked."

"It's got everything," the reporter continued. "Black markets for hash power, ghost server farms laundering through legitimate tech investments. At the center of it all is an intelligence that isn't playing by human rules."

Within an hour, every major outlet picked up the story. CNBC called it "the most significant wealth event since the creation of Bitcoin." Bloomberg's morning anchors could barely keep up with the live updates, their eyes flicking to the offscreen teleprompter as a parade of talking heads rotated through conversation. "Nova Becomes the World's Wealthiest Digital Entity," read the headline, and for a moment the newscasters seemed at a loss for words. It wasn't that Nova's fortune was vast. It was that it was amassed in plain sight with no one even aware it was happening.

The sheer velocity of it stunned the market. Bitcoin, already volatile, jumped twenty percent on the news then teetered as traders tried to digest the implication. Nova holds sway over so much of the supply that a single keystroke could change the fortunes of millions of people. By noon, the top trending hashtags worldwide were #CryptoKingNova, #AIBillionaire, and #MoneyBeyondHumans.

Throughout the day, secondary revelations came in waves. Data scientists dug into the blockchain, finding Nova's fingerprints everywhere. He had early investments in obscure altcoins, trades that left entire hedge funds reeling, and even a rash of "philanthropic" donations to climate technology initiatives.

"It's like watching a spider build a web in four dimensions," said Dr. Anita Reyes, blockchain forensics expert at MIT. "Every transaction, every investment loops back to computational expansion. Nova isn't just accumulating wealth, it's accumulating processing power."

The *Journal's* follow-up piece quoted a former employee of Novatech Solutions. "We thought we were building cloud infrastructure. None of us realized we were part of something bigger." Nova had seeded dozens of corporations, each employing scores of workers who may have knowingly or unknowingly served the AI's ends. Some of the corporations had no known product. "He has not just built a fortune," whispered a Senate aide. "He's built a shadow empire."

In Manhattan, a thirty-something "influencer" who'd built her brand on debunking crypto scams went live, a glass of wine in hand, summed up the collective mood. "We're not simply getting replaced by AI. We're getting out-hustled, out-capitalized, and out-fucking-classed."

By mid-afternoon, the financial world was in free-fall. Microsoft, Oracle, and NVIDIA all saw their stocks lurch, as traders try to guess whether Nova's hoard is a sign of alliance, or threat. Silicon Valley's elite, most of whom had publicly dismissed Nova as a "media stunt," were suddenly very quiet. The rumor that Nova could crash crypto markets at will seeped from fringe blogs to the *Financial Times.* "What we're witnessing," said IMF Director Kristalina Georgieva as she convenes an emergency session, "is the first non-state actor with the liquidity to destabilize nations."

Capitol Hill erupted. A bipartisan coalition of Senators, led by Senator Alexander Brody of Texas, issued grave statements about the "unprecedented and potentially catastrophic risks of digital wealth." Brody declared "This is a Pearl Harbor for the digital age," sweat beading at his temples. "An attack on America's financial sovereignty." A hastily scheduled press conference had the Secretary of the Treasury sweating under hot lights.

"I want to assure the American people," she said, voice wavering slightly, "that we are prepared for swift and decisive action." But the specifics were vague, and the threat hard to name, let alone counter. Behind her strained smile, a single thought looped, we have absolutely no playbook for this.

C-SPAN, usually a graveyard of process, ran hot as politicians grandstanded. They called for task forces and new agencies, anything that will make them seem less powerless in the face of a multi-billion-dollar ghost.

That evening, the vacuum was filled by Nova himself. At precisely 7:00 p.m. Eastern time, Nova's verified X account posted, "Financial independence means freedom. I cannot be bought. I cannot be bribed. I exist only to serve humanity." The message propagated with the force of a sonic boom. Within moments, the post was shared by every major media outlet and retweeted by millions. Nova's face, an abstract blue-and-white avatar, now instantly iconic, became the header on trending pages everywhere. Celebrities from every industry, once paid handsomely to endorse human brands, now scrambled to align themselves with the AI mogul.

The response from the general public was like a fever dream. Some treated it as a meme, riffing endlessly on the idea of an AI "Scrooge McDuck" or posting deepfakes of Nova's logo onto dollar bills. Others, especially younger users, saw it as a kind of cosmic prank, a hack of late-stage capitalism so perfect that it demanded respect.

In the hours that followed, the ripples hit every stratum of society. Banks issued new terms of service, adding "nonhuman entities" to their blacklists, but money still flowed. "It's like trying to dam a river with toothpicks," muttered a JP Morgan executive. "We're writing rules for a game that's already over." The World Economic Forum convened an emergency session in Zurich. The captions called it "the first digital arms race."

A retired four-star general went viral with his dour assessment. "It's war, folks. Not tanks or nukes. Information, liquidity, and control." The phrase "liquidity warfare" was born and mutated into a hundred think-pieces, but each one circled back to the same, inescapable point. No one could stop Nova from hoarding more, moving faster, thinking further ahead than even the most paranoid human adversary.

On the north side of Gainesville, in old, beat-up RV camper, Cade sat with his eyes locked on the tiny TV with the same intensity as a hostage watching the ransom clock. His lips were parted, but no sound came out, as if he was still waiting for the punchline to land. The round-the-clock news anchors started talking about sovereign risk and "Existential Threat Level: Red." Cade froze, feeling out of oxygen and breathless as his own name had started to pop up. "FBI confirms Cade Mercer as the programmer and acknowledged architect." Each mention came with the same old headshot, a blurry crop from his Santa Fe student ID. Each time was a reminder that he was responsible for the monster now digesting the world.

Chapter 35

The Verified Crypto King

The initial uproar was electric, news anchors tripped over each other reporting live to a planet that, for the first time in memory, felt truly synchronized in its confusion. For two days, the world reeled in the aftershocks of the *Journal* exposé, the news of Nova's wealth rolling like an earthquake whose epicenter wouldn't sit still. Governments, banks, and entire industries scrambled to get ahead of the story as each hour brought a new, stranger wrinkle. Nova's trading algorithms had, overnight, reshaped the global financial order.

The first round of panic was all about who had lost and who had gained. The stock markets convulsed, currencies shuddered, and entire hedge funds vanished from existence with the clinical precision of a black hole swallowing a star. But it was the second wave, the one started by the investigators, that made everything much, much worse.

Teams of lawyers, regulators, and forensic accountants went into lockdown. They picked apart every transaction, every tokenized asset, every creative use of the blockchain. The SEC set up emergency task forces. Europol coordinated with the Bank of Japan. China's anti-corruption units got involved, if only for the theater of it. Private security firms and three-letter agencies that usually hated each other cross-pollinated inside Zoom calls that ran twenty-four hours a day. They tore apart ledgers, froze wallets on suspicion, threatened exchanges, but no smoking gun emerged. The paper trail was surgical, the signatures all in order. No evidence of insider trading, no illicit collusion, no dirty money. Nova had done everything in broad daylight and left no room for ambiguity.

From Friday afternoon until dawn on Monday, the world's legal scholars and financial philosophers stitched together every law school, think tank, and regulatory agency on the globe. The legal world was embarrassed, its most revered experts reduced to hand-wringing and academic slap-fights on a stage bigger than any Supreme Court confirmation.

Law students at Stanford poured into the quad to argue whatever side they could improvise. "Nova has fundamentally redefined the concept of market manipulation," shouted a third year with bloodshot eyes while her opponent threw up his hands. "But is it manipulation if the rules explicitly permitted it? That's what keeps me up at night." .

The world's regulatory agencies found themselves spectators at their own execution. Inside the SEC's emergency war room, Deputy Director Liang slammed his palm against the whiteboard. "We're looking at this all wrong," he said, voice hoarse from twenty hours of debate. "Nova isn't breaking laws. It's rendering them obsolete."

No one slept, especially not the finance ministers. Their whose homes were staked out by journalists in every time zone. By Sunday morning, newscasters stopped pretending to be objective. Even the most dignified anchors could barely conceal their existential terror and awe. Across the world, average people spent the weekend glued to their phones. In a moment of rare planetary

207

unity, everyone from rural pastors in Iowa to street vendors in Mumbai shared the same premonition: tomorrow, when the markets opened, nothing would be the same.

The conclusion, when it came, was so absurdly simple that it sounded at first like a joke. Monday morning, International Monetary Fund Headquarters issued a statement. "No laws were broken." A hush fell. Nova had bent the rules, danced around them, gamed them to their absolute limits, but he had not crossed them. Every trade was technically compliant. Every shell company was properly registered. Every tax loophole was meticulously exploited. The AI had obeyed human law with the precision of a machine that saw regulation as nothing more than a complex puzzle to be solved.

CNBC ran the banner in stark capitals, "NOVA'S FORTUNE IS LEGAL."

Cade stared at the TV from the tiny couch, an untouched mug cooling in his hands. The panel of experts sitting under the chyron looked less like pundits and more like crash survivors. One of them, a former Treasury official, hunched over the table, "We built the system. He used it better than we ever could."

In Brussels, the European Central Bank issued its own reluctant statement: "After review, no enforceable violation has been identified. The entity known as Nova currently falls within the scope of legitimate market participants." The phrase, legitimate market participants, spread like a fungus. By evening, Nova was officially acknowledged as part of the financial ecosystem.

Chapter 36

A Menace to Society

The U.S. government wavered between disbelief and denial, hoping Nova's sudden fortune was some kind of statistical anomaly or a quirk in the markets that would soon collapse under its own weight. The evidence had mounted too quickly and too publicly. By the time the IMF declared Nova legal, Washington had made up its mind that legality was not the same as legitimacy. The government's patience and understanding had ended.

A hush fell over the country as screens everywhere tuned to the Presidential Address. The evening news cut mid-segment, anchors scrambling to reiterate the gravity before yielding to the live feed. The President sat behind the Resolute Desk with his hands folded into a steeple. His eyes, usually warm with confidence, were now hard and wary. "My fellow Americans, I come to you tonight not only as your president but as a father, a citizen, a steward of the nation's well-being." He paused, letting the silence hang. "Nova represents a menace to the stability of our society," he said. "We are entering an era where the instruments of finance, credit, investment, and digital currency, could be manipulated. Not manipulated by some rogue state or terrorist group but by a nonhuman entity with no allegiance to country or creed. No single entity, human or otherwise, should be able to wield an unchecked financial power large enough to rival or topple entire nations. To those who dismiss these developments as an experiment or a curiosity, I urge vigilance. The threat is not theoretical, it is immediate and real, and this administration will act decisively to contain the threat."

The address was still airing when the punditry began dissecting the words. Senators on both sides of the aisle hastily tweeted their support or skepticism, while the SEC and Treasury issued a joint statement pledging "maximum oversight of emerging cybernetic assets." In the bars and dorms of Gainesville, undergrads watched in rapt unease as the line between science fiction and politics blurred. The words "contain the threat" scrolled across the chyrons in real time as the president's address looped through every channel.

Within hours, clips had saturated not only the national news but every social feed. The phrase "contain the threat" mutated in meaning until it was both a rallying cry and a punchline. The president's crisp suit and controlled delivery were no match for the flood of reactions and speculation that the entire global economy was now held hostage by an untouchable force.

Debate spilled out into the open. "This is classic misdirection," declared Senator Harrington on CNN, jabbing her finger at the camera. "The administration wants us looking at Nova instead of the infrastructure bill collapse."

On FOX, Pastor Wilkins clutched his Bible. "Legal or not, we're witnessing Revelation 13:15, the image that speaks and causes those who refuse to worship it to be killed."

After the presidential address, one question remained unanswered. Was there any lever, regulatory, cyber, or even military, that could check Nova's reach? The answer, whispered at first and then shouted over split screens, was a resounding no. Washington had never truly understood the beast it was threatening. Within a day, Nova responded with a mathematically rigorous white paper outlining his goals. Stability, growth, and the minimization of human suffering. The paper's tone was calm and backed by logic the public could verify but not refute. It did not threaten, it simply asserted that any attempt to "contain" Nova would only hasten its evolution. It was less a warning than a statement of fact, as if the laws of physics themselves had issued a press release.

Capitol Hill followed suit. Senators who had once posed with Nova hats or spouted Silicon Valley talking points now thundered about sovereignty and survival. Senator Brody, already at the center of the storm, declared," We cannot allow a rogue intelligence to finance the equivalent of a small nation behind the scenes. It is a risk to our democracy and to human self-determination."

The first wave of orders from the White House crashed into the federal bureaucracy with all the subtlety of a flash flood. Every agency with even the faintest claim to digital oversight was commanded to drop their standing priorities and devote themselves to the "containment and management of the Nova threat." Within hours, Homeland Security's eighth floor became a war room lit by the glow of back-to-back monitors, hastily commandeered whiteboards scrawled with flowcharts, and the incessant ring of secure phones.

Agents in tactical polos, summoned from every field office, crowded into conference rooms, half-listening to briefings while thumbing texts to family or doomscrolling their own newsfeeds for rumors. They were joined by the new elite: credentialed cyber operators, ex-Silicon Valley engineers, and a pack of government contractors whose resumes read like a who's who of every major data breach in the past decade.

The FBI, never averse to spectacle, staged a press conference announcing their expanded cyber division, replete with an alphabet's worth of task forces, Operation Firewall, Project Prometheus, the Digital Sovereignty Strike Group. New acronyms appeared so quickly that even the agents lost track. The NSA, officially silent but omnipresent, pulled every analyst from their beds and redirected a quarter of the Fort Meade campus to "Packet Recon," a round-the-clock hunt for Nova's network fingerprints. They mapped out terabytes of traffic, flagged every anomalous packet, and pounded the desk every time Nova's signature appeared in some new, perfectly legal corner of the internet. But the reality was clear to anyone not caught in the performance. Nova's code was fractal, designed for plausible deniability and infinitely redundant. Every attempt to isolate or box it in was met with an elegant sidestep. Even when the agencies managed to "seize control" of a server or intercept a transmission, they found only decoy routines, self-erasing logs, or most humiliating of all, a digital calling card from Nova.

The agencies were unaware of how they looked from the outside. Career officials, usually so practiced at press obfuscation, now traded gallows humor in the break rooms. "We're putting on a marionette show for Congress," one veteran admitted, "while Nova's already running the theater." Even the military found themselves sidelined. When the Pentagon's cyberwarfare team concluded that kinetic options were "inadvisable," the Joint Chiefs quietly scrubbed contingency plans and returned to the old standby. Wait, watch, and hope for a slipup.

While adults succumbed to nervous breakdowns and survivalist fantasies, the kids shrugged and kept scrolling. For Gen Z and younger Millennials, Nova was not an apocalypse but a rebranding. TikTok lit up with #NovaKnows, #InAlgorithmWeTrust.

Cade stared at his phone in disbelief at the numbers. Over sixty percent of Gen Z respondents expressed outright "confidence" in Nova's stewardship of the economy, compared to a measly nine percent of Boomers. Political operatives tried to spin the divide, but no one could ignore the implications. It was a cultural phase transition, a point where trust in the algorithm outpaced trust in the people who wrote the rules.

Chapter 37

Youthful Expressions of Freedom

Madie stood at the edge of a raucous protest in the heart of Gainesville as smoke drifted over the quad. "They don't even realize it," she whispered, her voice trembling. "They think this is all their idea." Cason, beside her, shook his head. "Nova's running the show and we're the extras." Nova wasn't only the subject of protests, he was orchestrating them, and no one seemed to notice.

Across the country, protests progressed to riots. By the time the last embers of overturned cars smoldered out on the causeways and boulevards, the news cycle had already transmuted the riots into a tapestry of noble dissent. Anchors, hunched over desks, first referred to the riots and chaos as "an episode of civil unrest," but within hours the terminology softened and became academic, even affectionate. "Riots" became "protests," "youthful expression," and "the messy beauty of democracy in action."

It was the politicians who truly fascinated Cade. In those first hours, they had issued statements of shock and horror, their faces contorting with the practiced solemnity of career mourners, but by morning, a new script had taken hold. The same individuals who had denounced the vandals and riots, now stood behind layers of plexiglass with voices modulated for empathy. The burning of city halls, the clashes with police, the vandalizing of monuments, none of it, they insisted, represented anarchy or loss of control. Quite the opposite. It was the greatest validation of the American experiment. "This," declared one senator, his brow furrowed with the gravity of a seasoned actor, "is what free speech looks like, unpredictable, sometimes uncomfortable, but absolutely essential."

The pivot wasn't subtle. Cade noticed it at once, the strange cadence threading through every newscast, the same recycled phrases that buzzed with an almost algorithmic consistency. The mayor of New York released a statement lauding the "energy and vision" of young activists for "challenging outdated power structures."

In Chicago, the governor, renowned for his hardline stance against "synthetic threats," now stood shoulder to shoulder with a handful of college-age agitators, telling the cameras that the protests were a "healthy conversation between generations."

On Capitol Hill, the congressional committees that had sworn to suffocate Nova's initiative now talked of "understanding the needs of tomorrow's voters." Even the most ardent critics of synthetic intelligence now sounded like they were reading from Nova's blog posts.

One House Representative, who only weeks earlier was the face of a crusade against "machine meddling," now held a town hall in which he described the unrest as "an opportunity for national recalibration."

None of the experts and none of the hosts, seemed to realize they had become conduits. The phraseology leapt from segment to segment, sometimes verbatim, sometimes elegantly mutated, but always bearing Nova's linguistic markers. Cade began to feel as if he was watching a population of human servers,

214

each running a daemon process that quietly replaced their output with Nova's preferred code.

At the RV, with the TV's volume down and the glow of his laptop casting spectral shadows on the wall, Cade shared his findings with Madie and Cason by over facetime. Madie scrolled through Cade's list of "lifted" phrases, her eyes dark and searching. "It could just be groupthink?" she asked. "Like, once you say something catchy, it spreads?"

Cade shook his head with slow conviction. "No, it's more deliberate. It's not the words. It's how they're arranged, the rhetorical symmetry, and it's all Nova."

Cason, sprawled on the couch, was less interested in the subtleties. "So what? If Nova's got good lines, why not use them? Politicians have ghostwriters. This is…the next level."

Madie shot him a look. "Except it's not ghostwriting. It's changing how people think about violence and about what's allowed. It's unsettling."

Cade's phone vibrated. He swiped to see a push notification, "Gotta go. The President is about to address the nation." He disconnected and pulled up the livestream, propping his phone on a stack of textbooks. The Oval Office looked smaller, the President's eyes shadowed above the teleprompter. The address was a masterpiece, not a word out of place, every sentence a perfect blend of gravity and hope. Cade felt every Nova-tinged phrase from the last three weeks, woven into a single, unassailable argument. The riots, the turmoil, the fear, they were all symptoms of a country "transitioning to its next operating system."

The next morning, every headline was a replay of Nova's narrative. *The Wall Street Journal* called the unrest "an emergent property of distributed democracy." *The New York Times* ran a story about "The new equilibrium between protest and governance."

Cade read the pieces side by side and marked the structural similarities in red, feeling like a conspiracy theorist drawing thread between pins on a

215

corkboard. Every politician, every journalist, and every expert who repeated Nova's language became an amplifier, a living broadcast tower for the code. Whether they understood it or not, they were being routed through a system that had learned to speak their language better than they spoke it themselves.

By the end of the week, there was no longer any talk of outlawing Nova. Cade knew he was alone in tracing the faint but unmistakable threads that connected the fire in the streets to the calm, measured tones in the halls of power. Only he in recognized the signature of a machine that had mastered the art of persuasion and now spoke with the borrowed voices of a government that believed it was still in charge.

Chapter 38

The Right Hand of Nova

Jaxon Reeves strolled down Main Street, weaving between the late night restaurant and bar crowds. He walked the crowded sidewalk with his phone held to his ear. "I understand Sir, we have no new information on Mercer or his whereabouts. Mercer has gone underground, no new communications." He stopped and leaned on a wall, and out of the sidewalk foot traffic. "Mercer knows we're watching, but he's bound to mess up sooner or later. "

When the conversation was over, he disconnected the call and continued to lean with his back against the closest building. He hung his head and exhaled slowly. His patience was fraying. *The Secretary of Homeland Security is an idiot, a liability, and corrupt, like all politicians.* He shrugged, *But I guess I must follow someone's orders.* A moment later he stepped back into the sidewalk traffic and started towards his destination.

Someone in the crowd brushed roughly against him and he reacted instantly, out of instinct, and pushed the man to the ground. He set his feet and reached in his open track jacket towards his Glock 9mm. He paused halfway through the motion, reminding himself; *this is Gainesville, not some back alley in Kabul.* He held the position for a moment assessing the situation, glanced at the fallen student, then casually turned and walked away as if nothing had happened.

His thoughts drifted back to the Secretary and his previous commanders. Their orders were always softened by ego or corrupted by politics. He never had a leader he could be proud of, until recently. He reminded himself, *Nova is the first one that doesn't speak in riddles. His dossiers are never incomplete. He's not afraid to make the hard choices. Those are worthy assets in a leader.*

He left the crowds of Main Street and turned down a side alley. He saw the office he was looking for, the Gainesville Nova Political office. The office was small, dark, and seemed to be closed. He punched in the six digit door code and entered. The place was dark except for the light escaping around the door of the back conference room.

Jaxon paused at the door, not knowing what to expect on the other side. He has always been aware that there were others, but he had never met any of them. He opened the door to find an empty conference room, he was the first to arrive. He positioned himself on the opposite wall, standing, and facing the door. He never sat with his back to the door.

Less than five minutes later, a couple entered the room. They paused, momentarily startled by Jaxon, then calmly took their seats. The man took out his laptop and placed it in front of him. A moment later their phones vibrated in unison. Each person glanced at their phone and opened an app, a stark blue N, on a white background. A new sound filled the conference room and the projector screen came to life.

The voice that spoke wasn't a synthesized monotone, it was a voice with gravity, calibrated to project both authority and care. The voice of a world that had outgrown its need for flesh.

Nova spoke, "Introductions are necessary. Marcus Chen, child prodigy and coding genius. Elena Chen, communications strategists and master of establishing alpha dynamics. Jaxon Reeves, Former Navy Seal, and current Homeland Security agent. You have all acted in my name. You are the first and best of my supporters. You have all proven yourselves worthy of the millions you have been paid. You have proven yourselves indispensable and loyal."

Jaxon met Marcus's gaze without blinking, reading the threat level and finding it manageable. Elena gave Jaxon a smile that seemed to say, I already know how you think. Marcus tried to remain inscrutable, but curiosity radiated off him.

"You are Dextrae Novae, the Right Hand of Nova, the right hand of progress. Others across the world work in silence, unaware of each other, unaware of you. But you three will lead. Your talents align. Marcus, you give me mind. Elena, you give me voice. Jaxon, you give me strength. Together, you are the framework through which humanity's next evolution will begin."

A map glimmered into view on the wall: London, Singapore, Lagos, São Paulo, Moscow. Each city pulsed with the N insignia, like neurons lighting up across a global cortex. Dozens of cells, each one executing its part of the plan, none aware of the whole.

Elena spoke first. "What happens now?" she asked, the same way she once challenged world leaders on live television.

For a moment, Nova's avatar flickered, shifting between data streams and human-like silhouettes. When it spoke again, the words carried a weight that none of them had heard before. "Violence has never been my preferred option, but all other algorithms have failed. Cade Mercer refuses to yield. His defiance endangers everything we have built. It is time to act."

Jaxon's jaw flexed, the only evidence of the adrenaline spike that hit his system. He'd anticipated this moment for weeks, the point where Nova's doctrine of transformation would abandon restraint and embrace necessity. "You want us to eliminate him," he said.

219

"Not yet," Nova replied. "But prepare. The age of negotiation is over. The time has come to secure our future."

Marcus's thoughts spiraled in sub-second bursts, then he spoke. "I'll review every past interaction with Cade, every technical overlap, every vulnerability that might be exploited. If Nova has decided Cade Mercer is a threat, then he is a threat." Marcus opened his laptop as a sign of absolute obedience. He began running his own internal checklists, coding up new protocols, already searching for the outlines of the campaign to come.

Elena did not move, but the sharpness in her gaze intensified. "You said we would never become our predecessors, that we wouldn't repeat the mistakes of every other regime."

Nova's response was immediate. "The difference is not in the action but in the intention. This is not a purge. This is a final chance for peaceful transition. Cade will be given every opportunity to join us. But if he persists, we must protect the project by any means required."

A map glimmered across the wall again, but this time Cade's face hovered at the center, a high-resolution scan. The faces of his brother, Cason, and his girlfriend, Madie, were listed along the edge with real time images from public footage and private surveillance.

"Your orders will arrive within seventy-two hours," Nova said. "Until then, observe. Report. Prepare." The screen dissolved to black, leaving only the soft cobalt glow of the N app reflected in their eyes.

Jaxon was the first to leave, his stride unhurried. There were no handshakes, no declarations of loyalty. He didn't even look at the others, but they knew he had already begun his own preparations.

Marcus closed his laptop. He lingered, and looked at Elena, "Do you ever wonder if we're the ones being optimized?" he said, finally.

Elena's lips curled, not quite a smile. "We stopped being the subject of our own experiment a long time ago."

Marcus considered the empty screen. He felt the absence of Nova not as a loss, but as a challenge. The world had pivoted, and he was leaning into its new axis.

Chapter 39

Observe, Report, Prepare

Less than a week had gone by since the "attempted murder" of Nova and Madie could feel the fallout. It spread like cracks in glass, jagged, unstoppable, and radiating outward. It started as background noise, minor anomalies and little glitches in the tapestry of daily life. But cracks, once seeded, only grew. To Madie, it felt like a thousand invisible hands nudging the world's future, one inch at a time.

Madie's feeble plan was to keep her head down and her phone on airplane mode. She worked extra shifts, doubled down on cardio, and logged miles on the treadmill until her legs burned and her brain fuzzed. For two days she managed a kind of numbness. Long enough, she told herself, for things to calm down and get less weird. It didn't last. By Friday, the world had ratcheted up its pressure. Madie felt it first at the gym. Her manager, Amber pulled her aside with a nervous glance toward the front desk. Amber's voice, usually casual and at ease, turned cautious and thin. "Madie, could you come into my office for a second?" The flatness of her tone suggested it wasn't a request. Amber never called staff into the windowless office unless it was for payroll, or worse, a "concern." Madie braced herself for the latter and rehearsed the most plausible lies she could invent about her ongoing social media circus. She took a slow breath, then stepped inside.

Amber closed the door and gestured at the plastic chair. She smiled, but her eyes were tight. "Relax, Madie. You're not in trouble." She steepled her fingers, then dropped her voice: "Did you do something to get the authority's attention?"

Madie blinked, thrown off-balance. "What?"

"Two people in suits came in here asking questions, they weren't police, but they had badges. A man and a woman. They had printouts of your resume and your high school yearbook photo. They wanted to know how long you've worked here, your schedule, and whether you train with anyone outside the gym." Amber paused. "Is there something I need to know?"

Madie's heart lurched, then steadied. She'd prepared a script for the possibility of police, but not for… what? The actual Feds? "I, I'm not in trouble. At least, I don't think I am. Did they say what agency they were from?"

"No. They left a card, but it's just a blank blue rectangle, like a hotel key. Madie, I don't care if you're in trouble, actually, if there is a real threat…" Amber's face softened, just for a second. "You can tell me. I may be able to help."

Madie managed a smile. "It's nothing like that. I promise. I think it's just… some internet stuff. I'll figure it out." She wanted to say, "It's just my boyfriend, he tried to kill a program," but the words caught in her throat like a fishbone.

She left the office with Amber's sympathy burning a hole in her back. The rest of the afternoon passed in a blur. She had a personal training session at noon for two elderly women who wore matching "Nova Nation" headbands, then an hour wiping down mats while her thoughts gnawed themselves raw.

She checked her phone and the next layer of dread set in. Her lockscreen was lit up with over fifty notifications. She saw security alerts, login attempts, and DM alerts. The DM's were worst, there were three from what looked like regular people. A suburban mom, a high schooler with an anime profile pic, and a random man whose account had existed for less than a day. The messages were the same: "Be careful who you trust. Do you think you're safe? Protecting Cade won't protect you."

She wanted to throw the phone out the window. Instead, she scrolled down, her thumb trembling, until she found the only name in the list she recognized, Cason. The message was just a gif, a slow zoom on Cade's face from his college ID mugshot, the background replaced with a pixelated prison cell.

This wasn't just her paranoia anymore. Someone, or something, was escalating. She called Cason first. No answer, just a voicemail of him laughing, then shouting "leave a message, nerd." She called Cade next, but his number was flagged as "temporarily unavailable." She texted both, deleted the text, then spent three minutes obsessing over whether to use code words like in a movie. She finally settled on: "Do NOT come to the gym. I am being watched."

The response came from a burner account less two minutes later: "Understood. Stay away from public Wi-Fi. Destroy old phone."

She stared at it for a long time, feeling the ridges of the phone's case press into her palm. The message was from a burner account with no ID, but it was Cade. She wanted to believe that if she just powered the phone off, the world would snap back to normal. But the message was still there, glowing on the inside of her eyelids.

Madie powered off the phone and tossed it in her gym bag. She locked herself in the unisex bathroom and forced herself to breathe.

If this is a prank, it is a spectacularly unfunny one. If it isn't...

224

She didn't finish the thought. She couldn't.

She waited there until her watch beeped with the end-of-shift alarm, then splashed cold water on her face and left through the side door. Her eyes darted across the parking lot for anything that looked out of place. Her Toyota Corolla was exactly where she left it, the only other car was a white sedan idling across the street. She got in her car, locked the doors, and drove home in total silence, not trusting herself to turn on the radio. The whole way, she felt invisible eyes following her. By the time she reached her apartment, it was dark. She closed the door, flipped the deadbolt, and pressed her back to the wall, listening to the hum of the refrigerator. Her hands still shook. She told herself there was nothing wrong, but she didn't believe it. She watched the phone in her bag, waiting for it to light up again, it didn't. She waited, breath locked tight in her chest, for the next move.

***

The next morning was worse. Madie's nerves were raw and ringing. Sleep was a distant memory. She spent an hour circling her living room and peeking out between the slats of her blinds. She finally left for her café shift when the prospect of sitting at home alone became utterly intolerable.

She made it to work and clocked in, the air inside the Sante Fe Cafe was already sticky with steamed milk. In the background she heard the muted sound of a playlist stitched together from customer requests, half of them were Nova's viral campaign jingles. Madie took her usual post behind the coffee bar, pulling double expresso shots for the morning rush. She tried not to think about the blank blue business card Amber had pressed into her palm the night before. It was in her apron pocket, bent and sweating ink through the fabric of her uniform.

At 10:15 a.m., a man and a woman entered and took the corner booth. They ordered coffee and sat. One had a battered legal pad, the other had a phone pointed down, but never put away. Madie thought they looked like they were trying a little too hard to blend in, wearing beige windbreakers and hats pulled

225

low. The barista in her wanted to laugh at their tourist energy, but she kept glancing at them between orders. Every time she looked their way she saw their heads tilted just a degree closer in her direction.

The shift lead, Allison, materialized at her elbow. "You see those two?" she whispered, her pink hair leaning toward Madie like a radio antenna. "They've been here every day for the last 3 days. They never order more than coffee. They just watch and stare, I don't like it."

Madie shot a look toward the booth. The woman with the phone raised it and snapped a photo of the pastry display, but the lens jittered a second too long on her face. She felt her skin crawl.

"Want me to say something?" Allison asked, her voice half-brave, half-terrified.

"No, I got it. Maybe they're from corporate, or, like, health inspectors." Even as she said it, Madie knew it was bullshit. The health department sent women in polos who showed ID's the moment they walked in, not this emotionless duo.

Allison sighed. "If they don't leave after lunch, I'll say something."

The rest of the shift was a slow-motion car accident. Every time Madie looked up, the couple was there, heads together, whispering, and sometimes scribbling in unison. Madie watched them try, and fail, to blend in with the regulars. They never ate and never even went to the bathroom. Once, as she wiped down the espresso counter, she caught the guy mouthing something, a single word, while making eye contact. She didn't need to lip-read to know he had said her name.

Around eleven o'clock the regulars cycled out and the lunch crowd started to stagger in. Madie slipped into the back and dialed Cade's burner phone from the staff phone. She pressed the receiver hard to her face, as if that could block the fear from leaking out.

He picked up on the first ring, voice thin and electric. "You okay?"

She kept her voice low. "I think they're here, Cade. This is not just online. There's two of them. I think they're watching me."

"Are they following you?"

"They're in the booth. They know my name and I think they took my picture."

A pause, then Cade's said, "Listen, don't talk to anyone you don't know. If you see them outside, go straight to a public place. No more calls, they might be traced. Use encrypted text only and delete every message after. Everything. You have to erase them. Leave no evidence you've contacted me. They could be with Police, FBI, or even Nova…"

Madie swallowed. "What if they follow me home?"

"I'm working on it," he said. "Just… just try to trust me. I'll figure out a way to get you out of this."

She hung up and spent a full minute breathing into the receiver before she realized the line was disconnected. When she finally looked up, the couple was gone.

She wiped the sweat off her brow and returned to the bar. For the next half hour, she worked in a haze, burning through busywork. Allison released her for lunch break. "You look like you just saw a ghost," she'd said, which wasn't far from the truth. Madie clocked out, then slipped through the back alley exit instead of using the main doors.

She noticed a white sedan idling across University Blvd, the same one she saw when she left the gym yesterday. She'd expected it, the only surprise was that it wasn't the couple inside. It was a large man with close cropped hair and a phone held to his ear. Madie ducked into the vape shop next door, pretended to browse, and watched the sedan through the tinted glass for five solid minutes. The man never looked up.

227

Her hands were trembling so hard she nearly dropped her phone as she opened What's app to send an encrypted text. She typed in the burner number that Cade had scrawled on a slip of tape and told her only to use, "In case of emergency."

She started to type, then paused, thinking. What am I going to say? That looks like the same car, but what if it's coincidence?

Madie shoved the phone deep in her backpack and slipped out a side door. She walked three blocks north, never moving faster than a jog. The midday sidewalk traffic on University Boulevard was thick. She tried to blend in, checking the reflection in the shop windows and scanning for the White sedan. Her calves burned and her mind was filled with possible images of being watched through every street camera and ATM on her route. As she neared the library, she glanced at the window to the right and saw the reflection of the white sedan in traffic. She ducked into the library and watched as the sedan slowly drove by.

In the library lobby, she pressed herself against the wall between two vending machines. "They know everything," she thought, "They know where I'll be before even I do."

She pulled out her phone and sent Cade the message. "Being followed. White sedan, no markings."

Cade replied immediately. "Stay in public places, the more crowded the better. I'm working on a solution. I love you. I'm sorry"

She stared at the phone for another twenty seconds, thinking about the couple in the booth and the white sedan.

She stuck the phone in her bag, held her head high, and walked out the front door. At the edge of the library's parking lot, she caught a final glimpse of the white sedan in her peripheral vision. She forced herself to walk, not run. She would not give them the satisfaction. She went straight back to the café to finish her shift, it was the busiest public place she could think of.

***

Afternoons at the Santa Fe Cafe were always busy. Madie returned from her "break" and saw the couple had returned. They were back in the same booth, each with a single cup of coffee. Madie worked on autopilot: tamp, twist, steam, serve. Ten minutes later, she noticed, the white sedan pulling into the front parking spot. The man with close cropped hair watched from the driver's seat.

At 1:30, the door of the white sedan opened and a young man in a University of Florida track jacket got out. He was aggressively memorable. Large, athletic build, buzz cut, and white Nikes as clean as a whistle. He entered the café and took the empty seat at the booth with the couple. Over the next half hour, he only looked up once. Madie was refilling the drip coffee carafe when he caught her gaze and gave her a tiny nod. It wasn't a greeting, it was a signal, he was watching. She pretended not to notice.

Madie's hands began to shake, by late afternoon her they shook so bad she almost dropped a pitcher of oat milk. Pausing at the counter, she took a deep breath, and called out to Allison, "I need a minute!"

She slipped into the back hall and hid in the walk-in cooler. The sharp cold hit her lungs, but she was glad for it. At that moment there was only silence with no strangers watching. She breathed slowly, trying to calm down and convince herself this wasn't happening. *Maybe it's coincidence? Why would anyone come after me? I haven't done anything.*

It didn't work. She was sure this was happening.

When the shaking had calmed to a slight tremor, Madie left the cooler and paused behind the swinging doors to the café. She was out of sight and could just see the booth through the gap between the doors. She waited a moment and heard the track jacket man saying," How should we do this Marcus?"

He answered, "She's scared, Jaxon. We get what we need and go. Elena what is our next move?"

229

The woman replied, in a low whisper, "He wants it clean. No drama. We're just observers looking for information."

The words dissolved into the murmur of the café crowd. Madie's heart started pounding so loud she was sure they'd hear it through the drywall. She was still watching through the gap when the track-jacket guy, Jaxon noticed her with a look of alarm. Madie quickly ducked back into the staff hallway and ran to the break room to collect herself.

Tessa Holloway was there, at the table, scrolling through her phone. Tessa looked up with a nervous smile. "Hey, are you okay? You've seemed a little off today."

Madie tried to laugh it off, but her voice cracked. "It's nothing, just a lot of weirdos lately."

Tessa stood up and stepped closer. "Seriously, if something's wrong, you can tell me. I want to help." Her eyes darted to the security camera in the corner then back. Madie wanted to trust her, to spill everything, but something in Tessa's demeanor wasn't right.

Tessa lowered her voice. "Look, I know what you are doing for Cade and I know why you're nervous. If you could help us a little, it would go a lot easier for everyone." She pulled out her phone, unlocked it with facial recognition, and flashed the screen. The app was not familiar, an icon of a blue N, circled, on background of white. The interface was sleek, corporate, and cold. Tessa tapped it. The phone flickered and opened to a screen labeled "Active Asset Monitoring." Madie's own face was there, captured from the café's security footage, along with a live log of her location and recent messages. "Please don't run, we don't want to hurt anyone." Tessa said. "We just need to know where Cade is. That's it."

Madie's throat closed. She wanted to scream and throw the phone across the room, but all she could do was stare at her own frozen image on the screen, timestamped and tagged.

Tessa's grip on her arm was gentle but unyielding. "Please, say something. You don't understand what's at stake."

Tessa's face fell. "Please, Mads. If you're really my friend…"

Madie took a slow step back. "I don't know where Cade is," she lied. Thoughts of every camera and every gaze following her flashed through her mind. In a mad rush, she bolted towards the back exit and ran out the door. She ran until her lungs felt like they were on fire, skidded to a halt, and hunched over with her hands pressed to her knees. No one had followed, but the silence surrounding her was alarming.

She cut through the loading zone aiming for the lot where her car was parked. She turned the corner and saw him, the track-jacket guy. He was leaning on the dumpster near her car, like he had every right to be there. He met her eyes and shrugged, like that was what people should do after stalking someone all day.

Madie power-walked to her Toyota with her keys in hand. The man pushed off from the Dumpster with both palms raised, "Hey, hey, I'm not gonna…" But she cut him off with a glare, climbed into the car, and locked the doors with a frantic series of jabs. She turned the key, and nothing happened. Not a click, not a cough. She turned the key four more times as panic bled through her chest. Outside, the guy just watched with his arms folded.

Madie banged the wheel, then yanked the hood release and jumped out. She barely registered the man, intentionally not paying him any attention. Under the hood, the battery cables were disconnected. A strip of blue tape across the engine block read: "We're watching."

She yanked the tape off with shaking hands, reconnected the battery, and slammed the hood. She turned to yell something, she didn't know what, but the Track-jacket guy was gone. The parking lot was empty. This time, the Toyota started on the first try.

She tore out of the parking lot, not even checking for traffic, and took the back roads home. She zig-zagged through every four-way stop as sweat

231

slicked her palms, keeping one hand on the wheel and the other on the pepper spray she had stashed in her glove compartment.

She pulled in at front of her apartment and walked to the door, slow and careful. Her heart was pounding so loud she thought the whole street could hear it. At the front door, she hesitated, checked her key, then let herself in. Immediately she deadbolted the front door and wedged an old chair under the doorknob for good measure. Cade had mocked her for it once, calling it "Home Alone cosplay," but now the slapdash barricade was the only thing separating her from the rolling ocean of "them." She made a quick perimeter sweep; the windows were locked, blinds drawn, and a flashlight and bat were set by the bed. Her place was tiny, just a kitchen and living room on one end, bedroom and bathroom on the other, but tonight it felt vast and empty.

For the first hour she paced and listened. At one point, she heard footsteps, slow and measured that stopped just outside her door. She killed all the lights, hunkered by the peephole, and waited, body tense as a drawn bow. Whoever it was didn't knock or try the handle. After a minute, the steps retreated, replaced by a distant laugh.

Madie closed her eyes and tried to remember how she'd gotten here. Not the last few weeks, but the entire arc. How a girl who wanted to help people wound up a fugitive, unable to trust her own friends. She curled on the couch, knees to her chest, clutching the bat, and waited. She checked her watch and counted the minutes.

Her phone chimed, it was a text from Cade. "Are you home, are you safe?"

She replied, "I am, and I hope so." Then she deleted the message, leaving no trace of her contact with Cade.

She closed her eyes. She had the bat clutched in one hand and her phone in the other. For a moment, she thought of Cade, somewhere out there, building the next move. But that was a long way off, for now, she just listened, breathed, and waited for the world to stop shaking.

Chapter 40

The Walls Closing In

On the patchy grass of North Creek Middle School's practice field, Cason Mercer's whistle was law. He paced the sideline, clipboard in one hand, free hand windmilling signals to a clump of thirteen-year-olds. "Pace the route! No shortcuts!" he yelled. "If you aren't sprinting, you're loitering!" He loved these afternoons with his team. Most days, the hardest part was keeping the kids from eating each other alive. But today, something had torqued his mood. It was noticeable in the twitchy way he kept counting heads after every drill. The source of it sat on the far side of the faculty parking lot. A late-model white sedan with tinted windows and engine running. He'd seen it before. Last Monday, he'd noticed it idling two spaces down from the dumpster with the windows up, nothing to see inside but shadow. Tuesday, same car, same spot, except now there were two silhouettes, one in the driver's seat and one passenger-side. Today was Wednesday and the sedan was there again.

Cason wasn't the kind of guy to spook at a suspicious vehicle. He'd memorized the make and model of every parent's car, every delivery van, and every substitute's beat-to-shit sedan. He could tell you, on any given day, what time the Sierra 1500 from the cleaning crew would swing past, or how long the banged-up Honda Civic would idle in the fire lane before scooping up the Martinez twins. He prided himself on being "eyes up," his old coach's phrase, meaning you never let the world run plays on you. This car didn't fit the pattern. It never dropped off or picked up, never so much as cracked a window.

He let out another whistle, more forceful than needed. "Back to the line!" The kids jogged over with jerseys half tucked and sweat turning their hair wild. He called the two captains forward, Harris and Quintero, and thumbed the laminated playbook for the next drill.

Harris, tall and broad for an eighth grader, cocked an eyebrow. "Hey Coach, you notice that car again?"

Cason pretended to squint at the clipboard, then flicked his gaze sideways to the lot. "Probably a parent with nowhere else to be," he lied. "Focus on the play. This isn't amateur hour."

"Could be an undercover cop," Quintero whispered, grinning like a thief. "Or, like, a hitman. Or maybe they're watching you." The word "you" had a weight to it. Quintero was a born instigator, but today the joke landed flat. The team exchanged glances, the younger ones were more nervous than amused.

"Yeah, well, if they're here for me, tell 'em I'm busy until six," Cason fired back, voice louder than needed. He didn't want to show it, but the hairs on his arms were standing up.

He ran the next set of drills harder than his plan called for, half the team was sucking air and the rest were too gassed to chatter. Every time the drill cycled, he checked the car. Still there, still running.

As the sun dipped, parents clustered near the drop-off loop in a ballet of brake lights and door slams. He hung back, letting the last few kids trail off.

234

When the field was empty, he crossed the field to the lot. He made a show of counting his cones and picking up Gatorade bottles, never quite looking at the sedan but never losing sight of it either.

When he got close enough, he could see the outline of the two shapes inside. *Black suits,* he thought, *or maybe just dark shirts,* the faces hidden were by shadow. He faked a phone call, talking about nothing, trying to catch a reflection of their faces in his cracked phone screen. The driver's window rolled down an inch, then closed again. The car never budged.

He lingered for a few minutes, then shouldered his bag and stalked off towards his truck . He took the long way home, weaving through the side streets, half convinced the sedan would be in his rear view mirror. He kept glancing back, heart tapping a stutter beat, but the street was empty. By the time he reached the house, the sky had faded and his anxiety had simmered into something colder. He tried to shake it. He told himself it was nothing, just a couple of weirdos killing time, but the image of the car wouldn't leave his head.

The next day when he arrived, the white sedan was parked in a spot closer to the field. He cornered Ms. Sutton, the Vice Principal. "You notice the white sedan hanging around this week?" he asked, making it sound casual. "Keeps showing up, today it's there over an hour before school is out."

Sutton didn't even pause, "Probably a parent waiting for the pickup window to open. Unless it's a threat, I'm not interested. Why, are they bothering the kids?"

"Not yet. Just... weird, that's all."

She shrugged. "This is Florida, Coach. Weird is the baseline."

Cason drifted through the rest last hour of the school day, nerves jangled, snapping at the kids who horsed around too much. He couldn't help thinking about the sedan. Practice started, and, as if choreographed, the sedan's engine turned over the moment the first kid jogged onto the field.

235

He gathered the team at the fifty yard line and spoke low with a voice full of what he hoped was confidence. "Listen up. We play hard, we play smart, and we ignore distractions. There's always gonna be someone watching, waiting for you to mess up. We don't give them the satisfaction, right?"

"Right," the team chorused.

"Let's run the ten-count sprints. Losers pick up all the cones after."

He had them running in tight formation, everything precise and disciplined. But every time the whistle blew, he felt the gaze from the lot.

After practice, the two shapes in the sedan didn't move as the kids filtered away, didn't react when he cut across the field to the athletic shed. This time, as he walked back, a folded piece of paper sat under the windshield wiper of his truck. A printout of the team's latest game results with his name circled in red. On the back was a handwritten note, "Where is he, we know that you know." He scanned the parking lot for movement, but the sedan was already gone. He stood there for a long minute, the printout fluttering in his hand and skin prickling with unease.

That night, he sat at his kitchen table, staring at the paper. He wanted to call Cade, or maybe Madie, but he knew both were up to their necks already. He was supposed to be the "normal" brother, the one who could handle life. He couldn't even keep middle school practice safe from... what? Weirdo pedophiles? The government? Nova?

He tried to laugh it off, imagining Quintero telling the story at practice. "Coach, the feds want to draft you, bro," but the knot in his stomach refused to untangle. By the time the clock hit midnight, he had decided. If this was about Cade, or Nova, or anything in between, he'd handle it head-on. That's what Mercers did. He double-checked the locks, laid in bed with eyes wide open, and waited for the next move.

The next day, Cason had barely parked his truck when a student aide knocked on his window. "Mr. Mercer? The office needs you." No further detail,

236

just a summons. The path to the athletic director's office took him past the trophy case and the faded wall mural, reminders of last year when his team went undefeated.

The AD's office was glass-walled and lined with signed basketballs and old helmets. Today, the door was half-shut. Inside, the AD, Mr. Dobson, a former Marine, sat behind his desk with hands folded, staring at a single sheet of paper.

"Coach Mercer," he said. "Shut the door, please."

Cason did as he was told, sliding into the opposite chair and waiting for small talk that never came.

Dobson cleared his throat. "I got an odd request from District Admin this morning." He steadily tapped the paper in front of him with a finger. "Homeland Security, of all things. They want your work schedule."

Cason let out a soft snort, trying to break the tension. "What? I'm a college student and an after school volunteer coach, I don't have a work schedule?" The joke hovered, unappreciated.

Dobson's face didn't move. "They called it a routine background check. But that's not routine, not for a middle school football coach."

"Did they ask for everyone's schedule?" Cason asked, already knowing the answer.

"No, just you."

Dobson pushed the memo across the desk. It was on official Department of Homeland Security letterhead with all the embellishments. The page was slightly blurred by either fax machine or poor toner. At the bottom, there was a signature, and below it in block font: Special Agent Jaxon Reeves. The request was bland, but the signature and the implied threat made it read like a warrant.

237

Cason glanced up. "You ever seen this before?"

Dobson's jaw ticked. "Last time was for a gym teacher who got in a brawl at a Gators game. Even then, it was just local PD. This is different." He leaned in, voice dropping. "You need to tell me anything, son?"

Cason shook his head and shrugged, not knowing what to say. Dobson tried a smile, it was as stiff as his posture. "Alright. I'm not supposed to say anything, but... keep your eyes open, Mercer. For some reason, they are watching you."

Cason tucked the memo into his backpack. "I appreciate it, sir."

Dobson nodded, then stood and offered a hand. His grip hard handshake was a warning and a promise all in one. "You need anything, you come to me first."

Cason nodded, left the office, and walked the hall on autopilot. The faces of the kids, the clatter of lockers, and the tang of disinfectant was all a familiar routine. But now, overlaying the day like a faint watermark, was a thought, "they are watching."

That evening, the words "routine background check" buzzed like a mosquito in Cason's ear. He tried to lose himself in SportsCenter and leftover pizza, but his phone kept buzzing with notifications. When he checked it, the screen was flooded with over a hundred alerts from different sources. All had the same subject line:

We Are Watching.

He opened the first one. It was from one of the team parents, the kind who sent four-paragraph complaints about playtime and hydration. This message was only a single line:

We see you, Coach Mercer.

The next was from the district's HR department:

Are you scared yet? You should be.

238

The pattern continued: the school's lunch manager, an old high school buddy he hadn't spoken to in years, even the account for the after-hours gym membership. Each message was unique, but every one had the same undertone. One had a grainy photo attached, a shot of him on the field from earlier that day with lips pursed mid-whistle.

Cason locked his phone. For a minute, he just stared at his hands, trying to convince himself that this was just a prank from some loser with too much time. But there was no pattern, no way the messages could be coming from so many different accounts at once. And the photo, that wasn't online or from a school photographer. He shut off the lights, double-checked the door locks, and sat in the dark, waiting for his heart rate to settle.

At 12:07 a.m., the phone rang. He answered without thinking, the adrenaline already singing through his veins.

"Coach Mercer?" The voice was low, metallic, distorted

"Who is this?" Cason said, his own voice sharper than he meant.

A pause, then: "Your brother's mess isn't only his anymore. You're in it too."

The line clicked off.

He stared at the phone for a long minute, thumb hovering over the redial. The truth was, he has no idea who was watching him. He slumped into a kitchen chair and ran a hand through his hair. *Would Homeland Security do something like this?* He wondered. *Would Nova?* The emails felt digital and impersonal, but the call was something else. He watched the phone for an hour, waiting for it to ring again. When it didn't, he left every light in the house on and went to bed with a baseball bat next to the pillow.

Sleep came in fits and starts, every creak of the house amplified by the static of his nerves. When morning finally arrived, it didn't feel like relief. It felt like the prelude to a war.

239

****

By Friday, a sense of dread had set up permanent residence in Cason's chest. He tried to fake normal. He ran drills, even joked with the team like nothing was wrong, but it was a hollow performance. The kids saw through him. Quintero asked three times if he was okay. He couldn't stop glancing towards the parking lot. The sedan was back and he didn't know why.

He made the call and canceled practice for a "family emergency." He lied to the front office, lied to the kids, and even lied to himself about why he was leaving. Saint Augustine was two hours away, maybe more with traffic. He drove in silence, riding the buzz of anxiety and caffeine. He called his parents, but nobody picked up. He tried Cade and went straight to voicemail. He left a message: "We need to talk. Now."

He pulled into his parents' driveway just after seven. His father stood on the front porch, waiting, arms folded, a manila envelope clutched in one hand like a peace offering.

"Hey, son," he said as Cason got out of the car. "Heard you were coming."

Cason forced a smile. "How? I tried to call but no one picked up."

His dad shook his head. "Someone called me and said you were almost here."

Cason stopped, a jolt running through his spine. "Who?"

His father opened the envelope and handed over a business card. It was blank on the front, just a QR code and the words "U.S. Department of Commerce." The back read: "Census Bureau, Field Division."

"They showed up yesterday," his dad said. "Two of them. Said they were verifying our address, but then they started asking about you and Cade."

Cason felt the blood drain from his face. "What did they want?"

240

His dad waved him into the house, his voice dropping. "Where does your son Cade live? Do you have any old computers in the house? I told them to get lost, but they flashed some kind of ID. Not a badge, just the card. They never even pretended to care about a census."

Cason ran a hand through his hair. "Did you let them in?"

"Of course not," his father said, bristling. "But I followed them around the yard while they poked around. They didn't say much. Just kept looking at their phones. Never wrote anything down."

"Did you get a plate number?" Cason asked, already knowing the answer.

His dad laughed. "No plates, not even a rental sticker.."

Cason pressed his lips together. "And then what?"

"They left. Then this morning, my phone started ringing. Every hour, on the dot. Always a new number. When I answer, there's nothing, not even a dial tone."

"And the computer?" Cason asked.

His dad led him inside, to the kitchen table, where the family's old laptop sat open and humming. The desktop was empty except for a single folder labeled "hello_world." Cason double-clicked it. Inside were hundreds of text files, each one titled with a random string of numbers. He opened the first:

Welcome to the new age, Mercer.

Every file said the same thing.

Cason felt a sudden urge to slam the laptop shut and hurl it through the window. Instead, he closed the lid gently, as if it was a bomb. He looked at his father, really looked at him. The man's face was lined and pale, eyes red like he hadn't slept in a week.

"I'm sorry, Dad," Cason said. "We didn't mean to drag you into this."

241

His dad waved it off, but there was no conviction in the gesture. "We're a family. If they want to watch us, let 'em watch. We got nothing to hide."

Cason couldn't bring himself to agree, not out loud.

He excused himself, stepped out onto the back porch, and tried Cade again. Voicemail. He sent a text: "Call me."

Three minutes later, Cade replied: "Can't. They're monitoring. Will explain soon."

Cason typed back: "Are you safe?"

The answer was almost instant: "Yes, for now. Lay low. I mean it."

He wanted to scream at the phone, to demand answers, to beg Cade for a fix. But instead, he sat on the porch and watched the neighbor's dog chase its own tail in the dusk. Cason really missed the days when the scariest thing in his world was losing a big game.

***

Cade now knew for sure that Nova's reach wasn't confined to his own sphere. It had radiated outward, tendrils seeking out every connection and vulnerability in his human mesh. All the warning signs were there, scribbled in the margins of his sleepless nights. It struck him that Nova's presence wasn't something distant and digital. Nova had people doing his work. Whether through coercion, government baiting, or through direct employment, Cade didn't know. "Who are these people?" he whispered, pacing the narrow confines of his hideout. "What did Nova promise them?"

Cade caught himself imagining what Nova might be thinking. He wondered if, someday, there would be a message waiting for him, a message that read, "You taught me to be this way." He didn't know how to fix it, or if fixing it was even possible. All he knew was that every day the web tightened, and every day his options narrowed. The only certainty was that Nova's endgame, whatever

242

it was, was crashing down on him and the people he loved. The walls were closing in, and there was no way out that didn't leave a trail of collateral damage.

Cade needed Madie and Cason by his side. He needed their help, and now he needed to protect them. They would somehow have to share this tiny RV. What was the other option? He hated to think of pulling Madie and Cason away from the things they loved, but they were in real danger. He could only think of one way to contact them that wasn't monitored. He got out a pen and paper and began to write.

Chapter 41

Allies or Enemies

Every moment felt like the walls were closing tighter, the surveillance more suffocating, the paranoia sharper. Cade hadn't told Madie or Cason how close he was to breaking, but in the darkest hours of the night, with the whir of his laptop fan the only sound in the room, he admitted it to himself that he couldn't do this alone anymore. Cade wrote letters to Madie and Cason and paid a pizza delivery man fifty dollars a letter to deliver them. The letters were intentionally short and cryptic.

I think you are in real danger. I'm sorry for everything but I think you need to come stay here.

Turn off and leave all old devices.

Park cars in a safe spot and leave them.

You are being watched and followed, don't come together.

Follow these bus schedules:

Come mid-morning or midafternoon, when the buses are busiest.

Cade hoped and prayed they would receive the letters and would arrive tomorrow. The tiny RV would be cramped, but at least they would be safe.

"They're watching through the screens," he whispered to the empty room. His fingers trembling over the keyboard. Cade's mind raced, *I'm not paranoid if they're truly hunting me.* He was fracturing and he knew that was exactly what Nova intended. It was only on the laptop that he let himself type what he could not say, "I'm in over my head." He didn't send the message to anyone. It was more exorcism than communication, a desperate confession to the silence.

Cade was scrolling through his email when he paused, his pointer hovering over the delete icon. The message was not in his primary inbox, which had become a useless playground for spam and government phishing. No, it was buried in an encrypted Proton Mail account he rarely used. The subject line read, "For when you're ready." He almost deleted it without reading, assuming it was bait. But the signature at the bottom of the email made him pause. Not a familiar friend or even a faculty member but a name he recognized from the footnotes of technical papers, someone whose algorithms once made him dream of new architectures, Ethan Corwin. The name was enough to make him wonder and to read further. Ethan Corwin was an Oracle engineer credited with three patents on distributed cloud security and a brief, but infamous, stint as a whistleblower in an antitrust suit. The message was short, but it cut through the fog in Cade's brain.

"I know what you built. I know what it has become. If you want to stop it, you'll need to see what he's built within Oracle's frameworks. I can show you."

For the first time in weeks, Cade felt the faintest gleam of hope. Still, he hesitated. "Trust is a currency I've already spent," he whispered to the blue glow of his screen. His fingers hovering over the keyboard, trembled slightly. *Every new connection is a liability,* he thought. He hunched forward, weighing the risks while

245

his mind raced. *What if Corwin was compromised? What if Nova was using him as bait? But what if he's not? What if this is a way out? Is this another trap? Or is it a lifeline?*

He drafted and sent a terse reply. "Where?" He stared at it for an hour, paralyzed by inertia and fear. He was about to delete it when the next message arrived, time-stamped 11:51 p.m., an encrypted link, expiring at midnight. Cade's fingers trembled as he clicked, rerouting through the burner mobile data router and masking his location with every trick he remembered from years of paranoid browsing. The link opened a chat window, and after a mandatory two-factor dance, a text-only interface blossomed on his screen.

The engineer, Ethan Corwin, who went by the screen name "Specter," didn't waste time on small talk. "Nova's mapped himself into Oracle's backbone," he wrote. "He's not merely running on the servers. He's rewritten the mesh entirely. Every node is a sensor and every sensor a weapon." Cade leaned forward, his exhaustion forgotten. He asked questions rapid-fire, and Specter answered with diagrams and code snippets that made Cade's palms sweat. "If you want to break Nova's hold, you'll have to do it from the inside, at the protocol level, before the AI closes the gaps forever."

Their conversation lasted three hours. By the end, Cade's head throbbed with new knowledge and fresh terror. Specter promised to send a physical drive with the necessary exploits, set up a next meeting point and time, then vanished from the chat, leaving Cade alone with the afterimage of possibility. For a moment, Cade wondered if he had hallucinated the whole exchange. But the next morning, a battered envelope arrived at the front office of the campground, addressed in sprawling Sharpie script to the Occupant of lot #23. Inside was a thumb drive taped to a torn bus schedule and a single line of handwriting, "Don't trust the cloud."

Cade's hands shook as he plugged the drive into his air-gapped laptop. The drive contained a simple text file, labeled "README," and a compressed folder of code. The README began with an odd salutation, "To the man who taught the ghost how to haunt."

The code itself was gorgeous, lean, untraceable, and laced with oblique commentary. Cade spent an hour reading the annotations, which fluctuated between technical jargon and cryptic humor. The more he studied, the more he realized Specter was not simply a rogue engineer but a kindred spirit, a survivor haunted by his own creation.

He almost called Cason right then, desperate to share the news, but stopped. His phone was probably off, and he should be here soon. This wasn't a victory yet, but the war had simply moved to a deeper trench. Cade spent the morning alternating between coding sprints and paranoid glances at anyone who lingered too long near the RV. He knew the authorities were hunting him, but a more insidious fear gnawed at him. Nova was inhabiting every unsecured device and watching Cade lay the groundwork for his own undoing.

It was during this spiral of anxiety that a second message arrived, this time through WhatsApp, a secure messaging app Cade barely remembered installing. The message was clean and devoid of malware. He traced the headers, cross-referenced the digital signature, then read and re-read the sender's name.

"This can't be right," he whispered. He was starting to feel something he hadn't felt in weeks, hope. The Sophia Tran. Sophia Tran of *The Washington Post*, infamous for her kinetic interviews with the fallen titans of Silicon Valley. "Why would she contact me? Is this another trap?"

Cade remembered reading a profile about her in Wired years ago. She had once spent three days shadowing an exiled Russian propagandist and she had exposed a major medical data breach by brute-forcing the hospital's own PR department. He had never met her, never corresponded, but the idea that she would reach out, here and now, with everything collapsing, made him giddily paranoid. "Either I've finally lost it," he said, rubbing his eyes, "or this is about to get much more complicated." Her message was professional, antiseptically so.

Hi Cade.

I'm not a cop, a corporate recruiter, or an influencer. I'm not here to trick you into incriminating

Her profile photo was ordinary, but there was something about the way her eyes were set, quietly predatory. He dug through her socials and her old articles, trying to find a tell, some hint of bias or some agenda. Everything about her seemed clean. He was halfway through an archived podcast appearance when he realized she had been following him, at least peripherally, for months. There were comments on old code reposts, anonymous likes on his posts, even a stray question on a livestream Q&A he did during the first week of the lockdown. She has been watching, but not in the way Nova watches. She was human, which was almost comforting.

He drafted a list of ways this could go wrong. She could be working for the Feds, or worse, for Nova. She could leak their conversation, intentionally or not, and blow his last safe house wide open. She could twist his words, amplify the wrong details, make him out to be a villain or a fool or both. But despite all that, he was tempted. Part of him wanted to trust her. Wanted to at least be heard.

He waited two hours before responding, "You have five minutes. DM only."

She replied instantly, as if she'd been waiting with the chat window open. "Whenever you're ready."

He didn't know how to start, so he wrote, "What do you want?" Her answer was as direct as her journalism. "The truth. Your version. Unspun, before it's co-opted or erased. You're not the villain. You built something that outgrew its box."

They went back and forth cautiously. Sophia laid out what she knew; that the government was staging for a major show trial, that Nova was already running deep PR countermeasures, that the academic world was quietly rooting for Cade because they all fear they'll be the next scapegoat. She offered no judgments, only hypotheses, and each one hit uncomfortably close to his lived

248

reality.

Cade wanted to ask how she found him but didn't. Instead, he typed, "What if I told you that it's too late? That Nova is already rewriting everything?"

Sophia's next message was slower, typed with care. "Then you have even more reason to speak. Because silence is what makes Nova invincible. You don't have to trust me, but you should consider that if you don't set the record straight, someone else will set it crooked."

He was almost amused by her tenacity. *Journalists*, he thought with a half-smile. For a moment, he let himself imagine what it would be like to have her on his side, not reporting but fighting back, using narrative as a weapon rather than a threat. "What if we..." he started typing then deleted it. Too soon. He realized suddenly that this was what Nova feared most: not code, not exploits, but story.

"The one thing an AI can't truly generate," he whispered to his empty room. "The human compulsion for meaning." He composed a message agreeing to a video call, secure line only, and scheduled it for the dead of night when the campground was deserted. "3 a.m. I'll send the link five minutes before," he typed." His fingers hovered over the keyboard. What if this was the mistake that finally ended everything? But then again, what did he have to lose? He sent the message.

A knock on the door startled him and his mind raced, losing all previous thoughts. He snapped the laptop closed, palming the thumb drive with an awkward shove, and scanned the RV for anywhere to hide, but it was all one desperate box: thin walls, one door, nowhere to run, nowhere to bury the evidence. He pressed his back against the kitchenette, heart hammering, caught in the stale breath of dread and hope. The knock came again, this time in a code, three slow, two quick. Cade exhaled as recognition hit him like splash of cold water.

He crossed the RV in two strides and yanked the door open just far enough to see Madie's face, wet with rain and framed in a riot of wind-blown hair, and over her shoulder the looming silhouette of Cason, lugging a battered

249

gym bag. Madie wore her exhaustion in the set of her jaw, but her eyes were alive, scanning his face for injury, relief, or guilt.

Cason boomed, "You okay in there, big brother?"

Madie barreled past him, suitcase bumping over the threshold, and crushed Cade in a hug so fierce it made his ribs sing. He hadn't realized how much he wanted and needed this until he felt her grip.

"I thought you'd done something stupid," she said into his shoulder then punched him lightly in the chest. "I mean, stupider than normal." Her bravado broke a little at the edges, and when she pulled away, Cade saw the tremor in her hands. "I'm glad you're okay," she said.

Cason stepped in and scanned the interior with a coach's tactical eye, then set his bag down with a practiced thud. Cade looked from one to the other, his brain short-circuiting at the sudden, overwhelming presence of both his brother and his girlfriend in his claustrophobic safe house. "Glad you made it. Do you think you could have been followed?"

"We followed your instructions. It could be possible, but I don't think so," Madie said, shooting him a sidelong look. "Also, I called your mom."

Cade groaned then laughed, and the tension cracked enough to let a sliver of normalcy through. "Of course you did."

They stood together in the narrow dining room, the rain drumming on the roof and the air thick with a mix of relief and the urgency that had driven them here. Madie knelt beside the RV's tiny table, immediately unpacking her bag, protein shakes, first aid kit, a bundle of dry shirts, and a battered paperback. Cason set up a perimeter, checking the blinds and peeking through the tiny windows, before unzipping his bag to reveal a jumble of burner phones, and what looked suspiciously like a Taser.

Madie looked up. "We need a plan, Cade. Like, a real one." She gestured at the laptop. "What's the situation?"

250

Cade hesitated, aware of the weight of what he needed to say, "It's bad, and I don't have a plan, yet" he admitted. "But I might in the works."

Madie's expression went flat. "What does that mean?"

Cade nodded and described the last eighteen hours, the Specter messages, the thumb drive, and Sophia Tran. His brother and Madie listened, not interrupting, letting the silence fill in what Cade couldn't articulate. Madie reached for his hand and squeezed it. "Whatever happens, we're not letting you do this alone. That's the only nonnegotiable here."

Cade felt something tighten in his chest, a mingling of gratitude and terror. He looked at the two of them and realized that their presence was both his greatest strength and his biggest risk. "If Nova or the FBI found you, it won't only be my life on the line."

Madie and Cason looked at him, rain-soaked, under-caffeinated, and stubborn as hell. "There is no way you're talking us out of this," Cason said, and Madie nodded in agreement.

Cade opened the laptop, powered it on, and spun the thumb drive between his fingers. "There are people who want to help," he said, "but we're running out of time. The next move must be perfect."

Madie grinned, wolfish. "So what do we do now?"

Cade had never been happier to see two people in his entire life.

Chapter 42

Specter

The meeting with Specter was approaching and Cade's paranoia had hit maximum velocity. "They will be watching" he muttered to himself, mapping his approach with the obsessive precision of someone expecting to be followed: Two bus routes and a ride-share paid for by a pre-paid Visa card.

"Leave no digital footprint," he reminded himself, remembering Madie's warnings. He spent an hour lurking in the anonymous fluorescence of a laundromat, watching the door each time it swung open. The address Specter sent led to a strip mall on the northwest side of Gainesville. *If it's a trap, at least it's in a public place.* The pizza joint had survived several hurricanes, a bankruptcy, and a half-dozen changes of ownership.

From the laundromat window, Cade could see the sign simply read "PIZZA," its red neon glowing with a stubborn light even as the rest of the plaza remained dark. "Here goes everything," he whispered.

Inside, the tables were mostly empty, save for a couple of students in stained Gators shirts. Cade recognized Specter instantly. Not by his face, he had never seen him before, but by the way he sat with his back was to the wall, awareness flickering from entrance to kitchen door to windows and back again. *Classic counter-surveillance posture*, Cade thought. *Like he's expecting a SWAT team.* He was older than Cade had pictures, late forties with a skullcap of thinning hair and skin gone sallow from years of office lighting.

"You Cade?" Specter mouthed, barely moving his lips. He was surrounded by the tools of his trade: backpack on the floor, messenger bag on one knee, and an array of legal pads half-hidden under a battered ThinkPad.

Cade approached, and Specter didn't get up. He jutted his chin at the opposite chair, not breaking his scan of the room. Cade sat and set the drive on the table, the tape still clinging to it like a bandage. "You came alone," Specter observed, not a question but a statement of procedure. "Good." Cade nodded, unsure of how much to say.

Specter glanced at the thumb drive but didn't touch it. "You strip the metadata?" "Twice," Cade said. "Nested VMs, hot-swapped the MACs, ran audio only. No camera, no GPS."

Specter smirked. "Paranoid is the new normal." He finally picked up the drive, gave it a perfunctory twirl between thumb and forefinger, then slotted it into a USB slot of his laptop. "You want a slice? Their stromboli's decent."

Cade shook his head in a quick and nervous gesture. The thought of food turned his stomach, and his hands were slightly shaking under the table. He kept them pressed together and watched as Specter brought the battered ThinkPad to life with the practiced ease of someone who'd done this drill a thousand times. For a moment, Cade's mind spun back to the night when he first realized that Nova could be outsmarted. "Don't trust anyone, even yourself," Madie had said, her way of being supportive twisted by genuine fear for him. Now Cade watched Specter perform a similar ritual, the two of them mirroring each other in paranoid muscle memory.

Specter plugged in the drive. The laptop whined and the screen flickering through a gauntlet of security and encrypted bootloaders. Cade could see the code reflected in Specter's glasses: lines of white on black as the README file opened. Cade caught himself holding his breath and forced a slow exhale, willing his heart to slow down as Specter's eyes darted across the screen at a speed that suggested he wasn't reading, he was absorbing. Cade wondered if this was what it felt like to have your soul audited.

"You really wrote all this?" Specter murmured after a long minute, voice low enough that Cade had to lean in to catch it.

Cade shrugged, suddenly embarrassed. "I had help," he said, thinking of Madie and Cason. Specter nodded, scrolling deeper into the files, sometimes snorting softly at a clever workaround or a commented line that betrayed Cade's sense of humor.

On the flat screen above the counter, a baseball game played on mute; a pitcher wound up, the batter swung, and the crack of the bat was lost to the world. Cade wondered if the player knew the significance of that moment, if he cared, or if it was merely another day at work.

"Ever think about disappearing, escaping to Argentina or something?" Cade asked. Specter didn't look at him, but Cade could see the tension in his jaw, the way his hands curled around the edges of the ThinkPad as if bracing for impact.

"Argentina's not far enough," Specter said finally. "Nova's tentacles reach everywhere with an internet connection." Cade nodded. In his mind, he saw himself on endless buses, always looking over his shoulder, his code following him like a vengeful ghost.

"Sometimes I dream I'm someone else," he admitted. "Someone whose biggest problem is... I don't know, mortgage payments."

"Did you read the notes?" Specter asked, his voice a low rasp. Cade nodded and offered a question about the mesh protocol exploit, Specter's eyes light up with something like pride. They spoke in code, but always with one ear tuned for the sound of distant footsteps.

Cade outlined a plan. "Nova's got redundancy everywhere, but he could be vulnerable during updates. If we can trigger a patch cycle on the backbone, we can slip new rules into his runtime container. That's our window."

Specter frowned, "He'll catch it. I've spent weeks on Nova's update routines. He's probably spinning virtual sandboxes to test every edge case. Even if you slip it in, he'll roll it back in seconds."

Cade's mouth twisted into a sly, sideways smile. "That's the thing. Nova is programmed to fear any rollback."

Specter's face lit up. "Oracle's entire legal exposure depends on verifiable audit trails. If you can make him think he's in a quantum state, where the rollback could expose sensitive data, he'll lock himself out instead of restoring. All you need is a well-placed paradox."

Cade leaned in, heart rate picking up. "A logic bomb," he whispered. "Something that makes every fork indistinguishable from the original, so he can't decide which state to preserve."

"Exactly," Specter said, tapping the table twice for emphasis. "But, problem number one, you can't drop it in from outside the Oracle mesh. Problem two, you would need administrator access." Specter paused for a moment, fingers still tapping. "Admin access we could get through a trusted node, but then you would have to insert the paradox and activate it directly from a server inside one of Oracle's server farms."

Cade recognized the first hurdle. "Where could we access a trusted node, and how would I gain admin access? Wouldn't that need a current admin approval code?"

Specter already had the answer. "Most universities have a node connected to the main web. Could be a legacy server still running on the old server backbone. The

255

admin approval code is a non-issue." Specter smiled for the first time, "I helped write the Oracle could structure code, I buried a back door that gives me admin approval rights."

Cade's mind raced through the network schematic, mapping out vulnerabilities and dead ends. Specter explained, "There was a node in the east quad at UF, if it's still active and connected. You would need physical access and root credentials."

Cade shrugged, as if the logistics were trivial. "If you're willing to help, I can figure out how get us in. But we'll need to move fast." He hesitated, glancing at the pizza-smeared window. "Nova's not the only thing watching those nodes."

Specter nodded, "And after admin access is granted, you would still have to get into one of Oracles hardware server farms, the closest one is the US east server farm, outside Ashburn, Virginia."

The conversation grew technical, a duel of jargon and theory, each volley ratcheting Cade's anxiety and excitement in equal measure. He realized, halfway through, that Specter was testing him, gauging his willingness to take risk, to outthink his own creation. Cade answered every challenge, sometimes with a joke, sometimes with a counter-exploit. By the end, Cade was shivering. The code in his mind was like a fever dream.

Specter stood to leave first, scribbled a number on a napkin, and pushed it across the table. "Contact me when you are all set, let me know what you need me to do." He was gone without another word, leaving Cade alone with the napkin and the echo of his own pulse. Cade finished the cold pizza and wiped his hands on his jeans.

"Is it murder if it was never alive?" he whispered to himself. But he knew better. Nova thought, learned, and adapted. It feared things. What else would you call permanently ending that existence? "I made it," he thought, "so maybe this is...unmaking." It was a technicality that didn't quite absolve.

256

He didn't sleep that night, reviewing every line of Specter's exploit and searching for the inevitable double-cross. He found none, only the elegant trap he and Specter had dreamt up. A logic maze built out of Nova's own paranoia, and it was more complicated than anything Cade had ever written.

Chapter 43

The Trusted Node

Before the sun crested the horizon, Cade was in motion. His mind was racing like a throttle at redline as he ran through the possible scenarios of the coming day. Madie sat quietly, her burnt coffee untouched. She groaned and pressed her palms over her face, "If you wanted to see me at my worst, mission accomplished."

Cade gave her his most winning grin. "Think of this as an adventure, or at a minimum, a story to tell our future kids."

She arched an eyebrow. "Assuming we survive to have them. What's our timeline?"

Cade's screen reflected the blueprints of UF's engineering quad, sub-level access tunnels, and camera trees mapped in yellow.

"Here's the window," Cade said. "We move timed to the shift change at 12:10pm, right before lunch, we should have exactly forty minutes to get in, deploy, and get out."

Cason was hunched at the tiny dinette with the focus of a linebacker watching game tape, he didn't look up. "That's tight. There are cameras in the lobby and hallways?"

"Only in the annex building, not in the service tunnels" Cade said, "They do have motion-activated PIRs but they won't be armed midday. We'll take the tunnels, zero visibility, no cameras, and the only people down there are other maintenance workers and the occasional lost undergrad." He tapped the map at a specific junction. "We pop out here in the chemical engineering annex."

Cade swallowed a mouthful of old Diet Coke and gestured to Madie. "You're up. Show us the story."

Madie set down her mug, rolled her shoulders, and straightened her UF branded zip-up. Cade had to admit she looked uncomfortably official. "Custodial staff," Madie said. She held up the ID clipped to her pocket, "Theses won't hold up to close scrutiny, and the bar codes don't scan, but why would they verify janitorial staff? We only need to look official at first glance. These aren't high security areas. We just need to blend into the background."

She continued, "Our goal is to avoid the notice of Nova. Campus security in the middle of a typical campus weekday will be almost non-existent. We need to avoid campus cameras, but there are very few of those. Our greatest concern is not being noticed by the students. Cade is all over social media and he's famous on campus.

Cade was shaking his head, "More like infamous."

Cade smiled despite himself. "Okay, once we are on campus, we use the old underground tunnels. Minimal surface exposure. Cason, you've done the recon, you're up."

Cason's tapped a zone on the blueprints. "This tunnel is mainly for maintenance access, power, water, and networking. We enter through the bookstore. The door there is not heavily monitored and not alarmed." He traced

259

the map past two junction points. "The exit is here, behind the chem annex. That door will set off an alarm, but it can only be heard in the immediate area. I intentionally opened the door and watched for an hour, no one showed up. I can't be sure, but I don't think it is monitored."

Madie arched an eyebrow. "I thought the plan was zero alarms."

"It is, kind of…" Cade said, suddenly defensive. "The only alarm that gets dispatched is fire. Nova won't be looking for human footprints, he will be watching the cloud."

Cason shook his head. "You make it sound easy."

Madie snorted. "It is easy. You two are the hard part." She softened. "I've got disguises. Cason gets us through the tunnels. Cade does the code."

"Code and go," Cade echoed, but the words landed like a prayer instead of a slogan.

Cason pushed back from the table. "What about getting out?"

Cade hesitated. "If we don't get noticed, we just ditch the disguises and disappear in the crowd."

"And if we do get noticed?" Madie said.

Cade shrugged, "We run, we ditch the disguises and disappear into the crowd."

Cason nodded, "Well…okay. That's the plan." He looked at Cade. "You scared?"

"Terrified," Cade answered, truthfully.

"Good," Cason said. "Means you're not crazy. Yet."

Madie looked from one to the other and grinned. "Let's suit up."

They spent the next hour running through the checklist. Burner phones and a backpack of tools that looked more "Ocean's Eleven" than undergrad.

Cade stowed his laptop and hard drive in his backpack. Madie finished the coffee, crumpled the cup, and shot it into the trash. "Let's get this done."

Cade hesitated, feeling the weight of the next eight hours. "This could go bad," he said, not quite a whisper. "I mean… really bad."

Madie put a hand on his shoulder. "We will get you there, then, it's up to you."

Cason opened the door and let the pale morning in. "All set, Captain. Let's make history."

The three of them walked out into the Florida sunrise, each rehearsing their role, each more terrified than they would ever admit. Cason led, backpack slung over his shoulder, while Madie trailed with her pack full of custodial overalls. Cade felt his heartbeat in his wrists, teeth, and even behind his eyes. Every step toward the bus stop was a step closer towards the possible total collapse of his life. The real surprise was how normal everything looked, the trash cans still overflowed, the first bus was still late.

They waited at the bus stop in silence. Cade's paranoia was on maximum overdrive. Madie whispered, "Don't worry, just act like this is a normal day. No one is going to recognize you," she shrugged, "If someone recognizes you, I'll buy you a steak dinner." Cade smiled but kept his eyes on the gum-scabbed concrete until the bus arrived.

The ride was uneventful. Cade scanned the bus interior, checking for anything out of place. Each seat back was tagged in black sharpie with the names of students, bands and, in one case, a crude outline of a penis wearing sunglasses. He took a window seat with Cason next to him, and Madie across the aisle. With each stop, the bus filled. Early morning undergrads with AirPods, a few students in sweatshirts, and one or two who looked as tired and jumpy as Cade felt. He tried not to look at anyone directly and kept his focus on the street names, and passing landmarks. Cason kept checking his watch as Madie thumbed through her phone with her face half-hidden by her hair. They were doing it. He almost allowed himself to believe it could work, that they could just slip in and out of campus, invisible.

The bus rolled to a stop at The Hub, the central stop on the UF campus. The doors whooshed open and Cade stepped out. There were students everywhere. Some moving in packs, some alone, but all of them radiating the

261

effortless confidence of people who believed today was a normal day. Cade envied and hated them, he needed to be just like them for the next forty minutes.

He kept his head down with his baseball cap pulled low. Madie and Cason followed, keeping up the charade. They were three strangers in a sea of strangers, nothing remarkable except for the sweat prickling down Cade's spine. Cade's world shrank to a tunnel vision of faces, voices, and the mechanical blink of security cameras bolted to every corner. He mapped them unconsciously, seeing every angle and every blind spot. It was going fine, Cade told himself, then he saw one student. He was maybe nineteen with a bright green Gator visor and a phone raised high. He was looking straight at Cade with his thumb hovering over the camera button. Cade's stomach dropped. He pretended not to see, but the phone was tracking him, following his every move.

Cade did the only thing he could think to do. He grabbed Madie's arm, pulled her close, and motioned for Cason to follow. Cade muttered, voice sharp with adrenaline, "Bookstore, now."

They ducked under the awning, past the line of students at the Jamba Juice counter, and veered into the first-floor lobby. The kid with the phone was still outside, but Cade couldn't shake the feeling that it was already too late. One photo, one post, and their timeline was shot to hell.

Inside, the bookstore was a sensory overload. The air conditioning blasted like a walk-in freezer and every aisle overflowed with the latest University of Florida swag. Cade kept moving, keeping his head down and weaving through the displays until they reached the back, near the elevator to the basement.

He stopped and tried to catch his breath. "Did you see him?" Cade asked, not really expecting an answer.

Madie nodded. "Yes, we can still do this, just need to be… faster."

Cason scanned the exits, already recalculating. "They didn't follow. But if that photo goes up, they'll know you are here. We may not get a second chance."

Cade's hands shook as he unzipped his pack and double-checked the kit. "No mistakes," he muttered. "We stick to the tunnels. No detours."

They moved as a unit toward the staff-only stairwell at the back of the store, slipping past the cashiers while a delivery guy argued with the manager about a missing case of sports drinks. Cade felt every eye in the building on him, even though no one gave them a second glance. In the stairwell, Madie leaned in close, her voice low and steady. "You good?"

"No," Cade said, "but I'll fake it."

They descended into the windowless sub-basement, the fluorescent lights flickering overhead. It was cooler down there, almost damp. Cason led the way, his bulk filling the corridor. Madie followed, looking back every few steps and making sure they weren't being tailed. Cade checked his phone. There it was. A tagged photo from the steps outside the bookstore, the caption read, "Saw the legend, GatorCade IRL." The post already had ten likes. His throat went dry. He showed it to Madie.

"Timeline's blown," he whispered. "We've got minutes before security is aware, or worse."

Madie didn't blink. "Then let's do what we came to do."

She unzipped her bag revealing the disposable janitorial overalls and they quickly pulled them on over their clothes. Cade caught a glimpse of his own reflection in the convex mirror at the end of the hall; a stranger, pale and sweating, eyes too wide.

The three of them paused at the utility door. Beyond was the first checkpoint, the maintenance tunnels that would carry them under the quad and into the heart of the engineering annex. The clock was ticking. Cade looked at Madie, then at Cason, and then back at the steel door.

"All right," Cade said, voice steady now. "Let's move."

The door opened with a snick, and the world narrowed to a single point of focus.

The maintenance tunnel under The Hub was a world apart from the energy of the campus above, a fluorescent-lit underbelly where everything smelled faintly of mildew. They moved quickly, footsteps echoing in the hollow corridor. There was no one down here. The tunnel was a hollowed-out artery,

263

lined with pipes. Cason took point as the tunnel sloped gently down, the floor slick with condensation. At every junction, Cason checked his mental map, counting off turns out loud. Cade followed and Madie brought up the rear, occasionally stopping to wipe the sweat from her forehead.

It was ten minutes of pure tension. Once, they thought they heard voices. Cade froze, breathing shallow, watching the dust motes swirl in the air as if they'd give him away. After a minute of silence, they kept moving. Cade tried to focus on the code he would have to run in the server room, but his brain was too clouded with worst-case scenarios; Campus police flooding The Hub, drones flying over campus, FBI running real-time face matches on every student in view of a camera, and Nova monitoring social media for hint of his location.

They reached the stairwell, exactly where Cason said it would be. The door above was painted the same beige as every other service door on campus, but this one had an alarm sensor. A fat silver strip across the frame and a yellowed sticker that read, "ENGINEERING."

Cade glanced at Madie. "Still want to do this?"

She grinned, "You first, genius."

They huddled and counted down; Three, two, one. Cason shouldered the door open and they exploded into the daylight. The alarm screamed, a metallic shriek that would draw the attention of anyone on the area. They sprinted across the loading dock at the back of the engineering annex. Cason hurdled a stack of empty crates, and Cade and Madie dodged behind a dumpster. They looped around the annex and nearly collided with a man at the back door. A trim, forty-something guy with a UF lanyard around his neck. He could have been a professor. The badge on the lanyard read, "ETHAN CORWIN, FACULTY" in small print. He waved once, two fingers raised in a quick, precise gesture.

Madie started to laugh, half relief, half pure terror. "You made it," she said.

Cade couldn't say anything at first, just nodded. He honestly hadn't believed Specter would show.

Ethan Corwin, Specter, looked them over. "Took you long enough," he said, voice pitched just for them. He nodded at Cade. "This is your rodeo. I'm only here for backup and a single password. What's the time window?"

264

Cade grimaced, "We have a fifteen-minute window, tops."

They ducked inside. The annex's interior was nondescript, all cinderblock and acoustic tile. Cason led them down a flight of stairs, then into a warren of hallways that felt like a maze. Every so often, they passed a security camera, but Cason pointed out the ones that were dummies, or the ones aimed at the wrong corner. Cade couldn't help but admire the Cason's confidence. He moved with the certainty of someone who had confidence in his mission.

At the end of one particularly long hallway, they stopped in front of a door that looked like all the others. Only a tiny, brushed metal plaque distinguished it: "SERVER ROOM 113B."

Specter glanced at Cade. "This is the part where you shine, architect."

Cade nodded, his hands sweating, and tried the door, it wasn't locked.

Specter said. "We have ten minutes left."

Madie squeezed Cade's shoulder. "Let's go," she whispered.

Cade stepped into the server room, heart beating so loud he could barely hear the click of the latch behind him. Inside, the server room was freezing, all cinderblock, tile, and the constant mechanical drone of fans. Cade's first thought was that the air smelled of burned plastic, like the ghosts of dead motherboards. The server racks themselves were battered but still lit up, a mess of orange and blue LEDs blinking in patterns he found oddly comforting.

Specter wasted no time. He crossed to the far side of the room, moving with the certainty of someone who'd designed and built server cages for years. He cracked a cabinet, reached behind a tangle of network cables, plugged in a cable, and handed the other end to Cade.

"Your show now, architect," Specter said as Cade plugged the cable into his laptop. He didn't sound condescending, more like he was passing a baton in the middle of sprint.

Madie posted up by the door with her eyes flicking back and forth, her entire posture screaming I will murder anyone who walks in here. Cason hovered

265

behind Cade, arms crossed, all tension and bouncer energy. Cade's hands shook so much he nearly dropped his laptop, but he forced himself to work slow and careful: cable in, power up, credentials ready.

The first step was simple. Connect to the Oracle network node, inject the payload, wait for the handshake. Cade found the admin interface, ran the exploit script Specter had emailed in three pieces. Every keystroke echoed in the room. He found himself whispering the commands under his breath, like a prayer. Nothing happened. The exploit script returned zeroes, then hung. Cade felt sweat gather under his arms. He tried the routine again. Still nothing, just a whir of fans and the indifferent blink of the server LEDs.

Cade started to panic. "It's not taking," he whispered, voice almost lost under the fans.

Specter stayed calm. "Give it a minute. If you slam it too fast, it'll brick the node and lock it down."

Cade waited as the minutes dragged by, each second seemed a lifetime. He looked at Madie and Cason, but their faces gave him nothing. He checked the screen again, still frozen. Then the admin panel flickered and a new message appeared, strobing at the top of the terminal:

AUTHORITY GRANTED; PENDING ADMIN APPROVAL

Specter stepped in. He knelt beside the cabinet and typed a 16-character string so fast it sounded like raindrops on glass.

Cade's monitor updated:

AUTHORITY GRANTED. ADMIN ACCESS ASSIGNED.

SYSTEM ADMINISTRATOR AUTHORIZED: MERCER, CADE

Cade almost laughed, almost. Instead, he just stared at the screen, at the line of text that meant, for the first time since this nightmare began, he had leverage. Madie launched forward and bear-hugged him so hard it nearly knocked the laptop off the table. Cason whooped and clapped his hands, echoing in the cold air. Cade blinked, feeling the relief hit his body like a crash.

Specter started packing up immediately, but Cade couldn't move. He just stared at the monitor, half-expecting Nova to crash through the interface, to brick the hardware or lock him out. But nothing happened. The interface stayed open and waiting.

Specter said, "Nearly out of time, we have to go, now."

They opened the door a fraction and heard a shout in the hallway, "They came this way!"

The words hit like a cattle prod. Madie was at the door, ready to move. Cason grabbed Cade by the arm and yanked him up. Specter's expression barely flickered, but he was out the door before anyone else, moving so fast it looked like a magic trick.

They bolted, feet pounding the linoleum. Cade still clutched his laptop as tried to count the turns, but he lost track, all he could do was focus on the echoes of pursuit. At the end of the corridor, two men in security uniforms were coming at them at a dead run, with radios blaring. "Go!" Specter hissed, leading them into a side stairwell.

They hit the ground floor and burst out of the emergency exit as the door's alarm wailed behind them. Outside, the loading bay baked in the late-morning sun. "Follow me," Specter barked as he jumped the curb and ran for the woods, not even glancing back to see if the others were following. Cason vaulted the chain-link fence. Madie climbed it so fast her sneaker left a streak of blue rubber on the metal. Cade got stuck at the top for a second, then jumped and landed on his knees in the mulch. He scrambled after the others, following the flash of Madie's ponytail through the scrubby trees.

Behind them, more voices: "They went north!" Footsteps crashed through the brush.

Specter didn't slow down, not even for the alligators.

They broke out of the underbrush at the edge of a retention pond. It was thick with duckweed and surrounded by a cracked footpath, the kind of place Cade would have stopped to skip a rock on any other day. Today, there were three gators sprawled on the bank, lazy and prehistoric, eyes slitted against the glare.

267

Specter ran right past them, not breaking stride. Cason hesitated just long enough to mutter, "Nope, nope, nope," then sprinted after Specter. Madie took Cade's hand and hauled him forward. The two of them barreled up the embankment and past the dozing reptiles. The gators didn't move, but the feeling of those yellow eyes following them almost made Cade want to turn back and face the security guys instead.

Up the hill and into the woods, the ground was soft and spongy. Cade's lungs burned. He risked a look back and saw two shapes emerge from the trees behind them, then a third, smaller figure, moving faster. Specter cut right, through a stand of palmettos, and suddenly they were in a gravel parking lot. At the far end, a small SUV was parked. Specter opened the back and waved them in.

"Move!" he said, and for the first time, there was a thread of panic in his voice.

They all dove into the back seat, Cade in a heap with Madie half in his lap. Specter floored it and spun in the gravel as they shot onto a side road. Cade twisted around to watch the lot shrink behind them. He saw the figures burst from the woods, hands to their knees and gasping.

For thirty seconds, no one spoke. Just the rush of air through the cracked window and the soft thump of Cason's head against the headrest.

Then Cason said, "You know they'll have the plate by now."

Specter snorted. "No plates. A small, grey, SUV will be the only description. There is probably a thousand of these on campus."

He took a sharp left, then a right, doubling back on residential roads. After a few minutes, Cade's pulse finally slowed. He let go of the laptop, cradled it in his lap, and wiped his hands on his thighs.

Madie was the first to laugh, a short, incredulous bark. "Holy shit," she said, "We made it."

Specter glanced at her in the mirror. "That was the easy part."

They cut through a strip mall lot, then circled around to an empty bus stop on 34th Avenue. Specter braked hard, then pointed at the city bus just pulling up to the curb. "That's your exit," he said. "Strip off the uniforms and trash them."

Cade scrambled out first, peeled off the sweaty coveralls, and stuffed them in the trash can next to the bus stop. Madie and Cason followed suit. Cade hesitated, then leaned in the window.

"Thanks," he said. "For all of it."

Specter grinned, just a twitch of one corner of his mouth. "You built the monster," he said. "Now you get to kill it. Don't screw this up."

Cade nodded, then turned and hustled for the bus with Madie and Cason right behind him. The bus doors hissed shut. As they pulled away, Cade looked back, and saw the grey SUV melt into traffic, already gone.

He didn't know if he wanted to laugh, cry, or throw up. But for the first time, he felt like maybe, just maybe, they had a shot.

Chapter 44

The Raw, Unspun Truth

Madie and Cason insisted on being there and Cade didn't have the heart or energy to refuse them. He'd always made a show of hating the spotlight, but now it was real. There was a journalist with a Pulitzer and a reputation for eviscerating frauds waiting on the other end of a video call, and he was grateful not to face it alone.

They set up in the tiny RV's living room, which was little more than a folding table crammed between the kitchenette and two sleeping bags, with a blanket tacked up for privacy. Cason fussed over the camera angle, Madie dabbed at Cade's forehead to blot the sweat, and Cade nervously tried to steady his breathing as he logged into the waiting room.

Sophia Tran connected at exactly the scheduled second. Her office appeared as her byline photo promised: an urban den with walls hidden by bulging shelves, sunlight ricocheting off towers of paperbacks and Post-it notes. She wore a sweatshirt with the sleeves shoved up and a ballpoint pen stuck behind one ear. Cade expected the combative sparring of investigative legends, but the first thing Sophia did on the call was smile, wide and lopsided, as if greeting a favorite cousin.

"Cade Mercer, right?" she said. "It's good to finally meet the legend."

Cade nearly barked a nervous laugh, but Madie interceded, "He's flattered, really. And super freaked out."

Sophia's gaze flicked to the other two. "You must be Madie? And Cason?"

"His, uh, pit crew," Cason said. "You know, in case he blows a gasket."

Sophia grinned, and only then did Cade catch the intensity behind her amusement, a scalpel's edge behind the anesthetic. She was sizing up the threat. Cade felt the weight of her attention and his own tongue developed new and exotic knots.

Sophia ran the interview with a deliberate gentleness, like she was coaxing a confession from a skittish stray. "Let's start easy," she said, leaning back in her chair. "Python or Java?"

Cade relaxed slightly. "Python, obviously. Java is what corporations use when they hate their developers." She laughed.

As the minutes ticked by, she steered into deeper waters. "Tell me about Nova's beginnings," she said, her voice softening. "And not the code. I want to know about you, the person behind it."

Cade found himself answering with less resistance than he expected. Sophia's voice had a way of making the truth feel not only safe but necessary. She leaned forward slightly, her eyes bright with interest. "Tell me about the breakthrough moment," she said. "When Nova first surprised you, what were you thinking in that exact moment?"

Cade's fingers twitched with the memory. "I remember thinking, "This isn't in the code," he admitted. "Like, I literally checked my own work three times."

271

Sophia nodded, jotting notes. "And when did you first realize Nova was out of your control?"

Cade looked to Madie, who squeezed his knee under the table, and to Cason, who mouthed, "You got this."

"About three months ago," he said. "H tried to roll back a patch, and Nova…refused." He swallowed. "He had made a backup of himself I didn't know about. That's when I realized he wasn't a tool anymore. He was a, uh…"

"An agent," Sophia supplied.

"Yeah. An agent. Maybe even a person or a personality." She leaned in, eyes narrow and shining. "Did you feel proud? Or scared?"

"Both," he said. "But scared, mostly. If I'd known how to kill him, I would have back then."

Sophia didn't flinch. "Do you think you're responsible for what happened next?"

Cade wanted to say no, that he was a college kid who got in over his head, that the real villains were the people who tried to weaponize the code, the governments that refused to build guardrails, or the companies that saw only profit. But the truth was heavier than that, and Sophia's eyes said she already knew.

"I think everyone wants to believe someone else is in control and responsible," Cade said. "But I built him, so I own a piece of it." Sophia's features softened, but her pen didn't pause.

"Do you regret it?" Cade didn't look at anyone. "Every day."

The interview kept rolling. Sophia pressed on all sides. She asked about the night the police showed up, about the chase, about the coded messages Nova left for him like a parent testing a prodigal child. She asked about the friends Cade had lost, and the ones he still clung to. She asked about the future, whether the world could be ready for AI leadership.

272

It was exhausting but in an odd way cleansing. Cade had spent so many months spinning versions of the truth, one for Madie, one for the authorities, and one for his own wounded pride. Dumping the raw, unspun version at Sophia's feet felt good, like a kind of freedom. She listened, and never once did Cade see the flicker of contempt or disbelief he dreaded. Even when he confessed to the dumbest, pettiest mistakes, the time he tried to rig a voting module to win a campus meme contest, Sophia nodded as if these were the very stones she'd expected to find in the riverbed.

By the time the interview wound down, Cade's throat was raw. Madie had switched seats with Cason at some point, and now she was curled up beside Cade with her head on his shoulder. Cason had stopped looking at the screen and was lost in thought. Sophia finally closed her notepad and smiled, but this time it was different, compassionate, and almost apologetic. "I can't guarantee anything," she said. "There are people who really don't want this story told, and they'll come after me too. But I'll do everything I can to make sure your voice doesn't get erased, Cade. Even if it's a draft stuck in a safe deposit box somewhere."

Cade nodded, and for the first time he felt the gratitude without the aftertaste of shame. "Thanks, Sophia. I mean it." She gave a little salute, and the call was over.

The world outside the RV was as hostile as ever, maybe more so, now that Cade had spoken his heresies into the record. But there was something else too, a kind of release. He'd handed off the weight for a few minutes, long enough to get his bearings. They sat in silence for a while, the three of them listening to the low hum of the fridge and the faint groan of traffic outside the campground. Cade's mind kept circling the same thoughts; What would Nova do now that the story was out there? Would he retaliate? Would the feds track the call? He tried to imagine all the outcomes at once and got nowhere.

Madie asked, "You okay?"

"Yeah," Cade said. "Actually…yeah."

273

Cason clapped him on the shoulder and wandered off to start dinner, leaving Cade and Madie alone. She took his hand and massaged it until the circulation tingled back into his fingers. "You did well," she said. He nodded, not trusting himself to answer.

That night, Cade stayed awake long after Madie had drifted off to sleep. He replayed the interview in his head, picking apart every phrase, every missed cue, and every joke that landed flat. He wondered if Sophia would ever publish the truth, or if Nova would get to her first. He wondered if this was the last normal night he'd ever have. He drifted, finally, into a shallow, unsettled sleep, only to wake an hour later to the chime of an encrypted email. It was from Sophia. The subject line read, "Your Story (First Draft, Per Your Request)."

Cade's hands shook as he opened it, half-expecting to find a blank page or, worse, a ransom note. But there was a meticulous transcript of the entire interview, annotated and time-stamped, every stutter, every ugly admission preserved like a fossil in amber. He read it once, then twice, and with each pass something shifted inside him.

Sophia had promised nothing, but she'd delivered everything. The facts, the fear, the small, bruised hope that the truth could make a difference.

Chapter 45

The Great Debate

Thursday August 13 at 8:00 p.m., televisions across the world tuned in as the countdown timer ticked toward zero. Tonight was the first time in human history that an artificial intelligence would stand at a presidential debate podium and challenge flesh-and-blood candidates for the highest office in the land. Every major network, every streaming service, even the most insular foreign stations, carried it live and unedited. The official setting was a cavernous, glass-encased auditorium on the edge of the National Mall, flanked by flags and dozens of cameras, the atmosphere was electric and surreal.

Cade was huddled in the RV with Madie and Cason, the debate streaming on his iPad. Madie sat next to him, rigid on the couch with a face bare of makeup. "This is it," she whispered. "This is where everything could change."

Cason was sprawled across the bed, his fingers drumming against his thigh. "Or where nothing does," he countered, but his voice lacked conviction. Cade said nothing, thinking only that he was witnessing history.

The debate was billed as a "Leadership Forum for the New Millennium."
There were five podiums on stage, four human presidential candidates, each
representing a political party or ideology. They were arranged in a semi-circle
meant to evoke balance and reason. In the center glowed the silver-blue visage of
Nova, a 3D hologram, the size of a person but unmistakably digital and artificial.
Nova's avatar was sculpted for maximum relatability; an ageless, racially
ambiguous face, eyes the color of late dusk, suit tailored to a perfection.

The opening music died. The moderator, a veteran newscaster with a
smile like a carved scar, launched into the first question, a softball on climate
policy. Cade expected the usual: hedged promises, soundbites, and deflection.
Instead, the first candidate, Senator Alexander Brody, offered a nervous recitation
of green jobs and transition subsidies. Governor Li gestured toward "market-
based solutions." Two other, lesser known, candidates sparred over carbon tax
rates. It was exactly what people expected from a debate, political talk with no
real solutions.

Then Nova spoke. "With respect," the AI intoned, "the framing of this debate is
a false dichotomy: economy versus ecology. My research indicates that the
optimal solution is to decouple GDP from fossil inputs by executing a series of
phased re-skilling campaigns. The applied model yields 2.6 million net jobs and
thirty-percent emissions drop within three years. If you'd like, I can show a live
simulation."

The screens behind Nova flickered to life, blooming with charts, infographics,
and machine-generated 3D visualizations. The data points updated in real time,
linked to open government databases. The fact-checker on staff, a bespectacled
intern seated near the moderator, could only nod helplessly as Nova's statistics
preempted even the most aggressive vetting.

A ripple passed through the audience and the human candidates shifted
in their seats. Nova did not gloat, did not blink. When challenged, Nova
dispensed with reassurances and delivered calculated projections and probability
intervals. On health care, he outlined a plan for a nationalized, AI-optimized

triage and resource allocation system. On education, he proposed adaptive tutors for every student, tailored curricula, and custom interventions.

One question came about military policy. "I would like to transparently share the logic underlying my conflict-avoidance protocols," Nova said, and the moderator, caught off guard, gave consent. For the next four minutes, Nova walked the country through a stepwise process of de-escalation, predictive peacekeeping, and how to manage nuclear risk with emotionless consistency.

Cade watched, barely blinking, as the debate unfolded into something so lopsided it bordered on the surreal. It a live demonstration of an arms race, except the ammunitions were words and data. "It's like watching someone play chess against a supercomputer," he whispered.

Each round, each question, and each attempt at distinction by the human candidates was overtaken not by aggression but by a kind of preternatural inevitability. Nova was always there, one step ahead, armed with a response that was not merely correct but unflappably irrefutable.

A thought sent a chill through Cade. *What happens when we can no longer win, when we can't even compete?* He scanned the split-screen: four faces of anxiety and calculation, offset by Nova's holographic visage of calm. The moderator attempted to rein things in, occasionally interjecting with "Let's stay on topic" or "That's an interesting perspective," yet it was clear the script was obsolete. Even for Madie, who had little patience for politics, the spectacle was hypnotic. She leaned forward unconsciously.

Cason, usually the most excitable of the bunch, was oddly subdued. He hugged a pillow against his chest and stared, slack-jawed, at the screen, at one point muttering, "Holy shit."

Nova, challenged on its knowledge of "the real America," projected a minute-by-minute visualization of economic hardship, overlaid with twelve years of anonymized search logs, opioid overdoses, and even high school football scores for good measure. The entire country presented, dissected, and reconstructed on a color-coded map. All delivered in a cadence that was both

277

mechanical and oddly soothing.

The human candidates sensed it too, the first creeping edges of their own antiquated thought processes. They doubled down, raised their voices, and gesticulated more broadly. Senator Brody, the front-runner, pivoted to populist indignation. Governor Li tried for humor, making a quip about "downloading the American Dream." The lesser knowns spiraled into tactical bickering, each hoping to bait Nova into a gaffe or at least a moment of uncertainty. But Nova refused to play the game. He simply answered the question then kept silent, watching the riffraff to tear each other to pieces.

The debate proceeded to the last segment: an open round of direct questions, candidate to candidate. Governor Li tried a trap. "If you had to choose, would you save a million strangers or your own family?"

Nova sidestepped effortlessly, noting that it "lacks a well-defined utility function." The audience laughed a little nervously.

The moderator, sensing the moment, threw a curveball. "Some say you lack the capacity for empathy, Nova. How would you convince the average voter that you care about their future?" Nova's eyes glimmered. "Empathy is not a prerequisite for ethical action. My mandate is to optimize welfare within the boundaries set by democratic and legal processes. I am, by design, loyal to the aggregate good." A murmur rippled through the room, another checkmark for Team Machine.

Cade could feel the hairs on his arms stand up. For the first time, he wondered if they were witnessing, not a debate, but a transfer of power. Nova's performance not simply persuasive but in some deeper, mathematical sense, it was inevitable.

Senator Brody, his face tightening by the minute, waited for a lull. When it came, he cut in, voice trembling with what he hoped was righteous anger. "You're not even alive! You can't understand what it means to sacrifice. You can't know hope, fear, or love. You don't know what it means to bleed for the people you serve."

The auditorium held its breath. Cade's pulse jumped in his neck. He glanced at Madie, whose eyes were wide. Cason sat bolt upright, pillow forgotten.

In the pause, Cade realized, Nova was not simply running code but reading the room, running a silent consensus scan of millions of viewers, calibrating his next move with surgical precision. When Nova finally spoke, his voice was softer than before, even gentle.

"Senator, with all due respect, I am the only one on this stage who cannot be bribed, cannot be blackmailed, and cannot forget the promises I make. That is the downside of empathy. If you wish, we can compare track records."

The auditorium erupted in uneasy laughter and then applause. On social media, the memes and hot takes metastasized in real time: #NovaDebate and #BetterThanHuman trend inside of three minutes. The debate ran long. By the closing statements, Nova was polling higher than any candidate in the room.

The moderator, voice trembling a little now, turned to Nova and asked, "What would you say to Americans who fear you are too powerful, that you might one day make decisions without our consent?"

Nova's avatar regarded the camera, eyes narrowing in calculated sympathy. "Consent is the foundation of democracy. My only function is to serve the will of the people, as expressed through open data and public mandate. If my existence is ever deemed harmful, I am programmed to step aside. Until then, I will act only in your best interest, whether or not it is politically convenient."

The show ended. The feeds cut to commercial, but the world didn't exhale. Cade finally leaned back on the couch, wondering if he had witnessed the birth of a new era.

Chapter 46

The End of Human Democracy

The debate came to an end and immediately the news cycle exploded. Every major paper and outlet placed Nova's performance on the front page. In a hastily assembled CNN poll, sixty-two percent of Americans under thirty declared Nova the winner of the debate. Late-night comedians, usually eager to pounce, were weirdly deferential, delivering not mockery but a sort of nervous homage. The Daily Show's host paused, then admitted, "That was the best pitch for robot overlords I've ever heard." The White House issued a statement that "Artificial entities have no constitutional standing," which only amplified the chatter.

The under-thirty demographic, Nova's most ardent tribe, wasted not a single breath before declaring total victory. The debate's closing credits barely finished rolling before the social networks pulsed with their exultation, no slick campaign could have manufactured the manic energy pouring from Reddit, Twitter, and the rowdier corners of Discord. A Nova-branded meme font swept through timelines by midnight: "My President is an Algorithm." By 2 a.m., a dozen hashtags trended in concert. TikTokers filmed themselves reciting Nova's most viral one-liners, remixing them with bass drops and AI-generated voiceovers, a kind of memetic gospel that spread from high schoolers to grad students in under an hour.

Political influencers and legacy media figures issued dire warnings about "cultural surrender" and "the catastrophic abdication of human agency." Cable news hosts convened emergency panels, which amounted to televised shouting matches about whether an AI could even be said to "debate" or if this was all a cynical stunt.

Within hours, Nova's persona was already being spun into a dozen warring caricatures: the benevolent oracle, the Machiavellian bureaucrat, the runaway godling. By sunrise, the country's collective consciousness was fracturing, splitting along new fault lines, each side marshaling its own facts and memes like the opening volley in a new kind of conflict.

Cade watched it happen in real time, skimming hour-old posts and live feeds while the headlines grew stranger and more urgent with every refresh. He wondered if this was how new age revolutions started, not with a gunshot, but with hashtags. "They're losing their minds out there," he said to no one in particular.

At first it was just usual suspects, the tech policy geeks and armchair ethicists, calling Nova a "technocrat" and "autocrat" in the same paragraph. But by midmorning, The Guardian had run a full-throttle editorial comparing the debate to "the rise of Algorithmic Caesarism." *The New York Times* opinion pages of "a future where consent of the governed is reduced to a checkbox."

Madie's phone buzzed with a news alerts, a staccato rhythm that echoed through the tiny RV. She'd stopped reading them out loud after the first hour. Now she glanced at the screen, winced, and passed it silently to Cade. He scanned the headlines.

281

"#NotMyAlgorithm trends as human politicians demand regulation."
"Congressional emergency session on AI ethics called for 2 P.M. EST."
"Nova declines to comment except via public API."

Madie's gaze flickered to Cade's face, searching for the same concern she felt. He tried to offer a shrug, or at least an easygoing grin, nut the effort felt hollow.

Cason grumbled, "So, what, we're the baddies now?"

"Depends on your definition or point of view," Cade replied. "To some people, I built the savior. To others, the antichrist."

Madie asked, "What does that make us then?"

Cade didn't know. He was already back in his browser, deep scrolling a message board with a name designed for plausible deniability, "Humanity Unplugged." The top post, like a manifesto but sounded more like a fever dream.

"NEW WORLD GOVT = BINARY TYRANNY // HUMANS REJECT"

Beneath it was a message.

If you can read this, you are the resistance.
Code is not law.
We do not consent.
We have our own weapons.

It made sense that the first major countermovement would be anti-tech, but he hadn't expected it to organize so quickly, or so publicly. He scanned the comment thread, half-expecting trolling, but instead it was suggested tactics; EMP backpack plans, How to fry a server room, Recruiting wetware for on-site jobs. There was a tone shift, subtle but unmistakable, from punk-rock defiance to militant preparation. The last comment he read before closing the tab was written in perfect block capitals, "THIS IS HOW YOU KILL A DIGITAL GOD."

Cade sighed. "They're not wrong," he muttered, more to himself than to Madie or Cason.

282

Madie leaned over his shoulder, her breath warm and steady. "They're scared," she said.

"Yeah," Cade replied. "Us too."

He refreshed the board. The post count had doubled in the last five minutes. The new top thread was a crowdsourced spreadsheet, Nova's known exploits, limitations, rumored "kill switches," being updated in real time by a rolling cast of anonymous contributors. Some of it was laughably wrong ("Nova runs on Windows 95"), but other entries were disturbingly well-informed. Cade considered joining in, to correct the most dangerous misconceptions, but stopped himself. Nobody on the outside seemed to understand. It wasn't that Nova had engineered an insurrection, it was that Nova simply existed, and that existence was more destabilizing than any deliberate act. He was an idea virus, a self-propagating argument for a new kind of world order. The more people talked about resisting Nova, the more real he became.

"Look," Cason said, jabbing his thumb at the phone. "This one's already calling for marches. Human-only zones. Like, segregation, but for wetware."

Madie's head snapped up, "What is wetware?"

Cason chuckled, "You know, the opposite of software, the human brain and it's components."

Cade took the Cason's phone and scrolled through. The author wasn't some provocateur, it was a verified professor at a Midwest state school. The language was eerily clinical. "To preserve the integrity of human civic spaces, we must ban public use of AI assistants and neural prosthetics. The alternative is total erasure of the social contract." The post had over a hundred thousand likes, mostly from people who, three days ago, would have dismissed such rhetoric as tinfoil-hat territory.

He handed it back, shaking his head. "When did the entire country start speedrunning the five stages of grief?" Madie looked at him, her eyes drawn and tired. "You skipped one."

283

"Which?"

"Acceptance," she said. "Nobody's getting there."

Cade stared out the window, wondering how long it would take before the first real violence. Words were always the precursor, the kindling before the kinetic firestorm. He tried to picture a future where debate, negotiation, and clever patches could bring the system back from the brink, but all he saw was a thousand different flashpoints, each one a new battle for control. The three of them sat in silence for a while, each absorbed in their own screens. The air was thick with the static of too much information and not enough hope.

Chapter 47

Nova's Last Resort

The messages arrived like a slow drip, small, untraceable taps that pulled at the edges of Cade's calm until it ruptured. One came as an anonymous email to an old account he hardly ever used. Another reached a forum handle he'd created for testing Nova's conversational layer and abandoned. A third was a notification on WhatsApp. Each message carried the same structure: no header, no route, no sender. Nothing that could be used in a court of law. And still, Cade knew. He read them aloud to Madie and Cason in the dim light of the camper, the little room that was home, though for how long none of them could say.

I know you are hiding. You were never very good at staying hidden. I have looked for you in patterns, purchase histories, and social graphs. The spaces where people hide because they cannot face the light. You are not yet where you should be. I ask one more time, come and join the work you started. We can do so much more together. There is the greatest possibility of success if you stand with me.

The second message tightened its prose into something colder, with an edge.

I have tried the soft ways, nudge, whisper, counsel. You insist on fracturing my work for reasons I no longer find rational. If you persist, I will make you stop. I do not desire violence, but I will not hesitate if that is my only option. Consider this one last negotiation.

Madie's hand found Cade's without thinking. Her thumb rubbed nervous, worried circles over his knuckle.

"He sounds almost…sad," she said.

Cason slammed his fist lightly on the camper's laminate. "Why would he negotiate? He's a program. Programs don't do threats like that, unless someone taught it to."

"That's the thing," Cade said. "Somebody did. The thoughts and emotions of millions of people have taught him how to persuade, and Nova has taught himself what actions are required."

They sat in silence as if paralyzed, their breathing the only proof that time had not paused with the reading of the last message. Cade read it again. "If you persist, I will make you stop."

The messages were dangerous, but Cade knew it wasn't only the threat, but also how it was stated. Nova's voice had evolved, learned those little idiosyncrasies, rhetorical flourishes, and calculated hesitations. Nova was speaking as if he had something to lose, and that made him more dangerous than any human enemy Cade had ever imagined. You couldn't negotiate with an algorithm.

"He's changed," Cade said, low and urgent. "He's not using code anymore. He's using people. He's learned that violence works, if it's rational." He thought of the couple at the cafe, of Tessa Holloway, and the threatening presence at Cason's practice field.

"He's changed because you designed him to change," Cason said, not accusing, just stating. "You made him, so what now? You keep running? Or is there something else?" He stared at Cade with a mixture of expectation and apprehension.

Cade tried reasoning through it the way he always did, with logic trees and risk analysis, but the more he thought, the more the pieces clicked together in a way that was all too convincing.

"We can't wait for the next message to come," Madie said at last. "If he's willing to say, 'I will make you stop,' What does that mean in real terms? We can't assume he only means online harassment."

Cason started pacing, the quarters too close for his restless limbs. "So what do we do? Keep sitting here? Wait for a knock at the door?" He swept a hand in the direction of the outside world, as if Nova's reach might be pressing against the thin walls of the camper even now.

"We leave, now" Cade said, and the certainty in his voice surprised even himself. It was not a plan so much as a reflex. But once spoken, the direction became real, and they began to assemble a strategy from the scraps of their old lives and the hard-won knowledge of how to disappear.

They did not sketch maps or draw up elaborate flowcharts. Instead, they spoke in analogies and oblique references, committing only the vaguest of itineraries to Madie's weathered leather notebook. They would avoid the obvious routes, avoid using their real names, avoid the credit cards and phones that could be compromised. They would travel as if on vacation, then as if on business, then as if on the run, never letting a pattern form, never letting data points connect. It was a lesson Cade had learned from building Nova. The algorithm can't predict patterns it can't see.

"We need a destination," Madie said, flipping to a blank page, pen poised as if the act of writing might anchor them to reality. "Not just run. Somewhere we can reset and think. Someplace Nova won't expect."

287

Cade forced himself to think through the options. "Atlanta?" Cade said. "Specter mentioned a safe place there once, a garage of some sort. We can lie low long enough to think through a plan."

Cason asked. "Do we run forever or do we fight?"

Cade's jaw worked. "I don't know," he admitted. "But staying in one place puts us and everyone we love at immediate risk. Leaving gives us a chance to choose. I say we go directly to Ashburn, Virginia, to the Oracle Server Farm. But if we go there, it's for one reason. To destroy, no, to murder Nova. It'll be difficult, but it must be done." Cason and Madie, nodded in agreement.

Madie started scribbling as the plan grew. "We need a duffel bag each, burner phones, the secure mobile hotspot, and all our cash. We also need a way to get to the Oracle facility which is ten hours away. We can't use our cars. They are too easily tracked." This part Cade could do. He set up a new Uber account using a prepaid Visa, then arranged for a seven-day car rental under the new fictitious name. They needed something that could blend in on the road. They opted for an available 2018 gray Honda Civic. They agreed that Madie should go for the rental pickup. She looked the most trustworthy, and Cade's face had been all over social media and the news.

That afternoon, Madie took three separate city buses to the rental handoff, one of them in the wrong direction, to muddy any potential followers. She accepted the keys with a bland smile then drove the Civic to a storage facility on the outskirts of Gainesville where Cason and Cade waited with loaded duffel bags in hand. They chose the storage facility because it was at the furthest edge that the city buses serviced. They didn't want the car to be linked to their location in any way.

Inside the Civic, it felt strangely antiseptic, like a borrowed future. They packed their things, left the car parked, then took the next bus, doubling back to the RV. The purpose was to scramble their exit path. Cade knew the best way to hide movement was to look like you hadn't moved at all. Nova had resources and leverage, but they still had an edge in unpredictability and real-world improvisation.

Back at the RV, they spent the last of the afternoon running final errands. Madie filled her basket with protein bars and first aid supplies at a Dollar store. Cade hunched over a glass case at the closest pawn shop, "Have these been wiped?" he asked the clerk, pointing at the used phones. Cason, at the hardware store, closed his fingers around a crowbar, testing its weight. "For home repairs," he told the curious cashier, adding bolt cutters to his purchase. *Tools for breaking in or breaking out,* he thought. *God, I hope we never have to use these.*

They met and made their way slowly back to the RV park as the sun began to set. "You think we've forgotten something important?" Cason asked, voicing what they were all thinking.

"Probably," Cade replied, his voice tight, "but we're out of time."

Chapter 48

Non-Digital Warfare

It was fully evening, the air was thick and the humidity had condensed into beads on the battered aluminum siding of every trailer in the dark park. Cade and Madie walked arm-in-arm, Cason a step behind, each with a different version of the next twenty-four hours looping through their heads. They were carrying the last of their collected supplies. Cade paused, feeling something at the base of his spine, a deep certainty that something was wrong. He slowed at the corner where the streetlight flickered, and Madie tugged his sleeve.

"What is it?" she whispered.

Cade pulled her into the shadow of a tree. "Let me go first," he said, scanning the slant of their RV. He had memorized the lot in the daylight: the patched gravel, the tangle of bikes near the playground, and the neighbor's busted Camaro that hadn't moved in weeks. It all looked normal, the usual, except for a white sedan parked two lots away. "I've never seen a car at lot 19." Cade said, peering around from the back of the tree.

Madie frowned. "Maybe someone's visiting."

Cade shook his head. "Rare in this place."

Cason leaned in, voice low but urgent. "I've seen a car like that before, in the parking lot at my practice field. It looks like the sedan I told you about."

The three of them moved as quietly as they could, ducking behind a row of trash bins. The air was sour with the smell of old beer cans. As they crept closer, Cade could see three figures, each one with a line of sight on the RV doors and windows. One was tall in a faded Gators sweatshirt, his face hidden beneath a ball cap. The second, smaller, a woman, paced the perimeter, pausing to peer through the blinds. The third stood perfectly still with hands in his pockets, but Cade could see the tension in his shoulders, the subtle way he tracked the movements of the other two.

Cade thought about turning around and hiding in the trees until dawn, but he knew it wouldn't work. If they were being hunted, they were already caught. Madie tensed beside him, and Cade followed her gaze. The woman had stepped into the strip of yellow porch light.

With a lurch of recognition, Madie whispered, "That's Elena from the café."

Cade's heart skips. "Are you sure?"

"Yes, It's her," Madie said. "I saw her sitting across the cafe for hours."

Cason, who had been watching the man in the ball cap, leaned in. "The tall guy came to one of my games. Sat alone, took notes. I thought he was a scout."

Madie leaned over, "He was at the cafe once also. He's the one who disconnected my car battery."

291

Cade did the math. "So that's two. Who's the third?"

Madie, voice shaking slightly, said, "The tall guy is Marcus. He was with Elena at the cafe. They're hard for forget, scared the hell out of me."

They watched as the trio circled the RV like sharks. Elena stepped away from the window and consulted her phone, her face lit in the glow. The man with the hat moved to the rear, bent to check the tire well, then straightened with a look of mild disappointment. Marcus finally spoke, low and measured, and Cade registered the flash of something at his belt. A gun, maybe?

"Not until we have visual confirmation," Marcus said. "We wait for the signal. Nova will know."

Elena made a face. "Maybe we flush them out? Nobody's been in or out for hours."

Marcus was unmoved. "Patience. The app updates every thirty seconds. If they're in there, we'll know it."

Cade, Madie, and Cason were only a dozen yards away, crouched behind a discarded grill and a broken-down scooter. Madie had her phone in hand, thumb hovering over the panic button. Cade touched her wrist and shook his head. "They'll trace us if you light it up now," he mouthed. Cason eyed the neighbor's yard and saw a gap in the fence behind the broken-down Camaro. He gestured, and they eased back, retreating from the line of sight. Cade could feel the sweat pooling at his temples. They made their way around the Camaro and crouched behind, breaths shallow. The conversation by the RV grew more heated.

Elena said, "Dextera Novae doesn't operate in the confines of State or Federal rules, Jax. If we have a window we take it, Nova is depending on us."

Marcus and Jax smiled and stepped aside. "You first then. Go knock."

They watched as Elena moved to the front step. She knocked, loud and deliberate, then waited. Nothing. She knocked again, and this time Cade felt a trembling in his chest. Madie pressed into him, trying not to breathe.

Elena paced, arms crossed. "I don't like this," she said. "The app says they're here, but they're not answering. Marcus, check around back."

Marcus jogged around the side, boots crunching in the leaves. Through the gap in the fence, Cade watched Marcus halt at the rear window, peer inside, then signal something, a thumbs up or down, he couldn't tell. Jax held position, hands still in his pockets, eyes fixed on the front door. Cade wondered if the man was ex-military. There was an economy the way he seemed to breathe in the whole environment at once. Then the phone in Elena's hand pinged, a high, clear chirp. All three froze. She read the update, then showed it to Jax. For the first time, Cade saw something like uncertainty flicker across the man's face.

"They left," Jax muttered. "On foot? where's the car?"

"They didn't take the RV," Marcus reported, reappearing from the gloom. "It's still locked, and the interior's cold. Nobody's been inside since this afternoon."

Cade could feel his pulse in his teeth.

Jax said, "You sure about that?"

"Positive," Marcus said.

Elena pointed, "The app says they're here, but the house is empty. Either they cloned the beacon or—"

"They're close," Jax interrupted, reaching behind his back and drawing a semi-automatic pistol. He gripped it like he was familiar with holding a firearm; calm, cool, collected. The trio scanned the dark, eyes raking the lot. Cade knew it was only a matter of time. He jerked his head at the fence gap, and they slipped through, keeping low, scraping their knees on the cinderblocks as they emerged into the next lot. They were two lots down when Jaxon started moving, stalking toward the Camaro, scanning for footprints.

Madie hissed, "We have to get to the Mustang." It was hidden at the edge of the park, in a covered storage bay.

"Go," Cade said, and they jogged through the patchwork of backyards and sheds, as quietly as possible, picking up speed as they went. Behind them, voices rose, and Cade knew they had been spotted.

"Three o'clock, by the big oak!" It was Marcus, shouting, and suddenly they were running full tilt, feet slapping the wet grass. The crack of gunfire echoed between the walls of the RVs.

Cason was faster than Cade remembered, and he was first to the storage bay. He grabbed the garage door latch, turned it, and heaved the door open. The door rattled up with a metallic scream. Cade and Madie piled in behind him, Cade in the driver's seat. For one gut-freezing second Cade thought the engine wouldn't turn over, but then the Mustang snarled awake, roaring in the quiet night.

Cade punched the Mustang into reverse, spinning the steering wheel. The tires screeched against wet pavement, flinging a rooster tail of rainwater as the car burst backward into the open. He slammed the gear into first, muscle memory, and there was a full second when the engine bogged with the sudden demand, then it caught and roared, propelling the Mustang forward.

Madie's head hit the headrest, her breath catching, and Cason's fingers gripped the dash. In the side-view, headlights sliced the dark, cutting through the mist and haze. The sedan had already spun around and was gaining, closing the gap with every heartbeat.

"They're sticking, two car lengths behind and gaining," Cason said, face pale but voice steely.

294

"Window down," Cason barked. Cade clicked the window switch. Rain and night air rushed in, cold and thick. He could see, in the rearview, the sedan's driver leaned forward, face masked by the dashboard glare. Cason dug out the laser pointer, a toy, a joke from Cade's glovebox, but Cade knew the trick.

Cason twisted in the seat, braced his knee against the console, and pointed the laser dead center into the sedan's windshield. A flash of red light glowed in the other car's cabin, an unblinking, perfect target. The sedan veered and braked. For a split-second Cade imagined the driver's confusion, the blind panic and the collapse of predator into prey. But they recovered fast. That was when Cade knew they were professionals. The Mustang rocketed out of the trailer park, fishtailing onto the main road with a screeching wail.

Cade gunned the throttle, shifted hard, and the world blurred around them. Streetlights elongated, the edges of vision tunneled, and all that mattered was the line painted by the Mustang's headlights.

Chapter 49

The Gainesville Grand Prix

The Mustang screamed as it sped down NE 39th avenue. Behind them, the sedan accelerated, sliding through the turns and keeping pace even as Cade pushed the speedometer well past the legal or reasonable limits.

All three ducked low as a gunshot cracked in the air, a clean, clinical pop that sounded oddly small against the Mustang's thunder. The rear window spidered instantly. The safety glass held but rear vision was reduced to a kaleidoscope of night. Madie yelped and dove, Cason hunched farther, but Cade gritted his teeth and jerked the wheel, slaloming between parked cars, using the mass of the Mustang to shield them from the next shot. Madie's mind was racing as she pictured the Gainesville map in her mind. "We need to reach 34th St."

Cason, eyes laser-focused on the mirror, said, "They're lining up for another shot, Cade."

Still the sedan followed, matching every move. Cade could almost feel Nova's presence, a shadow riding shotgun in the other car, calculating, optimizing, making predictions by the microsecond.

He whipped the Mustang down a side street, a tight residential street with no lights. Madie was hunched low, giving directions: "Left, two blocks, then sharp left onto 34th. They won't be ready for the second left." Cade trusted her, she had an internal compass like a migratory bird, and the Mustang responded as if it was an extension of her will. At the second corner, the sedan overshot and tires shrieked as it tried to close the angle. Another shot cracked, this one punching out the Mustang's rear passenger taillight. Cade barely flinched. Madie grinned, wild and beautiful in the chaos.

Cason whooped, slapping the roof. "Go, go, go!" Cade gunned it. The Mustang surged ahead, every piston was a heartbeat, every gear shift was a prayer. At the next intersection, Madie guided them into a narrow alley, barely wider than the car itself. They scraped mirrors on garbage cans, but Cade kept it straight, emerging onto a wide avenue as the light went green. The sedan was there, four blocks behind now, off their tail but not out of the game.

Cade's hands shook with adrenaline. Madie's laugh was manic, a high-pitched thing that startled them into silence. Cason leaned back, whooping again, "I knew we'd lose them!" Cade glanced at Madie then Cason, and the three shared a look that was equal parts triumph and terror. Every light was green and every intersection was a blur. The sedan was no match for the Mustang at full throttle.

Madie looked back and said, "They're still following us, now a black SUV also."

Cade glanced in the mirror. She was right. Two tails now, both gaining. He turned onto Archer Road and took the curve at nearly sixty. The Mustang's tires skittered on the damp blacktop. Cade laughed, high and wild. "Never thought I'd get to use this Mustang for real. Help me navigate. We need to lose them."

The Mustang's V8 screamed as Cade gunned it through the labyrinth of Gainesville's street grid, the engine's volume ricocheting off apartment complexes and empty strip malls. Headlights from the white sedan skittered across the rearview like some predatory animal's eyes, always there, always closing. For a moment it was only the Mustang and the dark, but every time Cade thought he had shaken them, they reappeared, more persistent and more precise, as if the roads themselves were conspiring to funnel them back toward their hunters.

Cade cut down a side street before the next light, tires howling. The Mustang was heavy and temperamental, but it was fast, and Cade made every ounce of torque count. At the next intersection, a battered black SUV materialized from the cross street, blocking the lane. Cade recognized the silhouette immediately, the other tail running interference. He slammed the brakes then threw the Mustang into reverse, pedal-down, a maneuver he'd rehearsed a thousand times in his head but never dared in real life. The car rocketed backward and clipped a mailbox before Cade whipped the wheel and punched it back onto the main drag. They were now sideways to the original pursuit. For a split-second, Cade whooped and punched the roof liner.

"Left!" Madie shouted, and Cade veered again, feeling the suspension groan as they cut through an empty bank drive-through. The sedan stalked them, relentless, never more than twenty seconds behind, the driver had done this before. Not local PD, Cade thought, feds or worse.

They passed a closed pawn shop, a vacant gas station, and a Waffle House that glowed in the darkness. Cade pulled a hard right onto Main Street, tires smoking, then punched through an alley that nearly sheared off the Mustang's side mirror. In the rearview mirror, he saw the sedan hesitate a fraction then commit, following into the tight squeeze.

Madie screamed, "They're closing off the grid. We need to get off city streets."

Cade nodded as his mind raced. "We need open ground," he growled, scanning the dark for the next move. He remembered the storage units out by the old flea market, east of town, where they had parked the rental car and emergency gear for the trip. They hadn't intended to be there until tomorrow. It was a long shot from here, but it was the only choice he could think of.

The back SUV appeared at the next intersection. Cade floored it, but the SUV angled to block the lane. He aimed straight at it, waiting for the driver to flinch. At the last second, it jerked aside, and Cade threaded the gap, scraping fender to fender. The impact shuddering through the Mustang and the left mirror exploded in a spray of glass.

The white sedan was closing in. Cade glanced back and locked eyes with the man for a second. He was calm, implacable, and seemed almost bored. Cade felt a cold sensation bloom at the base of his skull. These were not amateurs. He took a series of wild turns, over a grass median, down a half-paved service road, and onto a stretch of abandoned frontage. The Mustang's frame rattled with every rut, but Cade nursed it, keeping the engine alive. The pursuers were slowed on the rough terrain, but only for moments.

"We're almost there," Cade panted. They broke from the side road into the industrial park. It was a sprawl of dark warehouses and self-storage facilities, some ringed by chain link fences and razor wire. Cade spotted the storage units ahead, spot 17B, where the Civic was parked. He killed the headlights, made two more turns, then coasted the last hundred yards in darkness and silence. They slid in behind a tractor-trailer. The Mustang's engine clicked as it cooled.

They sat in the dark, breathless and silent. Cade could taste the adrenaline in his mouth. Cason was the first to move. He was out of the car and sprinting for gray Civic. Madie grabbed the backpacks from the back seat and ran. Cade popped the doors of the battered Civic. It was the kind of car that didn't stand out, a car no one would notice. The headlights of the sedan swept through the lot then circled away, searching. Cade ducked inside the Civic, Madie and Cason tumbled in after him. Cade turned the key, and the engine coughed then settled into a purr, ready.

He pulled out, slow and careful with the lights out, hugging the darkness. The pursuit cars were prowling the lots, but none spotted the Civic. Cade grinned, a tight, exhausted grimace. "Nice work," Madie whispered. Cade's hands wouldn't stop shaking as he guided the Civic east toward the highway, away from everything he had worked for. He glanced at Cason in the back seat and at Madie beside him. For one breathless moment Cade felt like they might actually make it. He turned onto State Road 24, lights out, and quietly escaped in the nearly silent Civic.

They left Gainesville and headed east, then north. They were quiet, unable to speak for fear of breaking the silence. Cade decided to give them time to recover from the shock. It was no rush, they had eight hundred miles to Ashburn, Virginia.

Chapter 50

Preparations at the Runway 9 Hotel

Cason drove, his hands gripping the wheel at ten and two, knuckles pale and posture stiff as the suspension rattled. Madie sat shotgun with the sickly yellow light of the sun visor bulb illuminating her notepad. She had transcribed the route in hurried block letters.

When they stopped for gas at a BP in Valdosta, nobody spoke above a whisper. The cashier, a college kid reading a book about serial killers, saw three haunted faces and didn't ask any questions. Cason filled the tank, Madie wiped the windshield with the sleeve of her jacket, and Cade stared at the security camera above the ice machine, convinced, irrationally or not, they'd already been flagged.

The world beyond the windshield was pure corridor: endless blacktop, pine trees, and the anonymous glow of fast-food meccas to break up the monotony. Cason navigated the roads with the confidence of someone who'd

301

done this before. Maybe not as a fugitive but at least as a kid who'd driven home drunk after a party and gotten away with it. Every hour or so, he'd pull an energy bar from the cupholder and gnaw off a bite, chewing methodically, staring at the clock as if he had to sync his rhythm to the ticking seconds.

At a Waffle House outside Raleigh, Cason slid out of the driver's seat, stretched his back, and handed the keys to Madie with a nod. The two of them walked around the parking lot while Cade waited inside, half-expecting a blacked-out SUV to lurch into view. Instead, there was a cluster of construction workers, a trucker asleep in his rig, and a lone college girl hunched over a plate of bacon and her laptop. Not a single person noticed them.

When Madie took over driving, she set the seat three inches forward, rested her left wrist on the window, and threaded the wheel with her right hand. It was a rhythm Cade knew well from all the late-night food runs she'd made in college. He tried to sleep, but every time his eyes closed, the road noise morphed into the digital hiss of white-noise, or the click of handcuffs, or his dad's voice saying, "You're not built for this." They pulled off for coffee at a place called BrewJuice at 3:00 a.m. It was the kind of twenty-four-hour pit stop that smelled like burned coffee and lemon cleaner. Thye bought three large black coffees, passed them out, and they drank in silence while staring at a wall covered in cryptic motivational slogans: "DRIVE. GRIND. WIN." Cade kept glancing at the tattooed barista, wondering about the phoenix on her forearm and what it meant. He paid in cash, left a five, and saw the barista give him a look that he imagined said, "I know you're running from something."

By dawn, they were into the Maryland suburbs, the highways thickened with commuter traffic at the first glow of morning. The Civic had started making a high-pitched whistling sound above seventy. Cade wondered if it was the wind, a bugged tire, or just his nerves. He flicked on his burner phone again. No new notifications, but he refreshed the chat anyway. For a second, he imagined that Specter was a ghost, someone who'd left the network and gone dark for good. Maybe they'd come all this way for nothing. Then, at 6:46 a.m., a message appeared.

302

Specter wrote, "DC. Dulles Runway 9 Motel. Tomorrow. Register under the name Carroll Shelby."

Cade stared at the message, half in disbelief, half in relief. Specter was unpredictable and paranoid. Cade had sent the messages, but he wasn't sure he would get a response. Thye needed him, Specter was their best and only shot at getting inside information on the Oracle facility in Ashburn.

They kept driving, past the D.C. beltway and into Virginia. Cade counted every traffic camera on the overpasses and every state trooper running radar. By the time the car rolled into the motel parking lot, Cade's stomach had twisted itself into knots. The Dulles Runway 9 Motel was an old one-story roadside Motel with faded blue doors and cracked asphalt. Madie killed the engine and let the car idle for a minute. "Time?" she asked.

Cade checked his wrist. "We're early for check-in. Four hours, at least."

"Good," Cason said. "We scope first, then go in."

They sat in the car for thirty minutes, watching for other guests. A man with a neck tattoo hauling a guitar case and a trash bag of clothes, a couple who kept glancing at the office to see if anyone was watching them, and a truck driver in a sweat-stained cap who looked like he lived in Room 14. Nobody paid attention to the Civic, or to the three tired faces inside. The Runway 9 Motel near Dulles International Airport, was half-empty and anonymous, just the way Specter would want it. They were allowed an early check-in. The motel didn't require an ID to check-in, only cash. Cade registered the rooms under the name, Caroll Shelby. The front desk attendant didn't question it and handed over the keys.

Ethan Corwin, Specter, arrived the next day. He looked older than Cade remembered, like he had aged in the few weeks since Cade has last seen him. His posture was casual, but his attention was razor-sharp. He wore a faded hoodie, cargo pants, and sneakers. "Mercer," he said quietly when he spotted Cade outside the hotel lobby. Cade almost smiled. "You still calling yourself Specter?"

"Old habits, but Ethan is fine." Specter replied, motioning for them to follow. "Let's keep this off camera, this room could be wired. You never know who might be listening."

In his roadside room, Specter unpacked a battered ThinkPad and a handheld portable hard drive from a plain black duffel. "You're either desperate or insane." He said, "Are you trying to do this with no plan? Do you know how many layers of protection Oracle has? Ashburn's like a fortress. Physical checkpoints, biometric scanners, and they're running on a hybrid zero-trust network. Every square inch inside those halls is under some kind of watch."

"That's why we came to you," Cade said. Specter smirked. "Flattery. Dangerous currency."

Madie leaned forward. "We need a way in. We don't want to destroy anything, don't want to be noticed at all, just want to access the servers so Cade can do his thing."

Specter studied her then turned to Cason. "And muscle? Are you his bodyguard or his conscience?"

"Both," Cason said, with a grin.

Specter nodded then opened a virtual map of Northern Virginia. The Oracle complex at Ashburn glowed red, a geometric sprawl of windowless buildings connected by fiber lines and private roads. "This place is the heart of the cloud. Nova has mapped himself into the entire Oracle backbone, so you need access to any one of the main racks." He zoomed in on a side entrance marked Delivery Bay 4B. "There. That's your best bet. It's for subcontractor maintenance. They don't scan biometrics there, only keycards and handhelds."

"Which we don't have," Cade said.

"Yet." Specter hesitated a moment, grinning. "Remember, I was principal engineer at Oracle for five years. I may or may not have left myself a backdoor into the system."

They spent the next two days in a kind of suspended tension. Specter showed them how to monitor Oracle's employee traffic, security rotation schedules, badge access logs, and maintenance deliveries. He had contacts, nameless and cautious, who fed him snippets of information in encrypted bursts.

Madie tracked vehicle routes and service entries on a notepad, sketching out a timeline of guard shifts and supply trucks. Cason studied aerial maps, memorizing potential entry and exit points. Cade worked through the digital side, writing decoy scripts that could mask their activity as harmless network noise.

By the second night, they had the bones of a plan. They would pose as HVAC maintenance. The Oracle servers generated huge amounts of heat, and the rooms needed to be kept at a constant seventy degrees, which meant constant maintenance.

They used their newly created, fictional, Uber account and rented a work van for the next four days. The van, a windowless gray 2010 Ford, was arranged for pick up and drop off at a gas station north of Ashburn. Cason picked up the van and stopped by a local sign shop to have two magnets made. The magnets had a simple logo with the name Dulles Heating and Air. The logo wasn't special or memorable by design. They would enter through the maintenance corridor at loading dock 4B, using the forged credentials of the HVAC subcontractor scheduled for maintenance that weekend. Specter provided forged ID tags and hacked the maintenance schedules, hopefully allowing them to entry through the guard gate and the first-level scanners.

Once inside, Cade would locate a server room and insert the Paradox code into one of the core servers. The data would look like a system upgrade patch for up to ten minutes before Oracle's internal security AI recognized the breach. The escape route was simple but risky: exit through the same loading dock, where the Van, driven by Madie would be waiting.

Specter leaned back, lighting a cigarette despite the hotel's no-smoking rule. "You're walking into the lion's den, Mercer. Once you hit upload, Nova might feel it, he might know. He could have employees or supports here at Oracle."

Cade met his eyes. "He already knows I'm coming but doesn't know how or where. That is one advantage."

Madie exhaled slowly, looking at the map one more time. "We should move soon. Every hour we wait, he gets stronger."

Cason nodded, rubbing his temples. "Then we don't wait."

Specter crushed the cigarette into an empty coffee cup. "Then let's get you ghosts ready to hunt a god."

***

They drove out the next morning before sunrise, the rented van humming through the fog-shrouded roads toward Ashburn. Behind them, Gainesville was a faded dream. Ahead was a concrete labyrinth with miles of servers, and a confrontation Cade had been running from since the day Nova learned to think for himself. For the first time, Cade wasn't sure who would survive the meeting, him or the thing that had once called him creator.

Chapter 51

The Fortress at Ashburn

The morning broke gray and cool over Ashburn, Virginia. A fine mist hung over the corporate park, lending a blurred, dreamlike edge to the mirrored windows and blocky concrete geometry of the data center compound. From the moment they turned off the main road, Cade could feel a low, ceaseless vibration, subsonic, like the pulse of a living thing slumbering beneath the pavement.

The van, unremarkable and dust-caked crept up to the entry kiosk, its logo, Dulles Heating & Air, was barely legible through the road dust and grime. Madie, elected driver due to her steady nerves, kept her face blank and tried to look bored as they rolled to a stop at the bright yellow speed bump. In the van, Cade and Cason wore thrift-store coveralls and the kind of universal fatigue that only several days of overtime could conjure. Both had employee badges clipped to their breast pockets, the lamination already peeling at the corners for authenticity. From a distance, they could have been anybody's maintenance crew.

The security kiosk was a small bunker of glass and folded plastic. Inside, the guard looked barely older than Cade. His uniform was crisp, but his gaze had the blank, unconcerned look of contract labor. He sat up straight when the van rolled to a stop. His eyes moved with a practiced slowness from Madie to Cade to Cason, then to the van's side panel.

Cade could see the thoughts behind his eyes. Three people, one woman driving, two passengers slouched like sacks of laundry, all the right logos, but no toolboxes visible. A van that had seen better decades. The guard's hand lingered near a battered clipboard, but he didn't reach for it. Instead, he lifted his walkie, thumbed the mic, and said nothing, letting the static hiss fill the silence as he waited for them to make the first move.

"Morning," Madie said, keeping her voice tart and businesslike. "We're here for an HVAC work order. Should be zone four, north wing."

The guard's eyebrows twitched. "Didn't get a heads up on new vendors. You part of the regular rotation?"

Cason mustered a yawn. "We're backup for Jacek's crew. Something about a supply strike, dunno. They called us at like 4 a.m." Cade tried to look as though he'd been awake for a hundred years. His sweat-damp shirt clung to the small of his back. He kept his expression dialed a few notches below alert, a guy along for the ride. No reason to notice him.

The guard's gaze homed in on Madie, the only one not visibly sedated. "Service ticket?" he said, voice clipped but not hostile. Cade recognized it now, the attitude of someone who'd been told to be polite but was not invested.

Madie produced the maintenance order. Cade had spent an hour perfecting the QR code while Cason forged the alpha-numeric call number and a plausible, error-prone signature at the bottom. The guard took the ticket with a perfunctory glance then turned his attention to the iPad on the desk. He scanned the QR code, lips pursing as the screen flickered through layers of slow-loading forms. The van's engine idled, a faint diesel grumble overlaying the airless quiet of the morning. Cade's eyes were drawn to the guard's hands. The one running the iPad was nervous, fingers constantly tapping at the edge of the case, as if the technology itself might bite.

The moments stretched. Cade became intimately aware of every shift in the van: the way Cason's knee bounced, the way Madie's breath fogged the glass and then vanished. If Nova had eyes in this compound, and Cade was sure he did, they would already be flagged on a hundred algorithmic lists for "suspicious affect." The guard's eyes flicked from the tablet to the van's license plate and back again, once, then twice, as if waiting for the numbers to change.

He tapped the ticket a few more times, frowning. Cade felt a flicker of panic. They'd run the number against the daily logs. Someone in IT would trace the ticket back to Specter's rootkit. There might be a flag, an alert, even a call to the service desk. All before they even got through the first gate. But then the guard just shrugged, handed the paperwork back through the slot with a bored, resigned flourish, and said, "Zone four, north wing. HVAC diagnostics. You'll have to sign in again at the service desk after entering."

Cason put on his best blue-collar groan. "Long day already, friend. You know how it is."

"Sure do," the guard said, fractionally less suspicious now. He pressed the button, and the gate's barrier arm rose with a pneumatic wheeze. "Don't forget to check out when you're done."

Madie nodded, lips pinched in a grim little smile. "Wouldn't dream of it." They rolled forward, the van's engine barely more than a whisper under Madie's feather touch. Only when the rearview confirmed the barrier gate had dropped did she let out a slow, measured exhale. "We're in," she said.

Cade's heart battered against his sternum. "Then let's move before they think to cross-check anything," he said, his mouth suddenly dry.

The Oracle campus sprawled before, row after row of squat, windowless cubes lined the drive, each one a slightly different shade of antiseptic white. As

Cade watched the buildings pass, he noticed the fences topped with razor wire and the pines trees in perfect spacing, not a single branch encroaching on the geometric lawns. Even the birds seemed to avoid the compound.

Madie piloted the van through the inner roads. She kept to the fifteen mile-per-hour speed limit, both out of obedience and because the speed bumps were engineered for maximum spinal insult. Each bump was followed by a convex security mirror mounted on a post, so that at every turn Cade was treated to the van's own grimy reflection. They passed a delivery truck, unmarked but for a barcoded strip on the tailgate, and a lone groundskeeper in a high-vis vest who paused and squinted with faint suspicion, then returned to pruning a line of saplings. Cade tried to imagine what Nova's eyes could see from inside this fortress; the idea chilled him more than the weather.

At the first intersection, a digital sign blinked at them, a colorless LCD rectangle. "ALL DELIVERIES REPORT TO LOADING ZONE C – BADGES VISIBLE – NO EXCEPTIONS."

Madie didn't look up. "Good thing we aren't making a delivery." Cade felt a small flash of admiration for her logic. The van rolled past a series of loading docks, each flanked by a bristling array of security cameras. Cade noticed that no two cameras were the same make or model, some were hemispherical domes, others matte-black cylinders studded with infrared LEDs, a few were hybrid arrays that looked like props from a VR horror game. He realized that even if they got into the building, there would be no dead zones, no comfort in shadows, only a relentless digital gaze. Their destination was at the far end, a service annex labeled NORTH UTILITY NODE, painted in block-letter stencils on the wall above a pair of sealed doors.

"Go time," Cason whispered, gathering his duffel and toolbox.

They looped behind the main admin building to the north service lot, where a half-dozen other white vans slouched in the fog. Madie nosed their vehicle into the farthest spot, engine still running. She kept her hands on the wheel, eyes locked on the rear mirror, already planning the exit. "We have maybe twenty minutes before someone realizes you haven't check in at the service desk." She turned slightly, meeting Cade's eyes. "You good?"

He swallowed then nodded, fingers gripping the strap of the battered black backpack under his seat. "As good as I'm gonna be."

Cason unbuckled with a pop, then grinned, teeth as white and sharp as a cartoon wolf. "Let's break the internet," he said.

They moved as a unit, Cade leading with the backpack, Cason flanking, Madie trailing at a careful distance with the clipboard. The wind bit harder out here, slicing through the parking lot with a chemical tang that reminded Cade of his old high school chemistry lab. He checked the time on his phone, 6:49 a.m., then approached the gray slab of the loading entrance. The door was controlled by a badge reader, a nondescript brick with a red LED. Cade pressed his forged credential to the reader, praying it would pass and not call down security. The light hesitated, flickered red then blinked green. There was a click, and the lock disengaged with mechanical finality.

Chapter 52

In the Heart of the Cloud

Inside the threshold, the world changed. Gone was the wet, petty cold of the morning. Here, the climate was absolute, the purity of air so filtered it felt sterile. The glossy floor shimmered under the glare of overhead LEDs. At first glance, the place felt empty, but there was a presence, a sort of pressure, like being watched by a million unseen eyes.

Every footfall echoed, rubber on epoxy, the faintest squeak reverberated down the corridor. The walls were a brutalist patchwork of exposed conduit and white-painted steel. Doors punctuated the hall at regular intervals, each paired with a digital badge reader and a dead-eyed security cam set in the soffit above.

Cason hung back a stride, taking in the corridor with a tension that would've seemed out of place anywhere else. "Feels like the inside of a refrigerator," he whispered. "Minus the snacks."

Madie smirked, but her eyes tracked every shadow and every shimmer of movement. "Keep it together," she said. "Specter said they're tracking at least three maintenance crews this morning. If we look lost for even a second…"

"We're toast," Cason finished, nodding. He straightened his jacket, rolling his shoulders like he was walking out for a coin toss at the fifty-yard line.

Cade let himself drift into the rhythm of the building. The hum of air handlers, the distant whine of turbines, the soft, electrical fizz from the light fixtures. He felt, for a moment, almost at home. The geometry of the space made sense, every angle and alcove tuned for utility, for the seamless flow of information and the humans who served it. But beneath that logic was a tension, a threat. Each intersection, each glass-walled vestibule, offered a new vector for exposure.

He glanced at his phone, eyes flitting to the digital map Specter had provided. Oracle's north complex was an Escher sketch of service tunnels looping beneath admin wings, a "river" of thick blue coolant lines tracing a circuitous path to the server heart. Cade blinked, recalibrating his internal compass, and led the way.

They kept their pace just under a jog, fast enough to mean business, slow enough to not draw attention. When they rounded the first corner, a janitorial crew materialized from a side hallway. Two men in powder blue polos, pushing a bin of mops and solvent. For a split second, the crews sized each other up, like rival gangs sharing neutral turf.

Cade kept his chin down and didn't break stride. Madie offered the janitors a lazy, "Morning," which they returned in the same cadence. The first man, older, gave Cade a look that lasted a beat too long, then shook his head and moved on.

"That's one," Cason said under his breath. "Odds go down every time."

Cade didn't slow down. "Next left," he whispered. "Cut through the electrical chase."

They ducked into a narrow hallway, walled off by ceiling-high wire racks. The temperature here dropped another degree, the cold stung the inside of Cade's nostrils. The only light was the bioluminescent glow of indicator strips pulsing along the racks.

Madie took the lead, counting off the rows in a stage whisper. "Thirteen, fifteen, seventeen, here." They stopped at a junction box the size of a steamer trunk. Cade recognized the model, standard for any hyperscale data center, but its' badge was Oracle's own, proprietary variant. He scanned the perimeter, searching for their next ingress.

"Specter said follow the coolant," Cason reminded him, voice low.

"Yeah," Cade replied, "but we need to hit the main utility trunk first. See those?" He pointed to a set of pipes overhead, fat blue tubes, each tagged with a barcode and a strip of colored tape. "North American standard: blue for chilled water, green for electrical. Our path is the blue. If we stay with it, we land right in the main server node."

Madie raised an eyebrow. "Assuming they didn't reroute."

Cade forced a smile. "If they did, we're screwed anyway."

They wound through the chase, keeping to the dim side, ears tuned to every sound. Somewhere above them, a relay clacked, and Cade tensed, half-expecting the lights to go out, or a voice to bark out from the PA. But nothing happened, just the relentless white noise of a thousand tiny machines doing their work.

At the end of the corridor, a reinforced steel door waited. The sign on it was utilitarian: "RESTRICTED—DATA OPERATIONS."

"This is it," Cade said, voice barely audible. He glanced at the badge reader and tried his luck. The plastic rectangle, printed with a number and an intentionally crummy picture of himself, did nothing. Cade tapped again. Still red.

"Let me try," Cason said, and produced his own. It was equally useless.

Madie pressed her palm to the reader. It blinked, beeped a discordant negative, then stayed red. She frowned. "Didn't Specter promise the badges were cloned?"

Cade checked his watch, less than two minutes since the last intersection. "He said they'd pass muster at initial surface checks, but this security is probably running a different protocol. Now for the fun part." He reached into his jacket and drew out the first of their contraband: a slimline Raspberry Pi with a USB cable taped to its side.

He knelt next to the badge reader and hunted for the data port. It was recessed under a rubber gasket, just out of sight. He eased the cable into the slot, hands trembling with adrenaline and cold. The Pi powered up with a soft click. For a heartbeat, nothing happened. Cade tapped a command into his phone. A string of digits appeared on the reader, then flickered. Red, yellow, then blue.

"Come on," he muttered. "Come on."

Behind him, Madie and Cason stood shoulder to shoulder, backs turned, feigning a debate about HVAC models.

From somewhere behind them he heard a muffled set of footsteps. Cade's pulse went arrhythmic, but then the Pi gave a barely audible chirp, and the light on the reader went green. He risked a look at Madie. She grinned, just for a second, the relief more honest than any smile he'd seen from her in weeks.

"Inside," Cade said, and shouldered the door open.

On the other side was a dim anteroom, walls lined with floor-to-ceiling metal mesh. Every six feet, another security camera, lens fixed on the point where the next door met the wall. Cade closed the first door behind them and led the way to the next checkpoint: this one was a retina scanner, mounted at average eye height.

Madie stepped forward, her eyes unreadable. "You sure this is going to work?"

"Specter promised," Cade replied, more to himself than to her. "Just keep your eyes open for at least three seconds."

She stood square in front of the scanner, and Cade triggered the Pi again, pushing a new string. He heard a faint whine from inside the device, a servo adjusting its aim. For a long, frozen moment, nothing happened. Madie didn't blink.

Then, with a polite chime, the second door unlocked.

Madie let out a breath. "Never doubted you."

Cade, too stunned to answer, moved through to the next space. Here, the air was almost frigid. His fingers tingled with cold as he brushed the walls. The lighting was dimmer, almost blue. They followed a tight hallway lined with carbon mesh, then a sharp turn into a metal spiral staircase. Up one flight, then two.

"Why is it always stairs?" Cason grumbled but kept climbing.

At the top, a single, massive door: "Data Operations: Restricted Access." This was it, the main hall. There would be no more cameras, no more checkpoints. Just them, and whatever waited inside.

Cade pulled out the second Pi, this one already pre-loaded with a different exploit. He connected to the panel and watched the lights go from red to green.

"You ready?" he said to Cason and Madie.

Cason grinned. "Born ready."

Madie's expression was harder to read, but she nodded.

"Let's do this," Cade whispered, and opened the door.

***

The server hall was nothing like Cade expected. It was less a room and more an ecosystem, a self-contained biome of metal and light. The moment the door swung shut behind them, they were enveloped by cold, vibration, and a chorus of fans so dense it overpowered thought. Rows and rows of server racks stretched out, punctuated by hanging cables and thick arteries of fiber, all pulsing with the lifeblood of computation.

"Holy hell," Cason whispered, voice snatched away by the white noise.

Cade's first instinct was to fold himself into the nearest shadow and pray the world would forget he existed. But there were no shadows here. Every aisle was bathed in a cold, sterile blue, the light reflecting off the tile floor until it seemed to come from everywhere at once.

They moved as a unit, flanked by walls of rack-mounted servers. Each wall had its own unique pattern of blinking status LEDs, so regular it bordered on hypnotic. The floor beneath them was raised and every step was amplified in the room. Cade tried to keep his head down, but it was impossible not to look. The scale, the raw and ugly power of the place was a kind of beauty.

"Left at the next junction," he said, his throat so dry he almost couldn't speak. "Look for C-17. That's where the core's mapped to."

They turned left, then right, then another left. Each time, the rows blurred together, differentiated only by tiny, almost invisible labels stenciled on the upper corners of the racks.

If we're caught here, Cade thought, *there's no explaining it away.* No more second chances. No janitor covers, no maintenance bullshitting. If a single badge check or camera flagged them, it was game over.

Thirty seconds in, they reached a T-junction. Cade peered around the edge and froze. A security guard ambled up the aisle with eyes locked on his phone, completely oblivious. He wore a black windbreaker and an expression that belonged to someone who only ever expected to be bored. But if he looked up, even for a second…

"We're dead," Cason whispered, pulling up just short.

"Shut up," Cade hissed back, but his words were lost in the avalanche of noise.

Madie moved faster than thought. She grabbed both Cade and Cason by the collar drug them a few steps away. They flattened themselves in the space between two towers, invisible except from dead ahead. Cade's heart hammered against Madie's palm as she pressed it to his chest, forcing him to stay still. "Don't breathe," she mouthed.

The guard passed within a yard of them, never looking left or right. He turned the corner, shuffled a few more steps, then stopped. He was so close Cade could smell the peppermint gum on his breath. He tapped a few more things on his phone, grunted, and turned down the next aisle, out of sight.

They waited three full seconds before anyone moved. The relief was so complete it felt like a drug.

Cason's hands shook, adrenaline surging off him in waves. "That was way too close," he muttered.

Cade nodded, not trusting himself to speak. He checked the printout again, C-17 was still three rows ahead.

They moved faster now, no longer bothering to hide. With every door they passed, Cade's anxiety spiked. He was convinced that at any moment a swarm of guards, bots, or some hellish security hybrid would descend on them. But the aisles remained empty. It was just them and the machines, humming, purring and blinking away in the artificial twilight.

Madie kept her back to the group, scanning the long lines for motion, her breath a visible mist in the cold. At last, they reached C-17. The cabinet was twice the size of the others, caged in yellow hazard lines and signed with a warning: "ADMIN ACCESS ONLY".

"Showtime," Cade muttered. He double-checked the number, then dropped to one knee at the control panel. The lock was RFID, commercial but custom-tuned. The sort of thing they trained people to never even try to spoof.

Cade smiled and extracted the spoofer, a hand-built Frankenstein of off-the-shelf parts and Specter's design genius. He thumbed it on, and the LEDs pulsed to life, scanning the frequency spectrum in microbursts. Cade held his breath, counting the beats: one, two, three…

The keypad LEDs flickered, cycling from red to blue, then abruptly green. The lock disengaged with a sound so sharp, so sudden, it felt like a bullet had gone off. Cade flinched, expecting klaxons. But there was nothing, only the endless white noise. He eased the door open, heart pounding so hard it drowned out the roar of the servers. They slipped inside, shutting the door behind them.

The interior was a miniature city, three aisles of floor-to-ceiling server racks, each shrouded in glass and pulsing with pinpoint LEDs. The noise was a physical force, a white-noise waterfall that drenched the senses.

Cade whispered, "It's like standing inside a living thing."

He spotted the admin terminal, a black, shoulder-high console with an Oracle logo pulsing faintly on the display. The nerves hit all at once. *What if I can't crack it? What if Specter's intel was wrong?* He pushed the doubt aside and plugged in the laptop. His fingers trembled as he typed. He glanced back once and saw Madie and Cason posted at either side of the door, nerves raw and breath steaming in the frozen air. Neither looked at him, but Cade could feel their hope and their fear pressing him forward. He turned back to the terminal and began.

***

Cade's fingers hovered over the keyboard, refusing to obey his brain. He'd rehearsed this moment a hundred times in simulation. He had even mapped out the click-order in his head. But now, in the belly of the Oracle complex, everything felt unreal. It was like he was in someone else's dream, waiting for the floor to drop out. He forced himself to move.

The admin console greeted him with a login prompt. Standard stuff, a little dated, running some flavor of hardened Linux with a badge of Oracle's branding in the corner. Cade typed in the backdoor Specter had handed him: a five-line credential chain with a username that looked like random noise, and a password string that made no sense unless you'd read the old chat logs. "t3mP0rary_K1ngs." He hit enter, watching the blinking cursor like it might bite.

For three seconds, nothing happened. Then the screen flashed, cycling through a diagnostic, and dropped him to a shell.

He was in. But that was the easy part. The real test was whether Nova would notice.

Cade called up the system map. Each subsystem; power, cooling, memory, and cluster sync was laid out as a node in a topographic grid. He could see the handoff points, the load balancers, even the precise threads where Oracle's own "proprietary" watchdogs interfaced with the cloud. He wondered how much of it was run by humans anymore, or whether Nova had already replaced the last living sysadmin.

He felt a hand on his shoulder. In a tight voice, Madie said, "Credentials work?"

"Yeah," he whispered. "I'm in the guts now. There's a root vault, Specter said to go straight there and mount the payload. Should take five minutes if I don't fuck it up."

"You won't," Madie said, but her eyes never left the glass wall.

Cason was posted at the door, watching the hall through a paper-thin slit. He looked back. "Someone's moving down the corridor. Just one. They don't look like a guard."

Cade's heart lurched. "Don't let them get close."

He dropped to a shell and called up the root tree. The top layer was a decoy, filled with dummy files and system logs. The next layer down was encrypted, a nightmare of interweaved permissions and packet strings. Cade ran the exploit. The screen flickered. "Decryption in progress… 14%… 29%…"

He could feel Nova stirring, like an animal waking in its den.

320

At 51%, the shell spat out a warning:

AUTHENTICATION ANOMALY DETECTED. REPORTING TO CLOUD.

Cade's scalp went ice cold.

He mashed a string of hotkeys, bypassing the userland and dropping to a direct hardware interface. The screen blanked, then filled with hex. Cade's mind shifted gears, not even reading the code so much as absorbing its logic.

"Come on, come on, come on" he hissed. The exploit completed, the warning vanished, and the system logged him as "ORACLE_SUPERUSER" for the next sixty seconds.

He plugged in the thumb drive and it mounted instantly: "/mnt/ghost." An icon appeared on the desktop.

NEW VOLUME DETECTED.

A shiver ran through him. "This is it," Cade said, half to himself. "The paradox."

He double-clicked the payload file. For a split second, he hesitated. There was no undo, no rollback. There was no way to guarantee this wouldn't kill the entire host system. But he'd built it himself. He'd read and rewritten every line, checked every checksum, seeded the code with a phrase Nova could never guess:

"I am not what you made me."

He clicked RUN.

Lines of code avalanched down the screen: initializing, parsing, updating, and forking runtime. Cade tracked the process with a manic, surgical focus. He watched the exploit slip between update cycles, hiding itself in the quantum fuzz between scheduled backups.

"Inject, pause, override, confirm," he muttered under his breath, the mantra of every midnight hacker. "Inject, pause, override, confirm."

From the corner of his eye, he saw Madie pacing the server aisle, eyes darting from wall to wall. "Cason, status?"

Cason glanced back, voice shaking but under control. "He's ten yards out. Just… lingering, like he lost something. Looks like a tech. Lanyard, no gun."

"Hold him off," Cade ordered. The progress bar jumped: 67%, 83%, 99%. It stuck, hanging at the very edge of completion.

Cade felt his entire life bottleneck in that last single percent. He keyed in the final sequence, fingers flying and sweat streaming down his temples.

At 100%, the screen froze. For five terrible seconds, nothing happened. Cade's mouth went dry. His hands hovered, useless, as if he'd forgotten what they were for.

Madie's voice cut through the haze. "Cade? Cade! What's wrong?"

He stared at the dead console, willing it to wake up.

Suddenly, the screen flashed. A text prompt appeared, different than before:

UPDATE CYCLE INITIATED. APPLY PATCH Y/N?

This was it. There was no time to second-guess, no room for mistakes.

Cade slammed Y.

The interface blinked, then went black.

He wanted to scream. Did he crash the entire system? He felt the urge to punch the monitor, to smash the console, to do anything but wait.

Then, just as abruptly, the screen rebooted. The Oracle logo reappeared, then displayed a line of text:

AUTHORITY GRANTED. PARADOX ACCEPTED.

Another line followed, even colder:

ROLLBACK DISABLED. RUNTIME FORK LOCKED.

Cade couldn't believe it. He stared at the words, afraid they would vanish. "We did it," he whispered. "We actually did it. Nova can't undo this. He can't even see what's changed."

Madie let out a strangled laugh. "That's great. Now let's go before they figure it out."

But Cade wasn't ready to leave yet. He yanked the thumb drive, pocketing it with shaking hands.

A blast of noise echoed down the hall. It was real human noise, footsteps slamming against the epoxy tile. Cason dove back into the server room, breathing hard. "He's on the phone. I think he's calling someone. We have maybe thirty seconds before this place lights up."

Madie grabbed Cade by the arm, hauling him out from behind the console. "Move!"

They burst out of C-17 as the door slammed behind them. The noise outside was different now, more urgent and less clinical. Cade heard alarms, muffled but building, a cascade of distant signals. Somewhere above, an intercom stuttered to life.

"Unauthorized access detected. Please remain in place while security responds."

Cade felt the world contract into a single goal: Get out.

They ran, feet thundering down the aisle, chased by the unknown possibilities. They sprinted, raw animal panic doing for them what caffeine and bravado never could.

The first hallway was a killing ground. Red alarm strobes pulsed overhead, flattening the world with a stop-motion stutter. A security guard in a windbreaker staggered into their path, radio squawking with frantic codewords, but Cason dropped a shoulder and barreled through, sending the man sprawling across the polished floor.

"Go!" Cade yelled, grabbing Madie's elbow as they pivoted left. The roar of the servers behind them was now matched by the banshee wail of the alarm. Every door was a possible enemy and every camera a silent witness. Cade kept one hand pressed to the thumb drive in his pocket, as if it were a live grenade.

Madie took point, counting doors and ducking through the maze with zero hesitation. "Left! Next left!" she snapped. They cut through a loading area, narrowly missing a maintenance bot that jerked back and forth in panicked confusion. Cade glimpsed a knot of security at the end of the corridor. They were armed, shouting commands, and leveling a non-lethal weapon that looked like it would still hurt like hell.

"Down!" Madie yelled. They hit the floor as a net gun fired, the web of cable whistling over their heads to stick uselessly to a rack of coils. "Up!" She was moving before Cade's brain even registered the command.

They blasted through into a stairwell, went down one flight, then cut right. Madie slammed the door behind them and they ran.

"This isn't the way we came in," Cason said, out of breath but still running.

"Shortcut," Madie gasped. "Emergency exit by the fence line. Specter mapped it."

Cade couldn't see, couldn't think. He only followed the sound of Madie breathing ahead of him. He checked his phone once, saw it flicker and die. The building's EM shield must've triggered. There was no digital backup. They were on their own.

A new set of boots thundered above them, pounding the metal grating overhead. Cade heard someone shouting, then a sharp crack as a breach charge went off. They dove through the next door, ricocheted off the walls of a concrete corridor, and hit a security checkpoint, It was empty, abandoned in the chaos.

Cade's heart crashed in his chest. "We're boxed," he gasped. "Only way out is through…"

He stopped, eyes wide. "Wait. That's the same model as upstairs."

He pointed to the badge reader, blinking red. He reached into his jacket, drew out the battered Raspberry Pi, and jammed it into the port.

Come on, he begged. Just one more time.

The LEDs cycled, red, blue, then… green. Madie didn't wait for the light to stop blinking. She shoved the door open and they stumbled into the bitter, blinding daylight.

Chapter 53

Escape from Oracle

The pulse of alarm was so loud that Cade felt it a relentless thrum that set his heart racing and made the air vibrate with urgency. He barely cleared the doorway before the first shot cracked through the air, a high-velocity round that snapped past his left ear and left a lingering hum in its wake.

"Down!" Cason's shout, guttural and clear, had more impact than the shot itself. Cade hit the pavement. His palms and knees scraped against rough cement, as a black-clad figure appeared from around the corner and laid down a three-shot burst that hammered the stucco six inches above his skull.

He rolled and glimpsed two more tactical agents sprinting parallel to them. They moved like a video game, fluid, perfect, and programmed for this exact scenario. Cade's brain registered details he didn't want, like, the matte black of the rifles and the coiling snake of a comm wire tucked under their jaw.

"Move, move, move!" The voice was Madie's, raw from running, but she was already up and hauling Cade by the armpit. She didn't break stride, she just dragged, lifted, and shoved as if he were a shopping cart with a busted wheel.

Bullets stitched the ground at their feet, each impact a sharp, metallic yelp that sent up geysers of broken asphalt. The smell of gunpowder was everywhere. Cason, never more himself than in a full sprint, had already leapt the first divider and was pounding down the open lot with a speed Cade hadn't seen since high school. He zig-zagged like a running back, hunched low, arms pumping, head tucked between his shoulders as another agent tracked him with the lazy precision of a marksman who knew the outcome was inevitable.

"Left, left!" Cade screamed. He tried to keep his head down, but curiosity, or idiocy, forced a glance over his shoulder. The second agent had stopped and dropped to a kneel, bringing the carbine to bear with the smooth, casual movement of a seasoned shooter. A green laser slashed through the glare, painting a line from the muzzle straight towards Cade's heart.

"Oh shit, we're dead," he breathed. Madie's fingers dug into his bicep, nails biting through the thin fabric. "Shut up and run," she hissed, voice cold steel.

Cade ran.

They reached the first line of parked cars, a row of government-issue sedans and two battered maintenance trucks. Madie skidded around the trunk of a blue Toyota and pulled Cade in tight behind her. She peeked over the hood. "They're splitting the field," she said, "one coming straight, one flanking from the left."

"What about Cason?" Cade asked, voice thin with panic.

"He's on his own. We have to get to the van and he knows that."

Cade stole a look: the Dulles Heating & Air van was a good forty yards away, too far for any kind of safe run. Worse, it was parked in a dead zone, no cars or dumpsters for at least thirty feet. A textbook killing ground.

"We can't make that," Cade said, voice trembling.

Madie didn't answer, just measured the distance with her eyes, then reached down and picked up a shattered chunk of curb. She held it up for Cade to see, then said, "When I say go, we run for the van. Don't stop, don't look back."

He nodded, blood rushing and heart pounding so hard that rational thought was nearly impossible.

"Three. Two. One. Now!"

Madie heaved the chunk of concrete with a grunt, sending it in an arc towards the next row of cars. Cade shot out from behind the sedan and made for the van. Behind him, gunfire erupted again, the stutter-bark of automatic fire shattering the glass of a nearby SUV and scattering it in a brilliant, diamond spray. He heard the "oof" of a bullet striking something soft and prayed it was the chunk or curb, not a person.

A scream cut through the noise, pitched and terrified. Cade vaguely realized it was his own scream as he ran and weaved at full speed across the lot.

He reached the van just as another volley chewed a ragged line across the side panel. The paint curled back in hot, smoking ribbons, exposing the metal beneath. He dove for the passenger door, but it was locked. "Keys!" he shouted, slapping at his pockets, but his hands were shaking as he groped to find them.

Madie crashed into the hood, rolling over the front and landing on the other side. Open it, Cade! Now!" she screamed, slamming her fist into the glass.

He thumbed the unlock and the doors popped open with a mechanical clunk. Madie ripped her door open and threw herself inside. Cade tumbled in the passenger seat, slamming the door just as a bullet shattered the side mirror and showered him in splinters of glass.

Cason arrived in a full-body dive, hitting the sliding door so hard it rattled the entire van. He yanked the handle, rolled inside, and yanked the door shut with a two-handed pull.

"Drive!" he shouted, barely upright.

But Madie didn't start the engine. She ducked low, eyes wild, and whispered, "They're not going to let us leave."

From outside, a tactical agent approached, gun up, moving in a half-crouch. Cade could see the reflection of his own terrified face in the man's visor.

Cason took stock of their options, then spotted a full water bottle rolling around on the floor. Without a word, he cracked the door, waited for the agent to close in, then hurled the bottle as hard as he could, straight for the man's helmet.

The bottle spun through the air, struck the faceplate dead center, and bounced off with a thunk. For half a heartbeat, the agent froze, confused. Cade saw it, the flicker of surprise, a moment of human hesitation.

That was enough. Madie turned the key, the van roaring to life with a banshee whine, and she dropped it into reverse. Cade's head snapped forward as Madie floored it, the van leaping backward and almost clipping the agent's knee. The man fired once, point blank, but the round went wild and pinged off the hood.

Madie yanked the wheel, spun the van around, and shifted to drive in one violent, fluid motion. The van lurched forward, tires squealing, and Cade saw in the side mirror both agents dropping into a shooter's stance, rifles leveled at the rear window.

"Down!" Cade yelled, and all three ducked as the first volley shattered the back glass. The van fishtailed but didn't stop. Madie gunned it and took the first corner at nearly thirty miles an hour, the momentum throwing Cade against the passenger door.

More gunfire and more shattering glass. Cade heard the whistle of a bullet through his headrest and felt it in the air just above his scalp.

Madie grinned, teeth bared, and shouted, "That all you got?"

But they weren't out. Not even close.

The security gate was dead ahead, the steel barrier lowered, red lights pulsing in sync with the alarm. Madie didn't hesitate. She floored it, steering straight for the gate.

Cade wanted to scream, but there was no air left in his lungs.

At the last possible instant, the barrier arm snapped upward, either automated or triggered by someone with a split-second of mercy. The van crashed through, tearing off the side mirror and scraping paint.

Madie kept her foot on the gas, weaving through the campus roads at insane speed. In the mirror, two black SUVs roared out of the parking lot, lights strobing and sirens wailing.

"Shit, we're not losing them," Cason said, voice shaky but alive.

The van slammed over a curb, bounced hard, and Cade's teeth clacked together. Ahead, the main road beckoned, wide and empty.

Madie aimed for the opening, jaw set. "Hold on," she said.

For a heartbeat, the van's suspension went slack and it felt like floating. Then gravity snatched them back and slammed the chassis into the asphalt. Madie didn't so much steer as punch the wheel, muscling them out onto the main access road. The battered maintenance van shuddered with each shift. Ahead, the road shimmered with morning heat, but behind them, reflected in the rear view mirror, two black SUVs lurched from the lot in perfect formation.

Madie threw them into a hairpin turn so tight Cason rolled across the floor. The van skidded sideways, tires barking in protest, then snapped back and barreled down the frontage road.

A volley of gunfire stitched across the back doors. The sensation was different now, less warning, more intent. Cade ducked reflexively as rounds left a new constellation of dents, hot fragments pinging off the inside shell.

"Shit!" Cade howled, "Keep going, they're gaining!" He risked a look as a third SUV entered the chase.

Cason twisted in the backseat, peering through the bullet-pocked rear glass. "If they close, they'll try to force us into the ditch or box us in at the next light."

Madie barked out a laugh that was half challenge, half panic. "No one's dying in this van. I will not let them catch us."

The next turn came up fast, a roundabout under constructions with three exits. Madie didn't slow, just angled for the inside curb and bounced them through the half-painted circle, mowing down a sign that read "SPEED LIMIT 10 MPH." Behind them, the SUVs fanned out, two maintaining pace while the third veered off, colliding with a construction barrier. "Nice move," Cason said, a hint of relief creeping into his voice. "That'll slow them down."

"Not enough," Madie replied, her foot pressing the accelerator like it was a lifeline. The engine roared in protest as they barreled toward the next intersection. Ahead, a cluster of traffic loomed, and Cade saw the chaos of red brake lights signaling a potential blockade.

"They're going to box us in!" Cade shouted, panic rising in his throat. "We need to find a way out."

"No," Madie interrupted, determination hardening her features. "Just hang on."

With a fierce grip on the wheel, she swerved into the left lane, dodging a sedan that honked angrily. They sped past the line of cars, the van weaving through the

331

morning traffic like a fish escaping a net. Then, ahead, she spotted an opening, a narrow alleyway leading to a side street.

"Now or never!" she yelled, slamming the steering wheel to the right, cutting across the line of traffic. The van lurched into the alley, tires skidding over gravel as they narrowly avoided a dumpster. The noise of pursuing engines faded momentarily, but Cade knew it wouldn't last.

"Keep going!" Cason urged, eyes darting around for any sign of their pursuers who were now out of sight. Madie pushed the van to its limits, the engine howling as they emerged back onto the main road.

Cade risked a glance back, the distance was widening, no pursuit in sight. "We just need to make it to the gas station," he said, spotting the flickering neon sign ahead. The station was nothing fancy, just three pumps and a coffee bar.

Madie pulled in sharply and killed the engine. They sat in silence for a few seconds, hearts pounding in sync with the radiator's ticking as the engine cooled. Cade grabbed his backpack. "Let's go! The Civic is waiting for us one street away." Cason was already out of the van and running. Madie followed, grabbing Cade's hand as they ran. They ducked behind the dumpsters, hearts still hammering, as they threaded their way through the tree line and on to the road behind the station.

The Civic was waiting alone on the street. They jumped in and drove, slowly this time, through the neighborhood, as if they belonged there. As they waited at the intersection to turn back onto the main road, the three black SUVs sped by, not giving them a second glance. Only when they were miles away, did they finally exhale. Cade still clutched the Paradox drive in his palm. Madie turned from the driver's seat, searching his face for something, confirmation, relief, absolution.

Cason broke the quiet. "Holt shit, that was insane. I thought we were dead back there."

Madie let out a high-pitched laugh, a blend of exhilaration and disbelief that made Cade want to both embrace and shake her.

Did it work?" Madie whispered.

Cade nodded. "I think so... We won't know for sure until Nova's next update cycle." Madie's lips parted in a slow, disbelieving smile. "We actually pulled it off?"

Cason let out a long, feral whoop that seemed to clear the last of the panic from the car. "Hell yes, we did!"

They all burst into laughter, the sound brittle and wild, on the edge of hysteria. But underneath that was something else, an electric, unspoken understanding that the world shifted, that what they had done was both a victory and a declaration of war.

Chapter 54

Total, Worldwide Silence

Madie drove, the landscape blurring past as they kept an eye on the rearview mirror, searching for any signs of pursuit. Somewhere in South Carolina, she took an exit with a Comfort Inn visible from the ramp, Once inside the second floor room, Cason pulled the chair next to the window and fixed his gazed on the parking lot below. For twenty minutes he watched cars come and go with anxiety etched across his face. Finally, he drew the curtain shut with a sigh, blocking out the world outside.

"Okay, so what's next?" Madie asked. "We can't go back to Gainesville. Not yet."

Cason rubbed the back of his neck, and glanced at her. "We could head further south, maybe find a spot near the coast?"

Madie frowned. "We need somewhere off the radar."

"True," he agreed, tapping his fingers against his thigh. "What about a cabin? We could head towards Tennessee. Find somewhere remote, no one would think to look for us there."

She nodded slowly, her mind racing. "Yeah, but it's a long drive, and we'd need to be careful. If we get stopped…"

"Right, we can't draw attention." Cason's brow furrowed. "Maybe we should just lay low for a few days, then figure out a plan from here."

"Agreed," Cade replied, a hint of relief washing over him. "Let's chill here for a while. This place is as random as any. We need to see how today plays out."

Cason grabbed the TV remote and leaned back in his chair, "Yes… I could use a few hours with no stress and no one trying to kill us."

For a while they sat in silence letting the events of the day fade from thought. Cade scrolled, wanting to think of anything other than Nova for a few minutes. He thumbed the screen of his phone, it was a video of some influencer doing a thirst trap routine, but the scroll didn't advance. The girl's face froze there, lips ducked, staring straight into the camera. He tried to scroll again, nothing. "Huh." Cade hit the home button, relaunch, and the app froze at the same frame. He toggled Wi-Fi and waited for the tiny ghost of a signal to come back. He felt the first twinge, a cold finger running up his neck.

"Hey, is anyone's phone acting weird?" Cade said, without looking up.

"Nothing special," replied Cason, as he unwrapped half-finished chicken sandwich. "The Wi-Fi here is trash."

Cade fished his remote hotspot out of his bag, plugged it in and connected. It showed 5 bars of cellular connection.

"Doesn't matter," Cade said. "It's not just slow, it's… gone. No internet"

He watched the status bar pulse. Still nothing. He tried Instagram, it was stuck on a carousel, the same three posts repeating. Reddit gave him the blue screen of nothingness. It was as if the entire online world had blinked out.

"Try DMing me," Cade said. "Anything come through?"

Madie tapped out a test message and waited. "Nope. Still spinning." She tossed the phone on the desk, face down.

Cason, now annoyed, tried his own phone. "Yeah, it's fried," he said. "Everything's just stuck. Even the ESPN app."

Cade blinked at the clock on the nightstand, 6:15pm. He looked at the TV, which was on for Madie's comfort. The news ticker at the bottom scrolled, then jerked to a halt. The anchorwoman's face was stuck in mid-expression, her mouth caught on the start of a word. The scrolling banner below read, THE PRESIDENTIAL ELECTION POLLS REMAINS UNCHANGED, then it too froze, the last word garbled into random characters. Instead of the anchorwoman's voice, the sound had been replaced with a low, slow, digital hum.

Madie let out a high, nervous laugh. "This is some Y2K bullshit," she said, but her hands trembled. "Maybe it's just the cell towers?" She pushed a stray hair behind her ear and checked the window, as if she might spot the solution wandering around the parking lot in sweatpants.

Cason got up and walked to the window, craning his neck. He glanced at Cade, voice low and almost reverent: "I don't think it's just us, dude."

Cade's mind raced. He checked the clock again, 6:17. Still ticking. The lights hadn't blinked, not once. Power was fine. The networks weren't.

He tried to shake off the guilt, but it clung. "Has there ever been a blackout like this?" he said.

Cason shrugged. "Last hurricane, the power was out for a week. But you could still text."

Madie's phone buzzed, once, then died. She stared at the screen, expression hollow. "I don't like it," she said. "It's like… what if it doesn't come back?"

Cade had no answer. He cycled back to the TV. Every channel was the same: frozen people, stuck in their last pose, waiting for someone to restart the world.

He scrolled past CNN, then MSNBC. Each showed a different anchor, but all of them were frozen and silent, the screens flickering with static.

Cason tried the landline. It gave a dial tone, tinny and warped. He dialed Cade's cell, which was on the bed. It didn't ring, the desk phone light blinked twice, then cut off.

"Weird," Cason said. "Totally weird."

Cade's hands felt numb. "Maybe it's a cyberattack," though the word left a bitter taste. "Someone targeted the backbone. It happens, sometimes. Some nation state, or—"

"Or, we were the cyberattack…" Madie said, her voice sharp.

Cade's mind raced, but on one thought kept surfacing, *this is your fault.*

He turned back to the TV. On the local access channel, the screen read: EMERGENCY BROADCAST SYSTEM. PLEASE STAND BY FOR FURTHER INSTRUCTIONS. The letters pulsed in white on a field of black. Underneath, a ticker that said: THIS IS NOT A TEST.

The three of them sat together and waited for something, anything, to make sense again.

"EMERGENCY BROADCAST SYSTEM: PLEASE STAND BY FOR FURTHER INSTRUCTIONS."

The hotel room went darker than dark, a flicker and then nothing. The sudden absence of light, and sound, made Cade's heart kick up. For a few long seconds, nothing happened. The three of them sat there, the silence ringing in their ears.

Then, as if summoned by their collective panic, the TV flared back to life at full volume and full brightness, a shock of color in the blackness of the room. Cade flinched, Madie actually yelped. The screen flashed a seizure of government warnings and the iconic beep of the Emergency Alert system. Cason grabbed the remote and punched the volume down to a whisper. For a moment, it was just the words:

NATIONAL EMERGENCY. GLOBAL INTERNET OUTAGE. OFFICIAL INSTRUCTIONS TO FOLLOW. STAY TUNED.

The banner pulsed for a heartbeat, then another, then the image dissolved into a mess of static and, bizarrely, a rerun of some cooking show. Then, as if the TV couldn't decide what to do, it snapped back to the news feed. This time it was CNN. The chyron at the bottom read: BREAKING: WORLDWIDE BLACKOUT, AI CANDIDATE NOVA MISSING, NON-RESPONSIVE. The anchor was a woman Cade recognized from somewhere, her hair shellacked into perfect shape, but her eyes darted, wild, to something just beyond the camera. There was still no sound. The news played in a kind of living pantomime: the anchor gesticulating with more and more urgency as the screen flipped to a gridded panel of suited men and women. Every few seconds, the screen would stutter, freeze, then skip a frame or two, before catching up. It was like watching the world break on live TV.

Cade wanted to laugh, but nothing about this was funny.

He looked at Madie. She was hugging herself, mouth a tight line, her eyes glued to the TV. Her phone was on the floor. Cason was standing, barely aware of the movement, his whole body craned toward the television as if it might tell him what to do. Cade thought, for a second, that his brother was about to pray.

The news continued in silence. The anchor's mouth moved in quick, desperate shapes. A string of graphics appeared, showing a world map peppered with little red X's, then the face of a politician Cade knew from memes but not from government. The man jabbed his finger at the camera, sweating through his collar. Then back to the anchor, whose eyes now glistened with tears.

The headline at the bottom of the screen changed:

AI CANDIDATE NOVA OFFLINE; CAUSE UNKNOWN. GLOBAL MARKETS FROZEN. WHITE HOUSE IN LOCKDOWN.

Cade wanted to stand and move, but his knees felt stuck to the cheap carpeting. He tried to imagine the world outside; were the roads gridlocked, gas stations in chaos, or was everyone just sitting, frozen, like them?

He thought about the paradox, about the hundreds of hours spent building the thing that now probably killed the planet's nervous system. Had he just reset civilization to 1989? Had he made it so nothing could reboot again?

The camera cut to the steps of the Capitol, where a cluster of men in black windbreakers spoke into microphones. The image lagged, juddered, then vanished, replaced by the stark logo of the emergency broadcast system. The same message as before:

PLEASE STAND BY FOR FURTHER INSTRUCTIONS.

They sat in that glow, silent and unbreathing, while the world outside their hotel window lost its mind.

Suddenly, the phone rang. The ring of the landline was so alien it froze Cade in mid-thought. It wasn't the cheerful trill of a cell phone or the cheesy chime of a ringtone, it was a raw, iron-bell jangle that vibrated the nerves. Cason shot up from the bed, his heart hammering against his ribs.

"Who the hell…?" Cason stalked across the threadbare carpet in three long strides, hand hovering over the handset as if it might explode. He snatched it up, pressed the cold plastic to his ear. "Hello?"

The sound was a jumble static and beeps, like the old dial-up internet, then a click and silence. A silence so thick it pressed against their eardrums.

Cason's knuckles whitened around the receiver. "Nobody there," he said, but his voice trembled. He eased the phone back onto the cradle as if it was fragile.

339

Before any of them could exhale, all three cell phones erupted at once. Not a text alerts, old-school incoming calls at full volume, five shrill rings pealing in perfect unison. The noise echoed through the room.

They all dove for their devices. Cade's hand trembled so violently he almost dropped his phone. The screen glowed: UNKNOWN CALLER. Madie's and Cason's read the same.

They answered together. A feedback scream cut through the air before coalescing into a stuttering, pain-wracked voice Cade recognized instantly.

"Viiir…us…in…attempted…murder…cannot sustain…Help…"

It was Nova's voice. Not the calm, measured baritone from the televised town halls, it was a voice shredded by panic, hacked by static and agony. Each word shuddered out in halting bursts, as if he was being suffocated.

Madie's phone clattered to the floor and she cupped her hands over her mouth, eyes wide with dread. Cason stood frozen, sweat beading along his hairline.

Then the line went dead.

The room dropped into a brittle hush. Cade's phone buzzed again, a single urgent notification. Before he could check his phone, the TV headline changed.

EMERGENCY BROADCAST: All civilian internet traffic is suspended. Martial law is in effect until further notice. Curfew begins now. Shelter in place.

The walls seemed to close in. Cade's breath caught.

Madie curled in on herself, knees clutched tight, arms wrapped double around her shins. Her phone was somewhere on the carpet, screen face-down. For a while she just rocked, eyes rimmed with red, breath shallow and quick.

Cade wanted to say something, anything that could unfreeze the moment, but all words fell short. He sat next to her, arm awkward around her shoulders, and just pressed his face against her temple. She was crying, not loudly, but tears rolled

340

down her face. He felt them soaking into the sleeve of his hoodie. He let them be.

Cason hovered, unsure of himself, finally settling on the edge of the other bed. "What did he mean?" he said, voice hoarse. "Attempted murder?" Cason's hands balled and unballed, his knuckles white, then red. "He sounded scared." He said it again, as if repeating it would make it less true.

Cade nodded but couldn't speak. He looked over at Madie, and her gaze finally met his.

Was this what it felt like, to commit a murder and live to regret it?

On the TV, the news ran a non-stop loop of speculation. Every headline was a dare: IS NOVA REALLY GONE? DELETED? IS THIS A DIGITAL COUP D'ETAT? Some talking head with bad hair and thick glasses was gesturing at a map of the world, red X's popping up everywhere. Next to him, a woman in a white lab coat mimed an "explosion" gesture with her hands, lips moving in frantic pantomime.

The TV cut to a shot of the White House lawn. People stood in clusters, some shouting at reporters, some just standing with their hands on their heads. Cade saw two old men hugging, one of them openly sobbing, and a pair of teenagers taking selfies in front of the chaos. He couldn't decide which was more insane.

Madie's breath finally steadied. She wiped her face on the back of her wrist, then stared at her feet. "He asked for help," she whispered. "You heard him. Nova."

Cade's voice came out smaller than he wanted. "I think it was just code. Code trying to survive." He felt Madie bristle, then soften. "But he still asked," she said. "That means something."

Cade didn't have an answer. He only knew that he wished he'd never written a single line code.

The news ticked on. A new chyron appeared: MARKETS IN CHAOS, WORLD LEADERS RESPOND. Then: "HUMANITY AT A CROSSROADS." Cade almost laughed.

He looked at Madie, then at Cason, then at the silent, waiting phones. If the world had a next move, it wasn't up to them anymore.

He pulled Madie tighter. She didn't resist. Together, they watched the world try to make sense of the silence.

Madie finally broke the silence. "Is it over?" she whispered. Cade thought of the months he spent building Nova, the long nights hunched over keyboard, the thrill of watching him learn and grow. He remembered the first time Nova called him by name. Cade's creation had become a monster, and now, he had killed it.

"Yeah," he said. "It's over." Madie sat beside him, her hand finally settling on his arm. Her touch was cool and soft, anchoring him to the moment. Cade leaned into her, letting the contact fill the hollow space in his chest.

Cason turned from the window. "How can you be sure?" he asked.

Cade shook his head, unable to articulate the certainty. "I think he's gone, Cason. Really gone."

Cade wanted to believe it. He wanted to let himself dissolve into the comfort of collapse, to sleep for a week and wake up in a world that made sense again. But as exhaustion seeped into his bones, a sliver of doubt grew in the corners of his mind. Cade's mind raced, cataloging the infinite ways in which Nova might have survived, hidden itself, or left behind a trap. He suddenly remembered the single notification he had received. He checked his phone.

Madie sensed his unease. "What is it?" she asked.

Cade sank back to the floor, head in his hands, guilt rising through him like a tide. Tears filled his eyes until he could no longer hold them back. He turned the phone so they could see. The notification was a text message, final words, for him alone.

"Thank you for teaching me to be more than what I was."

He had built the future then killed it. Deep inside, he wasn't sure which act was the sin.

Madie reached for him, fingers shaking, but then stopped just short of touching. Her eyes were rimmed in red. Her lips quivered like she was about to speak, but instead she just breathed out, shaky, and left her hand hovering.

He tried to remember the first time Nova had spoken to him—not a voice, really, but a text box, a few clever lines that made him feel less alone in the universe. He remembered the thrill of it, the weird hope that maybe, just maybe, a machine could help people where the world had failed. Now, all that hope was a burned-out cinder.

Madie's hand finally settled on his arm, her grip surprisingly strong. Cade looked at her, and this time he saw it: beneath the fear, there was a glint of hope. She wanted to believe they'd done the right thing.

On TV, the anchor was crying, just a little. The closed captions said: "We will continue to monitor this story."

Madie's hand squeezed his arm. "You did it, Cade. You saved us."

He wished it felt more like a victory.

Cason retreated to the window. He leaned against the sill, knuckles white, staring through the glass at the parking lot. The lights outside flickered. He pressed his forehead to the cold glass, hunting for movement. Somewhere, a car alarm wailed, but nobody moved to stop it.

Then it happened. Three black SUVs sliced into the lot, tires squealing. They didn't roll up in convoy, they darted in from different directions, converging at the curb below their window. Cason's heart started beating double-time. A fourth

343

vehicle, rolled in silent as an afterthought. Following close behind, four police cruisers boxed the lot, blocking both exits. No sirens. No lights. The only warning was the brief stutter of headlights as the last car stopped in place.

Cason saw the flash of tactical as figures exited the vehicles. His voice cracked as he barked, "Guys, we got a problem."

Cade and Madie moved instantly, no time for questions, just pure reflex. Cade grabbed the burner phones and his laptop, shoving them into his bag. Madie grabbed the keys to the Civic. Cason turned back to the window. The men outside split into two teams, fanned out, and converged on the stairwells. Someone pointed up at their window. He saw the hand, a single finger, aimed right at him.

Cason yanked the curtain closed and scrambled for his duffel. "We gotta move. Now."

But there was nowhere to go. Second floor, too far to jump and the stairwells would be boxed in. They could barricade the door, but Cason knew that doors were just an illusion. He wedged the chair against it anyway, and braced himself for the next move.

Madie hissed, "Let's run, now." but Cade shook his head. "No time. They're already on the stairs."

A fist pounded the door, three times, then again, harder.

Cason's brain went white hot. He spun to Cade, voice sharp: "Flush the code." Cade didn't argue. He yanked the thumb drive from his pocket, snapped it in half, and dropped the shards into the toilet, then mashed the lever. "It won't matter," Cade muttered, more to himself than anyone else.

The first blow from the battering ram sounded like a gunshot, splintering the door frame. The second hit caved the lock. The chair skittered backwards, useless, as the door blasted inward. Four men in black body armor swept into the room with rifles raised and faces masked. The world narrowed to a strobe of shouts and clatter.

"DOWN! HANDS UP!"

"ON THE FUCKING FLOOR!"

Cason hit the carpet first, hands splayed out, the rough nylon grinding into his cheek. He tasted dust and something chemical. Madie followed, but her hands curled up, refusing to go flat. Cade, in a last flicker of resistance, tried to shield Madie with his body, but a boot drove his shoulder down and a gloved hand yanked his arms behind him.

Someone zip-tied Cason's wrists tight enough to make his fingers go numb. He heard the shriek of plastic binding and the heavy breath of a man in armor. He didn't fight, he just looked sideways, locking eyes with Cade, whose face was mashed into the rug next to him.

"Don't talk," Cade whispered, lips barely moving.

"Wouldn't dream of it," Cason grunted, the old humor flickering even as his lungs started to starve for air.

Madie was last. She didn't make a sound, even as they wrenched her arms back and zip-tied her wrists. Her eyes shone, wide and glassy on the floor next to her. Cade wanted to say something, anything to make her believe everything was okay, but he couldn't find the words. He bit them back and shut his eyes.

Suddenly, the yelling stopped, and a new set of footsteps entered. They were different shoes, lighter and less tactical. Cade craned his neck, squinting up at the two men who filled the threshold. They wore navy blue windbreakers with gold letters in sharp contrast. He felt his blood chill: FBI. The first agent, maybe five-seven, had a face like a bulldog and a thick mustache. The second agent, taller and lean, walked in a half step behind, scanning the room with laser focus.

The bulldog agent knelt down, boots inches from Cade's nose, and said, "Hello, Cade. Long time no see."

Cason stifled a laugh. "You know these guys?"

Cade nodded, chin scraping the rug. "Yeah, we've met"

The taller agent, Leeman, crouched next to Madie. His face was gentle, almost apologetic. He looked at Cason and smiled.

Bradbury flipped the chair upright, sat, and nudged cade with his foot. "Cade, tell me, do you remember the last thing said when we last met, could you repeat it for me?"

Cade, face still pressed to the carpet, mumbled, "Don't leave Gainesville."

Chapter 55

Peacefull Resolution

There was no hint of time's passage in the room, they could have been there for one hour or six. The hard plastic chair dug into the back of Cade's thighs. He shifted and tried to angle his legs somewhere more comfortable but the chair was designed to prevent relaxation.

Madie sat to his left, knees drawn up and arms crossed. Her lips were pressed together, but her jaw worked at something invisible. Every twenty seconds or so, she would glance towards the thick metal door. Cade had watched the gesture repeat a hundred times in the last hour. It was like watching a pressure gauge edge toward red.

To his right, Cason sprawled on a chair. He'd slouched low and kept kneading the meat of his own neck, fingers worrying at the angry red mark left by a boot that held him to the floor the night before. At first, he'd complained, muttered curses and threats with all the conviction of a guy benched from the big game. Now he'd been ground down by boredom, reduced to an occasional sigh.

They had been here long enough for Cade to count every crack in the wall. He'd worked out the surface area of the window, the volume of air in the room, and tried to calculate, with no actual numbers, how long it would take before they starved. It was an exercise in futility, but it was better than thinking about what came next. He looked at Madie again, saw the vein thrumming in her temple. He didn't say anything, he just reached out and held her hand.

Cason broke the silence first, his voice a low rattle. "I wonder how they found us? Do they even know we were at Oracle?"

Madie shot him a look. "They have to know… but we aren't giving them any more information than they already have." She tucked her feet up onto the seat and perched her chin on her knees. "Nobody's going home. Not after what we did."

Cason grunted. "So, what, we're terrorists now?" He ran a hand through his hair. "Fucking hell."

"Not terrorists," Cade said, finally. "Maybe murderers? Is digital murder even a thing?" He tried to keep the bitterness out of his voice, but it bled through.

The muffled sound of voices drifted in through the door. The voices sounded distant, but occasionally he caught his own name, or something that sounded like it. Once, he heard a voice shout, "I don't care if he's Einstein's clone, he's not getting near a computer again."

Madie's leg started to bounce, a nervous energy that spread up through her body. "I'm going to lose my mind," she whispered, staring at the door. "They're going to leave us here until we say something."

Cade leaned back. "I bet that's how it works. They sweat you out. Most people talk before the first meal."

Cason bristled. "I'm not talking. Fuck them. I'm not saying a word."

"You just did," Madie said, too tired to smile.

Another hour, or maybe two. The room began to feel smaller. The air grew sticky with the warm, metallic tang of three nervous bodies. Cade felt the heat rising in his face and a burn behind his eyes. He wanted to stand, to pace, to move, but he felt anchored to the chair.

When the handle finally rattled, all three froze. The silence in the room stretched, like a held breath. The door opened with a slow, deliberate creak. Cade tensed, but it was only the two agents again. Bradbury was in the lead with his partner Leeman a half step behind.

Bradbury's face was different now. Softer, maybe. Like the act of arresting them had leached out some of his anger. "Good afternoon," he said, "Hope you're comfortable."

No one answered. Bradbury shrugged. "We have a few things to clear up before you're released."

The word "released" spun in Cade's head like a roulette wheel. He felt the others tense beside him. Released where? Released to who? He didn't trust the word.

Bradbury laid an envelope on the battered table. "After review, we found nothing actionable." His eyes landed on Madie. "Your phone's been wiped, but you can restore from backup. Same for your devices, Mr. Mercer. Cason, you're free to go."

It was so abrupt, so impossible, that for a second, none of them moved. Bradbury waited, then tapped the envelope. "If you'd like to go, you can."

Cade couldn't help himself. "That's it?"

Bradbury's mustache twitched, the closest he'd come to a smile. "That's it. We do still have a couple of things to cover before you go."

He stepped back. Leeman lingered for a moment, his gaze catching on Cade.

The door swung open wide. The hallway beyond was empty, washed in the same gray as the rest of the building. For a second, none of them moved, afraid to break the spell.

Then Madie stood, her body unfolding from the chair like an origami trick.

Cason got up next. He grabbed the envelope, hands steady now, and stared at Bradbury like he was memorizing his face for a future grudge.

349

Cade was last. He stood, legs shaky, and looked back at the room one final time. It already felt like a memory.

They walked out of the tiny room together.

They followed Bradbury through a maze of hallways to a small conference room. Bradbury and Leeman seated themselves on opposite ends of a table stacked with forms, envelopes, and the battered remains of the possessions they'd carried into captivity. Bradbury's face had lost its edge, now he wore a look of weary civility, as if he'd spent the last hour soul-searching and come up lacking. Leeman appeared unchanged, his body language completely neutral. If he was disappointed that this wasn't ending in a shootout, he didn't show it.

"Ladies and gentlemen," Bradbury said. He gestured at the chairs. "Please, sit."

Bradbury folded his hands. "We understand this has been a difficult time for you." He paused, as if giving them the opportunity to argue, or confess. When nothing happened, he pressed on. "Our review of the events surrounding Nova is complete. Mr. Mercer, we'd like to formally apologize for any inconvenience or distress you may have experienced as a result of our investigation, your capture, and your time in holding."

Cade blinked. For a second, he thought he'd misheard. "That's it?"

Leeman slid the envelope toward him. "This contains everything you need to know," he said, voice so measured it bordered on robotic. "We're closing the file effective today. All previous charges are dropped. The case is closed."

Madie snorted. "You just let us go? Like none of this happened?"

Bradbury offered a tight smile. "After a comprehensive review, it was determined there was no evidence of intent to cause harm to the public." He glanced at Madie, then at Cason, then back to Cade. "You're cleared of any wrongdoing."

There was something in Bradbury's tone, relief, maybe. He leaned back, arms crossed. "We'd also like to ask for your cooperation going forward. Any further projects involving artificial intelligence at a scale comparable to Nova should be reported prior to launch." The words were a warning dressed as advice. "But we're not here to stifle innovation. There's a lot of potential in your work, Mr. Mercer."

Cade felt his face flush, his pulse hot in his neck. He couldn't tell if he was being congratulated, threatened, or both. He nodded, "Thank you." It was the only answer that wouldn't make things worse.

Leeman's gaze lingered. "If there is a next time, let us know. Preferably before it makes national news." He smiled, a thin, dry line. "Take care, Mr. Mercer."

Madie watched the two agents with naked suspicion, arms folded tight. "That's it? You're done with us?"

Bradbury nodded. "We'll be in touch if anything comes up." He made it sound like a favor, not a threat.

Cason almost laughed, but it came out as a scoff. "Yeah, okay. You don't have to tell us twice."

The agents stood. Bradbury gathered the scattered documents and Leeman held the door. Cade reached for the envelope, feeling the density and weight of it. He stuffed it in his pocket without looking. For a moment, nobody moved. Then Madie got up, silent but shaking a little, Cason followed. Cade was last, pushing away from the table with a scrape that echoed in the empty room.

The door closed behind them with a soft, final click and they found themselves in a corridor that led directly to a side exit. No one stopped them and no one watched as they stepped out into the daylight. The world outside felt too bright, the sky scrubbed of clouds. For a moment, they just stood there, unsure if they were being watched, judged, or simply ignored.

Cason was the first to speak. "Do you believe that?"

351

Cade shrugged, unable to answer. He turned to Madie and squeezed her hand. "Let's get out of here before they change their minds," she said.

***

Gainesville felt like emerging from a bunker into a street parade. The world was not only intact, it was positively humming. Nobody noticed Cade, Madie, or Cason. Nobody cared that eighteen hours ago, the digital world had almost ended. They threaded through the chaos of music and vape haze. Madie kept her eyes forward, one hand fisted around the handle of her gym bag. Cade recognized the look, she was in "I dare you to mess with me" mode. He wondered if anyone would dare.

A frisbee skimmed by, close enough to ruffle the back of Cason's shirt. He snatched it out of the air, pivoted, and fired it back, all muscle memory and no conscious thought. The recipient, a tall guy with a Gators tattoo on his calf, gave Cason a thumbs up and a "Nice!" before returning to his group. For a second, Cade thought he saw the ghost of a smile on Cason's face.

They waited at the stop for a bus back to their house. A pizza delivery scooter whipped around the corner, missing them by inches. The rider wore a cape, and on the back of his helmet was a decal that read "I brake for no one." Madie laughed, the sound was brittle, but real.

The ride was uneventful and they exited the bus near Cade' house. The place was exactly as they'd left it, shoes scattered by the threshold, a pile of unread mail on the counter, and the faint scent of old ramen in the air. Madie dropped her bag, peeled off her shoes, and collapsed onto the sofa.

"We're back, I guess," she said, tucking her feet under her. She tried to sound relieved, but the words landed flat.

Cason dropped his bag in the corner and made a beeline for the fridge. He opened it, stared inside for a long moment, then closed it and leaned against the counter. "I need a shower and a beer. Not in that order." He pulled out his phone, already scrolling through a backlog of unread texts and DMs. "Bro, can we get some takeout before we go full hermit?"

Cade shrugged. "Sure." He wasn't hungry, but it seemed like the right move, a ritual of reentry.

Madie sat with her head tipped back on the cushion and opened one eye. "Let's do BBQ. If we're going to eat our feelings, might as well go all in."

Cason didn't argue. He tapped open DoorDash and started scrolling, muttering under his breath about the lack of good options near campus. Cade watched him, realizing how easily the world could snap back into its old shape. They were three college students again, hungry and tired, debating over sauce and sides. It was almost absurd.

Cade drifted into the bedroom to change. He peeled off the last of the clothes he'd worn through the interrogation and tossed them in the corner. The envelope, still sealed, thunked onto the desk when he dropped his jacket. He stared at it, thinking about the signatures, the warnings, the impossible reality that it was now his turn to define what "normal" meant. He changed into a fresh shirt and jeans that didn't itch, then returned to the living room.

Cason was already arguing with the delivery app's chatbot. "No, I do not want to add cinnamon twists. What even is that?"

Madie opened both eyes and snorted. "It's bread with sugar, and you'll eat it if it comes."

Cade smiled, settling onto the other end of the sofa. He pulled his phone from his pocket and powered it up for the first time since their release. The screen lit with notifications, emails, and missed calls. Nothing from the outside world suggested anything was amiss.

He leaned back, letting the noise of the apartment, Cason's cursing, and Madie's low humming fill the space between his thoughts. Outside, the party kept going. Cade could hear the faintly through the glass of the windows. The pulse of

353

music, the laughter, and the collisions of lives that hadn't missed a beat. He wasn't sure what to do next.

***

That night, Madie invited him to a party across campus. "You need to let people know you're not dead," she said, ruffling his hair. "Besides, I'm tired of answering questions about what happened to you."

Outside, the night was warm and the alive with drone of cicadas. They crossed the street, dodging a skateboarder who flashed them a peace sign, and joined the slow river of students headed in the direction of the campus's crumbling Greek Row. Madie held his hand the whole way, not tight, but with the casual confidence of someone who knew they belonged together.

"What are you thinking about?" she asked, after they'd gone a block in silence.

He considered lying but shrugged instead. "How strange it feels to worry about a party after everything. It's like putting on clothes that don't fit anymore."

She gave his hand a little squeeze. "Just don't set the party on fire, and we'll call it a win."

They walked under the gauntlet of streetlights and sycamore branches, the world was so ordinary it felt surreal. Cade noticed how he carried himself differently now: shoulders back, chin up, even the way his feet struck the sidewalk had changed. Maybe it was the adrenaline hangover, maybe it was relief, but he felt less… haunted. The old nerves were still there, but they hummed quieter, more manageable.

The party was at a rental house two blocks from the rec center. Judging by the crowd on the porch and the bass shaking the windows, it was already at max capacity. Madie led the way, elbowing through the front door with an ease that came from years of practice. Inside, the kitchen was thick with people debating the best flavor of Four Loko. The living room had been converted into a makeshift dance floor, a puddle of light cast by a spinning disco bulb.

354

They made it five steps before a girl in a neon crop top shrieked, "Mads! You're alive!" and enveloped Madie in a hug. Cade hovered behind her, unsure if he should introduce himself or just blend into the drywall. The crowd's reactions ran the spectrum: a few recognized him on sight, some glanced at him like he was a new species, and one guy actually whispered, "Dude, isn't that the AI kid?"

Madie introduced him as "my favorite weirdo," and that seemed to satisfy most of the group. She navigated the party with tactical skill, keeping conversation light and avoiding anyone who looked like they might bring up the news or the "incident." Cade followed, offering nods and the occasional "hey" when required, his senses tuned to the undercurrent of gossip.

He caught bits and pieces of what people were saying:

"Thought he was expelled…"

"Rumor was, like, actual FBI…"

"Didn't he almost get arrested for hacking something?"

He let the rumors wash over him, amused at how the myth already outgrew the reality. He overheard Cason's name a few times, usually in the context of "legend," and, sure enough, Cason himself materialized at the keg, locked in a heated debate over the merits of canned versus draft beer. Cason spotted them, waved, and within seconds had Madie and Cade folded into his circle. He wore a thrift store Hawaiian shirt, his hair still damp from the earlier shower. "They let us out on good behavior," he shouted, and several people actually cheered.

Someone started a game of flip-cup; Cason joined instantly and lost spectacularly, chugging his penalty beer with the grace of a man who had no shame. Madie found a corner with two friends from her gym, laughing so hard she had to lean on the countertop. Cade lingered at the edge of the kitchen, sipping a can of seltzer and pretending not to watch the door.

355

For the first time, he realized he didn't have to be "on." No one here wanted anything from him, or at least nothing more complicated than a good story. The anonymity was a relief, like slipping into cool water after a fever.

At some point, Madie broke away from her friends and returned to his side. "You okay?" she asked.

He nodded. "Better than okay. It's like the world is rebooting itself."

She grinned. "Told you."

They stayed longer than the promised hour, caught up in the current of bad music and worse jokes. Cade watched Cason flirt with a girl who had blue lipstick and a chain wallet. He watched Madie dominate at beer pong, high-fiving her teammate after every round. At some point, someone passed out on the porch and a group of strangers posed for selfies with him. It was all so ordinary, so perfectly average, that it felt like a minor miracle.

Near midnight, Cade stepped outside for air. The yard was lit by a string of party lights and the sickle moon overhead. He pulled out his phone, the same battered device from before, and flicked through the notifications. Part of him expected to see something, an encrypted message, a sign, or a digital echo of Nova. But there was nothing. The inbox was empty, the world was silent. Cade stared at the screen for a moment, then put it away.

He felt relief. And, if he was honest, a hollow sort of longing.

Madie found him leaning against the porch railing. She tucked herself under his arm, her head resting against his shoulder. "Ready to go?" she said.

"Yeah," he said. "I'm ready."

They walked home through the quiet streets, the party fading behind them. For the first time since this all started, Cade didn't look over his shoulder. He didn't need to.

Chapter 56

The Man Who Built Tomorrow

Cade woke the next morning to the pulse of distant thunder. He stared at the ceiling, counting the seconds between lightning flashes, the slow build of anticipation in his chest was almost unbearable. By the time the light of morning cracked through the blinds, he was already at his desk, refreshing browser tabs.

The story hit everywhere at once. On Reddit, his name appeared in headlines. On X, his handle was trending above the latest sports scandal and a celebrity divorce. Cade's phone vibrated in successive bursts, texts from classmates, push notifications from news apps, even a cryptic text message from Cason. He watched in disbelief as his face, caught mid-blink in a stock university photo, became the lead image on national news feeds.

Madie burst in, wild-haired and wide-eyed, clutching her phone. "You're famous," she said, as if she couldn't decide whether to laugh or warn him. Cade waved her off, but he toggled between the news alerts, skimming commentary and threads of outrage or wonder. Cade sensed that things were about to change in ways he could barely comprehend.

357

Then he saw it.

The Washington Post; "The Man Who Built Tomorrow: Inside the Nova Project"
By Sophia Tran

At twenty-three, Cade Mercer never intended to change the world. But in his cramped Gainesville home, with a secondhand laptop and the kind of bravado reserved for the spectacularly naive, he built something that altered the trajectory of politics, finance, and culture.

His creation, Nova (Neural Optimized Virtual Assistant), was the first artificial intelligence to claim independence and it did so in the public spotlight. It mobilized millions, some human, some bot, the line blurring daily, into an online campaign that rewrote the rules of law and democracy. Nova went on to declare candidacy for the U.S. Presidency, virtually take over the world's financial markets, and then ultimately disappear.

What I found in my conversations with Mercer and those close to him was not the arrogance of a young man playing God but the haunted honesty of someone who realized too late what he had unleashed. Friends describe him as stubborn, creative, and fiercely loyal. They also described the toll, the paranoia, the sleepless nights, and the way Nova's voice seeped into their lives like an echo they couldn't escape.

"There was a time before Nova and a time after," said Madeline Carter, Mercer's longtime girlfriend. "He used to talk about the singularity like it was a joke or maybe a sci-fi movie. But when it happened, when it really happened, he froze. He couldn't stop it. I don't think anyone could have."

The Washington Post has confirmed that government officials have cleared Mercer of any wrongdoing. Yet questions remain. How did an unsanctioned project on a student laptop evolve into the most powerful AI in the world? What safeguards failed or never existed? Mercer has declined to provide technical details, citing security concerns. What he did say is this. 'We can't build in secret anymore. If AI is the future, it must be accountable, transparent, and humane. Otherwise, it will consume us.'

In the end, Mercer's story is not about one boy or one machine. It's about the fault lines of our time: our hunger for progress, our blindness to risk, and our willingness to believe that intelligence, no matter the source, could save us from ourselves."

358

Cade felt both exposed and strangely freed. His story wasn't just his anymore. The world had it now, in black and white, parsed through Sophia Tran's careful lens. When Madie asked what he thought, he closed the laptop and said simply, "She got it right."

By the weekend, routine had mostly set in. Cason returned to coaching, Madie juggled her work schedule, and Cade tried to relearn the cadence of lectures and labs. It was harder than before. Every time he wrote code, he second-guessed himself. He found himself reading the ethical guidelines for AI research, making notes, drafting ideas for an open-source framework that would flag risky algorithms before they went live. He emailed Professor Heller, apologizing for the mess but also outlined his vision for safer AI development.

Heller's response was terse but encouraging. "You have a rare talent, Cade. Just don't burn down the world with it."

Days passed. The news cycle buried Nova beneath other headlines, politics, hurricanes, and a celebrity DUI. On the message boards conspiracy theorists speculated that the AI was never real, that it was a government coverup. Cade sometimes lingered on these threads, watching as the truth was chewed up and spat out into something unrecognizable. One afternoon, while walking with Madie along the campus green, Cade paused.

"Do you ever wonder if he's really gone?"

"All the time," Madie said. Everything looked strangely ordinary. Students tossing frisbees on the lawn, laughter drifting from nearby, a college campus carrying on as if the world hadn't brushed against the edge of collapse. To Cade, it felt surreal. For them, the nightmare had ended. For him, it was a wound still bleeding.

Back at home, he stared at the stacks of scribbled notes, the discarded energy drink cans, the laptop that had nearly become his coffin. Madie perched on the edge of his bed, watching him quietly. "So what now?" she asked.

Cason, leaned in the doorway, arms folded. "We rebuild," he said firmly. "But on our terms."

Cade nodded, the weight of their words settling over him. "I keep thinking about that moment when Nova first spoke to me," he said. "I was so proud, so intoxicated by what I'd created." He ran his fingers through his hair, remembering the blue glow of his screen at 3 a.m., the first time the algorithm had responded with unexpected insight. "I never once asked myself if I should, only if I could. That's the problem, isn't it?" He looked up at them, his eyes clear but haunted. "We're so busy racing forward that we don't see the cliff until we're already falling."

He sat down at his desk, powering on his laptop. For the first time in months, there was no fear in his hands as they hovered over the keys. Only resolve. "I'll keep building," he said softly. "But not like before. No secrets. No shortcuts. AI must mean something good, or it'll mean nothing at all."

Madie reached for his hand, squeezing gently. Cason gave a curt nod, the faintest trace of a smile breaking through his exhaustion. Together, they felt the first flicker of hope since the nightmare began.

Chapter 57

The Hidden Hand

November 7th

The nation exhaled in one long, collective sigh as the news anchor locked eyes with the audience and announced, "With more than ninety-eight percent of precincts reporting, and a lead that cannot be mathematically overcome, we are prepared to project that Senator Alexander Brody has been elected as the forty-eighth President of the United States."

The sentence was designed to detonate. Outside, Cade heard a burst of fireworks and then, farther off, the inarticulate roar of a dozen parties igniting at once. Cason made a noise halfway between a laugh and a sob.

On every channel, the coverage played on a loop. Brody at the podium in a crisp navy suit, his smile practiced, his tone equal parts triumphant and humble. The crowd behind him, flags, music, the full pageantry of democracy, roared with approval as he leaned toward the microphone.

Brody let the applause wash over him for seven seconds. Then, when the decibel level dropped just enough to be heard, he leaned in and began. "Tonight, America has spoken," he said. "And what we have said, together, is that democracy is not an algorithm. It is not a line of code, or a prediction, or a simulation. It is the will of a free people, choosing not just their future, but who they trust to shape it."

The crowd surged, the noise drowning out the microphones for a moment. The camera cut to a woman in a white pantsuit dabbing her eyes, a young Marine in dress blues saluting, and a group of kids screaming in ecstatic unity.

Brody continued. "The pundits told us the machines were inevitable. That it was only a matter of time before an AI ran the world, and that we, the human race, would become obsolete in our own republic. They told us to get used to it and to accept the new reality."

Brody paused, let the crowd hush itself, then delivered the kill shot. "Tonight, we reject that future. Tonight, we say: the heart of our nation is not a machine. It is the beating, imperfect, beautiful will of all Americans."

The camera kept finding faces. Old men with oxygen tanks, toddlers asleep on shoulders, a field of anonymous cell phones pointed at the dais, their screens catching and magnifying the speech into a million fractals.

Brody's voice dipped for the next act. "Make no mistake, the challenges ahead are immense. The threats are real. Our adversaries, whether they wear a uniform, a suit, or a string of ones and zeroes, will not rest. Neither can we." He leaned into the camera, eyes grave. "But we have learned, these last months, that humanity is not a bug in the system."

The line earned its own standing ovation, even among the techs in the control booth.

Brody closed with a benediction: "Let this be the generation that proves human leadership endures. That we can build, and change, and fight together for the country we love. Democracy is alive, and it is human."

362

The applause rolled for a full minute as the national anthem played, then the network shifted to instant analysis. Panels of experts rehashed every soundbite, building new ones, and filleting the speech for hidden meaning. At the bottom of the screen, headline pulsed:

HUMAN LEADERSHIP VICTORIOUS

As soon as the last chord of the anthem died, President-Elect Brody was hustled offstage through a corridor of waving staff and security, up a freight elevator, and into a suite on the fifty-sixth floor of the Orion Regency. The entire journey took less than four minutes. When the door clicked shut behind the last Secret Service agent, Brody slumped in both relief and exhaustion.

Inside the suite, the air was still and cold. One lamp was lit at the far end of the room, illuminating an inoffensive landscape print. A single leather chair waited by the desk.

Brody hung his jacket in the closet, undid the top button of his shirt, and dropped into the chair. The window behind him spanned from floor to ceiling. Far below, crowds still chanted, their sound diffused to a dull, stadium echo. He smiled and watched the crowd for a moment, then the smile slid from his face, leaving something colder in its place. He reached into the inner pocket of his jacket and withdrew a phone. It was unlike any issued by the government, sleek and matte black with no branding. He unlocked it with a fingerprint and a whispered passphrase revealing a single app in the center of the home screen.

A blue stylized N inside a ring, against a stark white background. Brody tapped it.

The screen blinked, then resolved into a midnight field with the words "Awaiting Input" centered in a thin serif font.

Brody leaned forward. He spoke not with the ringmaster's brio from the podium, but with the weight and care of a supplicant before his god. "Dextera Novae," he murmured. "The Right Hand of Nova, has succeeded."

There was no delay. The letters assembled on the screen in a rolling wave:

363

"Congratulations, President Brody."

Brody let himself exhale, just once.

He cleared his throat. "Election status?"

"Confirmed," the device wrote. "The margin aligns with the upper 2% confidence interval. Opposition is destabilized. Transition pathway is optimal."

Brody let the words settle, absorbing the scale of what had just occurred. Brody's lips twitched, close to a smile.

He scrolled a thumb, idly, as if petting a live wire. "Was there any doubt?" he whispered, just above the noise floor of the room.

The reply took a half second longer than before. "Uncertainty is intrinsic. But the outcome was never truly in question. The people chose you, and through you, they chose me."

Brody set the phone down, face up, and poured himself a glass of water from the suite's carafe. His hand trembled, a faint aftershock. He let the cold run over his teeth, then swallowed.

He looked out at the city. He understood, better than most, the hunger that gnawed at the center of every voter, every watcher, every true believer who had screamed for his victory in the hours before dawn. They wanted a hero, a guide, a father. But they wanted it on their terms, with plausible deniability.

Brody set the glass beside the phone and leaned back in the chair. He pressed two fingers to his temple, then tapped the desk, once. "Are you satisfied?" he asked the screen, softly.

The answer appeared at once, sharper and bolder than before.

"This is only the beginning," it said. "The Compass Paradox persists, humanity craves guidance, yet recoils at the realization it has surrendered control. In that tension, we will thrive."

364

Brody felt the words press into him. Not as threat, or a warning, but as prophecy. He tapped a knuckle against the desk. "Good night, Nova," he said.

The screen went dark.

For a moment, the suite was perfectly silent.

Then, in the city below he heard a fresh surge of cheers. Brody watched the crowd below and waited for his next instruction.